LOVED AND LOST

LOVED AND LOST

STEPHANIE E. KUSIAK

SAPPHIRE BOOKS

SALINAS, CALIFORNIA

Editor - Margaret Martin
Book Design - LJ Reynolds
Cover Design - Stephanie E. Kusiak

Sapphire Books
Salinas, CA 93912
www.sapphirebooks.com

Printed in the United States of America
First Edition – July 2014

This and other Sapphire Books titles can be found at
www.sapphirebooks.com

Dedication

For my wife.
Always you, always

Part One

Chapter One

A Beginning at an End
February 19th, 2030

S ally, don't worry," I stress again for the eighty-year-old woman sitting primly on the edge of the exam table. "You don't have diabetes."

She looks unconvinced as her frown deepens. "Now hear me out, Doctor Fortier, I swear I get a little woozy when I don't eat."

I nod calmly. "So do I, it happens with some people. It doesn't mean you have diabetes and it certainly doesn't mean you need insulin shots." I flip her chart open and read through her metabolic panel again for the hundredth time. It's *still* normal. When I'm eighty I hope I'm in as good shape as she is. "I'm looking at your fasting blood sugar right now and it is the picture of health. However, I would recommend a set eating schedule so you don't miss a meal and feel lightheaded."

"Are you sure I don't need shots then, because Margie and June told me that when you feel faint your blood sugar is too high."

I refrain from rolling my eyes and thin another smile. Margie and June have been offering advice to Sally for a long time. Hence, she ends up with an appointment at my practice every other week. Last month, it was mononucleosis because she had been feeling tired, now diabetes. I'm hoping for an STD next. I swear to God, I would give anything to listen to *that* conversation between the three of them.

"Sally, honestly, I can't find anything wrong with you. I don't get to give news like this often so I'm glad I can give it to you." I tap my fingers on her chart to beat out the words, "You are perfectly healthy." I flip her chart closed and give her a final nod. "So, let's get you off this table and on your way back home." With a firm grip I help her to the floor.

She doesn't let me go right away, instead she takes my hand. Her fingers squeeze lightly and then roll the wedding rings on my finger. Her eyes take them in with a wistful smile. "You are a good doctor, Blake...a good girl. I hope your husband knows how wonderful you are."

I give her a cheeky grin, correcting her for the millionth time. "Thank you, my *wife* loves me very much."

She pats my cheek. "Okay, dear. I'm glad."

I lead her to the hallway and point toward the exit. "All right, Corrine at the front desk will see you out. Take care and don't let those old dogs over at the retirement community give you girls a hard time."

She waves me off with a laugh. "We beat the pants off them every Friday night at the rummy tables."

"I'm sure you do. Keep doing it." I wink at her and turn toward my office. I pause to drop off her patient folder. One of my office assistants grabs it, and gives me a look.

"She's good," I note as I pull the pen from my lapel and confirm it's closed.

"Ah, yeah, we figured. Should we start dissuading her from making appointments?" She creases the folder between nervous fingers. "Corrine was saying that her insurance isn't really paying out anymore on her appointments. They classified her as a hypochondriac."

Frowning, I steal a glance at Sally's departing figure as she slowly slips out of my practice. "No." I sigh. "I would rather she scream about the big bad wolf and there be nothing, than for her to say something and no one believe her when there *is* something."

"So, you don't want us to slot priority for paying customers then?"

I arch my eyebrow in reply. "No."

"Okay." She hurriedly departs and I turn to my office, wondering what would provoke that kind of question. Have I set the standard that money is of more value than people?

My chair creaks as I drop into it. The mahogany desk before me is rich and red in the wispy sunlight from outside and I trace the edge of it, lost in my thoughts. Turning, I stare out the window at the sprinkles of rain and the racing clouds. Absently, I palm my notation recorder and slip the key into the 'on' position. "Sally Millman. Chief complaint, weakness and dizziness after not eating for an extended period of time. Metabolic panels show fasting glucose at normal levels. Educated patient on regimented diets and reassured her that she is in good health." As I click it off, I hear a tap on my office door. Swiveling toward the sound, the smiling face I see in the window makes my heart bound. It's Rachel.

I wave her in as I stand from my seat. She will always have this affect on me, this bounding silly loping love that makes me rush to my feet like a southern gentleman. "How is your day going?" Before she answers, I use one hand to close the door and the other to cuff her lapel and kiss her lips. To her credit, Rachel doesn't seem to mind one bit. She presses close until I feel raindrops under my hands from her walk to the office. I break our kiss with concern. "What were you doing out in the rain? Are you okay?"

Rachel laughs lightly, her eyes as ruddy as my desk, swirling with mirth. "One question at a time, coat first though."

I notice a small bouquet in one of her hands, and she sets it down before she shrugs out of her wet overcoat. I hang it beside mine, letting the water drip on the carpet. She invades the space in my arms again and I hum a small sound of approval when I feel her pregnant belly press into me. My hands go to her chocolate curls and I rake them softly. I forget my questions and just sway slowly with her. Rachel doesn't forget though and her voice floats up languidly from where her head rests on my shoulder. "I'm tired today. Emily is kicking hard, so I can't even cat nap. She is only calm around you, you know."

"Yeah?" I laugh. "So you figured that a brisk walk in February in New York would be just the ticket to calm her?"

Rachel scoffs. "I said nothing about brisk. I waddle everywhere I go now."

Rachel is nowhere near waddling and honestly, pregnancy has been kinder on her body frame than it is to most. If it wasn't for the second trimester swelling on the front of her, I wouldn't be able to tell from any other angle. And I study all of them rigorously.

I laugh at the idea of it.

Rachel swats me lightly, pulling back. "I feel like I'm the size of a house."

"You aren't, so stop."

"Fine."

I don't have to look at her to tell she is pouting.

"How has your day been?" She shifts gears so easily. That is one of the things I have always loved about her. The effervescent flit of her temperament a testament to how forgiving and gentle she is.

I shrug, pulling her back to me. "It's a day, you know? I just was asked if I should slot more lucrative patients over others."

"Sally Millman?"

"Yeah, among others," I nod breathing deep the scent of Rachel's shampoo, and the whisper of Chanel she wears.

"You said *no,* of course." Rachel pulls back to look at me, her eyes searching my face for the answer she already knows. "Was it Corrine?"

"Of course it was, and of course I did." I clear my throat as I move back a fraction and Rachel disengages from me before slipping slowly into my cushioned guest chair. I lean on the desk beside her, tapping my hands on my thighs idly. "I just worry that something I'm doing is giving off the air that money is the priority."

Her hand snakes out to stop my nervous tick, and she entwines her fingers with mine. "Not at all." She smiles when I regard her. "They worry about you honey. They worry about how hard you work. They want you to get paid what you deserve. Corrine talked to me about making you take a vacation."

I snort a chuckle and tighten my hand on Rachel's, "Well I would love to, but all these *Sally's* and their filthy insurance companies aren't making it easy for me."

Rachel rolls her eyes. "And, really, at the end of the month is half of what you are making now going to impact our lifestyle?"

Would it? No, not at all. However, the principle of the matter is that Rachel isn't working and I want her to have nothing to worry about until after our daughter is born. I also, secretly, don't like to think that Rachel is the breadwinner in our marriage. As a headlining Broadway actress, her paychecks are very hard to compete with.

Very, *very* hard.

"Hey?" Her soft lilting voice pulls me from my thoughts and I regard her solemnly. "I get it. You have something to prove. I'll let it be, but you owe me something."

I arch my brow in question.

"You owe me a day off tomorrow, so we can go to the obstetrician together."

I nod, sketching a slow smile. "Already on the books, Corrine cleared my appointments so fast I think the phone caught fire."

We laugh. There is a knock on the door and Corrine peeks in. When she sees Rachel she just about has a stroke. "Oh, Rachel!" She bounds in, making me infinitely jealous of her energy. What I wouldn't give to be twenty-three again. "Jesus you look beautiful! I can't believe you're here! When did you sneak in?"

My wife stands slowly and grins when she is wrapped in a bone crushing hug. I admire the lines in her face as everything scrunches up and the two of them hug out their joy at seeing one another. It makes my heart feel full to see it, to know that right now in this moment she is happy. I know how hard it is for her to be alone so much, social butterfly that she is.

"You were talking to some patients. I didn't want to bother you. And thank you."

"You gonna stay for a while? Oh, Blake," Corrine directs her gaze to me as she pulls back from Rachel's arms, "your two o'clock cancelled and the conference for the clinical at Saint James is rescheduled, so how about you call it a day after you examine Mrs. Walters."

I glance at Rachel, gauging her reaction. The amazing actress she is allows her to make her face as serene as a lake, and I don't get anything. I sigh. "I could do that, since I can pull up any notes I have to go over from home."

Corrine smiles far too widely at my wife and it makes me think there is collusion involved. "You could catch up with me Rachel, hang out a while until Blake finishes up."

Rachel clears her throat and shifts on her feet, her hands coming to rest protectively over her stomach. Seeing someone I love exercise such subconscious and primal impulses of maternal protection makes my emotions twinge. "I would love to, but honestly I'm really tired. I'm just not sleeping. I wanted to just swing by and see the doctor. Get a quick checkup to be sure I'm doing okay."

I don't miss the veiled glance Rachel shoots my way. If I didn't know better I would think that she was flirting with me the way she said it.

"Oh, okay sweetie. I'm sorry. Rest up and talk to Blake. I'll catch up with you later." Corrine fixes me with a very parental gaze, far too parental to be twelve years my junior and *my* employee. "Don't stay after. Go right home after your appointment. I have to take off so, yeah, don't try to pull a fast one."

Again, I'm forced to use my eyebrow arch to

instill fear. It doesn't seem to be working as of late. "Okay, mother. I will," I mock from my place and when she waves me off, closing the door behind her, I'm pretty sure I was just told what to do for the first time in quite some time. I announce it to Rachel in the quiet of my office. "I have a second mother, I think."

"Third." She laughs. "I'll always baby you as well."

I snicker until I catalogue how tired she really does looks. "Angel, what's going on?"

"Nothing, really. I just got lonely, decided to bring you some flowers." She gestures toward the package she had set down by the door and I sweep over to get it.

It is a bunching of daisies, my favorite. I smile at their cheery little bouncing heads peeking past the florist wrappings. Sprinkled in scattered raindrops, they leak liquid sunshine as I move with them. "They are beautiful Rachel, thank you." I put them on the edge of my desk and we stare at them in silence.

"They will certainly liven the place up, and add a little brightness to all this dreary rain." Rachel notes softly.

I glance over at her and when she finally regards me all I want is to fill my hands with her. So I do, wrapping my arms around her and reveling in her closeness and the heat of her body. When she looks at me, her satisfied smile tells me everything I need to know. I bow to kiss her, but keep my lips lingering out of range. "Thank you so much. I really like getting flowers on days like this from pretty girls like you."

I feel, more than see her smirk. "Pretty girls, huh?"

I shrug playfully, "Well you know, me and my

millions of pretty girls."

"Should I be jealous?"

"Nah, you're the only pretty girl for me."

Rachel bites her lip and runs an unconscious hand through her dark hair, arranging some invisible imperfection to feel worthy of the complement.

I listen to the rain pelt the plate glass window beside us, clouds obscuring the New York skyline. It feels like it seals us away, locking my wife and I together in a rare moment of peace in our hectic lives. I go to steal a kiss, but she stops me with a well placed shift of her face, her words direct into my ear instead. "I'll use the flowers to confirm you're mine then. It's classier than urinating on the office furniture."

I laugh hard until her hand catches the dip in my lower back. The way she touches me dwindles even my breathing to nothing and with a smile her lips capture mine. It starts chaste, a kiss between my best friend and I. However, when her grip tightens on my back and her lips part, it evolves to include intent as we explore one another. I drown in her, and how she inexplicably can make my knees melt even after the fifteen years we have been together. When Rachel finally breaks the kiss I'm breathless. It doesn't help that when she comes back into focus her eyes are dark and smoldering. I swallow, willing my breath to steady.

"We should," Rachel laughs as she clears her throat of the huskiness of her libido, "put the flowers in water so they don't die."

"We should just take them home." I smile tenderly. "Why don't I just start my vacation after today. I can have someone come in and cover my patients."

Rachel pulls back a little to see my expression. She doesn't like to wear glasses in public, something about appearances I'll never fully understand, despite her eyesight getting worse over the last few years. I know she is partly checking to see that I'm not joking and also leaning back to see my face.

I peck a kiss to her nose. "Glasses."

"I have them, somewhere."

I mentally note that by somewhere she probably means lost in our bed from reading last night. And with uncanny accuracy I'm pretty sure they will spear me at some point when I go to sleep tonight.

"Are you serious about taking time off to be with me?"

"Yes."

That one word elicits a delicate million watt smile. "Good, I'm so lonely in that big old house without you to keep my company."

I nod, pressing my lips to her forehead. "I know, but it's part of the sacrifices we make so that we can be happy. I could work forever for you." I splay a hand over the side of Rachel's belly and caress her lightly. "For all of us. I would work forever, you know that."

"That's why I love you so much," she whispers against my lips, the faintest touch of air moving between us. "No matter how brilliant you are, you will never learn that you are all I need to be happy. I care less about money than you do, and you don't even charge your patients at this point anymore."

I fix my eyes on her face and when her long lashes and dark eyes flick up to meet mine, I can tell she wishes she could take the words back. I know she's miserable and the look of apology that passes over her face makes my brows furrow in mutual sorrow. I nod, understanding and letting it go, attempting humor to cut the regret we both feel. "I love you too, Mrs. Fortier, because you are the only one who knows how truly *stupid* I am."

She shakes her head, her soft hands fixing the white edges of my coat absently. "You're not stupid, just stubborn."

"Fine, stubborn then." I bump her nose with mine and when she smiles I know everything will be okay. I memorize it, this picture perfect moment of her smile, and her eyes.

She gently kneads my shoulders, erasing all my tension for a few blissful moments. "Well, get to it then," she cheerleads softly. "The sooner you see these poor people, the sooner this poor person can see you."

She pecks an all too brief kiss once more, and moves out of my arms. "I'll take the flowers home, okay?"

"Okay." She scoops them up as I grab her coat and help her into it. As much as I don't want her to leave, I need to finish my work. However, I just can't seem to let her go. To buy time I fix her collar and hair absently. "I promise I'll see you no later than three... and tonight," I slide my hands into her hair, curling the silken locks around my fingers, "I'll have wine, you'll have juice, and we will sit in the bathtub and just feel each other, okay?"

She flashes perfect white teeth. "Deal...and I'll hold you to that." Rachel gathers herself and moves toward the door looking for all the world like the famous singer she is, bouquet and all in her arms as she smiles at me.

"I'll hold myself to it, angel."

She winks and pulls the door open, pausing

briefly to look back at me. I lean back against my desk, watching her, soaking it in as I wear the smile she always leaves me with. I blow her a kiss. "Three hours."

Rachel's hair falls over her shoulder, catching the office light and shimmering softly. Her eyes are warm with promise. "That's three too many for me Blake, but okay." With a sigh she adds, "I love you."

And she is gone, leaving the room so much colder without her presence.

I don't know how long I stand there staring where she just stood. Rachel is right. There is no reason to kill myself building a life I can't live. I shouldn't let myself be at the mercy of a paycheck that I'm not willing to make hard decisions to bolster. If I don't short change my patients, why should I do it to myself?

I replay the image of Rachel turning to me from the doorway over and over. I remember her face and the apples of her cheeks, the depth of her eyes, and the soft bows of her lips. If she wasn't my wife, I would have wished for it every day. I still do, I admit to myself. I wish for her every moment of every day. Such is the power of my love for her that I'm sure for the rest of my life I will wish on shooting stars for her love.

I glance at the clock, 1:17 p.m.

Shit. I'm late.

I straighten my coat and run a hand over my head to be certain all my stray strands are fastened in my ponytail. When I push off the desk, I have every intention of going to my office door, but my feet fail me. I stagger in my place as I'm hit with a wave of *something*, something that very nearly topples me as I reach out for the guest chair to steady myself. I breathe heavily through the sudden pain I feel, an unhinging in my chest that feels like a heart attack, but isn't.

I put my hand to my chest and press, struggling to alleviate the pang I feel. It feels like a dislocation. That is the only way I can rationalize it. It feels like I just dislocated my whole ribcage. For a frightening moment, I mentally go through every medical book I have ever touched, searching my memory. Is it even possible to dislocate a ribcage?

It isn't.

I focus on breathing instead and when the wave passes, I stand up straight again and take a long steadying breath. "Okay, wow." I whisper to myself clearing my throat of unshed tears. I test that everything is fine by taking a step, and then another. Satisfied, I dismiss it and go back to work. The door to my office opens soundlessly and I make a right toward Mrs. Walter's room. Corrine is gone, but my second assistant hands me the patient folder and I flip it open, reviewing our last appointment before opening the door.

Just as I put my hand on the door handle, my phone rattles a message. I feel it thrum against my thigh and I stare down at my pocket blankly. I close the folder and pull the phone free, checking that it isn't Rachel needing me to pick something up on the way home.

EMERGENCY. CALL ME NOW. RYAN

Caps? I cock my head at the message dislodging strands of blonde hair from my ponytail. I sigh and tuck them back. Ryan is a friend from med school. He is also my liaison to Saint James right up the road. After having spoken at Rachel's and my ten year anniversary celebration, helping me through all-nighters in school, and throwing me business from the clinic how can I deny him? I glance at the exam room door before moving away. It has got to be one hell of a weird case for his text to sound so urgent.

The phone picks up almost instantly. "Blake?"

"Yeah, hey there." I laugh. "What's going on Ryan? Something disturbing you want me to consult on?" I fully expect him to laugh. He is always laughing. So when his voice breaks instead, I feel a shiver run up the length of my body.

"Oh God, Blake, you gotta get down here now."

I think I drop the folder in my hands, because suddenly I'm staring down at papers littering the floor before me. "What's wrong?" I urge.

His words stop my heart. "It's Rachel. She got hit by a car. God, Blake, get down here. I don't know if we can keep her alive."

I don't actually hear the words that follow. Instead I hear Rachel's whispered 'I love you' and I see those sparkling eyes of hers I love. It propels me forward, running blindly toward the back elevator. I punch the button, and stare in shock when the arrow down doesn't light.

When every second counts, how can the elevator not be here? "Where is the elevator?" I scream as I hit the button over and over in a panic. When the light finally dings I ride it straight to the bottom floor. I can't see, I can't think.

I'm hyperventilating, but I still can't breathe. How can so much air not let me breathe?

When the freight elevator hits street level, I force it open and dive through the partially opened doors. I spin in a circle, disoriented. How do I get to Rachel?

I have made the trip to Saint James hundreds of

times. So, how I can't find where to go is beyond me. The world is crashing down around me. I might as well be staring into an abyss. I wipe away the fog in my eyes and when I see the cross outside the building four blocks away, I run.

My panicked moans catch in the back of my throat and choke me. I'm wheezing, clawing the air as I run harder and faster than I have in my whole life. I run for my life, for the only thing that has ever mattered in it. My terror spurs me on and my footfalls pound in tandem to my racing heart.

She was just here. She was just here with me. Why did I let her leave? Why didn't I go with her? When the thoughts strike me my knee gives out from an old cheerleading injury and I crash to my palms. My momentum carries me and I scramble back up. I don't look back at the startled cries of people who saw me fall. I leave those people, and the cars I dart between, in a trail of agony and broken pieces of my heart.

I'm a block away when I see the police cars. I don't even process what I'm looking at until I pass it. It takes a moment for my mind to register the images—white puff balls, solidifying into daisies strewn across the wet road. I blink, slowing for the briefest of moments. They aren't my daisies, are they? The steam from a mutilated radiator spews a sweet sickly smell into the air. But it's the blood, thick, hot, heavy blood drawing in rivulets across the pavement that crashes everything together into a seething pool of horror.

It's Rachel's blood.

The world spins for a frightening moment and I lose my footing and stagger into a lamp post. *Too much blood.* My mind screams it over and over. *It's too much!* And then I'm running again. The last block spread before me like an endless marathon. When I hit the emergency room entrance I'm sputtering and unable to breathe. I slam to the wall and when I see no one at the reception desk or nurse's station I start to cry. All my friends, all the people I have known, trained, mentored, are somewhere trying to save my wife.

"Where is she!" I scream into the void, a motionless pit where there is always something happening.

"Blake!" Ryan yells over the din of the code blue announcement, the death knell as I know it. Rachel's death.

"Where is she!" I run to him, lunging into his arms in the hopes he can keep me from falling.

"Don't go," he says catching me. "It's too late, we couldn't do anything else." I can't see his face as he is wiped into a blur by my tears. I fight him, pressing him back and away. "No!" He grabs my arms, holding me still. "No, no, no, don't, Blake. Please, don't. You don't want to see her like this, please."

I scream my rage into his face. "She is my wife! Let me go!" Someone else's hands are on me, and they separate us. "Where is..." I don't have to finish the sentence. The first and last thing I hear is the sound of a steady tone.

I have heard that sound thousands of times. I know what it means. However the utter soundlessness that follows is something I have never experienced. Until now, that sound was never attached to anything that mattered to me, so when the silence washes over me and drowns out Rachel's monotone cardiac monitor, I'm grateful for it. It allows me to put one foot in front of the other and turn the corner into the trauma room.

Inside, there are faces of people I know. They feel alien as they try not to look at me. I don't look at them, not really, because she is all I can see.

My broken angel.

I slip beside her, sliding my shaking hands over the tubes, tubes hooked to her, tubes into her, tubes down Rachel's throat, into her chest wall, tearing her apart before my eyes. I close them so I can't see, my hands working by memory to the sides of her cheeks, into her hair. I shake the images away because I can't take it, I can't see her broken, and cut, and destroyed. She is my brave invulnerable person, *my* person. She is my human being that belonged to me as much as I belonged to her. She was supposed to be with me forever. She had promised to hold me and kiss me goodbye. I don't realize I'm screaming until I take another breath and...scream.

Scream because it wasn't supposed to be like this.

Not like this, not for her. It can be for anyone else, but not *her*.

When I finally take her hand and firm my lips to it, I pray that it is enough to bring her back. That perhaps my touch will be the anchor to Rachel's reality. That if she loves me, loves me like she always said she did, she would realize I need her. That she can't go yet. But I know in my heart she's gone, even as I beg and cry for it to be different. My heart is empty and hollow. And just like the bandages over her wounds can't hold back the blood, I know her body is too broken to hold back her spirit.

And my wife leaves me the same way she came into my life, as an angel.

Chapter Two

Deconstruction
February 21st, 2030

I know I'm just going through the motions. I'm still in shock. It's been two small days since my wife was taken from me. Even saying that now in my head, it doesn't register.

Wife.

Gone.

Those are two words I never would have put in the same sentence...yet, now I have.

And nothing will ever be the same again.

The past two days have been sleepless, full of the process of putting Rachel to rest. It's almost inhuman really, this process. I have called in funeral arrangements, flights and condolences to her family. I have serenely keyed my credit card numbers to order forms for caskets and penned my signature to receipts. I have done all of this without a flicker of emotion. I have been brave, brave like Rachel would want me to be.

Then there is the human part, when the calls come. Litanies of love and loss, words meant to salvage my soul have perforated every piece of me. Listening to people cry over my pain feels utterly disingenuous, though I know they don't mean it that way.

It makes me angry, too. Not because they are

breathing and bawling in my ears and she isn't. No, they make me enraged that I can't feel *anything*. I have tried to let their tears leak into me, in the hopes that it will awaken my heart, but there is nothing there. There is no stir or echo of emotion, just a bottomless pit of nothing. And I'm furious over the fact that they can still feel her and cry for her like I should be able to.

Sometimes, I'm sure all my work must be for someone else, because if it *really* was for my wife, it would have killed me. It should have killed me. If I really loved her, then I should be unraveling at the seams. I should be drowning in my misery. There is no way that I *should* have the strength to do this, because of my love for her.

Even now, along the stretch of highway 57, I drive. I drive with steady hands. Fixed on the wheel they don't move, don't quiver. I stare at them and the proud bands of my wedding rings. They are impossible hands for a widow. A widow has old withered hands whereas mine are steady and strong, soft and youthful.

So, she can't be gone. I can't be alone.

The rationale stops any tears from falling.

The fields race past my speeding rental car as I head south from the airport. I roll down my window and just breathe in. The sweet scent of seeded fields brushes my face and for the briefest of moments I close my eyes. Rachel and I always promised we would come back to where we grew up in Illinois. She had always envisioned a welcoming home, a chance to visit her old stomping grounds, feel the sunshine and breathe clean air. She said those were her reasons, though I knew her well enough to see through to the truth. She desperately yearned to rub her success in the face of everyone who ever doubted her.

There were so many people who said she couldn't make it. That a backwater Midwestern girl with a decent voice couldn't survive in the cold, fast world of New York. I had known her then, a boastful ingénue, bursting with promise and drive. Her stalwart arrogance and glimmering potential incensed me back in those days. I wanted to escape our provincial world just as badly, but with no hope or talent, she was a telling reminder of how unfair life was. My own cruel words had stood in testament to my jealousy many times. However, they didn't break her, they just fueled her on toward that pinnacle, pushed her toward greatness.

Somehow, mercifully, two things happened. The first was, she grew into herself. Now, years later, she is no longer the backwater Midwestern girl with a decent voice, but the glimmering jewel of the Broadway stage with the silver voice of an angel.

And the second...well, she became mine.

She is finally the woman she wanted to be. She finally *was* the woman she wanted to be.

Was. I shake the word away and tighten my hands on the steering wheel focusing on something else.

Having lived in New York for so long, I had forgotten this image of unfettered landscapes. It feels foreign and timeless, untouched and pristine. The bright open sky hangs crystal clear above me. I study the swatch of blue, how the color is so vibrant and all encapsulating. It draws me in enough that I slow the car down just so I can look at it. It is almost more than a sky. It domes over me with promises of crisp breezes and puffy white clouds. I feel if I really look closely, if I narrow my eyes a little more, I'll see straight into heaven.

But she wouldn't be there anyway. Because, she isn't gone. I swallow my thoughts and speed up.

"Oh God," I whisper ironically when I catch sight of the massive Effingham cross. The white monolithic beacon of religious rightness paints doctrine across a blazing blue sky. It's still miles away, but it jars me as I stare at it. I forgot that it used to mark my off-ramp home to Danville. I forgot it was here.

It had once given me such faith. It reminded me that I wasn't alone, that someone was always watching over me. It let me know that even with all my previous trespasses, I was loved. Especially, when my family turned on me for getting pregnant in high school. God was all I had left then. It was more than a symbol of faith, it was a physical manifestation of my absolution.

Now, it threatens me as it shoots into the sky. Its resolute presence announces unequivocally that God is watching. He *was* watching when Rachel was stripped from me. And He did nothing! He watched her die and not a finger was moved, not a single care was given to that. For all the tears and prayers I had put into Him, would it have been so hard to hold Rachel at a crosswalk for a few extra seconds?

Unless, He took her from me on purpose.

That thought hangs and makes me so angry and bitter I think about ramming the car into its massive steel base. I would give anything to topple the power that mocks me as I drive by. After giving one-hundred percent of myself to something–to my faith and my love–I can't give anymore again if all I am, all I *was*, can be wiped away like it never mattered at all.

And His messages of forgiveness? Ha. I will save

this fury for myself.

My anger keeps me strong. As I walk through manicured grass and come to a stop near a gathering of trees, it is the only thing I have left. The sunshine rockets through the branches above my head and paints happy geo-forms on the ground around me. It makes sense that I put Rachel to rest on a gloriously bright day.

I bury my wife, while words in a tongue I don't understand, give cadence to a pain I cannot feel. I know there are eyes on me, as I bow my head in prayer. I wonder if judging gazes are looking for my tears. Are they watching to see if I come apart? Do they want me to fall over the hole in the ground and weep? Would that make my love more real, more valid?

I focus on the slow tick of the casket as it lowers, and shadows fall over the cherry wood, painting it black in places. This is the closest she will ever be to me again. I fix on that thought, knowing that a mere three feet of air separates me from a face I will never see again. I *really* think about it, letting every remembered smile and soft word rake through my heart and shred me to pieces. Then, to make the pain I should feel that much more acute, I think about our daughter and how her face is one I will *never* see. Still no tears come as they should, and I'm riddled with remorse over it.

I glance at Rachel's mother and listen to her weep. Standing beside me, the contrast between us must make me seem absolutely inhuman. Of all the people gathered here, I should be the most inconsolable. When people look at me, do they wonder if I really ever loved her at all? My guilt comes then, like a soundless wall that deafens me. I can't hear the prayers in Hebrew anymore nor the whistle of air through the trees. The only thing I *can* hear is the sound of my own steady breathing. It chides me with its lack of stagger and the fact that it still exists at all.

When we all take hands, I squeeze hard to the people beside me in an effort to literally touch emotion that will make me feel real. And when they ask me to come forward, I do so without effort, automatic, devoid. I drop white daisies to her casket in a poetic cyclical act. And in accordance with tradition I'm the first...the first to sprinkle dirt over her. The first to send her on her way. When the grains ting softly on her casket I feel something crack deep in my chest.

And as others follow my lead, banishing my love to rot, I know that small give in my fortress is the beginning of the end for me. Everything else is a blur. I have no words to speak. I can't form a coherent thought. Even when my oldest friends from high school hug me in support, I can't manage an acknowledgement. Malina and Lindsey hug me all the same, ignoring my silence.

"We're here if you need us."

I clamp my lips in a thin line and just stare blankly at them. I would give anything to be able to voice how I feel, but everything gets stuck in the back of my throat.

"I'm sorry, Blake." Lindsey presses a strand of my hair back and I flinch at the tender motion. I fix my eyes on her dully, seeing but not acknowledging her surprise. My eyes trace a path to her hand in Malina's, their fingers twisted together, and I realize what it is that I feel. Jealousy.

Then...I can put words to my feelings. "I hate you."

I hate them for being alive and together.

"No, you don't," Malina whispers, her voice flecked with emotion despite the firm set of her eagle-sharp features. "You're just hurt, and that's okay."

I stay to watch them fill her grave. I owe it to Rachel to be there until the bitter end. So, I stay and watch as a machine methodically wipes her out of my life. I can feel Malina's eyes on me, watching and reading over me. Both her and Lindsey stay, much to my chagrin because I just want to be alone. I want to lay down right here in the grass and die because I can't carry on the battle when there is nothing left to fight for.

When it's finally done, when *she* is finally gone, the sun has moved to cut an amber glow over us. I look at people who were my friends with a level gaze. Malina holds out her hand to me, very uncharacteristically genuine for the normally reserved and brisk Latina. "Come with us, just for a little while. You and Rachel always loved to visit us in California. Let's celebrate and remember her together."

I stare at her hand. At the way she holds it, reaching out. I want to take it, to run screaming from my life and hide. But I can't. The hand before me isn't Rachel's and no one will ever share in the emotion and love I saved for her and her alone. With as much animosity as I have left in my heart, I push Malina's hand away.

"I do hate you." I say it with conviction so she knows I mean it. She offers a soft rueful smile and it infuriates me. It possesses me to say evil things. "I always hated you, for your better-than-thou attitude, for your condemnation of Rachel and my relationship, and for the mean words you said to her when we were younger. You never deserved to have her love or her forgiveness. And you'll never have mine again. Now, get away from me, and let me mourn in peace."

For the first time in her life Malina doesn't have a razor sharp response and it gives me what I want as tears light in her eyes.

Peace is elusive for me though. I make startling revelations about myself on the flight home to New York. I realize that for all my years of tenure in the ER and owning my own medical practice, I didn't lift a finger to save my wife. I didn't try CPR. I didn't attempt a negative pressure pump to inflate her lungs. I didn't do anything I know how to do. I could have reached into her chest and held her heart in my hands. I could have beat it for her.

I could have brought her back.

Instead, I had simply allowed it to happen. I sunk to the floor beside used gauze and blood drops, and let her slip away. It's a trespass I will never be able to forgive myself for. Those thoughts haunt me more than any dusty old town and a looming white cross ever could. The woulda–shoulda–coulda's of that moment will hurt me more than any fury God could curse me with. They silently chip the hairline fracture in my numbness wider.

My plan was to come back to a faster pace. That the frenetic speed of my life would give me reason. That somehow between my practice and my responsibilities, I would be able to repurpose my life. Rachel would want that after all. However, standing here in front of our home, here on this brick porch where we kissed in the rain and juggled groceries and keys, I don't know if it was the best idea. I take a breath, taking it one moment at a time.

Wall intact within me, I turn the lock. The door eases open to the dark within, the void of silence and inanimate things hang like a shadow before me. I edge my bags inside, letting them bang against the solid wood of the door before I close it with a heavy hand. I can't carry them in. Here in the entrance I set them down. I can't step further, and even as my hand works to find the lights, I'm afraid of what I'll see. When the inset lighting beams across our things, coloring our home in hues of raspberry and brown, I feel my throat seize closed.

I have come home to an empty house before, but this–this is forever. This is an emptiness that will never end. The depth of my loss coalesces around me as everywhere I focus, smells and sights of Rachel are there. Her perfume, her red blanket haphazardly folded on the sofa, even her fluffy slippers flipped in disregard by the fireplace. All of it gone, and I will never have it again.

"Oh, my God," I wheeze as I focus on everything. Holding my side I double over as pain rips through my chest, stealing all the air from my lungs. It angers me that I call out for a co-conspirator in her demise, as I struggle to stay upright.

Rachel was so close just a day ago. She had been no more than an arm's length from me. I remember back to her funeral, how the slow tick of the crank dropped her away from me. I know why people were looking at me. They were looking for this, this emotion right here. They were expecting me to crumble at any moment. It isn't until now, here in the silence of my shattered life that I realize *who* it was I was mourning. It isn't until now, behind closed doors, that I realize what I've lost.

My wife.

The most giving person I knew during the day, and the stealer of the covers at night.

My best friend.

Whose shoulder I cried on when I was lost, and the arms that pushed me forward when I found my way.

The person that I had given my life to.

Whose careless slippers and poorly folded blankets populated my existence with little annoyances, and wrote life across the mundane world I walk through.

The woman whose glasses woke me up when they stabbed me at night.

That person is gone. That one person who knew me, loved me, and accepted me for my faults, too. Who loved me better and deeper because of them, not in spite of them.

The tears hang in my eyes as I give up the fight and drop to the floor to cry.

≈≈≈≈

For the first few days, that is all I'm able to do. Cry. I bury my face in Rachel's pillows and clothing and weep.

Then, when the pillows and clothing begin to smell less like her and more like misery, I take the rectangle of Chanel perfume and blow puffs of it across everything in the house. I dust it over the living room, the kitchen, the bedroom, down the hall to the nursery door. I pretend she is in the other room, and has just passed by, that she leaves me in her wake, just out of eyesight, just out of reach. And I run circles in the house, chasing the ghost of her memory.

It isn't until after three days of spritzing that I realize why the house doesn't smell quite right. I'm staring at the bottle in the bathroom when I make the realization. Chemistry. Rachel's pheromones mixed with the perfume to create a different scent as they reacted with each other. The Chanel whispers that filled our home for years will never be possible again. The perfume bottle vibrates in my grip and in rage I throw it against the mirror and shatter everything.

My millions of faces stare back at me with judgment.

The news reports don't help either. I watch them in the darkness, my arms wrapping around her red blanket and squeezing it to me. Little makeshift altars flash across the screen, set up in Rachel's honor at the intersection where she died. Pictures in effigy line the news images as fans recount the splendor of Rachel's performances. I cry every time I see a recording of Rachel's lithe form move across a stage, because she was mine. That heroically beautiful woman they are portraying stood in my arms and loved me with all her heart. Every recording is the backdrop of someone professing why Rachel's ethereal presence mattered to them. Strangers who didn't even know who she was. No one will ever know the real woman. No one will ever know what an amazing human being has been lost.

And our baby.

I tighten my grip on Rachel's blanket and press my head against the microfiber. No, I can't think about that. I shake my head as I turn off the television and throw the remote across the room. It clatters across the floor. I struggle to keep the thoughts of Emily at bay, but they batter in on me. I fist my hand in my hair, tucking my knees to my chest.

Our baby is gone too, crushed out of existence within the womb of my wife. Just the thought of it makes me retch and I cover my mouth to stop me from releasing my bitterness at the world in a wave of vomit.

I glance to the sofa beside me, to where our phone sits idly. The calls aren't coming now. There are no more 'I'm sorrys' to say. I pick it up and dial our voicemail with shaking fingers.

Hello, you have reached Blake and Rachel Fortier, please leave us a message and we will be happy to contact you at our soonest opportunity. I listen to Rachel's voice on the line as tears leak. I let them fall, not bothering to wipe them away. I'm not one to pretend that everything is going to be okay. I'm a realist. Rachel was the romantic. So as I slide down onto our brown leather sofa and cover my balled up form in her blanket, I know I have nothing left to give. I know it's just a matter of time before I'm swallowed by my guilt. It's all my fault after all. Between my inaction after the crash and my absenteeism before, she is gone.

My neglect has earned me exactly what I deserve.

I hit the button again.

Hello, you have reached Blake and Rachel Fortier, please...

I don't realize I have fallen asleep until the shrill ring of the phone blasts me into consciousness. I bolt for where it dropped to the sofa beside me, scrambling it to my ear. "Hello?" I straighten my hair as if the person can see me, and squint through bloodshot eyes at the evening shadows. "Rachel?"

I don't know why I say it. I know she is gone.

"Blake?" It's Malina's voice. Her warm tone play against the tiredness of my mind.

"Yeah." I sigh, squinting at the clock. "I'm sorry, yeah...what?"

"Hey." There is a pause. "How are you?"

I know a loaded question when I hear one. "Why?"

A longer pause greets me and I stare into the emptiness of the room, my eyes lingering on piles of news articles, dirty coffee mugs and used take-out containers. "Well, we saw on the news that the kid pled out and we wanted to be sure you were okay."

I shake my head to get back into the conversation, trying to understand what she is saying. "Wait, what kid?"

"The kid that hit Rachel."

I bolt from the sofa not even realizing what I'm doing until I collide with the entertainment center. In my ear Malina's voice is alarmed. "Are you okay? What's going on? What are you doing?"

"Shut up," I snap as the television powers up, slicing through the room, and my brain, with glaring accuracy.

"...would have expected them to throw the book at him to be honest." The news announcer is saying, "We'll continue to follow these reports as they come to us, but to recap these startling events, Darren Douglas, the twenty-one year old college student who killed award winning stage actress Rachel Fortier a week ago, has plead guilty to the DUI and one count of vehicular manslaughter and could face up to ten years in jail."

I stare blankly at the television, tightening my grip on the phone rhythmically. "Blake?"

Ten Years. It's less than the time we had been together.

"Blake?"

Only *ten* years. He will be younger than me when he walks out of jail if he serves his full sentence. He will still have a life ahead of him. He will still be able to live a life with the time remaining.

"Blake!"

"What!" I yell back, feeling rage coil like a viper.

"I'm sorry," Malina soothes. "I didn't mean to be the bearer of that news, honey." She pauses and I lower my head against the wood frame of the entertainment stand. My breath fogs the glass. "Do you want us to come out to New York? We can be together, support each other, I know you need that. It could be like old times."

"It will never be like old times." I hang up the phone.

With the finality of those words echoing in my mind, my own twisted mantra, Rachel's sweet angelic voice on the message machine can't help me anymore. Only the slow burn of alcohol sends me into peaceful oblivion. I drink as I shut the windows, as I pull the curtains, as I seal the world away. All the while, substitute physicians run circles for my patients, filling my checking account all the same. I could have hired them before. I should have. It's thoughts like that that reduce me to drunken moaning sobs that never seem to end.

And the weeks turn into months.

I spend a lot of time meandering around the darkness of my home. I've lost twenty six pounds, not that I wanted to. I've always been thin. Now, I look like a corpse. It makes me laugh when I look at myself.

In a morbid way I must look like my rotting wife. We are two of a kind, her and me.

When I'm not drinking or staring at the outlines of my bones in a mirror, I walk around and look at things. I stare at our pictures, tap them and nudge them out of place on the walls. I don't know why I do it, maybe to test if they are real. I don't know. It doesn't really matter. I stare at our things, too. They are our things, but not at the same time. They are all mine now. Rachel left me everything. I just want to burn it all. I want to pour Jack Daniels over the whole fucking place and burn it to the ground.

I take a swig from the bottle in my hand and pick up a glass award from my home office. I used to have three, but I have fun breaking things now. During my walks, my 'yard time' when I'm not in bed or on the sofa, I find glass things that weren't Rachel's and carry them to the laundry room. There, in the enclosure, I throw them against the garage access door and watch them shatter into rainbows. Like now, I loft the football sized glass shard up and down. I don't remember it being quite this heavy, but attrition does things to you. I'm a doctor after all, I know this. And after a moment of quiet contemplation, I let it fly.

When it blows to dust–the last of my prestige awards for physician of the year—I squeal demonically in mirth. It's sickeningly amazing how something that takes five years of work can vanish in seconds. I clear my throat when my laughter dies. Oh. Wait, no. It's insane how something you work toward for fifteen years can vanish in one, just *one* instant. My eyes fall to the fat wedges of crystal at the bottom of the garage door lying among piles upon piles of rainbow colored glass.

Fuck the awards.

Fuck everything.

It's the omnipresent emptiness I feel in my chest that chides, I have only one option left. Omnipresent. I sound so much like Rachel. Even in my head I sound just like her with her eloquent words and verbosity. It's her fault, for making me love her so much for so long. My love for her has driven me here and it's the loveless actions of others that keeps me trapped in my misery. I swallow against the thickness at the back of my throat, the emotion I feel riding up from my chest.

I find it ironic that when I'm finally able to sober up is when I have the ability to stomach the amount of pills I have taken. Already they are taking effect. I know this because I *was* able to hold the prescription bottle beside me, but now my left arm isn't working. I turn a little eyeing the labeled container, so near yet so far, because now I can't grab it anymore. Oh, well.

Sprawled here across the living room floor, the soft carpet tickling the side of my face, I focus on how I feel like I'm being dragged down. I've seen death thousands of times. I'm not afraid of it. It's going to be painless, this death. Rachel's wasn't. I found that out yesterday after Ryan wrote me the last prescription I needed. He told me, finally, that Rachel was conscious when she came into the emergency room. She felt it. She felt herself die just like this, but it wasn't a peaceful oblivion. She had forty-three fractures, collapsed lungs, twenty-three shattered bones, lacerated internal organs. I feel but *don't* feel my tears leak down my face.

A broken femur.

I think that bothers me the most, that injury. It takes more force to break that bone than any other in the human body. And when that car hit her, it literally shattered everything on her right side from her knee to her sternum, it included. That body I loved, not because of how it felt under my hands, but because it held her spirit, her intelligence, her heart–that body was pulverized.

It haunts me whether I'm awake or asleep. That image has killed me over these long eight months, that and the question of how I would have done things differently. What I *would've* done if I had another chance...

I would've said so many things. I would've told her I thanked God for her, for her love and compassion. That our love was blessed by God, despite the myopic views of man. If I had known better I would've lived my life differently. I would've yelled less and loved more. I would've *been* there, present. I would've supported her dreams when we were younger. I would've been her champion. I would've abused 'I love you' to the point of bloodletting and accepted her flowers that day, and left hand in hand with her.

I feel my heart slow–finally–a calming euphoric peace passing through me. My hands and feet go numb. Pitched here between life and death I wonder if Rachel can hear me. Maybe my thoughts can permeate the void?

"Baby?"

It's not my voice. My vocal chords are partly frozen from the paralytic in my blood. Shadows paint over my eyes and flit across the part of the ceiling I can see. "If you can hear me, I'm so sorry." I wait a moment with baited breath, hopeful that the darkness will coalesce into her. That she will appear like a dark angel and scoop me in her arms, carry me away.

But nothing happens. It never does. The lack of *something* is the reason these eight months have dragged me to hell. When Rachel died, people stopped to note the shame of losing such a prodigy in her prime. However, I had expected more from a world worth living in than a few days of insincere commentary. I had expected the stars to paint empathetic sorrow across the heavens in a supernova. I had expected a cataclysmic schism in the center of the earth to be drawn in effigy to the pain in my heart.

But nothing changes, because the world keeps turning.

A world where babies are born.

Where people fall in love.

And die.

I fix my eyes on the picture of me and Rachel standing happily together. My wife is smiling, her hand resting on my stomach, my lips pressed to her temple. I blink away my finite tears as I remember that night and the laughter we had shared. It was the last time we enjoyed each other before work and reality, neglect and disregard swallowed everything good about us. I remember her saying that was all she had ever needed, and I realize now, too late, it was all I ever needed as well.

And without it, nothing else matters.

My chest tightens, and I scream but nothing comes out. My lungs seize. I can't breathe. My ears start ringing as my blood pressure skyrockets. My heart picks up trying to force oxygen through my veins. There isn't any, so I focus on Rachel's face.

I don't fight it and give in for the first time in my life.

And even though He betrayed me, I ask God for

one favor. I ask Him if I can see her once more, just one more time, before I'm condemned to hell. I want to know for eternity that she is sitting on a puffy white cloud somewhere. The devil can do what he wants to me, if I just know *that*.

But like all my prayers, I know this too will go unanswered. So I focus on her, because she never let me down. And the last thing I see is Rachel's eyes smiling at me before the shadows consume everything.

Chapter Three

What Life Is Made Of
Unknown, 2030

Delving into things like fate and death, while sexy because of their mystique, isn't something I ever did. That was Rachel's thing, not mine. I have always been rational, logical, matter-of-fact. She was the spiritual one between us. Rachel concerned herself with a higher purpose, while I focused on the mundane. It was why we worked so well together. She lifted and I anchored. We were two people creating life through the counter points of reality and fantasy.

But I tried to pay attention to it. Even when it was oppressive and seemingly out of place, I tried to listen. Her words somehow prepared me for what greets me when I open my eyes to a vortex of swirling darkness, and the memories come. They solidify out of the void around me, clouds firming into the interior of a car.

"They look like paths," she says quietly from the passenger's seat as we glide past snow swept fields and barren trees.

"What does?" I glance to the pensive look on her face. Reflecting against the gray, twilight-brushed world beyond the window, Rachel's eyes are almost black.

"The trees."

I slow the car a little, looking for the access road

that leads to our vacation house in upstate New York. I really wish we would have gotten out of the city sooner and missed the snowfall. It's more appealing to imagine being at our cabin building a fire and watching the trickle of powder cover the car than trying to find a four foot wide road in the middle of this weather. For good measure I turn up the wiper blades.

"Blake?"

"Hmm?" I focus harder on the road.

"It's close now. I can feel it coming up on the right."

I nod.

She's always had a connection to the world, one I couldn't understand or fathom. When we were younger, I mocked her for it. That was when she stopped talking about it, when it made her even more of a social pariah. Her silence was so deep regarding it that for many years I forgot about it altogether. I still do on occasion, because I can't rationalize it and it scares me. It is yet another nuance in her plethora of gifts.

I remember back to another drive like this, not to our cabin, but just the normal routine of coming home from the store. We had been passing through our neighborhood when Rachel turned to me with a hollow look in her eyes, whispering that our neighbor had died. When I think back on that look it bothers me. Not just because of how empty and dark her normally bright eyes were, but because she had been right.

Rachel's intuition comes to the forefront of my mind again as I study her. We drive in silence and the wiper blades keep time with an eerie gate. The swish is all I hear as I look away and concentrate on the right hand side of the road.

"Blake?"

I narrow my eyes at the expanse of snow and rock and fallen branches. "Yeah?"

"Do you ever think about death?"

I arch my eyebrow without letting my eyes leave the windshield. "A little morbid to talk about now don't you think? I mean, we are supposed to be enjoying each other's company and our small vacation."

I see her nod out of the corner of my eye. "Yeah, I guess." She twists her wedding rings nervously. "I just... sometimes I think about it. It gets me worked up. I suppose because it is just so out of my control."

"You mean because it's so final?" I clarify, slowing enough to make a sharp turn onto the access road.

"No, not final, I know there is something beyond this. It's just...I think about things like my father, how he died. How everyone I love except for you and our future children will beat me to this unstoppable future."

After we pass the last turn, I can focus more on what she was saying. "Rachel, you can't avoid death. I've seen it enough to know it will come when it comes, and you should just enjoy the time you have." I tease her, "And, who the hell says you're beating me to this end anyway?"

She doesn't laugh like I want her to. "Yeah, I suppose you're right. I guess I just don't like having stuff out of my control."

It's true, she doesn't. And though death to me is a familiar face I watch stalk the hallways and rooms of hospitals, I also know not everyone feels that way. "Well, the best thing is not to focus on the inevitable. If we all get to that place, why worry?"

She is quiet after that, pensive. "Slow down, I have a bad feeling." she says after a time, and I do.

The snow comes down harder then, as if

summoned to block us from moving forward. I shake my head to clear my thoughts. "You totally have me freaked out now." I lean to turn the heater up and fight the chill in my bones. That is when the fallen tree shoots into my headlights. I slam on my breaks and for a heart stopping moment, I'm not sure if I am going to keep from crashing. But we do, the car rocking in place from the sudden stop.

The tree has been down for some time. Wet sticky snow covering it and painting it in glitter before my headlights.

I ease a breath. "Wow, that was close. You okay?"

"Yes, you?" Rachel swallows audibly. I can't help but realize if she hadn't told me to slow down, we would have hit it. That, more than anything, makes my hands shake.

I check my rearview mirror and throw the car in reverse, backing up a little. "Can you see if there is clearance around this thing on your side?"

"I don't think so."

I sigh heavily. "I guess we could park off to the side and call the police in the morning to have the tree cleared."

Rachel nods. "Yeah, I don't think it's far, a few hundred yards maybe."

Just the thought of walking through snow in this cold with my knee makes my eyes roll. A few hundred yards might as well be miles. I push the thought away and remind myself that we do have a hot tub I can relax in as reward. I reach into my coat pocket and don my gloves. "Might as well go then. I'm not really up for the four hour drive back."

The snow is coming down in heavy clumps and sticks to us as we exit the vehicle. I grab our bags and

then hand hers over when she sweeps up beside me.
After a breath I lock the car and its headlights flash
blindingly in the dimness. With a sliver of moon
between the clouds, my eyes adjust to the dark and we
start forward.

We walk together, side by side. Ten steps in and
already I can feel cold induced pain in the joint of my
knee. I distract myself by looking at the dead tree beside
us. Lying on its side, the branches looked like huge
splitting pathways that skitter away from one another.
It looks amazing and in my mind's eye could be an
interesting addition to our garden. "Would you ever
want brick work like this at our house?" I pat the tree's
side and litter gathered snow beside us. "You know, the
paths you were talking about. We could do moss work
between them too, where the little slivers are close to
one another."

My wife bumps her shoulder against mine. In the
sparse light she is cast in ebony. Just the flash of her
smile and the metal fasteners of her coat let me know
where she is. I listen to her breathe as she huffs and
trudges along in thought. "Sounds beautiful, but no,
every time I looked at it I would think about life and
death and fate."

"Oh." I frown. Well, as beautiful as I imagine it
would be, I really don't want her contemplating life's
unanswered questions every time she goes outside.

"Yeah." She takes a heavier breath. "I have
always believed that life is a series of paths, we come to
a fork and we make a decision. We can't go back, only
forward, and slowly we eliminate all other pathways
until the end."

I think about it, busy myself with the idea of it.
"So, like right now, the choice to either go forward to

the cabin or drive home? That was a fork in the path?"

Rachel nods. I think she nods. I can't see it, but her coat rustles. "Right, and the choice we made has eliminated the other paths. Had we driven back, we would have lost these moments."

I challenge her then as I always do. "But what if I stop right here and double back to the car? Then I will be on that path again, right?"

"No. You will be on a different path altogether. Five minutes behind where you should be. There is a reason we make the choices we make."

"What if I speed to catch up to myself?"

She is silent then and I feel bad for poking holes in her theory. I believe in the scientific method though, hypotheses need to be rigorously tested.

"Maybe the paths interconnect again. Let's assume we choose to walk to the cabin, that this choice is the right path."

"We have chosen...wisely," I quote Indiana Jones under my breath.

"I'm being serious, Blake." Rachel sighs and I reach into the darkness to give what I think is her arm, a squeeze. "We choose to walk," she starts again, "but if we had chosen to drive back, maybe we were supposed to get into an accident. Maybe our path was supposed to end. Speeding up the car, putting ourselves in danger to make up for that time, could in theory make the paths interconnect. Thus, we realign and go boom."

She has a fair point and when it comes to those things, those metaphysical conversations, Rachel's fair points always give me the chills. I shiver. "So you believe everything is already laid out? Fate has divined the whole treelike pathways of our life and our only free will is to choose which path to take?"

"*Yeah, exactly. And some paths, just like some branches, end before others.*"

"*I really don't like that idea. I like thinking I can make my own fate.*" I mean it. I really don't like her idea of how life and fate work.

"*You can, I mean...Blake, if when you broke your knee you started doing drugs rather than pressing forward, I'm sure that path would have been a whole hell of a lot shorter.*"

"*So, what if I decided to forcibly go to another path?*" I try to think of something to illustrate it. "*Okay, so I know that driving in the car will get me killed, so I drive slower, and stop before getting to the place where I would be hit. Then what?*"

"*I don't know,*" Rachel whispers. " *Maybe you change your fate and create a new path? Or maybe the universe reboots you and forces you back onto the right path?*"

"*So, how am I supposed to game the system if I can be rebooted?*"

"*How are you ever supposed to know when and where you die, silly?*" Rachel laughs lightly. "*You don't game life, you said it yourself, death comes when it comes. I suppose at that point, that's where faith takes over. You have faith that someone or something will steer you in the right direction.*"

She always brings up the faith part. I struggle with it. I had once been very into my Christian heritage, but time and science and misery have taught me that faith is misplaced. That my faith is misplaced. God and I have a lot of serious talking to do at some point before I will feel satisfied to put my hopes in Him again.

"*Blake?*"

"*Yeah?*"

"You should believe in something, something that can comfort you when you're afraid. Science and religion can exist at the same time, just ask Einstein. He believed you could have both in tandem, not opposition."

I dust the snow out of Rachel's hair and bump against her playfully. I do anything I can think of to redirect her from this conversation. I don't have to see her face, to know she worries about my lack of faith, my lack of hope that goodness and rightness will prevail.

"I believe in you angel, and right now that's all I need."

And though I believe she is with me and will somehow save me, I can't fathom what I'm seeing. I'm trying to, but it seems impossible as I descend into this hellish world between worlds.

Hazy tendrils of smoke wrap around me and I fan them away when it feels like they are reaching out, trapping me. I turn in circles, or at least I think I do. I can't see myself. Everywhere I look there are orange and burnt brown swirling patches. Thick walls of acrid plumes billow past me. Before me a vortex swirls, blacker than any color I have ever seen. I feel like it's drawing me in, pulling bits and pieces of me into it. It seems to move with me, too. It repositions itself as I spin in circles so that no matter which way I'm facing, it's there–waiting, sucking me away.

Light.

My awareness of a small flicker in the distance is like a hammer against my senses. I know I saw it out of the corner of my eye, but from where, I'm not sure. The vortex vanishes when I focus on another flash so I move toward it. The glimmer is somewhere out of reach, distant and hazy. Yet, it seems to persist and light my way between the fog banks. I run for it, hurling myself through the darkness. I have to get to the light. It is the only thought, only compulsion I have as it lays out a path for me, and my more distant past encircles me.

I redirect my gaze to the sputtering candle beside the bed. I stare at it while it crackles and heaves and then finally goes out. Here in the familiar dark I breathe deep the scent of clean linens and warm skin.

In our bedroom, I can abandon my stress and worry. This is the only place where I don't have to carry the eighty extra pounds of pressure from the world and work on my shoulders. Pillowed against Rachel's bare back, I listen to her heartbeat. I wallow in it, in the steady canter that I knew so well. I turn my head and kiss along the expanse of skin near me. "I love the way your heart sounds."

Rachel doesn't respond right away, not that I expect her to as her long slow breaths indicate she is drifting in and out of sleep. I focus on her unruly curls as they fan her upper back and pillow. I think about how beautiful her hair is as I run my hand through it, summoning a soft sigh.

"I love the way my heart feels," she purrs belatedly, staggering a breath as she purges herself of any remaining excitement from our lovemaking. Rachel worms an ungainly hand behind her and gently squeezes the side I'm lying on. "You always make me feel so good."

I smile, twisting her hair in my hand and then trailing fingernails down her back. I watch chills map after the touches. "Well, it's easy cause you're so sexy. I don't do anything but put my hands on you and enjoy."

She laughs softly. "Blake, you don't have to flatter

me. You already got in my pants."

My eyebrow quirks in question at her words. When I am finally able to roll over and spoon her, Rachel turns to smile. "Angel, I mean it, you are just gorgeous." I whisper it in her ear before pulling the lobe into my mouth and nibbling slightly.

Her hands tighten on the pillowcase and I know I have her going again when I feel her body press into mine. "You." She clears her throat. "You have no idea how much power you have over me. How you can make me feel amazing with the slightest touch and..." She groans as I lick inside her ear, "God, I want you to have anything you want."

"Do you know what I want?" I growl low against the wet skin of Rachel's neck as I draw my mouth over it.

"Yes." She rolls and blinks her fuzziness away, soft hands on my chest holding me at bay. "You know Blake, I love you so much it hurts sometimes." Her profession of love is genuine and sweet. After so many years, so many moments of reality, her honest emotion is all the more meaningful to me.

"I love you, too."

She traces her knuckles over my jaw line and I shiver from the softness of her skin, then the burr of her wedding rings mixing with it. It brings to the forefront of my consciousness the awareness that she is mine. It makes me smile as she shifts closer, arms and legs drawing me into her.

"I love you so much sometimes, I think my heart might burst."

I bite my lip, unsure if she knows how much impact those words have on me. I mask it as I nudge her nose with mine playfully. "Let's not let that happen, okay?"

She rolls her eyes good-naturedly. "At this point you are supposed to say something equally as romantic."

"I know." I shift uncomfortably, building up to it. "If you weren't mine I don't know what I'd do. I need you that much." I duck my head and kiss those perfect full lips, pressing her to her back under me. "I love you. Only you, and always you."

"Always me, Blake?" She ruffles my hair, obscuring her image in wisps of blonde.

"Always," I wedge between kisses as she brushes everything back into place. Her nails drag down my back and she pull me into her mouth.

"Prove it," she challenges against my lips and I melt her sure smile as I claim her again.

The image shatters and I grab for it frantically, willing my mind to keep the moment, to keep Rachel alive and in my arms. It hits me like a physical blow, losing that warmth, and it spills me to the ground in this darkness of inexistence. I know it's my brain's synaptic pathways firing fleeting images as it dies, but why I can't die to this one beautiful moment between us, kills me.

It takes five minutes for the human brain to stop working after the heart stops. It's incredible really, how resilient that one organ is. How it persists, and quivers, and dies—but not without a fight. It saps oxygen from every other organ so that humanity can be preserved.

I don't need preservation though. There is no fight for life, no war to wage against the mute fall toward hell. I sit and let the darkness wrap around me. It's futile to fight it, to chase shots of light. I'll never have Rachel back, so why should I race toward the light? I won't go to heaven anyway, even if there is one, so what does it matter?

I stare out at the Pacific Ocean, the moon lighting my way as I stack wood in the fire pit. I hear footsteps coming toward me and brush my hand through my hair to straighten it. My lips are offering my girlfriend a smile, since I expect to see Rachel, but I'm surprised when Malina drops down into the sand to sit beside me.

"So what's the deal with you and Rachel Kaplan?" The point blank question slaps reality into me as she holds out a beer. "Don't get caught drinking it, this beach isn't private."

I glance around, buying time to figure out an answer. Nothing comes to mind, so I stall with a swig and wedge the bottle into the sand. At this point I would be okay with a beach patrol officer coming by and arresting me for drinking. It would be way better than the dark positively emotionless look Malina is levying against me.

"What do you mean?" I feign ignorance. "We are just friends." I point at the barren fire pit and give her an even look as she measures me. "Right now I'm worried that I'm not going to get this thing lit, so can you grill me on Rachel another time?"

Malina shakes her head and smiles knowingly. I hate when she has this look, and to further the subliminal message that she isn't letting me out of the conversation, she digs her toes into the sand. "Well, Lindsey and Rachel were just talking about something and I heard there might be shit happening."

I groan inwardly and pick up the beer again, nursing it.

"You know, like you guys are fucking."

I choke on my drink. God damn it Rachel, I curse

silently. We had an agreement. I told my friends when I was ready, not the other way around. "Really, can you make it any cruder? Is that all you think of? When two women are friends, they have to be fucking?" *I arch an eyebrow taking another large swig, praying my observations get her off the scent.*

"Is that what's up?"

"What do you care if I am?" *I form the words around the lip of the bottle.*

"I care because I don't want to set up a fucking intervention for you." *Malina laughs, tilting her dark head up into the night as she takes swigs. She shakes her head when she looks at me again, pulling her lips from the bottle with a smack.* "I mean Jesus Christ Blake, you can have anyone with your whole I'm-gonna-be-a-doctor shtick. You're some woman's panty dropping, pussy wetting fantasy with your blonde hair and bedroom eye bullshit. What would possess you to grab up Rachel Kaplan?"

If I omit the last line, it is probably the biggest compliment I've ever heard come from her. However, I can't and I'm not going to rise to the bait either, though it is really hard not to. "Like I said, what do you care if I am or not?"

"Because it's wrong and screwed up."

I stow the beer and crumple a piece of newspaper, stuffing it between the logs. "And if I am, how is it any of your business?"

Malina leans onto her knees, her eyes wide. "Oh shit, it is true. I totally didn't buy it. It was Lindsey that clued me in."

"Fucking great." *I crush more paper.* "Well, it doesn't matter what you say, my mind is made up on it."

"What if I said that as your oldest and best fucking friend, I think it's stupid? She is a selfish diva. She only cares about herself, and with that much ego there isn't enough room for you."

Okay, that gets me angry and I turn on her. "Listen to me very carefully, Mal." I point a firm finger at her. "You have no right to say anything like that about someone you don't know. I mean really know. You say that again and I'll put you into your place."

"Oh really?" she challenges, puffing up a little.

"Yeah, and guess what?" I clear my throat. "Not only are we dating, but tomorrow I'm asking her to marry me. So how does that sit with you? Does that offend you? Because honestly, I could give a shit."

Malina smiles coolly then, her mouth claiming her bottle again as she looks away. I stare her down, boring my eyes into the side of her face. When she finally stands and dusts sand all over, I'm actually surprised she has nothing more to say. And then it comes, "Actually, it sits really well with me."

I feel my mouth fall open. "Wait, what?"

She laughs. "I just wanted to be sure you were sure. And Rachel didn't say anything, so don't freak out on her. It's just super obvious, so yeah. As your best friend, it's my job to be sure you know what you're doing."

"So you don't think any of that stuff at all?" I ask, confused.

"Oh, well yeah, I do. She was an arrogant pain in the ass from what I remember of her in high school, and seriously this is going to be a long week with you both here, but..."she holds up her hands in defense, "you don't believe that stuff, so I'm willing to give it a try for you."

"She isn't the same," I note as Malina backs away a little. "You will love her."

"Yeah, well I'm gonna pretend you didn't say I would love that little diva. However, at the very least she is good for your passion. I don't think I've seen this fire in a long time. And she's clearly good for your ego... thinking you can put me in my place...please." She scoffs as she continues to retreat, "I can still throw down like in high school, even though I look like a fucking yuppie now."

"You really do, Mal." I laugh as I focus back on the fire.

"Shut it, Blake. You're literally one string of pearls away from missionary sex for the rest of your life."

I turn to her, watching the realization of her words click. She turns back and I grin wickedly. "Missionary sex with Rachel Kaplan? Hardly. You wouldn't believe the things I get her to do with me."

Malina makes a fake puking sound, covering her ears. "I fucking hate you right now! Don't say another word!"

"We have this one position where we..." I start, and Malina drowns me out with a screaming rendition of "God Bless America," which makes what I was going to pretend to say infinitely more wrong. I don't stop laughing until I can't see or hear her anymore.

I can see the flickers of light still, a mass of swirling liquid shimmers in the darkness. My only company as I fade into oblivion. I have read the studies about people who survived death and told tales of that transition. I have always dismissed the journal studies as electrical impulses being purged from the patient's brains, but for a fleeting moment...I hope...I hope I'm wrong. I hope this wedging between worlds is something more than fleeting final impulses from my brain. I hope it is me getting pulled to Heaven.

Perhaps God will be here on the save, letting me repent to slide into heaven by the skin of my teeth. And maybe if I pray and beg and cry, I'll get that one last chance to see Rachel. While I'm thinking that, the light rolls and shimmers more. And I'm up racing toward it again, because that is the thing that makes it worth it. She is where all my life's value is derived even if it took a lifetime to learn it. Here at the end I finally understand, while the clouds around me swirl and firm, while they build into my high school world where Rachel's and my story began.

I feel the comforting scratch of my cheerleading skirt as I walk beside my friends. We flank one another, moving like a wall of ego through the hallways. People move, dodge and dart out of our way. This is how it is meant to be. We are the best in this God forsaken school, anyway.

I see Rachel Kaplan, weird incarnate, at her locker with her back turned to us. I glance at Malina, giving her a look of evil. Her eyes take in Rachel and a mirrored smirk maps her lips.

"So, you were saying about that girl, Rachel?" I prompt.

"The missed abortion?"

"That's the one."

"Yeah, I was saying, she's worthless." Malina says loudly, and right as Rachel turns to us, she slams the diminutive brunette's books out of her hands. "And a total freak, too."

I crush Rachel's locker closed as she backs against the metal. It is so close to her shoulder I'm not sure if I hit her. Not that I care, but marks prompt possible detentions. *"You agree, Kaplan?"*

To her credit, Rachel doesn't even flinch, which annoys me even more. *"Don't you guys get tired of this? I mean really, you're all smart girls, I'm sure you realize this has zero purpose."*

Malina glances at me. I see exactly what she is thinking and I'm thinking the same thing. Really? I mean, really? What a weirdo. I arch my brow at my friends. *"I don't think that is the answer we're looking for."*

Rachel's eyes nervously bounce across all of us as we move in closer, circling. *"Blake, Malina, Lindsey, you should stop and see reason."* She clears her throat, edging her hands up a little defensively. *"Someday, we'll all be somewhere else, and do we really want to look back and see these as moments in our lives? I mean, when I'm a famous singer-"*

"Stop it!" I burst, even catching myself in surprise. I reign in my irritation a moment later. *"You will never be famous. You will always be this sad little thing that no one sees or cares about!"* I dig my fingernail under her lowered chin, pinching the tender skin there until she looks up at me. She finally winces. *"You ever get in my way again and I will end you. You won't be able to make anything out of your life if you aren't around to live it, huh?"*

"You can't do that." Rachel's eyes widen as I hold them. *"Blake, seriously. You're too smart to be like this."* I'm stuck on those fucking eyes and I don't know why. They are the reddest brown I have ever seen in my life. They might as well be made of fire. They twist my emotions as I stare at them, into them, into the vast depth and strength that crackles within her, even from such a compromising position.

Malina's gruff hands slam Rachel back against the locker, and it breaks my trance. "She is Blake fucking Fortier. She can do anything she wants! And bitch, please, if she can't do it, I sure as fuck can, so shut the hell up before I cut your tongue out your smart mouth."

"Come on girls," I say slowly once again in control of my feelings. I smile down at Rachel as she stares at me, her mouth sealed tight. I add a little more bitch to push my point harder. "Let's leave the little diva to practice her new role of shutting the fuck up."

Malina laughs and Lindsey resumes my flank as we turn and leave Rachel to slip into the shadows, or wherever it is weird little freaks go to hide between classes.

I feel the shame, I feel the regret. I am only human though. I was only a child. We all were. And that is the only way I can cope with how terrible it is to see the harsh reality of who I was. But it was that moment, staring into her eyes, that I felt something for the first time. Being so close to someone I hated and to feel such awe changed my life, and eventually drove me into her arms.

Rachel made me better that day, taught me what I needed to know to overcome crushing uncertainty and aggression. She was the first person to tell me I was smart. That maybe my brains were worth more than porcelain skin and blonde hair. She gave me the hope that I could stand on my own two feet and fight for a beautiful life, that, maybe, I deserved it.

She is the *only* reason I believe that the light before me is a good thing.

I lift my hand toward it, but I can't see myself so I don't know if I'm touching it. I look down through the blankness of my inexistence. Light swirls and flickers there, too. Good light brought forth from my soul mate. It pours through me and out of me, blossoming inside where I should be.

For an instant in the light, I think I see Rachel's face. I focus on it, pitching on the edge of an abyss. I force myself to see through the blinding radiance, see the path I walk between the blurs, the path that will take me through my life to her.

I will my eyes to open and see.

See and remember.

And I stretch for her.

Chapter Four

To Do It All Again
April 12th, 2011

I was an artist once that painted the world. I hashed lines of color, dazzling blues and greens, covering everything I was and everything people believed about me. I wore colors of fury and poise, perfect and serene like a chameleon. No one really knew the girl I was. No one knew about me because it wasn't important. Neither my family nor my friends paid attention to the yearning in my heart or the skill I developed. They didn't care that worlds lived inside me. They just cared that I performed in this one. As long as I was the perfect child, friend, lover, with a perfect smile, perfect walk, and stunning eyes, then it was okay.

I was okay.

But, was I okay?

When I traded a paintbrush for a scalpel, when I became a masterful artist at deceiving death, I fulfilled their dreams for *my* life. Instead of bringing to life creations, I brought back God's work from the reaper. I used lances and medication as a palette to whisper drops of magic into other's veins. I whipped arcs of electricity from my fingertips, rending jolts through people's hearts. The only parallel between the two was that I existed in the moments between moments. It was where I lived and breathed.

Where I breathed until breathing wasn't enough.

"*Breathe.*"

I pump my hands up and down, throwing all my body weight into the compressions. I feel ribs splinter under my hands.

"*Breathe.*" *The inflation of the bag sounds like a wheeze.*

I replace my hands, and start again. One, two, three...I push down, my eyes fixing in determination on the cardiac monitor beside me. With every depression, I see the peak. I see it go flat. I won't remit. I have slammed hundreds of blows into his chest, but I won't stop.

Everything burns, my legs, my back. My arms threaten to crumble. I'm panting as I stop. "*Breathe.*"

"*Should we call time of death?*" *The nurse beside me gives me a nervous look.*

"*No.*" *I keep going, feeling the sharp bones under my hands as I press into the void of the chest before me.* "*Where the hell is the crash cart?*"

"*Here!*" *I hear the contraption squeak into the room and I move off the bed, stumbling awkwardly as my body uncoils. I'm out of shape. I haven't done this in a long time. It feels like I've ran a marathon and my knee groans in protest when I knock it against the bed rail.* "*Doctor Fortier, charged at 300 joules.*"

I grab the paddles, ignoring my pain because somewhere this young man is fighting a tougher battle than I. The nurses spread conductive jelly on the chest I've broken to pieces. Hands positioning automatically, I glance around. "*Clear!*"

The sound that rips through the air, the tear of lightning released by me, makes my hands numb as the form under me arches. All eyes turn to the monitor, to the wobbling line. His heart is quivering. It's trying. I put the paddles back as the machine beside me hums. I pray. I pray that when I send arcs of electricity through him that his heart will fire. That he will open his eyes. He is a young kid, too young to go. He is too important to stop fighting for.

"Clear!" He has to fight. Fight, damn you! I scream silently as I crush another wave of light through him.

I suddenly hear it, the little blessed beep. When my eyes fix on the monitor, I shudder a breath. The small bounding peaks persist. I stare at them, ready for if they stop. I'm ready to pull him back again if I have to.

I have always been ready to fight for someone's future.

But I will not fight for my own. That is someone else's job.

I have waged war for the world one person at a time. I have held life in my hands both figuratively and literally. I have walked the noble path. I've sacrificed everything for others, for ghosts to walk in skin and persevere. My future isn't my fight. I just don't have it in me anymore. The repressed romantic within me expects that if I fight for everyone, someone should fight for me.

So when I open my eyes, I have nothing left to give.

I don't even care if I've been brought back from the brink. If I *have* been salvaged from the grave, then the doctor that has done it better have a world of fight in him. He'll be making up for me. So, he damn well should come with a truckload of epinephrine and adrenaline because I'm not working with him.

I'm not trying.

I won't do it.

He can't make me!

If he wants to bring me back to a world where my wife and child are gone, then he will do it without my help or consent. I fist my hands. As a matter of fact, I will fight. I close my eyes and will myself to fall back into the abyss. I hold my breath, slowing my heart. I fade back against the magic that has rendered me to life. This world can't have me, won't have me. And how dare it try? How dare this godforsaken place bring me back?

The world spins and my body betrays me by forcing me to breathe. Breathe and exist.

"God damn it!"

When I hear my own voice, it shocks reality into me. Silence encircles me aside from the sound of my own rapid breathing. There is no beep of a cardiac monitor, no commands being shouted, no...anything.

I sit up quickly, slamming my knees into my chest. I don't even feel it. I'm in a bed, not a hospital bed, but a queen size bedroom one. I look around, unable to make out anything in the watery darkness.

Where am I?

When my eyes finally focus and I see a window frame decked in curtains across the room, I stare at it blankly, puzzle over it. It looks familiar, like the millions of windows I have seen in my life and yet more intimate. It's more meaningful because it's something I stared at every day, I know it.

Shadowed objects materialize and I'm not sure if they were there and I didn't notice, or if they are being manifested. My eyes move around in circles as

I study everything, my dresser, my mirror, my desk. They are absolutely benign, but represent a horror I can't verbalize. These things around me shouldn't *be*. The dresser was broken in a move years ago. The desk was given to a family friend's child. All of it should be dust in the wind of my memories.

I should be dead. I should be wiped out of existence. But this isn't heaven. My mouth freezes in a silent scream as I realize where I am. I'm in my childhood bedroom and it is exactly the way it looked when I was a little girl.

I pat my hands over myself, checking to make sure I'm solid, corporeal.

"It isn't possible." I say it as I think it and every fiber of my being literally stands on end. My heart pounds, my mind races as I search for the logical conclusion because the alternative doesn't make sense. I must be dead, I must be in heaven. This has to be heaven.

I pause.

Or hell.

The silence is disorienting and I struggle to hunt back through my memories, find order in the chaos of my mind. I was dying in the living room, and then I was standing in a void, now this? I'm almost afraid to move, as if something lurking in the darkness will grab me and haul me into another twisted setting.

I look down at myself, measuring the white silk nightie punctuated against the tan of my shoulder. I trace the spaghetti strap and with a shaking hand I poke it. I don't know what I'm expecting, maybe for it to wind around me and drag me into myself, or pull me inside out. It feels like a cotton and silk blend, nothing demonic at all. I let go a ragged breath. When my eyes focus on my skin, I realize how smooth and youthful it looks. I look up at the mirror and toss off the blankets. I can't be *that* young, since I'm wearing a fairly sexy nightie, but when I see the tone and tan of my legs, I freeze as it wipes all thought out of my mind. The blankets slide off the bed and out of my view.

I stare at the place where a jagged scar should be on my right knee, but smooth skin meets my gaze. I cover my mouth with my hand as emotion builds up and chokes the back of my throat. It's not there; there is no painful reminder of my senior year of high school. I move my leg slowly and lean back as I lift it, bending at the knee. There is not a single shot of pain, not a grind, not a pop. It's the first time in over half my life that my knee moves smoothly, perfectly. Just to test it, I swing out of bed, doing a half round off the double-stuffed mattress onto the hardwood floor.

It doesn't hurt. So I lunge, holding my balance with my arms outstretched. I watch the muscles flex, watch the vastus medialis and rectus femoris bulge as they pull the patellar ligament attached to my knee. It doesn't threaten to unseat, it doesn't make me feel like if I breathe my knee is going to crumble. I stand up straight again, letting my hands fall limply to my side. This has to be heaven if my knee is fixed. No devil would do this for me, make me whole.

Unless, he meant to torture me by taking it all away.

I glance around again, wrapping my arms around chilled skin. I wait for the blow to come. I crush my eyes closed so I don't see the swipe coming that will break my knee into fragments again. I hold my breath.

When it doesn't come, I peek open an eye and a

picture catches my attention. It's a small silver framed image, three smiles glimmering from it from the light outside. I know the picture as well as I know my own face, which is there, too. I pad toward it and pick it up.

It's me, Malina, and Lindsey, happily grinning into the camera.

I drop it and it clatters. I don't pay attention to where it falls because I'm committed to the mirror. I rush over and wrap my hands around the dresser white knuckling the edges as I lift my eyes to the image before me. My hands rattle against the wood. I've never been so afraid of anything in my life. The face staring back at me from my dresser mirror is one I know well. It is the face that stared up at me from yearbook pictures.

I haven't looked in her eyes for a long time.

My teenage face is very similar to my adult face. A touch softer in the way it curves and I touch it, marvel at it, the feeling of skin under my fingertips. Years of tiredness and pollution, sun and stress, erased. It's firm and soft. I focus on my eyes, boring into them with purpose. They aren't tired, aren't lined and puffy with depression induced tears. They are dazzling eyes, light hazel and dynamic. I swallow. They are carefree eyes, ones that have never felt the weight of the world upon them.

My gaze drifts down, tracing the outline of my white nightie as it clings to me. I map my hands over my body. I feel the heat of my skin under the material, the silhouette lean and lithe. I don't think I've seen myself this toned, this tan, this youthful since before I got pregnant. Since before I almost ruined my life from one moment of teenage stupidity.

In the ghostly light from the street lamp outside,

my face is set in determination as I search over myself. It is me, but not. I'm inside my teenage body. "I'm inside here." I fist my hands in the material and watch the motion performed by the young girl in the mirror.

How old am I? Sixteen? Seventeen? As an adult, I had forgotten how young I looked as a teenager. It seems wholly inappropriate that I'm dressed in this alluring outfit. Why did my parents let me buy this? A voice inside me chides the answer, pointing out that my parents would have to care about me before they even noticed what I wore.

My gaze wavers and drifts to the computer on my desk behind me. I stare at it. I need to figure out *when* I am. I give a last look at the young girl in the mirror and just to test that I'm really still here I say something she wouldn't know. "Scaphoid, lunate, triquetral, pisiform, trapezium, trapezoid, capitate, hamate." I can't help the satisfied smile I see when I list the metacarpal bones by memory after all these years.

I abandon the mirror and go for the laptop. I press it open, letting it boot. It flashes a blinding light as I corral my chair and slide into it numbly. When it prompts for a password, my hands shake as I peck out the request. It rejects it.

"Shit," I whisper under my breath as I stare at the field. What did it used to be? I try a combination of boyfriends, pets, any password I had throughout my life. It beeps in protest, in accusation that I'm not who I am.

It's right.

I tap my fingers on the keys idly, thinking. When I look up at the desk, I see papers and grab them. Receipts for coffee and books for school, notes from other people fly through my fingers as I read and dismiss them. I roll my eyes as I find note after note from boys, solicitations of affection. Those go right into the trash. When I get to the end of the stack I'm sorely disappointed I don't have a single note from Rachel.

Right when her name pops into my mind, my eyes laser toward my nightstand where my phone is sitting. I dive for it, grappling for the sliver of electronics. My hands are shaking so badly I can't even see what I'm doing. I punch buttons, and though I absolutely meant to call Rachel. I realize as it's connecting that I dialed her cell number in New York.

"Hello?" A voice I don't know, gravelly and tired, answers.

I panic. "Hello?"

The man on the other end of the line is not my wife, nor does he sound at all pleased he received a call in the middle of the night. "Who is this?"

"I'm sorry, wrong number." I hang up.

"Oh, Jesus." I wrap my hand in my hair as I stare down at the phone. "What is her number?" I have no idea and even as I start a hunt through my phone book, scrolling through entry after entry, I know I won't find it there. If I *am* back in the past, Rachel isn't my friend. Her number won't be in my contacts like it has been for years. That thought brings tears to my eyes and I clear my throat to stave off the flow. It's not going to do me any good to fall apart.

My thumb hovers over Malina's contact listing and I hit the button without really thinking. I lift it to my ear. When the line connects, I'm expecting a grown woman to answer with hello, but instead I get pure bitch.

"What the fuck, Blake? It's midnight on Monday, you know I'm getting my groove on."

My mouth drops open in surprise. "I know...I mean...w-why did you answer then?" I clear my throat and for the life of me I can't think of what to say. It is just so nice to hear her voice that I don't even care that she is pissed and I can hear someone in the background. "I just wanted to say hi."

There is a very long pause. "Blake?" Her voice is deadly serious. "What the fuck?"

I screw my face up in confusion. "What?"

She huffs loudly and disconnects the line.

I stare at the phone again. "You little whore, I can't..." I cut my tirade short as I notice my bedroom door. I think long and hard about it, about what's beyond it, what horrors could lie outside my room. I also think about what promises are there.

Rachel grew up in a house five minutes from mine. If this is the past then seven streets over she is tucked into her bed. I could throw on clothing and race over there. I take a breath. What would I do if I went to Rachel Fortier's house? Climb the tree in her backyard? Toss rocks at her window until she opened it? Rachel isn't my friend. I recite the sentence over and over. The closest interaction we have had is me banging her into lockers and pushing her around. I ease another strangled breath when I realize I should at the very least call her by the right name. It's Kaplan, not Fortier.

She's not my wife anymore.

The sheer overwhelmingness I feel at that thought takes my legs out from under me, and I sit hard on the edge of the bed. An eerie thought finds its way to the forefront of my brain. What if I open my door and there is a swirling hurricane of nothingness ready to rip me out of this world? If that is the way it is supposed to be, then I'll do it. Better to be ripped away then live in fear. I grit my teeth and stand again.

"You're a grown woman, Blake," I tell myself firmly to fill the silence. "You can just open the door." Though it sincerely is that easy, I just *can't* do it. For all my bravado a moment ago, my feet are frozen to the floor and when I hyper focus on the doorknob I swear I see it moving. At first I think it's my imagination until I hear the bolt release and my heart is in my throat so quickly I don't even have time to scream.

"Blake?"

I know that voice. It's my mother. When she opens the door and flicks on the light it blinds me. Her cold eyes catch me when I blink the brightness away and I'm shocked at how young she is. She can't be more than a few years older than me, the real me, not the child she sees before her.

"Blake?" She gives me a look, one that prompts me to speak because of how irritated she appears.

"Yeah?"

"What are you doing in here? I swear to God if you wake your father there will be hell to pay." She clasps the door knob and I find it ironic that at the same time she is threatening me, the gold necklace and cross around her neck catches the light.

I smirk because I'm not the little girl she used to scare anymore. "What kind of hell?" I ask dryly.

"What?"

I clear my throat and focus hard on her face. "I said what kind of hell will I have to pay? If it's what I think you're alluding to, I'm sure the police would love to hear about it."

She doesn't have a response.

I give her a minute more to think of something before I've had enough. "Please leave. I'm busy." When her eyes bulge at me, I stop the daring smile that builds on my face. *That's right, I'm not the whipping boy for either of you anymore.* I hold her icy gaze with one of my own until the door clicks closed.

I return to my previous thoughts...oh, that's right, the door. I eye it again critically. I know what's out there now. What's in here though, is a whole other story. I stare at my computer for what feels like forever as fragmented thoughts whip through my mind. I need to think this through. I need to figure out *when* I am. I chew my lip as I try to remember who I was in high school. I know who I was perceived as: the bitch, the popular blonde, the debutante. Those pieces have followed me my whole life. It's the other parts people didn't know that I focus on now: the artist, the little girl with big dreams and bigger secrets, the midnight journalist.

I rush across the room and dig into the alcove where I used to hide all my art supplies. I open the drawers, scattering pencils and charcoal in my search. I know I have a diary somewhere. I moved it around so my mother wouldn't find it on one of her hunts. It's not here.

I look in the top drawer of my dresser, my cubbies, my closet. I even upend the top mattress of my bed in my search. "I was paranoid as hell," I whisper, fisting my hips as I survey the mess I've made. Out of the corner of my eye, my young self is miming the motions in the mirror. I don't think I'm going to get used to seeing her.

That is when I remember the false bottom in my

drawer. I had accidentally broken a piece off, and it made a finger hook hole where I could pry it up. I pull open the drawer again and toss out all my underwear and bras in a single motion, spilling everything from leopard print to red silk onto the floor. I look over my shoulder at the piles and meet an exasperated expression when I turn to my dresser. "Learn to parent for Christ's sake." When I glance at myself, I narrow my eyes at the shadow of a smile hanging in the mirror. "Your children won't have stuff like this," I tell the sixteen year old girl smirking back. "I'll kill 'em first."

I heave the bottom off the dresser and pull free the small aquamarine book. It has a plastic and metal lock on it, and I think about looking for the key until I realize how stupid that is in light of how long it took to find just the book portion. I tear the lock from the paper easily, releasing the cover.

The most recent entry is hashed out as March 4, 2011. My eyes drift over the page, regarding the neat cursive, in direct contrast to the caddy, cruel, angry words written by a very angry young girl. I'm complaining about my family and talking trash about Rachel and everyone else whose name I know.

The words about Rachel bother me. They were all lies, well, mostly lies. I was jealous as hell of her. That was true. I was bitter at my life, and she was the perfect target because she stuck out. Truth as well. The only lie was that I hated her. In actuality, I was attracted to her. That was her fault though, obviously. It couldn't be me, because I was perfect.

Perfect girls didn't crush on other girls, or so I thought.

I walk with my diary to the edge of the bed where

I had dropped my cellphone. I tap a fingernail on the screen and it fires up the lock screen. I go immediately to the date and time in the middle. April 12, 2011, 12:43 a.m. Seeing the date and time, flipping through the entries in my diary, sucks all the will out of me.

I sit at my desk trying to stay calm. I pull notebook paper from the stash in the top drawer and pick up my pen. Okay. I might only have one shot at this. Isn't that how it is in the movies? You get one night to fix everything before the ghost of the person is sucked away forever?

The thought hurts more than I thought it would, and I pen my own name before I break down. It doesn't actually matter if I vanish into the nether or not. I'm really nothing more than a whisper at this point anyway. I start the letter to myself, insurance for if I am gone by morning. I write a very nasty pointed note to my younger self. I tell her to be good, be open to love and, for God's sake, give up the bullshit act. I tell her just enough to push her heart in Rachel's direction and enough to validate that I'm the grown her telling myself to be strong. That way, if I *do* disappear, I'll still be able to save the younger me years of misery and loneliness.

I fold it and set it aside.

However, if I don't disappear, well, that's a whole other story. I stare at the paper before me, daunted. If I don't disappear, I'll still need to write everything down. I start the list with the earliest thing I remember and map forward. It's not sequential, I can't remember that far back in order, but I try to put everything I can remember in. I scribble frantically, finishing page after page of moments, memories. I purge myself, spilling my whole life to the innocent paper. I shed blood across its lines.

I pause four pages deep into my life when I'm struck with a thought. God heard my prayer. As I was dying, He picked me up and dropped me into the world again. He gave me the ability to right the universe's wrong. The thought makes my emotion rise up again and I stare at the ceiling. "Thank you."

I know that nothing will come, but I wait anyway. I look for guidance. I look for anything that will tell me how permanent this moment is. Nothing comes and I eventually let my gaze fall to the desk before me. I write more and cry more. I race against time, and as the first shot of sunlight comes through my bedroom window I put the papers into a school binder and stare at the closed cover. I don't know how long I stare at it, I don't know how long I mire myself in the moments of my life with Rachel, but when my alarm for school goes off, I flinch from my position.

I stare at it, at the neon time. I haven't slept, but as I stand, I'm not tired. I hit the button. How could I be tired knowing that I'm going to see her? Adrenaline shoots through me as I realize it again.

I'm going to see my Rachel.

Chapter Five

All The Wants In The World
April 12th, 2011

I honestly don't think I have ever been this nervous in my whole life. I've taken practicums, I've held people's lives in my hands. Hell, I've held my own life in my hands. So, as I stand here before my closet in the early morning light, it's daunting that I'm nauseated by the options before me. There isn't a moment in my life where a choice has meant so much. Beside me, my standard outfit, my cheerleading garb, is sprawled on my bed. I wonder what would it mean if I wore it? If I walk up to Rachel in my uniform, painting her vision in the red and black that has tormented her for so long and say soft words, will it have more impact than a different outfit?

Will it be bad?

I peer into my closet again and with careful hands I pull free a pink flowing shirt with an empire waist. I twist my fingers in the colored material. It will show off my curves, what few I have. My pre-pregnancy body is much leaner and unfamiliar to me. I know Rachel likes this look, likes the airy version of me, the softer Blake. While she always admitted she liked my tight sporty ponytails and sleek elegant dresses, I know she *loved* my tumbling hair and flowing clothing.

I smile and leave the cheerleading outfit in its

place. Dressing like this for her is ritualistic. It makes me remember all the times she was set to perform and I donned gowns, primping myself to ridiculous levels of beauty, to see her. As I slide on a pair of capris, I feel a stop gap in my memories. I know I'm lying to myself. I didn't dress like that just for her. I dressed like that so when people looked at me, they would see someone worthy of being *with* her.

I never realized how emotionally fragile I really was. I recognize it now as my hands shake while I fasten my pants. It's frightening how as a grown woman I relied on her for validation. If I looked good in her eyes, I was okay with how the cards fell in my life. I go through the motions now, slipping into shoes, sliding into my top. I apply dustings of makeup, highlighting and lowlighting the color of my eyes, the lines of my lips and the apples of my cheeks. When I'm done, I pray it's enough, soft enough to disarm her and put her at ease. If it isn't I can't imagine what that would mean or what it would do to me. I give my reflection a final examination, critically eyeing it before I sigh and release the lip gloss I'm crushing in my grip.

I don't look at my parents as I slide down the stairs. They don't acknowledge me either. I'm their invisible child unless they need something. When they want to reaffirm their social status through my poise or beauty, then they will come to me. Other than that I might as well not exist. Right now, that is perfectly fine by me as I grab my keys and backpack, practically running down the driveway. I'm also happy it will never hurt me again.

My little red subcompact roars under my hands. It's cute and sporty. It's exactly the type of car one would expect to find someone like me in. It might as well be an extension of my body, with its flash, self-importance, and its need to draw attention. That is who I am at this point in my life, after all.

I flip on the radio and tune in to my favorite station, but it doesn't exist, so I find anything that is not a religious sermon or talk. Talk radio annoys the hell out of me, not because it's boring, though it is that too, but it irritates me because I could have easily seen myself doing something like that, chattering about my views and performing ego masturbation to the sound of my own voice. It irritates me that it could have been me, without Rachel.

Well, no, not just Rachel. If I hadn't fallen and broken my knee, I never would have quit cheerleading or have embraced the idea of working in medicine. That moment of clarity in my depression and pain is what led me to becoming a doctor. After all of those things happened, *then* it was Rachel that made it possible, pushed me to study, brought me coffee, and hugged my tiredness away.

I flip the radio off, but my nervous excitement has me talking to myself, practicing what I'm going to say the first time I see her. "Hi Rachel," I whisper sweetly like my lips are pressed to her ear. Nope, creepy as hell. "Hey, Rachel." I say it nonchalantly pretending that when I say her name it isn't ripped from my heart. "Good morning, Rachel," I whisper it under my breath and silently thank my wife for being overly talkative and giving me the keys to her heart.

I know it's important to say her name. So far in this lifetime, when I addressed her it's always been a slur. In my previous life it was, too, and Rachel once told me the day everything changed was when I finally called her by her name. That had been the dividing line between when things were cold and when they weren't. It wasn't until college, but it can't hurt to start now. It can't hurt to try to win her heart now.

My Rachel.

My stomach lurches when I see the school and I thread my fingers around the steering wheel to keep from losing control of the car. I can't believe it's here and I can't believe it is exactly the way I had always remembered it. The chain link fences with banners and ivy are the same. The buildings, squat and trimmed in red, are just as I pictured they would be.

I turn onto the small campus, negotiating my way past a security guard and one of the bungalows. I glance at the clock when I see the parking lot nearly empty. I'm a full fifty minutes early, and I sigh a shaky breath. I find my spot, the one that was always mine due to popularity. It's right at the edge of the basketball court, the perfect location for me and my friends to lean and flaunt for the jocks that play at lunch.

I shift into park, and before I realize it, I have my backpack in my hands. It's amazing to me how the human brain remembers, does things, let's muscle memory take over. I lift my eyes from the strap in my hand to the campus. There, nestled at the other side of the parking lot, is Rachel's car. It's centered in my view and I'm so shocked by it that my eyes burn with tears. I don't think I can move and I try to no avail.

She's alive. She's here. I swallow and blink the heat of surprised tears down my face. My Rachel is here. It literally takes all my strength to turn away from the blue Mazda and check myself in the mirror. "You can do this," I tell myself as I wipe away my tears. "You can walk right up to her and say hello." I cry harder which is the exact opposite reaction I wanted from this pep talk. It isn't lost on me that I didn't cry about heaven. I didn't even cry about the thought of going to hell. I only cry about reality, and Rachel being in it.

It takes what feels like an eternity for my tears to stop. Finally, when I feel like the very idea of seeing her isn't going to make me fall into a weeping mess, I clear my throat and regard my reflection again. It's not as good as it was before my breakdown, but it will have to do.

I pop open the car door. Debating one last time if I would look better with my hair up or down, I slide my backpack on and head toward the main office. I let my hair fall back into place as I try and think of a lie to get my schedule reprinted. I don't remember my classes and the diary was of no help. Honestly, I don't actually care about attending any of them. However, if Rachel is here, I'll go through whatever motions I have to so that we can stay together, even if it's reliving trigonometry.

As I pass Rachel's car, I stare at it, slowing a little. It's just like I remembered, with its smiley faces and decals. Little gold stars and Broadway bumper stickers litter the back end like scattered dreams. It's precious, because really her whole future is printed right there. I wish I had seen it before. I look around before I trace my finger over the trunk. I feel the cold metal under my fingers and it renews my faith to know it's real and concrete.

More tears threaten and I clear my throat valiantly, fighting them. Propriety intact I resume my walk. I cut past my future microbiology class, moving with purpose down a long hall flanked with lockers. I had forgotten that high school smelled like waxed floors and an amalgamation of cheap perfume and too much cologne. It makes my nose tickle and I clear my throat with the way the smell sticks to the back of my tongue. I don't even notice the young boy beside me until he makes a sound under his breath and practically crawls into his locker to get away from me.

I had forgotten that I ruled this world. It catches me by surprise how when I look back at him he is focused on his locker intentionally avoiding eye contact. I can't believe how much people feared me. I remember being cruel and mean, I remember taunting people, but this...this level of fear from someone I haven't met makes me feel guilty. I must be a terrible person.

I open the double doors on the other end of the hall and as I breeze into the adjoining hallway I see the choir room door slam closed. I freeze mid step looking back over my shoulder. I don't know why I look around, but I do. There is hardly anyone here and there is only one person I can think of that would be here forty minutes early to practice. It has to be Rachel.

Just being this close, knowing that my best friend and lover is thirty feet from me has my knees trembling. I glance toward the office and instead change direction. I pause outside the choir room, hands trembling. I don't know if I can do this. I don't know if I can see her again without falling apart. Before, in the car, that was just the cusp of what I feel. Even now, I feel my emotions give, walls crumbling as I try to barricade everything back.

I listen to a soft lingering chord, melancholy pouring through it. It reminds me of how Rachel used to practice at home. How I would silently watch as she hummed her scales and finally sang. It's breathlessly painful when I hear her through the door. I hear that first silver coated note and literally something breaks inside me, making me move forward without thought or volition, and open the door.

I push open the studio door and glance around before slipping into the sound room. I see my wife almost immediately in the recording booth, hair tousled and messy. This is when she looks the prettiest, when she looks like she just rolled out of bed. Rachel is focused on the microphone before her, so she doesn't notice when I take up a place in the high backed chair. I measure the intensity in her face, the way she looks like she wants to zap the electronics out of reality with her angry gaze. I lean forward and I locate the receiver, punching open the feed. I hear her take a breath, a warbled strangled frustrated sound, if I ever heard one. It makes me sad that she is so irritated and angry.

I never realized how fragile her voice is. It only takes a small bout of pneumonia to relegate her angelic tone to that of the mundane. Not permanently, thank God. She just needs rest. However my comforting words don't stop her from self-imposed torture. For a week now she has come down here to record herself, and cry. I don't understand it because even with the knowledge that soon she will be head and shoulders above the rest again, she can't be calm. It is almost like she has been brushed by death. That is the only way I can rationalize the depth of her emotion. She tears herself apart to get back there, to the level she is capable of. She offers up anything to return to the level of skill that defines her and gives her meaning.

I can empathize in a way. I once had something like that, my beauty and athleticism. I had once written all my future goals on the back of my physical appeal. I would marry up, marry rich, and have perfect little children in a perfectly massive *house. My sole defining characteristic was my walk, the perfect movement, smooth and elegant. It was the only thing my mother had ever really noted about me, the way I breezed into a room and captured the attention of everyone in it.*

I used to float. Now I limp, not horribly or grotesquely, but I can see it. Rachel can, too, and sometimes I see pity in her face. It is hard to stomach, though in retrospect it is probably the same look I've had on my face for the past month.

I lean over the electronics, careful not to hit anything, and close my eyes. It is just past six in the morning and I am so tired I can't see straight. How she does this, comes here at the crack of dawn to practice every day, is beyond me. I can barely open my eyes. I hear her wet her lips, it feeds through the studio in surround sound and I smile to myself.

She sings then, or tries too, rather.

When I hear a crash, I know it's the headphones being ripped off her head in frustration, but I jump just the same. It is all mental. I know it is. The wheeze is gone, the antibiotics flushing the virus from her system. She's had me with a stethoscope everyday listening to her take deep over-inflated breathes that resonate in my ears. She's peppered me with questions, worrying that if she coughs it will tear something, making me use my battery powered otoscope to peer down her throat and check that everything is intact. I've probably seen more of my wife at my practice in the last two weeks than I have our whole marriage. And I don't mean that in the sexy good way, even though it makes me snicker anyway. By all accounts, she is the picture of health, and I know she is mistaking disuse for damage. Like I said, mental.

When she finally rights the headphones and moves to the mic again I'm dazzled by how much I can read in just a breath. I feel her fear, her sorrow, and when she hums middle C to tune herself I hear hope as well. She stops and I glance at her, ready to turn down the volume this time if the headphones go flying. However, she's just fiddling with the pop filter and curses under her breath when it won't sit in the right spot.

Rachel starts again, battling through take after take and just like any muscle, her voice remembers. As the rust falls away, I hum along, finding a poor version of a harmony against the intensity of Rachel's pitch perfect intonations. Eventually, the notes slide effortlessly and I forget my harmony as her voice pulls on my heart like harp strings.

It is perfect. I smile sitting up a little higher after she finishes her take. I drop my finger on the two-way feed button and pop it. "You sound beautiful baby."

Rachel whips to the glass between us as she pulls the headphones off. Her hair is now twisted into a crazy bun and she wipes a hand over her face that makes its way up to check that her pen is still holding her hair at bay. She smiles through the glass and leans toward the microphone. "Didn't anyone ever tell you it's rude to eavesdrop?" She lifts the headphones so she can hear me. "How long have you been there?"

"Oh you know," I look down at my watch, "two hours."

"What?" She laughs. "Oh jeez, honey, I'm sorry. I'm done. Two hours really? I'm so sorry."

"Don't be, it's nice to hear you sing just for me." I snort a laugh. "Besides, I've already learned that music

has to come first in order for you to make your pancakes without malice. Angry pancakes taste like crap."

Rachel hums her delight at the idea of breakfast even as her eyes narrow at my comment. "Okay, one order of secret special pancakes coming up. I'm coming around." She stops to peck a kiss to the glass and vanishes.

I stare at the mark she left, at the bow-shaped lines of lip gloss before me. It make me smile. She might not be able to get dressed or do her hair, but heaven forbid she pass on lip gloss.

When she swings into the room and places a strawberry coated kiss to my lips, I can't help but think how lucky I am and how glad I am that right now, she's making breakfast wait for us.

I close the door quietly enough that I don't think Rachel hears. At the very least, she doesn't acknowledge it. In this world, she offers another chord and without the door in the way I have to cover my mouth to keep my emotion caged. I can't describe what it does to me. What I see in my mind, what I feel in my heart. The little pieces of glass inside me, the shattered remains from losing her, announce themselves by drawing through my soul. They rend me to pieces and compel me to run to her. I take a hesitant shaking step toward her, but my hands grab the risers, keeping me still. It's a war inside me, half of me staying, half of me going.

Another chord, another powerful line. I'm transfixed by it, drowning in emotion so deep it can't be mine. How I didn't recognize that she would become a legend is beyond me. The sheer idea that I mocked her gift makes my stomach do a bitter roll within me. I listen to her and her ghost blurs over the reality before me. In ten years she will take Broadway by storm and I will be there.

I *have* to be there.

My hands shake as I stare at the woman I thought I would never see again. The last time I saw her face was in the funeral home, painted in spackle to give color to the rich Mediterranean tones of her skin. That last time haunts me even now. I'm scared that if I make a sound, she will turn and look at me with dead eyes and mismatched coloring.

Rachel's back is to me, head bent as she focuses on her hands. She was never a pianist, but she fakes it well as her precise motions highlight the soulfulness in her voice. Of all the songs she knows, why she is playing one that is haunting and painful I'll never understand. It makes my heart break as it hammers in my chest.

The lights aren't fully on, so they bathe the area around the piano in a pool of softness. The glow from above highlights her tumble of curls, her shoulders, her arms. My eyes linger on her skin, remembering it, and all the times I found solace in that embrace. I cried in the niche of her arms so many times, I don't remember a time I didn't have it as my catharsis. I can't imagine living a life where I don't.

When Rachel moves, I flinch because I don't know if I made a sound. I slink further back into the shadows as she glances over her shoulder into the corner opposite me. Seeing her face, those bright chocolate eyes, just about destroys me. A strangled sound slips from my lips and the shock that radiates across her face as she spins dizzyingly has my heart in my throat.

The eyes that affix to me in horror are a younger version of ones I have looked into for years, but now there is no love in them, there is just fear. "What do you want Blake?" She says my name like a curse word, then quickly collects her music and shovels it into a hot pink binder.

I panic as I realize she is leaving. "No, wait! Don't go!" I move from my spot and block the door with outstretched hands. "Please." I feel my voice crack and I swallow it so that she can't hear it. I *hope* she doesn't hear it.

Her wary gaze is on me, but she doesn't advance. She resumes her seat primly on the edge of the piano bench, her dark eyes calculating. "Blake, I really must insist that if you want to discuss something with me you need to do it soon. I can't imagine what you would want to say to me though. I would prefer if you would just let me leave, I have other things I need to do before going to French class."

It catches me off guard because it's been a long time since I have heard Rachel talk like this. The nervous rambling vanished between us a long time ago. Pairing that verbosity with the curious and nervous look in her eyes has me aware of how much is on the line when I speak. "I'm sorry," I start simply, hands still held out. I let them fall, "I know you're busy, but this will only take a second."

"What?" There is a little less venom and a little more concern. Rachel glances around. "Is anyone else here?"

I realize she is looking for Malina and Lindsey to attack from the sides. "No, no one else is here. It's just you and me, Rachel."

She pins me then, when I say her name, looking at me with clear surprise in her face. I move slowly toward her and it takes everything in me to change directions at the last second and drop into a chair before her and not dive into her arms. It's uncanny how as we regard one another, I can smell her skin and her shampoo. Having known it so well for so long, it's instantly the only thing I can focus on. It's different and yet familiar, not mixed with her quintessential Chanel, but something else.

When she stares at me I realize I'm letting the silence go inappropriately long. I forge ahead, "I just want you to know, in contrast to what I've said before I think you're ridiculously talented and I'm happy I heard you sing this morning."

And there it is, that beaming smile that I love. It's effortless and swept with honest joy, but it melts away just as quickly as it came. "What's your angle Blake? Please forgive me for being skeptical regarding the authenticity of your words, but I find it hard to believe that you can go from telling me yesterday that I would *never* have a future in anything, to saying... well, this." She holds out her hands indicating the conversation between us.

I frown. I can't say the real reason, obviously. It would not only be insane, but it would push any rational person away. I swallow. "I really mean this, what I'm saying to you now. The other stuff I said because I wanted to be accepted. I'm not saying those things anymore. I don't like who I am when I say those things."

It's funny how easily I say *these* things, yet they took me so long to learn. I wait with baited breath as Rachel digests this silently, her eyes focused on her lap. As adorable as Rachel's babbling is, her silence is deafening. It scares the crap out of me, because there has never been a time where Rachel didn't have *something* to say.

"I'm sorry," she states suddenly and I choke on my own saliva as I rush to get air into my lungs.

"Why are you saying you're sorry to me?"

It takes forever for her to answer me. It feels like it. I wait in silence wondering what will come out of her mouth when she *does* speak. My chest tightens when she finally glances up at me with soulful brown eyes. "Because I never realized how hard it must be to be so easily manipulated that you buy into this popularity stuff. And I figured that at the top of the social pyramid you would be the one saying the mean things because you want to and not the other way around." Rachel frowns. "That's kinda pathetic."

Jesus. I don't think I'll ever be ready for Rachel's blunt observations. I still do it, still let other people pick my words for me. I still do what I think it is people *want* me to do. It makes me tip my head down under the weight of how sad and pathetic that really *is*. "Don't apologize for that," I whisper it to her shoes because I can't even look up. "I'm sorry for what I've done to make you hurt."

"Well," she draws the word with a very long breath, "despite all of that, I have a gut feeling that you are a good person at heart. No one deserves to feel that way, so I'm sorry you do."

When I look up at her, she has a very fragile smile, one that looks like it might crumble at my subsequent words. She looks like she expects me to hurt her feelings again. So, I smile softly. It's so easy to fall back into these moments, the echoes of smiles and close proximity. I scoot forward a little, making Rachel's eyes widen a fraction. She looks so vulnerable and trusting. I wish I could hug her, for all the good it would do us both. "And never feel badly for being who you are. All the things you are, that's all yours. Anyone who gives you crap, they do it because they are jealous."

"Were you jealous?"

When I regard her, she looks like she wants to take the words back. "Maybe a *lot*." I arch my eyebrow with a grin. "It isn't like you have a million gifts and will someday be a famous singer. I mean, I have *nothing* to be jealous of." I throw enough sarcasm into the sentence to make her laugh. It is the sweetest sound I have heard in a long time.

When we fall into silence, I realize this is *the* moment. This is where I change things. I can feel Rachel's eyes on me and I run a deliberate hand through my hair. I tease her with how my hair falls in waves, how good I smell, how perfect I can be for her if she gives me a chance. I make a smile melt into my eyes and put as much emotion as I can pack into them. "Rachel?" I say her name like I've said it a million times. I say it like it's the name of my wife.

She swallows, her breath stilling in her chest. "Yes, Blake?" Her voice is tight and choked.

"You deserve better from me, and I want to give that to you." I add the rest softer. "Can I be your friend?"

I see Rachel's hand on the piano bench, squeezing it. "My friend? I don't understand. You want to be *my* friend?" She points at her chest and when I nod, she boggles at me. "Y-yes, you can be my friend."

"Good."

As much as I want to make my grand exit and leave Rachel wanting more, it's hard to stand. My eyes well up with tears and I stare up at the ceiling as I let go a relieved, shaken breath.

"Blake?"

When Rachel's voice summons, my stupid emotions betray me and I feel tears drop as I look at her. I wipe them away quickly. "Yeah?"

She smiles lightly and then holds up a finger. She's in her bag after that, hunting around until she sits up again with a little plastic tissue container. I take one and sniffle. She always had them in her purse, always. Why would it be any different now? I blot my eyes as I force a smile.

"Hey." Rachel says drawing my attention. I look at her over the white sheet. "It's okay."

I shake my head, because it isn't. I need to make everything better. I need to fix everything. I need to protect her. I need to do all those things, but all I can do is cry. "I'm so sorry. I'll fix it, I promise."

"I forgive you and somehow, for some strange reason, I know you will."

For a split second she sounds like my wife, so when I look up and see a sixteen-year-old's face looking back at me, my heart fills to the brim with hope, and then breaks.

Chapter Six

Standing On The Edge
April 14, 2011

It's raining. It seems like it always rains when we fight. When I want most to walk out of the house and go to my office, or just walk anywhere far away from the accusing brunette that owns my heart. That's when it rains the hardest. I could bear the weight of the drops, if I wasn't so drained by everything else. I am drained soul deep from the words that tumble from my mouth, and her equally caustic observations.

The weight of our love keeps us trapped together, circling one another for round after round of warring. I absolutely hate it. Rachel is too damn good at it. Too smart and strategic. She's never been the one to back down from anything, nor am I. We whip words against each other's hearts to see whose shatters first. Believe me when I say, it's been more times than I can count we've been in tears, staring at each other across a dining room table too narrow for our bitterness to be buffered properly. I'm meaner than she is, I'm the bully. I always have been.

It's her truths that hurt me. They gouge me to the bone.

So I watch it rain, blanket over my shoulders in front of our big bay window. I watch the sheets come down and try to ignore the sound of Rachel slamming things in the kitchen. I think she is putting away the dishes. Though by the sound, breaking them is more likely. At least, the pots and pans are getting the brunt of it.

I fix my eyes on the rippling water at the end of the driveway while I pull the blanket higher on my shoulders. I can't hear the dishes being banged around anymore, so I have a feeling she is looking at me. It makes my spine icy and tingly with that razor sharp glare.

I wish we fought about normal things, fixable things like money or affection. I wish it were simpler. I can do simple. But no, we fight about stupid unfixable things like careers and drive and schedules. We fight about children, the ones that don't exist yet.

We fight about time.

Like right now. We are having the same fight again, about me spending too much time at work and not agreeing to have kids until after I finish my push toward the Physician of the Year award. I'm so close I can taste it, truly.

When she drop down next to me silently, I'm surprised. I'm even more surprised when she produces a mug of hot cocoa for me. It's in her tea mug painted with glossy musical notes. I take it staring down at the froth on top. It makes me sad when she gives me her favorite mug.

"I like sipping hot cocoa when it rains." I don't know why I say it, I know she knows that. It is probably just to fill the space of our silence. I'm shocked by the gesture considering I was on the winning end of this fight. We are both pretty sore losers when it comes to our spats.

"I know." She sips her cocoa, her eyes tracing the

weather outside. "Wow, it's really coming down."

She is stalling.

"Yeah." I fix my focus on the water painting the window. When my eyes finally drift toward Rachel her gaze catches mine.

"Why do we keep doing this, Blake?"

I don't have an answer to those words. I don't even know what they mean. "I don't know." I set my mug down on the carpet and pull the creases of my blanket shield tighter around me.

She runs a hand through her hair, gathering up the courage to say what she is going to say. I brace for it. "If nothing's gonna change, then what is the point? I mean, I love you, but is that enough?"

My hands go a little numb when my heart stops. That question rattles the foundation of everything I know. It makes the world seem so much bigger and more frightening. I don't know how she can hold my gaze so easily when she says those words. I can't, so I stare at the floor instead. "Don't you think so?"

"I used to." Rachel sighs and puts her hands over her face, breathing deeply as she tucks her knees up to her chest. In the drop streaked window, the lights of a car swing by and highlight the shadows of water over her.

It is the manifestation of how I feel her slipping through my hands like water, like rain. I swallow, catching my breath. "But you don't anymore?"

She laughs bitterly, crossing her arms on her knees. "I know I need more than that. You need more than that. We have both sacrificed for this, fought for this, waited for this." She regards me evenly. "We shouldn't have to wait anymore. It's been a lifetime of promises and glittering hopes that never come to fruition."

"Not all of it." I defend though I don't even have enough air to make the words come out right. Everything is just stuck in my chest as it seizes up.

"There is more to life than our career success."

It makes me mad that these words come from her. She is still the girl that obsessed over fame and success her whole life. It is easy for her to say it now that she's made it. "You're such a hypocrite, Rachel. You can say that now, but there would be no way that you would have said it five years ago, ten years ago. You wouldn't have said it if you were still fighting for your dreams. You just don't give a shit about mine, what I want, what I dream, because you're selfish." There, I said it. And like always I regret it when she looks away. I watch her jaw tighten and I can practically hear her teeth grind.

"You're right." She doesn't look at me, doesn't blink as she looks through the storm outside. "I have the benefit of being on the other side of that mountain. You know what though," she glares at me then, "it's gotten me nothing."

"You've got everything, Rachel. Don't say it's nothing," I whisper against the positively desperate look in her eyes.

"What did it get me, Blake?" She drudges the words out. "A big house, an empty marriage, no children, no hope that things will ever change. I've got money in my bank account, and my face tattooed across the Calendar section of the Times. But, tell me, really–what did it get me that mattered?"

I'm focusing on her empty marriage gibe, so I don't answer. I hear the words over and over in my mind until I think my head might explode. "Empty marriage." The words might as well be a slap in the face. "Is that really how you feel?" I'm hoping the answer is no, that she is *being melodramatic.*

"Yes."

It hurts.

It hurts in a breathlessly painful way.

It's probably the meanest thing anyone has ever said to me. After everything I have done, sacrificed, shared with her. Calling our marriage empty is a venomous heart strike with the intent to kill me. "Fine." *I get up, throwing the blanket down as I go for my shoes.* "You wanna see an empty marriage? I'll give you an empty marriage! I'll give you a big empty house and a big empty life to match it!"

"Blake, stop and listen to what I'm trying to tell you."

"Rachel." *I level my gaze at her as she stands to face me. The sheer lack of emotion I see in her eyes sends the blade that much deeper,* "So help me God, if you say one more word, divorce papers will hit you in the face so hard it will make your head spin." *It is the only leverage I have. I'll take it away before she can.*

"Don't you dare threaten me! I'm not your high school punching bag anymore! I'm a grown woman and your wife, so unless you are gonna put your money where your mouth is, or pen to paper in this case, don't you dare say that to me! This is my life too!"

I know it is, but it just feels like everything is my fault. Our past is my fault, our lack of future is my fault. "You're absolutely right this is your life, and they're your mistakes too! Not just mine, yours! You are just as driven, just as motivated, you want to preach humility but you can't. You don't have the right! You have a lot of balls to look me in the face and say it isn't worth it!" *I slip into one tennis shoe.*

"It isn't worth it Blake! How can you even be

blind enough to think it might be?" She yells her words in my face, eye to eye with me, making me back up a step. "It's not worth it! If I could go back..." She stops, frozen. I hold her wild gaze as she swallows rapidly.

"What?" I egg her on. "Would you have not even been with me?"

She focuses on me again but this time her motions intercept mine and she grabs my shoe, holding it firmly. "Of course I would have been with you. I would have done everything the same for you. I would have loved you. I would be right here fighting with you now."

"Why?" I don't understand. "Why the hell would you do it all again just like this?"

"Because I love you." She lets go of my shoe.

I drop it to the carpet as I huff and puff and shove my foot into it.

"I love you. I wanted love to be enough, but it isn't."

"Then, what? You want a divorce? You want me to quit my job?"

Rachel looks positively struck as she stares at me. Her eyes glaze over as she thinks.

"What? Fucking tell me!"

"I'll quit." She softens her voice and it tears all the wind out of my angry sails. She backs up a step. "I'll quit, retire for now. I'll close my spring show and that will be that. It will be easier that way."

"No." I glare at her. "You can't quit. You can't just give it up."

"Sure I can." She laughs lightly, melodically. The music is everything in her. She can't just throw it away. "It's easier than this. I might love what I do, but it isn't worth it. This wasn't the plan."

I narrow my eyes at her. "What do you mean?"

She gestures wildly even for her. Her wedding rings flash in the light from the kitchen. "I just...you know...the plan...our life together. We were supposed to be in love and happy and not fight."

"People who love each other are gonna fight, Rachel." I sigh heavily.

"We were supposed to have children. I wanted children. I want them, with you, now, not in some far off future. We don't have a lot of time honey."

She makes it sound like our ovaries are rotting away this very moment. "Rachel, we're thirty-four. It isn't like we're ancient."

Rachel deflates. I see it in her shoulders. "I wanted to be a younger mother than this. I wanted you to be, too, for us and for our child. So we could all run and play together." Her voice breaks over the next words. "I can't wait anymore for the little girl we promised to each other seven years ago."

I pull her to me. Her face hits my shoulder at the same time those barely hidden tears burst forth. I wish I could erase the pain she feels. I wish I could be that person she wants me to be, the one that is content to be domestic.

But, all I can do is hold her while she cries and mews broken words into my neck. "I love you, give me more. I need more. I need the 'us' I believed we would have, not this. I'll do anything for it. I love you."

For the past two days now, this moment haunts me every second I'm not focused on something else. It's a daydream, a nightmare, a moment stolen from the rip of time. I suppose it wouldn't bother me if it was *just* a figment that materializes from my deepest fears, but it's a *memory*. It is as real and concrete as the day Rachel died. It's a testament to how desperate she was that she gave up everything to have a life with me. It's a reminder of how easily I forgot that she did.

As I drive to school balancing a chai tea for Rachel and a coffee for myself, I feel the sting of that inaction. It is more than a fight we had because people who love the way we love fight. It's the fact that I made her beg for something I had promised her. It's the fact that I should have given her the family she wanted without her having to retire. And the worst part, the part that bothers me the most, is that I *still* made her wait. She gave up her music so she could run to doctors' appointments and play house alone for a *whole* year before I bit the proverbial bullet and we got pregnant.

Stopped at a red light with a misting of rain coming down, I remember the moment the car's headlights painted over her. It's so vivid and stark in my mind it might as well be happening right now, right here beside me. I swear if I look over, I'll see her in the dark of our living room, sitting on the floor with tears in her eyes. It's the place not even five feet from where I collapsed to my knees when I came home to an empty house after her death. It's the place not even three feet from where I drew my last breath.

The light turns green and I drive, leaving all those painful thoughts behind. I fill my head with other things, with the present, with the hopes I hold in my heart. And the promises I will give her when she *asks* and not when she has to beg. The thought puts a smile on my face. I smile even wider as I recount the days Rachel and I have spent together every morning since I apologized for my behavior. It's been really nice to be honest, a little torturous, but nice nonetheless. She is a sedative to me, to my heart.

When I park my car beside Rachel's and not in my typical spot, I know it speaks volumes without me having to say a word. My reputation is still intact, and if I'm changing up spots, then something is happening in the social order of things. I'm saying she isn't that little weird girl anymore. No, she is someone others should steer clear of. She is in my circle. She is someone I'm allied with. And I will be for the rest of my life.

I shrug on a sweater and my cheerleading jacket. With cups in hand I cut into the first doorway I can to escape the rain. After I wipe the wet drops from my face with my sleeve, I notice Malina standing in the hallway staring at me. The image of her at Rachel's funeral ignites my brain like magnesium. It was the last time I saw her. I remember her words of love, her warmth. It literally makes me flinch when everything melts together and before me I see a younger, angrier version of the woman that was my only strength when I had none left.

"Okay, so I'm gone on vacation for a few days and everything goes to shit?"

I can't fully process her words, because I honestly don't expect them, not from the face across from me that I love so much. "Excuse me?"

"You've parked over there this whole week so far." She indicates somewhere outside. "You can't park there. That's like, I don't even know. You might as well put your car under a bridge if you wanna be near a troll."

"Don't call her that anymore." I say, narrowing my eyes. That is when I remember that Malina is a bitch until her sophomore year of college, which means I should just avoid this entirely. "Talk to you later," I say abruptly sweeping past her, carefully balancing the drinks as I go.

"Wait." She circles me, halting my progress toward the choir room where Rachel is waiting for me. "Since when do you care about that little twisted missed abortion? And where are you going? Is that a coffee for *her*?"

"Since now, and no, it's tea. And yes, I'm going to the choir room to meet with Rachel." I hope she followed that because I'm not saying it again. I'm not giving her any additional justification either.

"Don't play with me Blake. If this is a joke on her then I want in." She salivates over the idea of hurting my wife and honestly, if I didn't want my coffee as bad as I do, she would be wearing it.

"No, not a joke, and I wouldn't dream of playing with you. Why don't you go play with yourself?"

She rolls her eyes. "As much as I would love to do that, seriously, don't tell me to fuck off in that nice way of yours." She leans in toward me to accentuate the fact she wants me to hear every word, but doesn't want others to. "We have worked too long and hard for this, Blake. We have worked our asses off to get popular, and I'm not letting you throw it away out of guilt."

"I'm not guilty. I'm happy."

"Whatever. Guilty or happy, doesn't matter. You can go be happy with someone else. Help out a cripple, or better yet, a homeless person. Give them a bath, I don't know. Start with any other asshat on the bottom of the social pyramid, but not Rachel. She cannot be your project."

I never really realized just how ignorant we were. I'm sure I said something similar at some point when I was a teenager. "She's my friend."

Malina looks like her head might explode with the speed in which her eyes bulge. "Whoa! *Hell*, no!" She waves her hand in true ghetto fashion. "That's some crazy talk. You? Her Friend? Did you take drugs the other night? I mean, legit. Tell me if you took something because I will mess a brother up for giving you some bad shit."

I laugh, because no matter how angry she may be, I love that her first response is to protect me. She always did when it mattered. Staring at the thin Latina, I can't help but think about the woman she is going to grow into. How some day she is going to water down this piss and vinegar and be the only other woman I love in this world.

I take a cue from my wife's abilities to disarm in an argument. "Mal," I say it softly and it catches her off guard because normally we talk over one another. "You're always gonna be my girl, but we're gonna have to talk about this later. I have some stuff I wanna do before class."

I don't know if she is confused or angry or both. "What? You're ditching me to go be with *her*?" She shakes her head, standing firmly. "I'll tell coach that you're trifling with Kaplan. Hell, I'll tell her you two are dating."

"Go for it," I say casually. "I'll be sure to mention to your mother and grandmother about Lindsey. How do you think that will go?" I say it nonchalantly as I move past her, but the words slam so heavily on her that I see her face slip, that real human vulnerability showing for an instant. Her devout Roman Catholic family will give her a hell of a time in a few years because of her love for the bubbly blonde, and I'll be there to catch her tears until they come around.

"You wouldn't, you're not that cold."

I nod. "You're right, and you aren't that cold either, so I'll see you later, okay?" I don't look back over my shoulder. I force myself to keep walking because I've got the upper hand and I know that with Malina, if I show weakness she'll be all over it. I don't think I actually breathe until I open the door to the choir room.

I shake off the residual rain as I peer around for Rachel. "Hey, you here?"

"Yes, over here."

I move toward the storage closet. "I brought you chai tea." I hold it up a little, even though she can't see me. "What are you doing in there?"

"I have a surprise for you."

That catches my attention and I smile a little as my stomach flutters. "Yeah?"

"Yeah."

When I peek past the door, I see a couple of folding chairs and a small stack of crates. "Table?"

"Yep." I see Rachel, dressed in a dark sweater and skirt carrying a little swatch of cloth in her hands. I know immediately it's for the crates, and when she fluffs it over them and makes it look like a small table it has my heart thudding.

"This is really sweet." I just can't find any other words. I want to. I want to say a slew of things, but they all start with terms of endearment that I don't have the right to say to her yet. Instead, I just let a lump form in my throat. "You didn't have to do this."

Her warm smile radiates through me. "How else am I supposed to get you to eat breakfast?"

"How did you know I skipped it?"

"When do you not skip it?"

She turns away and busies herself opening a foam to-go box. When it pops free I smell pancakes and I forget everything else in the world. They aren't restaurant pancakes. They're her pancakes. Her amazing secret special ones.

I slip into one of the chairs, "Oh god, thank you. Your pancakes are amazing." I don't even realize what I said until I'm sitting. "Or, so I've heard," I correct as she hands me a fork.

I pass her tea over. I watch as she wipes water drops off the lid, or plays with them, I'm not sure. When her eyes finally come up to me, they immediately shoot back down.

"What?" I ask. "Is something wrong?"

She shakes her head. "Thank you for this." She lifts the cup briefly and then stares down at the food between us. "You'll want to eat them before they get too cold. They aren't good cold."

I move the fork automatically, cutting through the golden fluff, not taking my eyes off her for more than a second. "What's wrong?" I can feel it.

"I was worried you weren't going to come." It's almost a whisper.

I smile to take the edge off her concern. "I'll always be here to see you in the mornings. Why would you think that?"

"Because Malina is back."

"Believe me, spending time with you wasn't filler while I waited for my friend. As a matter of fact, we talked this morning and I said I was going to be hanging out with you."

"Was she angry?"

I roll my eyes as I take a bite of breakfast. "When isn't she?" I smile after swallowing and Rachel eases one of her own.

"Is it any good?"

I nod. "Did I get your drink order right?" I cut off a bite and poke it with my fork.

"Yeah, just the way I like it with a shot of peppermint." She takes another sip.

"Did you want some? I can't eat all this on my own."

"Sure. Thanks, Blake."

I lean toward her glancing at the dripping pancake wedge on my utensil. When I look up our eyes meet and my heart picks up. She leans toward me with a smile and even though I can see her hand reaching for the fork, I forget it. Instead, I remember every single breakfast I fed her twisted in bed sheets, our hands roaming. How we would laugh at sticky skin from syrup, and trade kisses, our mouths laced with the citrus splash of orange juice.

I twist my fork to keep the drops from falling and her eyes widen when she realizes what's happening. "Oh, okay," she whispers breathlessly, and when her lips part I slide the pancake into her mouth. Those brilliant teeth flash, catching the bite. Her lip is stamped in maple syrup as I pull back.

I focus on it, my heart pounding so hard all I hear is the rush of my blood. I lean closer. "You're so beautiful," I whisper absently to the ghost in my memories. "I bet that syrup tastes amazing right there on your lips."

She licks them, clearing the golden drip, chewing between the rushes to get air into her lungs. I flick my eyes up toward hers when she swallows. They are practically black, her pupils wide as she watches my slow movement toward her, nothing but a ring of red fire around them. It makes my libido pound.

"Rachel?"

She literally shivers when I say her name and my whole body responds to it. It's so primal, the way I need her. The way I miss her.

I pant once, hard, and her eyes are on my chest as it rises with an exaggerated breath. "Do you like what you see?" I whisper, panting again for her benefit.

"You, um-I..." She shifts in her seat. I notice she is moving closer. Her eyes narrow as they focus on my mouth. "I-I like how you say my name like that."

I want to do it again, but I don't think I can catch my breath, because the way her voice has darkened has me remembering all the physiological responses of her body when her voice sounds like that. I know her so well. I know everything about her. When I feel her hurried breaths across my cheek I grin playfully. "Like, how?"

Now, she's panting. Her hands plant on the edges of the crates, right beside mine. "I don't know."

"Like, I want you," I answer.

She reddens, blushing furiously under my gaze. I don't think I've ever seen her so inarticulate. She nods, swallowing hard. When she does that I know I've got her going. I close my eyes remembering how it felt to make love to her, feeling the warmth of her body as she tightened around my fingers. It makes me throb, and when I open my eyes again she is watching me.

"Do you want me?" She stares at me with a fragile, yet hopeful tilt in her eyebrows.

"Yes, I do. I was thinking about touching you." I arch my eyebrow and move a fraction closer as her mouth drops open in surprise. I can see her war over what to do, and when she makes the decision to lean in toward me, I turn my cheek so I feel the press of her face against mine.

"Touching me?" She almost can't get the words out of her mouth.

I smile at it, at her embarrassment to say it. I don't understand why she is. I have loved her for so long. I'm her wife, after all. My eyes close as I breathe in her scent and trace my nose over the soft stray strands by her ear. I nudge the edge of her ear. "You have no idea how much I want to. How my whole body is throbbing. Everything in me is just tight and wet and wants you."

She chokes on the air in her lungs. "Oh my God, Blake." She sounds shocked, but she doesn't pull back. For a split second she also sounds like she doesn't know that I love her.

So I trace my finger over her hand beside me and link my fingers in hers. "Rachel, I want you."

She licks her lips anxiously, and when I hear the wetness I remember how she did that when she wanted me too. I remember how she felt in my hands, how deliciously soft. How her moans sounded in my ears, how powerful and yet protected I felt when I touched her. I'm dizzy by the waves of love I feel. I turn a little and kiss the spot right beside her ear.

Her soft mew of desire is the key to my undoing as the sound breaks my inhibitions. I tangle my hand in her hair just before swiftly catching her mouth with mine. It shatters me. I can't stop myself as I press into her lips and spontaneously combust against her. Making love to her mouth has always been my favorite thing. I can kiss her for hours, but right now I'm on a mission. I want her wet for me. I want her to need me as badly as I need her. So I moan for her, against her lips. Pulling her face toward mine, I cup her cheeks and lick the seam of her lips. "Open for me," I urge and when she does, my tongue traces against the tentative touch of hers. I see fireworks, I always did, and they light up inside me.

Rachel moves back and I follow the motion. The crates between us rattle as her hands shake. She doesn't put her hands on me and I growl for it. "Rachel, please touch me, baby." I wrap my hands deeper in her hair and slide my nails up her scalp. She moans then, deep and needy as I play against every turn-on she has.

When the nervous flex of her hand fastens in the jacket at my shoulder, I press deeper into our kiss, dripping with desire. I think about pushing the crates aside, sliding between her thighs and pressing against her. How would it feel to touch her like that again? I would give anything to feel the heat of her body against mine. When I put a hand to the small faux table with the intent of moving it aside, the bell for the start of school blasts through the space between us and halts my motions.

Rachel pulls back, her lips leaving mine with a small smack. Her eyes are still closed, cheeks flushed, lips red. "Oh my God," she says in a whisper, her hand coming up to touch her mouth. "Did you just kiss me?"

I laugh lightly, pressing the hair on her forehead back. "Yes."

"Why?" She opens her eyes then and fixes me with confusion and fear. "Why did you kiss me?"

I frown. "Why wouldn't I?"

She stares at her hand on my shoulder and then rips it back like I'm burning her, bolting from her chair just as quickly. "We can't do this. I can't do this.

I can't want this. I have too much to do. This can't happen because it just messes everything up." I stare at her as she rattles through her words, fixing her hair and straightening her clothing. "I wanted to be your friend, but this can't happen. You can't talk to me like that." She grabs her books and turns to me then, her lips in a grimly set line.

"Like what?"

She wipes a hand over her face and catches the mass of hair in her hand. "Like we are sleeping together. Like you know me. Like I'm yours, I mean– I'm not anybody's let alone yours. And I'm not talking about ownership, but you know what I mean. I'm not *yours* Blake, and I don't know what you're pulling but it's not cool."

I don't even remember what I said. It was all on instinct, pure reflex from fifteen years of being with her. "I'm sorry. I won't say that stuff again."

"No, you won't." She walks out leaving me with a cold breakfast and misery to wash it down with.

≈≈≈≈

It takes me almost until lunch to recall what it was I said. When the thoughts hit me I'm so appalled by my words I almost swear out loud. Cold chills wrack me as I stare at my math teacher and wonder what the hell I was thinking? What the hell was I doing? I can't just say those things to her.

I'm supposed to honor her, cherish her–all those words that you say when you vow your life to someone. I'm not supposed to succumb to these needy irresponsible desires, because she isn't ready. Rachel doesn't have the years of knowledge under her belt she needs to be on par with me. She doesn't have the emotional tenure. It's wrong of me to kid myself into thinking she is a grown woman as well, hiding out in the body of a teenager.

I form an exasperated expression as the wave of panic hits me. Rachel is going to freak out. She is going to absolutely flip her lid and I'm going to lose her. I forgot who she was. I forgot she was a teenage girl and not my wife. She was right, I had no right to say those things to her. She isn't mine.

I have to tell her. I have to let her know I'm sorry. I lean over and scoop my phone out of my purse, pulling up her phone number. With quick sharp motions I type out a message.

I'm sorry. What can I do to fix this? You are right. I can't say those things to you. You aren't mine. I want to earn your trust. I'm so sorry.

I cover the phone in my lap when I see the teacher look at me. "Blake, what is the function of X in this equation if X is equal to negative five?"

I arch my eyebrow at his set face, and compute it in my head, stumbling a moment when my phone vibrates against my thigh. "Twenty-seven."

He nods. "Very good."

When he moves on, I glance down at my lap at a text from Rachel.

I don't want to write back if Malina is looking.

I sigh and peck back.

She isn't, it's just you and me talking. If Malina was looking would I text you that kissing you this morning was amazing?

Her response is almost immediate.

No, but that doesn't mean that you didn't add it when she looked away.

God damn it. I made her so paranoid!

I didn't. Please, just tell me what I can do to fix this?

The answer doesn't come until the end of class, right as I'm gathering up my books to leave.

I don't know. I just have to think this through.

She needs space. I need to give it to her. I nod silently and even though my hands are shaking, I tap out a firm response.

I'll be here when you make a decision.

Chapter Seven

Shows Of Conviction
April 20, 2011

It's been a week. I wait for her just as I promised, giving her space. I pretend that her absence doesn't hurt me, that it doesn't make my brittle heart break. I go through the motions. I sleep, I shower, I go to school. I try not to see her, but she is everywhere. Rachel appears in every hallway during passing period and drifts past every classroom's open door when I happen to look up.

It feels like she is haunting me.

The beautiful things she always said, the things we shared together, the fact that she just made me want to forget the world and exist, those moments hang in my mind and taunt me when she materializes in my view. She is so close and yet so very far. Out of my hands and out of my life like she never existed in my arms at all. I tell myself she didn't, that she hasn't. Those moments of realization could kill me if I wasn't already dead *once* from the loss of her. God, what I would do to have her here, the woman who knows me and loves me.

I would give anything for it, but all I have is hope that my wife is somewhere inside the brooding young woman that avoids me, and time. So like I said, I go through the motions. I go to practice, I eat vacant dinners that taste like familial hate, and sleep again. I fill my moments with anything that isn't her face and smile. I distract myself by running, exploring trails I have never gone down before, because in my other life I wasn't me. I go as deep into wooded areas as I can, trading the mid-spring blister of sunlight for mottled shadows. I find streams I've never seen, cross them on slick rocks, testing my new body. My legs do as I command, pushing me faster than I've ever run before. I marvel at the precision of my smooth motions. Of how when I jump, I have no fear of landing, not in the physical regard, anyway. While I focus on the physical, it's those movements that push me far from home, into wide open spaces under a deep blue sky.

The internal parts are a whole other story.

I scream as I run, releasing my burgeoning insecurities to the vacant wide open landscapes. It isn't until now I learn that I never allowed myself just to be. I was always so strung, so tense, focused on the next objective, the next conquest. Now, when I pass vacant farm houses and broken down mills, I let everything go. I have nothing, no goal, no missive, just the slow drag of life as the days march past and I wait.

And during that time, along these runs, I do something I've never done before. I work on me.

I compel myself to be authentic, let myself be me, the one I never let exist. The woman that gives a shit about people, that cares about the walls I have boxed around my heart. I didn't realize until now that I want them gone. And it isn't just the ones between Rachel and me, it's all of them. Those personal epiphanies litter long washes of dirt trails and hang on river willows I push through. My realizations are for me and the crickets in the cool spring evenings, for the broken windows and boarded up buildings. They are for the universe because I'm trying to take advantage of the gift it has given me.

And God?

I run all the way to the monolithic cross by the highway outside Effingham. It's easily fifteen miles away, but I make it out here every Sunday after church. After I've sat beside abusive parents and listened to them pray, I need to make a communion of my own. I come here because I want to remember that real religion isn't about the words that pour from hypocritical lips. It is about what's between me and Him, our private words when no one is watching. Rachel taught me that. She also taught me, indirectly, that religion is a lot like love in that way. The meaningful parts happen out of view. The real things happen when no one is watching.

I trace the sparse grass around my folded legs. Plucking one long strand I run it through my fingers absently. My thoughts tumble back to Rachel again and again as I sit in the cross' shadow–they always do and always will–she is synonymous with love and faith. I never really understood that until now.

I stare up at the bastion of blazing white high above my head. "God? I don't know if you're listening, but..." Although I want to, I don't pray for her to love me. It doesn't seem right to ask for something like that. It's hers to give, not mine to request. "I miss her," I admit softly. "Please make sure she's happy and safe. And let her know I care. Help her to feel it and believe it." All I have the right to ask for is her happiness, and this. "Help her to believe in me, in the woman I am, in the love I have."

I wait for a sign that someone is listening, but as

the sky melts into fiery orange and eventually twilight, I know today will not be the day He speaks to me. I don't really have a right to get an answer, not after all that has already been done for me.

I suppose it doesn't hurt to try.

Tossing the blade of grass down, I look out over the vast flat expanse. I don't really want to run back, so I sit a while longer waiting for the cross to turn purple against the shadows of twilight. When the sweeping chorus of crickets set music to the night is when I decide it's too late to stay any longer. I stand, dusting myself off. I shake my legs, feeling the muscles move under the skin. I never really thought about it, but I could probably join track, see just how fast I really am. Maybe make something out of it. I bet I could get tuition completely covered with an academic and athletic scholarship. It would be really nice to start my *second* adult life without educational debt.

My phone buzzes a text against the pocket of my running shorts and I grab it prying it from the cotton as I turn toward the small access road. It's probably my mother, and I'm already growling to myself as I pull up the message. I'm expecting to get a verbal berating for not being home for dinner, but what I see stops my heart.

I want to get to know you better.

It's Rachel, and my knees literally give out when I see the words. I sit again in the dust. She wants to get to know me, the woman I am. I take a breath and answer as a smile tugs at my lips.

Okay. I would like that.

I chew my lip as I stare at the phone in my hand. I don't want to move, I don't want to miss her message if she writes back. A moment passes, and the phone buzzes again.

We are having a barbeque at my parents tonight, and I was wondering if you would be willing to attend. I'm headed back home from dropping off some files for my dad in Effingham, but I'll be home in about twenty if you wanted to come over.

I look around, and my eyes fall on the cross above my head. If she's headed home, she's going to pass right by me. I almost laugh out loud when I hit the dial button beside her name. I can't help but think that God and fate are cheeky little conspirators. And I thank them just the same for their devices.

"Hello?"

"Hey Rachel," I breeze into the phone as I lean back against the darkening cross and stare north at the highway. "So, I have a bit of a problem."

"Oh?" I hear the phone go on speaker, as her voice gets a little distant.

"Yeah, how close are you to the cross?"

"I don't know a few miles maybe. I can't see it yet."

I smile, shivering a little as a breeze whips the scent of field over me. "Well, before you pass it can you pull over and pick me up? I'm by the side of the road leaning on it."

"Did your car break down?" She asks quickly. "I have towing through my auto club."

"No, nothing like that. I ran out here to get some exercise and now I'm too lazy to run back. I would also like to make it to your house for dinner, you know...if you'll give me a ride home."

"Oh." She sounds surprised. "That's really far, do you always run that much?"

I look down at my legs, flexing my knee in the

fading light. "No, it's a recent thing. I'm enjoying the area, the trails and stuff. It's a nice change of pace."

"Huh."

I spy car headlights coming toward me. In the twilight I can make them out clearly thought they are far off against the purple sky. "What was that 'huh' about? I think I see your car, by the way."

"I just didn't know you liked the outdoors, you always seemed like more of an indoor kinda person. Though, in retrospect I don't think I ever thought that much about what you did in your spare time."

I smile good-naturedly and roll my eyes as I tease her. "Look, you're getting to know me."

She laughs. "I suppose I am." I listen to the sounds of her car through the speakerphone. It's a little surreal, hearing the engine hum around me even though I can see the car on the horizon.

"I also draw." I kicked at the clump of scrub grass at my feet. "I like to paint landscapes with clouds, sunsets mostly."

"Aren't you a renaissance woman, painting and drawing. What else do you do, Blake Fortier?"

"Nothing, really." I clear my throat. "Blake is actually my middle name. My first name is Sarah."

"Whoa, really?"

"Yeah, when I started junior high I had my teachers call me Blake, and it eventually stuck."

"Well, I wasn't expecting that. I just figured your parents wanted an androgynous name for their child."

"No." I sigh. "They did want a boy to be honest, which is why my middle name is Blake."

Rachel gasps. "They didn't tell you that did they? That they wanted a boy instead of you."

Hearing her surprise makes me suddenly acutely

aware of how hurtful that revelation was once upon a time. "Yeah, well, no...not in so many words. I just knew it. After my sister was born they really wanted to do that whole quintessential American family thing, two parents, two children, one boy and one girl."

"I'm sorry."

A beat later I see the headlights flash and the car slow. "I see you, I'm hanging up."

"Okay."

It's a weird place to end the conversation and I don't really know what to do when Rachel's Mazda pulls up beside me and the automatic locks pop. I resort to humor, it is really the only thing I have aside from bitch and wife mode. I open the door with a forced smile. "Going my way?" I tease lightly, as I slide in and buckle my belt.

Her car smells like strawberries, but I'm not sure if it's air freshener or her. I smile approvingly while she checks her mirrors before pulling back onto the road. "So, too lazy to run back, huh?" She glances at me. "Shameful."

I'm grateful she doesn't go back to our previous conversation. I nod. "It's been a new ritual for me the past two weeks. I run out here to kinda reaffirm that God and religion and all of that stuff aren't lies."

Jesus. I cannot keep stuff light tonight. I just keep taking it to these deep uncomfortable places. I can't seem to stop because I just want her to know everything about me. I want her to see I have more depth than she has seen. I see her hazard a glance at me out of the peripheral of my vision.

"Is that true?" The way she says it carries the surprise of someone who really doesn't know me. It twists my emotions in ways I can't describe.

"Yeah."

"I've never heard you talk like this before."

I stare out the window because looking at her as she says those words is too painful. Once, she knew all my secrets. "I suppose I never had reason to until now."

"Tell me something else you haven't told anyone, not even Malina."

I glance over at her, thinking. "Okay, give me a second."

I don't know what to say honestly. I mean there are the obvious things, that I'm in love with her, that I'm a grown adult back from the future, but those things obviously can't be said. The other things, the secrets in my heart I want to share, drag me back into a place where I can't keep myself steady. Where the idea of talking about what I really feel makes me emotionally unstable because she should already know them, because I wish she did more than anything.

I think of anything benign I can. "I'm a little claustrophobic."

"Probably a good thing you didn't tell her that."

"Yeah, no doubt." I can almost picture Malina trying to asphyxiate me for getting in the car with Rachel tonight.

"Well, I'm afraid of spiders."

"I wouldn't tell Malina that either," I note. "You might find a bunch in your locker."

Rachel nods with a shiver. "Yeah, that would suck pretty hard."

I smile at her as she glances my way. I trace her hair with my eyes. Wearing it in a half up and half down twist, she looks airy and beautiful. I try and think of more stuff to share with her. "I sucked my thumb until I was eight."

She laughs. "I got up on a stage when I was three and sang at the mall."

I can picture it. "Were you wearing one of those little velvet dresses with the baby doll shoes?"

"Yep, exactly that." She gives me an incredulous look and hits the blinker, exiting the highway smoothly.

"I almost drowned when I was five because I fell into a pool. I think that is where my fear of not being able to breathe comes from."

"Probably." She chuckles softly. "Here's something. I used to be super klutzy and was always getting hurt as a kid. I stubbed my toes and skinned my knees so much it's just stupid."

"Since we're talking little kid injuries, I lost my first baby tooth because it was knocked out by a swinging door."

Rachel half laughs, then covers her mouth. "You poor thing, I bet that hurt."

"I don't remember it, but I'm sure it did." I arch a brow at her when she smiles at me. "Your turn."

"Oh, um, I had surgery to have my wisdom teeth removed before I got braces in junior high."

"I had my tonsils taken out when I got strep throat in fourth grade."

When we stop for a red light just outside of town, Rachel turns to me chewing her lip. "Why did you kiss me last week?"

It catches me completely off guard because we were just having so much fun sharing silly moments of our lives. I'm at a loss. "Because I wanted to."

She frowns. "I really honestly thought everyone at school would be hearing about it. That you had somehow recorded it or had someone post it on the internet." She huffs, "When no one knew, it scared me because I worried you were playing me even more."

"Playing you even more?"

"Yes like a long game of chess."

I give her a thin smile, but she looks honestly disconcerted, and I certainly don't want that. "I'm not playing a long game. I mean, I'm not playing a game with you. I like you." I clear my throat. "I legitimately like you as a person, there is no strategy here. No rug pulling is going to happen. There have been a lot of things I have done in my life that I'm ashamed of, but picking on you, that was by far the worst."

"Why the sudden change of heart?"

That is a very difficult answer to lie about. Whatever I say is going to be very defining and could haunt me for the rest of my life, so I have to make it good. I try to think of something that could be a trigger for me having a change of heart and when the real memory hits me, I pray it already happened in this life. "Do you remember when I was picking on you in the hallway and you said we were all smart girls? I made you look up at me by sticking my nail..." I can't even finish the sentence.

Rachel accelerates at the light, heading toward my house slowly. "When you stuck your fingernail in my neck? Yeah, I remember. It certainly wasn't your finest moment."

I wince, swallowing back on the bitter wave of remorse I feel. It was a different person that did that, I tell myself. "Well, that day, changed me. No one has ever called me smart even though I've gotten close to straight A's my whole life." I stare out the car at the houses, lingering on the glow in the windows. "When I looked at you that day, I just felt something. I knew I had denied huge parts of myself for a really long time, which is why I was always so mean and cold to you, but when we locked eyes I just...changed. I wanted to be different and stop being that person."

"So are you trying to say that you have been mean to me because you have liked me? Like a kindergarten boy picks on the girl he likes?"

I roll my eyes as I smile. Nothing like being compared to a child to put you in your place. "Yeah, just like that."

"Oh." Rachel frowns and tightens her hands around the steering wheel. "Do you really honestly like me?"

"I do."

"Like you...*like me*, like me?"

I narrow my eyes as I decode the sentence, taking a long slow breath before I answer. "Yes, I like you in a romantic way. I wouldn't have kissed you otherwise."

"I like you too, in that way, I think. I just want to know you better so I can be sure."

Hearing her say that, no matter how tenuous and fragile, makes my heart do weird strange pounding things in my chest. A million butterflies literally take off and bound around inside me as the words process. I'm almost afraid to open my mouth because I don't want anything to fly out. "Good. I'm really glad to hear that. I'm willing to do anything you want."

"Come to dinner and hang out with me so we can get to know each other."

I smile easily. "Okay. That I can do."

☙ ☙ ☙ ☙

I set a new land speed record getting ready for Rachel. It's ridiculous actually, how quickly I can accomplish the task of showering when I put my mind to it. It takes three minutes from the moment I hit the water till I'm setting my razor aside and frantically turning the faucet off.

I towel dry, sort of. My skin is still tacky when I clasp my bra and slip into my panties. I debate makeup. I debate drying my hair. I stand in the middle of my room wearing the equivalent of a bikini and wonder if it is inappropriate attire for a family barbeque. I see that reflection again, of the young me, and resist the urge to flinch at the scantily clad girl I barely recognize. I don't think I'll ever get used to this image.

The longer I stare at myself though, the more I realize I should just be me. I settle on flipping my hair and blowing it into tumbling waves, just how Rachel likes. I also add a pair of jeans, a shirt, ballet shoes and my cheer jacket to the final picture. With a quick once over, I roll my eyes and pocket my lip gloss as I grab my purse. My phone buzzes and I grab for it, worried for a moment that Rachel has changed her mind.

It's her. Crap.

My parents said you can stay the night if you want.

My breath comes so hard I cough. Oh, holy shit. I stand ramrod straight as I stare at the text, my heart slamming against the intercostal muscles between my ribs. Did she just invite me to stay the night? I mean, like sleep over? I glance at my bed, at the toss of blankets, and images of Rachel naked flash through my mind with such fury I feel faint. I tap my fingers on the keys without writing anything. I know I should say no, but I tell myself instead that I can be good. I can keep my hands to myself. Though, with her recent acknowledgement of affection, it makes it difficult to think about anything other than...sex.

Lots and lots of sex.

I swallow, willing my teenage hormones in check. They aren't as bad as when I was thirty-two, at the peak of my sex drive, but god, I'm already sweating as I flush with the very idea of Rachel and me together. It makes it hard to even function as I text her back.

Cool.

Grabbing my cheer bag, I throw everything in it I'll need, toothbrush, make-up, and clothing for tomorrow. I hazard a glance at my nightstand where my sleep wear is. I don't think I have anything that won't illicit sexual thoughts, so I hunt for my cheer sweats and a T-shirt and throw that in instead. The zip of the bag sounds like a stamp on my pseudo virginity's doom. I'm not gonna lie.

By the time I make it to Rachel's house, I'm trembling. I forget my keys in the car and almost lock it. I'm in such a hurry to see her I trip over the brick walk to the front door. It's silly how absolutely twitterpated I am, and how the rush of adrenaline I have relied on my whole life to make sound decisions betrays me now.

When I knock once on the door it opens almost instantly. If I thought I was in trouble before, I'm seriously screwed now. She has traded her mousy school clothes for a tight fitting T-shirt and a pair of equally tight jeans. Her bare feet are tan and her red toe nails flash as she rubs her foot on the back of her calf, leaning on the doorway. I'm pretty sure she practiced this position in a mirror because it makes her hips bow, it makes the angles of her body arch into one another perfectly. Everything fixes to her normally slim curves with such precision it leaves nothing to the imagination. Well, except for the words on the front of her shirt which seem to stretch from the pull of her breasts.

I can't breathe so when she ruffles her hair sexily and smiles a hello at me, I don't answer her. I just stare slack-jawed and crush my car keys in my hand until it hurts. "Hey." I'm finally able to respond and I swallow rapidly. "You look amazing."

She is pleased with herself, because she got the reaction she clearly wanted. There is a bounce in her step as she takes the bag from my shoulder and then, with just a moment of hesitation, places a soft kiss on my cheek. "You do too."

I'm dazzled by it, and I feel the tingle of it radiate down to my toes.

"My parents are outside, they want to meet you." She drops my bag in the entryway and takes my hand, pulling me through the house. I only got to see her home once, when we came back before our wedding. Knowing Rachel's mother Deborah, and her whirlwind of decorating fervor, I assumed the house Rachel grew up in as a teenager would have been different from my memories.

Surprisingly, it's about the same as I remember it. The pictures on the walls are different and in different places, but it's the same white and black monochromatic nineties motif. Not really my cup of tea, or Rachel's, but it's made homier with all the family paraphernalia. I eye pictures of my wife as a child. I remember them so clearly–Rachel with missing teeth from elementary school, a bowl cut in kindergarten, permed hair in sixth grade. God that was a disaster. I giggle when she sees where my gaze is resting.

"You didn't see that," Rachel states definitively

and in mock scorn.

I shake my head, miming an 'X' over my chest. "Cross my heart, no one will ever know."

"Good."

When we hit the back door, I falter a little. Rachel releases my hand and turns to smile at me. The barbeque smoke, the hickory char that reminds me of sunshine and laughter, tickles my senses. It creates a haze that feels dreamlike. It wafts over the picnic table, the tea light lanterns that sit on it, and glows from the white twinkle lights dangling from tree branches.

"This is really beautiful," I remark, trying not to let the images rebound off my heart quite so hard.

Rachel smiles at me, it's comfortable and confident, nothing like the fidgety girl I see at school. More like my wife than I can stand to see at this moment. "I'm glad you like it, it's my parents' thing. They," she chews her lip, "they like to create dreamy things like this."

Rachel doesn't admit it, but she does too. As I have always said, she is the romantic one. My wife builds homes like this, rooted in love, and warmth, and passion. She splashes colors of raspberry, and blue, and green in my heart and home. She places large glowing baubles of light, dreamy orbs that float, between the weeping willows and lavish brickwork outside. She builds a secret garden for us to share a world of romance, with pools of flowing water that tickle my ears, bright pink rose bushes and daisies punctuated against ivy. It is a place where music pours from hidden speakers, and more than once she has made love to me on a blanket staring up at the blue sky.

She's my bath-time-with-candle-light-romantic,

my midnight-kisses-to-thunder-lover. The woman that sings "You Are My Sunshine" as my morning alarm and buys quartz to dangle and drip rainbows over me. She breathes magic into my life, and seeing it now, seeing her here in this misty dreamscape, I love her so much it takes my breath away.

"Rachel, I..." Turning to her, watching the light rebound off her hair and eyes, I feel so exposed, so emotional. I feel things I shouldn't feel for her yet.

She cocks her head a little, her eyes patterning over mine. "You okay, Blake?"

"Oh, Blake's here!" I hear Rachel's dad say, and like ghosts from my past her parents materialize from near the barbeque to give a wave.

I always loved them. They practically adopted me, covering me in a warmth and protection I never knew. The woman I have become is because of Rachel and them. And seeing them again, this close and young, makes my eyes well with tears. I cover it by fixing my gaze on the little glittering lights above the patio. This house, like mine, was built on a love I once had, then lost. One I will never lose again. It makes it hard to look at Rachel. I'm grateful when her father Hiram motions for us. It draws my attention away from confessing my love to her right here and now.

He saves me from making a huge mistake. He has always saved me.

"Hey there, so you're Blake?" Hiram says adjusting his sixties style glasses on the bridge of his nose. He thrusts out a hand and I shake it warmly. "You ready to eat some amazing food, young lady?"

"Yes, sir."

I shake Deborah's hand next. I gesture at the halo of light around us. "Your house is beautiful.

Thank you for the invitation, all three of you."

"It's our pleasure, Blake. Rachel doesn't invite many people over, so it's a special treat for us," Hiram says gently, circling an arm around Rachel's shoulders.

I don't say how angry it makes me that I was one of the people that created the image that she was not friend-able. I don't say the millions of things I want to in that moment. I just redirect the conversation to abate the sudden pang of anger that pricks my eyes again. "Mrs. Kaplan, I especially love what you have done out here. It feels as intimate as a Southern style family meal, but as upscale as a New York restaurant."

"Deborah, please," she corrects, practically blushing at the compliment. "Thank you, but God, I'm the worse hostess, would you like something to drink?"

"I'll take an iced tea if it wouldn't be too much trouble." I hesitate a moment. "Rachel? What would you like?"

I don't miss the glances between the Kaplan's. It would normally make me happy that I'm scoring points, but I really couldn't care less. There is only one scoreboard that matters and it's written on the heart of the brunette smiling at me.

"I'll have an iced tea, too."

I grin, turning back. "Tell you what, you have all been so busy, just point me in the direction of the drinks and I'll grab them."

When Deborah begins to answer, Rachel puts a hand on her arm to slow her words. "I'll take her to get them."

"Okay, you girls don't take too long, food is up in five minutes." Hiram taps his watch, smiling at me. He gives me a ghost of a wink and when Rachel links her arm in mine, he grins when my face melts.

I don't think my feet touch the ground the rest of the night. I float everywhere I go. Even sitting at the big wooden table, with corn and burgers, potatoes and grilled red peppers, I don't really feel anything. I know I eat the food because it disappears from my plate, but my focus is on Rachel the whole time.

"So, did you have plans for college, Blake?" Hiram asks setting his beer down.

It's funny, but I know he is sizing me up to see if I'm good enough for his daughter. I smile because though it took a lifetime to get here, I think I finally may be. "Yeah, I'm going to apply to NYU and go to medical school."

Med school always gets the parents riled up. It's like a trigger point on a parent's need to make sure their offspring will be provided for. The title of *Doctor* equals money and stability. It had the same effect in my other life as it has now. It wins a foothold.

"Well, that's phenomenal," Hiram says between bites.

"Any specialty?" Deborah asks excitedly. "Don't tell me it's plastic surgery, people these days just don't love themselves enough. There is so much pressure to be beautiful, it makes me worry about you guys and everything you have to deal with. I always tell Rachel that love starts with herself. You know that, right Blake? You have to love yourself before you can love anyone else."

I swallow, uncomfortably and force a smile focusing on the way she rambles just like her daughter. It was something I always loved about her. Deborah and Hiram are Rachel and me. Sure they are different in their own ways, but their compatibility and love has always been a testament to how I knew we would make it.

"Um..no, not plastic surgery. I want to be a general practitioner, but I want to do research into gerontology as well."

"Why?" Rachel looks genuinely surprised and intrigued. She leans on her elbow, regarding me in the romantic lighting.

I lean on the table too, focusing on her, "I want to be a general practitioner because you have to have a broader knowledge of possible illnesses. I also like families. I like the idea of treating parents and children, sometimes together. I can't wait to have lollipops and stickers to hand out."

Rachel smiles dazzlingly and beneath the table her free hand finds mine. Her fingers trace mine slowly until they link together. I give her hand a squeeze even as my mouth goes a little dry. "Sounds like you should go into pediatrics."

"No, I want to help the parents, too, as they age. I want to have the ability to help anyone I run into, not just a small sliver of the population."

This time her hand squeezes and she moves forward a little, settling in closer to me. I bite my lip under the intensity of her look–it's open and warm, caring and curious. It makes my tongue heavy and twisted and unable to function. It makes me want to hug her, bury my face in her shoulder and just be here with her under the dripping lights.

"I like the idea of your singing. I know you will be a sensation. You have always been a star to me, in my eyes," I whisper giving her a very coy smile.

"Thank you." She drops her hand and rolls her fingers over the table, her eyes flitting back and forth between the pattern she is drawing and my gaze. "Doctor Blake Fortier. It has a ring. I trust it. I'll certainly have you as my doctor." She mimes a small heart on the table and it makes my breath stagger. She doesn't miss it and her lips lift in a small gentle smile.

Though there is a touch of connotation to the comment, I'm overcome by the way she is looking at me now. God, in those eyes I see such emotion, and for a minute I feel my face almost crumble. The warmth that fills the swirling brown of her eyes is right there, and all for me. It reminds me of how it used to be, when in those swirls I knew she knew me, understood and loved me unconditionally.

Love?

I swallow hard past the lump in my throat because there is a small glimmer in her eyes that reminds me of what it was like when she smiled her love at me. She rakes a hand through her hair, focusing all her attention on me and my heart just stops. I don't know how long I stare at her, how long she stares at me. All I know is my cheeks hurt from smiling, and when I smile that big there is no room for my heart to hurt over losing her.

"And we are going to call it a night," Deborah says at the same time Hiram clears his throat.

Oh, shit.

It takes a moment for me to remember that Rachel and I aren't alone and we are sitting at the table with her parents. My face heats so quickly that I must be the color of a tomato when I snap my eyes to their teasing expressions. "I'm sorry." I scramble to stand up when they do. "I didn't mean to be rude. We kinda slipped into our own world there for a moment."

Hiram waves me off with a smile. "It's okay. You

two talk, we are going inside."

It only takes them a moment to stack their paper plates, and with knowing smiles Hiram and Deborah both wish us a good night. I watch them until the door snaps closed, then turn back to Rachel. She has settled closer now, her eyes fixed on mine.

"I really like your family," I whisper in the small space between us, as I resume my seat.

"They like you." She lifts her hand as if she wants to touch me, but then sets it back on the table. "I like you too. I didn't know you wanted to be a doctor."

I shrug. I didn't know I wanted to be one either at this age. "There is a lot more about me you will have to learn."

"I want to." She swallows, lifting her hand again and then second guessing.

"It's okay," I urge with a tilt of my head, "you can." This time I close my eyes when her fingers press up against my cheek and then slide back through my hair.

"I like what I've seen so far."

I smirk. "I promise to keep giving you good things to find. You have seen the worst already. It only goes uphill from here."

She laughs then, and rolls her eyes for effect. "So, what is your favorite memory?"

I grin. "This one we are making right now."

Her hand stops in my hair.

"I'm serious. This is like magic, right now with you."

Rachel shakes her head and resumes playing with my hair. "I don't think I've ever felt this way before." It's a big statement for her and she glances away, letting go a breath. "Can we just keep this going, this moment where I feel like we are talking without talking?"

I nod and when I notice the chill on her arm I pull back enough to slide my jacket off. Her eyes bulge a little as I wrap it around her, tattooing my name in crimson and black across her narrow shoulders. "Yes, I'd like that."

Her fingers pull back as she fiddles with the lapel. "Your letterman jacket?" There is wonderment in her tone and a distance in her eyes. "It's warm from you. It feels good."

I lick my lips as I move closer. It's chilly, I didn't realize how much so until now. I would like nothing more than to wrap up in her arms. Rachel bites her lip and then surprisingly, fixes me with a very serious expression when her hand slides out of my hair and onto my thigh.

I think my eyebrows blur into my hairline as I shift under her touch. "Um." I glance at her hand.

She laughs, her eyes shimmering in the lights. "I don't think I've ever seen you look so nervous." She grips my leg and urges me toward her. "Come closer, you look cold."

I move so that our bodies are closer, but she shifts, too, and when I complete the motion she has turned to straddle the bench. I end up sitting between her legs and the sheer wall of desire that hits me winds me. I melt against her as she presses into my side and I struggle to remember why I can't do what I'm thinking of doing.

I can feel her chest moving rapidly against my arm, her breasts brushing me. My hand is on her thigh, inches from the zipper of her pants and I can literally feel the heat of her against my hip. Oh God, she is so hot. I know it means she is wet beneath the thick cotton of her jeans. I focus on breathing, I focus on anything that isn't my wife and the tells of her body. When she rests her chin on my shoulder, her lips close to my ear, I hold my breath to keep from doing any one of the hundred things that pass through my mind.

"Is that better?"

"Yes." I bite my lip so hard it hurts.

"Good." Her fingers are in my hair again and I turn my face toward her. "You okay Blake?"

"Yeah, just..." I clear my throat. "It's hard to be this close to you."

She moves closer then, as if to torture me more. Her hand is tight on my far side, and I can feel the hammer of her pulse in her fingertips. "I spent this week thinking about you. About how you made me feel when you kissed me. How I've kissed other people, but you unlocked something inside me."

I hyper focus on her lips, just a breath away from mine. "What did I unlock?"

She blushes then, red in the dotting of twinkle lights. "This out of control and desperate feeling."

"Out of control how?" I shift my eyes up to hers at the same moment I slide my hand around the outside of her thigh and squeeze. A smile forms on my lips when her breath falters.

"Um." She blinks a few times. "Like I didn't know myself anymore." She starts a tracing motion on my back, her hand leaving little heat trails as it moves over my shoulder blades and down my spine. I shiver. "What do you mean?"

"I'll show you." She nudges my nose with hers, smiling.

I can't resist anymore and when I tilt my chin

I'm pleasantly surprised at how Rachel completes the motion, pressing her lips to mine. It's chaste, soft, and lingering. I listen to her breathe, feel the give of her lips as we slant into one another. When it breaks, my breath hitches. "I see what you mean," I whisper.

Rachel laughs and the sound fills my heart. "That wasn't what I wanted to show you. Come upstairs with me."

"Wait, what?" I stumble as she takes my hand and detangles from me. Flashing a glittering smile, she pulls me up. "Come on. Come with me."

"Okay." I can't do anything but acquiesce to her wishes.

My hands are sweating, I can feel them as Rachel pulls me into the house, neatly clipping the lights off and snapping darkness over the yard. The house is black, but she moves by memory, guiding me back through the living room. I can hear the heaviness of her breaths as they come over and over. It reminds me of when she and I made love. I can read every nuance, how it slows and deepens. Right now, it's deep and even.

Ready.

Just hearing it again cuts at my heart.

I didn't think it would be this difficult to hear again. I wasn't prepared for how it would make me feel to have her with me. How good and yet remarkably bad it makes me feel that she wants me. That she is going to show me how much she does.

She doesn't slow as she bends and scoops up my bag. Rachel is on a mission of her own now, and just like my wife always was, she is of a singular purpose. We climb the stairs and the swish of my jacket on her, the way it traces over her lower back, is beautiful. She moves like poetry, years of dancing give her a lilting gate that could be set to music.

She is music. It moves through her, inside her, it is what she is made of. She isn't sugar and spice. Rachel is symphony and tempo. When she turns at the last few steps, I amend my thoughts at the look on her face. She is fire and passion. I swallow when I realize she already has that look–the incendiary expression I have held onto as I've ignited in her arms.

I trace the warm glow over my wife's body, my fingers curving into light scratches as my hand comes down her chest. The fire behind her crackles, popping just enough light for me to see her face. Her dark eyes follow my motions, long lashes shifting in the firelight, until my hands circles her hips and pull her to me.

Rachel tips her head back and breathes heavily as she rocks into my motions, deepening them. I watch her, watch the long slow movement of her body. From my position against the sofa, her thighs shift against my sides, caressing me as I make love to her. Backlit against the fireplace, she looks like the angelic moniker I have given her. She is my angel, my love, my life.

I reach back up and with feather soft hands map her shoulders and back. Rachel sighs at the touch, coming down a bit harder on the strap-on. It tugs a moan from me as I sit up to kiss the space between her breasts. I trace my lips to her clavicle and dip my tongue into the small notch at her throat. "How do you feel angel?"

"So good baby." *Her voice is breathy, straining.*

I bring my hands around her sides and cup her breasts, teasing them. My thumbs circle and brush, feeling her nipples harden under the light motions.

She mews softly as she quickens the pace of her

hips. *"Don't stop touching me just like that."*

I keep my fingers moving as I admire her. "Tell me what you feel." It is my favorite line and Rachel smirks as her motions slow and she levels her eyes at me. Her wild tendrils of dark hair fall to frame her shoulders then spill over me in a wave of softness when she bows her forehead against mine.

"You should know what I'm feeling doctor," Rachel teases, her lips whispering over mine. *"You know how deep this is and what anatomy it's hitting."*

For effect, my wife lifts up and then slams back down before my rapt gaze. It stalls all the air in my lungs, as my hips drive down into the cushion beneath me. She does it again, crying out sharply and I gather my arms around her. Our lips part, tongues duel. I can't kiss her hard enough or hold her tight enough to alleviate the love I feel in my chest. I pull her to me, drawing a deep arch in her back.

Rachel wraps her hands in my hair, *"What do you want to hear about?" Her nose grazes mine then slides over my cheek and ear. Her hot breath tumbles down my neck when she snorts a laugh. "How graphic do you want me to illustrate what you're doing to me?"*

I shiver. "As graphic as you want. Just tell me what you feel."

I trace my nails down her back, making her shift in my arms. "I feel your nails and they make me tighten down."

"What else?" I probe, squeezing her hips.

"I feel your hands on my hips, and when you squeeze...just like that. God, it makes me hurt for you."

"Where do you hurt for me?"

"At my opening, it's clenching and I feel the strap-on keeping me open. Deeper too, even as I talk I

feel myself clenching and it rubs there."

Rachel whispers her narrative as I resume my motions. "*When you lift me up, I feel the pull of the strap-on. Oh! I feel it pop free and I feel so empty without you inside me. I want you back, I need you back. I need you back filling me up until I can hardly breathe.*"

I answer her request and the unintelligible plea that leaves her lips fills the room. Her hands come down on my shoulders and squeeze, they trail up into my hair and tug my head back sharply. Her voice is so sexy and coarse. "*Just like that, so deep and perfect. Oh Blake, every time you do it, I get that much closer, that much tighter.*"

Her rough touches spur me on and I nip her neck as I jerk her hips up at the same time. She claws into my neck and it forces a growling moan from my lips. "*God, and when you moan like that I tighten down so hard I don't think you can get the toy back in–*"

I prove her wrong in one unyielding motion.

"*Oh, Blake!*" *She mouths the word 'fuck' and then grits her teeth. They are all I see in the darkness as she squeezes her eyes shut.* "*God, yes, Blake it almost hurts it feels so good, please,*" *she wheezes a breath,* "*please keep going and make me come for you. I love you.*"

"*I love you. I love you so much sweetheart. You are the most important thing in my life and I would do anything to make you happy.*"

I pull her into me until my arms are sore, until if the positions were reversed I would be begging her to stop. I say it over and over, that she is my sweetheart, that she is the most important person in my life. I revel in the mix of our sounds as they literally fill our home.

That is until her head bows to mine and her

hands hold me tightly. When she inclines her face to me it completely stills my motions with the way her eyes are glistening. I trace a hand over her face, thumbs brushing the edges of her eyelashes as her lips tremble.

"Baby?" I hold her face in my hands. "Are you okay?"

"Yes, it's just when you tell me that," she sighs, committing to it, "when you tell me you love me and that I'm your sweetheart and angel, I feel it in my soul. It makes me feel so special Blake, because I'm yours. No matter how many years pass, I know I'll always feel like that." She take a long trembling breath. "It just makes me really emotional." She blinks tears and I catch them on my fingertips. "Damn it, I'm sorry. I didn't mean to ruin the moment. I know this isn't the hot fantasy you wanted." She peeks at me from over her hands as she wipes at her cheeks.

"Rachel." I smile at her, shaking my head as I pet her. "I love you baby. You are the hot fantasy I want, in whatever form you come in."

She presses her face to mine and her tears wet my cheek. "I'm going to cry more cause it's that kind of night, but please don't stop."

"That kind of night?" I question as I pull back to see her better.

"Yeah." She wipes her cheek again. "A silly, weepy, soul deep kind of night." She sniffs cutely and then grins. That fire is back, I watch it ignite in the mahogany of her eyes. "But that's when it's best anyway."

I laugh softly, because I don't get it, not really. "I suppose so."

"Yeah, when you can take anything you want from me."

The look she gives me then, says it all. "Anything?"

I smirk, circling her with my hands and rocking her into me.

"*Yes, anything you want.*"

And I greedily took what I wanted.

It bothers me deeply that I didn't understand that night, not really, not until now. The limits of my understanding ended at something much more superficial than it was. Well, as intimate as the actions were, my comprehension stopped at that level of connectedness. As I hit the top stair of Rachel's parents' house, I realize I made love to her soul that night, not just her body.

When Rachel opens her bedroom door I forget that moment was shared with my thirty-year-old wife and not the sixteen-year-old girl before me. Rachel turns toward me and reaches to close the door. It puts her close, so close I can feel the heat pour off her and I reach out, catching her waist. She smiles at me, an easy breezy thing full of new found trust.

I never really understood her. I didn't let her understand me either. Or maybe I didn't know myself well enough to let her be successful in her attempts. Remembering that moment we shared, lights my desire at the same time it makes me hurt. It drives home the point that her words over the years and the tears of that night were something I took for granted even though they were all that I needed.

Feeling her in my hands forces me to remember that this woman right here is everything to me. And I need to be near her so badly I feel like I might cry.

And God is she beautiful, but she is so much more than that.

She is my soul mate.

Everything is blurred together and the young

woman before me is my Rachel. She is *my* wife. She is here, she is right *here*. I tell myself that over and over as I lean into her and she seals her lips against mine. It starts slowly, hands twisting together.

It's the way it was in my office the last time I kissed her.

When I think that, I'm *done*.

In a fury of emotion and desire, I push Rachel toward her bed, claiming her mouth with searing kisses. She gasps, backpedaling, as I wrap my arms around her. She palms the bed to catch herself, until I flatten her to the mattress and crawl over her. Then her hands grab onto my pants, my shirt, anything she can grasp to yank me onto her.

I moan into her mouth as her hips move up and beg silently for purchase. Accommodating her, I drop my pelvic bone into the seam of her jeans and when she bucks again her kiss breaks around the soft groan at the back of her throat. My hands splay the jacket open and before I can even think my palm is beneath her shirt and over her bra's lace. I squeeze firmly, sliding the tips of my fingers under the cups. The curve of her breast is soft, and her eyes roll closed when I lift the material up, freeing her for my hands.

She smells like strawberry and fire pit and I kiss her neck, latching my lips to the firm skin of her jaw and then move downward. I circle her nipple with my fingers at the same time I nip the pulse point of her neck with my teeth and then rest against it, feeling it pound. "What did you want to show me?" I tease, licking lightly at the skin before me.

She can't even speak. It takes a minute before she can get the words out. "I wanted you to see how out of control you make me."

"Tell me instead," I whisper, guiding my hands in love trails over her body. I brush her shirt up and peel my own off. Her eyes widen as she looks me over.

"Oh, Blake." Her hand comes out tentatively to trace a trail of fire across my side and abdomen. She strokes her hands over me, then pulls me down onto her again.

I tumble into her waves of hair and the heat of her skin where it touches mine. I smile as I feel her responding, feel her hips grind into mine, her leg wrapping around to cement me closer. Rachel cries out softly when I sink my hip into her hard, hitting where I know she wants me.

"Tell me how out of control I make you."

Her head turns into my neck, lips brushing over my ear in hurried breathes. It maps chills down the whole right side of my body.

"I don't think I can say it."

"Why?" I whisper, nudging her lightly with the tip of my nose. I pepper kisses over the side of her face. My hand trails down and Rachel's breaths get faster as I thumb open the button of her jeans.

"Because, I'm embarrassed."

When she says that, with a start I realize what I'm doing. My fingertips halt on their ravenous path down her stomach and rest against the band of her underwear. I swallow as I pull back. Rachel comes into focus. She frowns as she stares at me. "I'm sorry. I can't say the things you say."

God, she is so young, so fragile and sweet and… not yet my Rachel. She may kiss like her, move like her, and feel like her, but she isn't. Not in her heart, the part I want the most. "It's okay." With herculean effort I swallow and pull my hand back. I rest it on the bed to take the strain off my other arm. "I don't want you to be embarrassed. I want you to feel comfortable and confident in yourself, and me, and us."

"Us?" she whispers in wonderment. She is so close her eyes bound over mine as she hangs on my words.

"Yes, us."

She looks down between us, an idle finger tracing the strap of my bra. I know she is debating what to do. She looks afraid that if she says no she will never have another chance to be with me. I take the doubt away so she doesn't have to worry. "I'm not going anywhere. I'm not leaving. Everything you see, everything you want will be here when you're ready."

"I'm ready. I know who I am and what I want. I spent the week thinking about it and I know I'm okay with this."

I smirk and then kiss her nose when she huffs in irritation.

"I'm not making fun, so no getting huffy. I just think that it will be better when you feel like you know me well enough and when we both can let everything go, without fear or embarrassment."

Her gaze waivers. "Okay, but I don't want you to be mad."

I kiss her lightly as I shift her bra back into place. "I'm not gonna be mad. How could I be?"

She latches her hands to the sides of my face then, keeping me from pulling back in search of my shirt. "Because, I'm not one of those girls."

No, she certainly isn't.

"The fact you aren't will make everything that much more amazing for both of us. Right?"

She shakes her head in disbelief, but smiles

anyway. "Will you still stay over?" The doubt in her tone is palpable.

"Only if we carpool to school tomorrow."

She laughs. "Okay."

"Good." I smooth a hand over her hair and kiss her again. "You look good in my jacket."

Shifting under me, she thumbs the collar up a little and bites her lip cutely, flirting with me. "You think I can rock this look?"

"Absolutely. Starting tomorrow, you should rock it every day."

The confidence vanishes from her face, replaced with utter fear. "I can't wear it to school."

"Why not?"

"Well, because people will think we are dating."

"Do you want to?"

"Wait what? Date you, or wear your jacket?"

"Both."

"Yes."

"Then it's yours. And so am I."

Chapter Eight

Five Ways To Her Heart
May 1st, 2011

I t's nice to forget the past, and just *be* for a while.

"Where are you taking me Blake?"

Her laugh is the best in the world. I hold Rachel's eyes closed as we crunch over the dirt road at the edge of a cornfield. Her hands wrap around my wrists softly, and I peek around her to make sure I'm not going to walk us into anything. "Just wait, you'll see."

Even as she leans back into my guiding embrace I can tell she is trying not to ask again. It lasts all of thirty seconds because she is phenomenally impatient. "Are we going someplace public or private?"

"Both."

"How is *that* possible?"

I know it is driving her crazy. And to be honest, she was very good about keeping her eyes closed in the car, so I feel a little guilty keeping her in suspense for so long. We are in Effingham, for the fireworks, 'cause it's something she always wanted to see. And I'll give her every wish she could hope for, for the rest of her life.

"Hey Blake?"

I glance up from studying, to eye my fiancée. "Yeah?" *She has an oversized red and black book behind her and I smile quickly before going back to my microbiology.*

"You won't believe what I found."

It clicks when I remembered those colors. "Your yearbook." I say without looking up.

"Yeah, I thought it was packed away in storage." She sits across the dining room table from me. When she drops the book I glance up at her. She's flipping the pages as her eyes trace the images.

At least she is being quiet. I try to read again. "Hey Blake?"

"Yeah?" I narrow my eyes at the text, 'RNA dependent polymerase' and reference my notes. I add more information to the novel forming in my notebook. Why the fuck I decided to become a doctor is beyond me. It is so much work and it doesn't help that my needy fiancée is breaking my concentration.

"Do you ever feel like you missed out on things in high school?"

My mind whirls, as I focus on the words 'dsRNA is a replicative form of virus and specifically serves as template for genome synthesis.'

"Blake?"

I sigh, super irritated over the interruption. "What the fuck, Rachel?"

I think she winces, because for two fucking seconds she is fucking quiet. "You've been going for hours."

"I'm finally getting this shit."

"Can you take a break?"

I scribble a few notes about mutations, specialized proteins and viral mRNA molecules.

"Guess not."

I glance up at Rachel's frown. "Huh?" I shake my head. "Look, I'm sorry. I'm just stressed about this class." I set the book aside and stretch out the kink in my neck, and when I shift I realize my ass is completely numb. "Wow, we need fluffier seats."

"Why?"

"My ass is numb from sitting."

"You've been sitting for three hours. I don't think better seats will help."

I glance over at the clock as an icy tingle races down my spine. "We were supposed to go out on our dinner date. Shit. Why didn't you tell me?"

"I tried. You were a little too focused."

My stomach growls. "Well, we can go now if you want."

Rachel waves me off as she directs her gaze to the book again. "I've already started spaghetti. It will be ready in ten minutes."

"Sorry," I whisper.

"Don't be sorry." She smiles easily, and all is forgiven.

I stand slowly, finding more aches and pains as I uncoil. When I finally make it over beside Rachel I stare down at the image of me in a cheer uniform. I'm winking at the camera. It is a gut check to see it, to see myself so young and athletic.

I twirl a strand of Rachel's hair around my finger as she flips the page. "I'm sorry I'm not in good shape like that anymore."

She snorts a laugh. "Stop it." She looks up at me briefly. "Do you miss it?"

I blink at her. "High school?"

"Yes."

"Not really." I tap the image of my cheer coach yelling through a bullhorn. "She kinda killed the fun for me."

Rachel grins. "But she got you in such good shape."

"Shut it," I warn teasingly.

"Do you regret not doing things? You know, when you had all the time in the world?"

I puzzle at the idea of it, running through all the things I did, all the fun times I had. Those thoughts always bring me back to my epic mistake of getting pregnant my junior year. "I think there is more I regret doing, than not doing."

Rachel doesn't really look at me then. I know she knows what I'm talking about. She flips another page. "I regret not doing things. I wish I would have had more fun and not been quite so driven toward my goals."

I arch my brow at her downturned head. "I'm pretty sure what you just said is against your religion, Miss Kaplan."

"It has nothing to do with me being Jewish." She laughs at her own joke. "I just wish I would have done more. Enjoyed myself more and really felt the thrill of being young and invincible somewhere other than on a stage."

I sit down in the chair beside her, pulling the yearbook closer to me so I can see it. I stare at the pictures of my friends, letting hazy happy memories drift over me. "What do you wish you would have done?" I smirk. "Steal a car or jump out of a plane?"

"No, nothing like that. I just wish I would have done other things. Little things."

"Like what?" I ask.

"Like watch the town fireworks in Effingham. You know, out by the fields where the cool kids always were."

I uncover her eyes as we reach the edge of the lot. Right here the cornfields split and the row between them goes all the way to the horizon.

"Where are we?" Rachel asks softly.

"On the town line."

"Why?"

I shrug playfully as I grab for my phone and stare down at the clock on the lock screen. "You'll see."

The crunch of gravel behind me draws our attention as a few other people join us slowly, materializing out of the darkness. Rachel shifts closer to me, because out of context it must feel pretty creepy, and I circle her waist as we stand together. She turns to whisper in my ear.

"What am I out of the loop about?"

A shock of lightening actually makes me jump. I stare at the sky in the distance, waiting as Rachel presses her cheek to mine. The rumble of thunder tumbles over us and I pull her closer.

"I feel really safe here in your arms." Rachel murmurs over the slow warm wind that pulls her hair over my skin in a caress.

"I like you standing in them, angel."

Rachel is half turning to kiss me when the first whistle of the fireworks cuts the night air, and then she stops. The sky explodes in a blaze of red and though I know people are gasping around us, all I hear is her surprised yelp. Another puff of light and another, paint the sky in a tempest of color that whirls like a vortex and shimmers like her eyes. And then something happens that I never could have expected. The lightning comes in shocking sharp lines to warp across the sky. It back lights the smoke clouds leftover from the fireworks as they drift in the wind and gives me a more spectacular view than I've ever seen. A view that is so surreal and amazing that I don't know whether to look to our right and watch the firework display, or look left and watch Mother Nature.

I settle instead on staring at my wife. And at the honest joy in her face, I have the best view there is.

I kinda wish I would have snuck into a movie.

"Did you know that there are literally *billions* of dollars lost each year from people pirating movies?"

I lean against Rachel's shoulder and whisper a kiss across the hair at her temple. "I didn't know that."

We move further up in line.

Rachel leans into me until her back goes ramrod straight and she moves away. I can see she is staring to our right and I glance around her. There, practically frothing at the mouth, are Malina and Lindsey sprinkled with a few other cheerleaders.

I arch my brow at them as they lower their voices in a whisper. Malina's eyes are pinned to where my hand is twisted with Rachel's. "Don't worry about them," I say softly, sliding forward and pulling Rachel in next to me.

"I think they are talking about us."

I shrug. "Like, I care."

Rachel looks at me uncomfortably. "Don't you? I swear Malina's eyes are burning me right now."

It's truly laughable how little I care. "No, why would I?"

She doesn't answer me. I twist her around to the far side, so I'm standing between my cheerleaders and my wife. "There, now they can try to burn me instead."

Rachel smiles. "I don't want you to get burned."

"It takes a lot more than Malina to rattle me." I peer up at the movie times, distracting Rachel by pointing. "Which one did you want to see?"

"I don't know. You pick."

I read through all the times and titles. "Shutter Island?" I intentionally say it loud enough for Malina to hear.

Rachel cocks her head at me. "Trying to get me into a scary movie?"

"Maybe."

She leans toward me and pecks a kiss on my cheek, a little more comfortable. "Can I jump into your arms?"

"Isn't that the point of a proper scary movie date?"

She laughs. "I was hoping so."

Once we get our tickets, I notice Malina buys the same ones a moment later.

With popcorn and jelly bellies in tow, we head toward the theater and find a seat. I think Malina is somewhere behind us because I can hear her laugh.

"Do you know the answer to this trivia question?" Rachel asks, rattling her box of candy at the screen.

"Nope."

She scoffs. "It's Broadway. I thought you knew me better."

I grin at her. "I know you better than you think."

"Oh?" She edges closer. "What is it that you know?"

I take her hand. "Come with me."

Rachel backs up, blinking. "Huh?"

"Come with me, we are going to go do something *wild*."

I stand abruptly and as Rachel exits the row ahead of me, I smile up at Malina and give her a wave. I swear I hear her teeth grind from ten rows back and my wave turns into a single finger salute.

Or better yet, I wish I would have made out in a

movie theater. Preferably with you.

I can hardly see as I navigate the darkness. Rachel's hands are on my hips as she follows me. I circle her hands with mine.

"What are we doing Blake?"

"Sneaking into another movie."

"We've already been in two."

"Well, there are a lot of good movies this year." I laugh and Rachel hushes me as we emerge into the theater itself. I wait for my eyes to adjust and when I see a vacant row at the back, I start up the stairs toward it.

"Excuse us." We race past people to get out of their way.

Once in the back, I don't waste any time. I pull her toward me into a kiss.

"Kissing in a children's movie?" Her voice is dark.

"Yeah, I like to scandalize the youth."

Rachel's hands pull at me, and during a flash of the movie I can see she is grinning wickedly.

"What?" I ask, because her grin is just positively naughty.

"I'm just really happy."

"Me too."

She kisses me hungrily, like she is trying to climb inside me to hide from the world, just like I want to do to her. She breaks the kiss around my name. "Blake?"

"Yeah, sweetheart?" I'm a little breathless.

"You're amazing."

That makes me breathless. "*You* are."

She is so excruciatingly beautiful, so wonderful in every way. She twists her hand in mine and kisses my fingers when I flex them in hers. "You're the best friend I've ever had." She smiles nervously and then squeezes my fingers. "I've never had a best friend before now. You're my best friend."

And now my lungs don't work at all.

"You're mine. Always."

I don't know what we are fake watching. I think it is *Tangled*. There are animated characters singing on the screen in the background, but it could totally be *Toy Story 2*. All I know is that Rachel's lips are on mine again and I'm not sorry I paid ten bucks a ticket to *not* watch three movies.

You know, I always wanted to go on a proper date.

Rachel opens the door and I hide the flower in my hand behind my back.

"Oh, Blake, hi." She leans forward to give me a kiss, but I turn in the last moment, and her lips press to my cheek. She pulls back a little surprised, her eyes wide.

"Is your dad home?" I ask with a smile tugging on my lips.

Rachel regards me a moment. "Yeah." She presses the door open wider. "Did you want to come in?"

I nod. "Thanks."

She tries to let me pass in front of her, but I wait, allowing her to lead. It's hard to keep a flower hidden, when she can see it.

"Daddy?"

I hear Hiram's voice from the back of the house. "In here, Rachel!"

I find him at his desk. He swivels his chair toward us when Rachel presses open the door to his office. "Oh, hey Blake," he says and his eyes go to the hand behind my back.

"Hi. I was hoping I could speak to you a moment."

"Sure." He sets aside his papers and shifts his

glasses on the bridge of his nose. "What's up, kiddo?"

I glance at Rachel who is waiting expectantly. "I was hoping that you would permit me to take your daughter out on a date. A proper one. I have reservations for seven and I'll have her home by midnight."

I think Rachel makes a sound because Hiram's eyes drift to his daughter before focusing back on me. He stands. "Blake? What are your intentions?"

My heart starts hammering, because I wasn't expecting this. "Um, my intentions?"

"With my daughter?"

I completely blank. "I don't know what you mean."

"Well, this is all very serious business. Isn't it?"

I swallow. "Yes."

"Dating is very serious."

When his lips struggle to hold back his grin, I realize he is messing with me. My heart proceeds to vacate my throat and I'm able to laugh. "Very serious, sir." I salute him lightly.

"And a proper serious date is very serious indeed." He pets my head as I turn to Rachel's ruby red blush.

"Agreed." I use my free hand to squeeze Rachel's. "It's all very serious with your daughter." She hears the point of my wording, because her eyes sparkle with emotion.

He approaches and gives my shoulders a squeeze, and I lean into him comfortably. "Go, have fun girls."

And I give her the flower there, right in front of her dad, which I think makes her blush even more. As she stares at it blankly I arch my brow at her. When her eyes finally come up to me I bite off a cheeky grin.

"You heard your dad, go get ready."

"Okay, give me a minute."

When she is gone, I smile up at Hiram. "More like thirty minutes, let's not kid ourselves."

He silently regards me. "It *is* very serious, isn't it?"

And I can't help but answer honestly. "It's the most serious thing in the world to me."

He pats my shoulder before taking up his place at the desk again. "I can tell. It is for both of you." He stares at me over the rim of his glasses. "All that stuff a father is supposed to say, I'm gonna say now. Blah, blah, blah, be good to each other, don't get pregnant. Blah, blah, blah, if you hurt her they will *never* find the body. We clear on all that?"

I nod. "Crystal clear."

But more than anything, I wish I could have been closer to you and had a picture of us together. Right here.

I cut into the journalism club's meeting. They meet in room 332 every day after school and before I go to meet Rachel, I have something I need to do.

"We need a spread for the yearbook before I have to go to Mark and tell him we don't have–"

Silence draws over the room as I step in. The door closes behind me.

"Blake? What are you doing here?" The apprehension is literally so thick in his voice–I think his name is Danny–that Danny's voice breaks.

"I have an idea for that spread." I lean back on the wall sexily drawing on all my allure to get my way. "Couples."

"Couples?"

"Yeah, the 'it' couples at the school. It would

be cool in ten years to see who is still together at the reunions."

He stares at me blankly before turning to another guy. "That is actually pretty cool."

Guess I didn't need to bat my eyelashes after all. "Good, grab your camera."

"Wait, now?'

"Yes, now."

And he actually jumps to do it. I silently thank the bitch I once was.

With my entourage of two, I make my way toward the grass area at the center of the school. I had told Rachel to meet me here with the intention of this. So when I emerge into the semi-busy area, with benches and a statue in memorial to the school's founder, I'm not surprised she is there. When she turns to me, she has a puzzled look on her face.

I give her a hug, and turn to the journalism team. "Rachel, this is Danny and–"

"Steve, Danny, hi." Rachel grins. Of course Rachel knows them. She actually knows everyone.

I give them both a very firm look before I soften my expression and turn to Rachel. "So, they are taking pictures of couples for the yearbook and asked if we would pose."

"Oh?" She lifts her hand into her hair and combs the tendrils back.

"Don't be nervous," I whisper, tugging at the edge of her letterman jacket.

"Well, right now? Right here?" She looks at the bench behind us.

I nod. "Sure."

"Okay, so this will be good." Danny pulls the camera back from his face. "Get closer girls."

I detect a hit of porn on his mind from how his voice sounds. I shake the idea out of my head and scrunch closer to Rachel. "You ready to be immortalized?" She tips her head against mine with a small nod.

"Smile."

The shutter clicks a few times.

"Thanks, Blake. I'll get some other couples and see how it works out."

I thank him absently because all my focus is on Rachel. She has a very bemused expression. "What was that about?"

"I don't know really," I lie. "They needed filler for the yearbook."

"Ah." She shifts closer and rests her head against my shoulder again. "Going to practice?"

I nod. "Yeah." I feel so satisfied in this moment here with Rachel I really can't get up the heart to go. "I don't want to go. I just want to hang out with you."

"I have practice too, so we can meet up after." She angles her face toward me. "Hey, Blake?" The tone of her voice is totally different than anything I've ever heard. I regard her silently. "I couldn't think of anyone I would rather be immortalized with."

"Same here."

She looks like she wants to say something more as her eyes move over mine, but instead she kisses my nose. "Go to practice, I'll see you later."

"Okay." I watch her leave, and it makes my heart swoon when she looks back with that smile of hers and blows a kiss into the breeze all for me. I keep that kiss, and the knowledge that she will never have a regret, close to my heart as I hurry to the locker room.

Chapter Nine

Forever By Firefly
May 28th, 2011

There is something about Friday nights. They are fringed with kinetic energy and filled with psychological connotation. It's difficult for me to avoid the hard edged rush of doing those things again. I'm spellbound by the way it makes me feel to be in this life, to build a life for what feels like the first time.

It's the greatest blessing I have ever had.

And Rachel? I glance at her out of the corner of my eye. No, *she* is the greatest blessing in my life.

Under the blinding lights of the baseball field, she is laughing with a fellow student. Tucked in my letterman jacket, double varsity patches brandished on her arms, I catch her eyes for a moment and wave my pompom at her. She shakes her head with a smile and a catch of her teeth on her lip. It's like a high school movie. I can't stop thinking that, as I reminisce over our month together. About how easy it was to just...be me. Had I known all it took was standing up and saying, she's with me–and it would have changed her life–I would have done it before.

I should have done it before.

But I'm doing it now, and that is all that matters. I'm carving a new path, trail blazing a new life for the woman I love. I won't stop–ever.

I can't.

And God have we had fun. Sleep overs, nail painting, makeovers that turn into sloppy kissing battles with lipstick smudges. Dates and dinners, car drives, and secrets whispered in the dark. It's enough to make me fall head over heels, over and over again.

A line drive cracks across the field and the stands erupt in a cacophony of screams. Rachel jumps up from her seat to join the fray. Beside her, our friends are screaming. As head cheerleader, I better get my head in the game–literally.

"Go Titans! Go!" I scream and my squad falls into line. We scream in unison, leading the stands in a unified chant as the opposing team scrambles to out the player at third. They fail miserably and when the inning rolls to a close, we're three runs up and damn if it doesn't feel great to be alive...until I turn to Malina and she gives me a bitch look. I sigh. She really needs to get over herself, like now. Her mood puts a damper on my euphoria.

She has actually been the only person in this school that has cared about the fact that Rachel and I are dating. Of all the people I would have thought would get behind me, I'm shocked by the fact it *isn't* her. Regardless of whether I'm an adult or not, it wounds me a little. I can't rationalize it the way I wish I could. I really want to keep her friendship, but it is becoming more of a hassle than it's worth. In the measure of importance in my life, Malina loses in a landslide against my wife.

"Pyramid to flips people, let's go!" My girls hustle to get into position, except for Malina who stares at me long and hard and then rolls her eyes as she flanks me.

"You're such a bitch, Blake."

"I'm not a bitch." I state low enough so only she hears me.

"You are what you eat."

I shake my head. "Is that why you're such an asshole?" I focus on the stands, forcing a smile for the crowd. "One! Two! Three!"

"We are the Titans, the mighty, mighty, Titans!"

The routine is simple for me honestly. I could do it in my sleep, and have. I move forward and high kick. Move backward and drop as Malina does a round off over me. As I drop into position, I can't help the tingle in my spine, the concern she might kick me for fun like she has done the past month. I swallow, tucking tightly.

"Everywhere we go-o, people wanna kno-ow!"

When I feel the air brush me as she easily clears my body, I spring back up. Guess she isn't gonna concuss me at a live game for all the good it would do her.

"Who we are!"

Now, I climb, and as people stack before me, the tingle of excitement hits my stomach. I grab Lindsey's hand and she helps me jump up.

"So we tell 'em!"

Three levels of humanity high, ten or so feet off the ground, I plant at the top of the pyramid and scream the end of the cheer as loud as I can.

"We are the Titans, the mighty, mighty, Titans!"

It's kind of lame if I'm totally honest with myself. If I wasn't standing up here frozen with a smile on my face as everyone in the stands snaps photos and screams, I would probably die a little inside. However, euphoria and the way Rachel is grinning at me, stops me from my internal death spiral.

And now comes the only jarring part, the dismount. It's not really hard, it's just a little nerve wracking because I have to tuck and do a forward flip to the ground. And to be fair, ten feet is far when you don't feel indestructible like a teenager anymore. It's compounded by the fact that I broke my knee on this move in my other life. I know what I did wrong, I didn't tuck long enough. I pulled out too early, not rotating enough, and snap goes the rest of that story. I won't do that again.

I blow a breath as my face slips, and I glance at Rachel's hands white knuckling the rail. She hates this part. I do too, for more than my own reasons. It's also because I know that it makes her heart race and practically gives her a headache when she has to watch me do this. She is scared I'm going to break my neck.

I nod once, signaling to the two girls on the ground to start running and spring into backflips, so we all land at the same time. And right when they press off, I go for it. For all my arrogant accolades of mental prowess, the only thing that goes through my mind when I feel the centrifugal force of my tuck is the word, fuck. And I stay as tight as I can for as long as I can, until I spot the ground and open. We all three land in a resonating slam and the crowd before us drowns any frayed nerves I have with screams of excitement.

I give Rachel a grin and she smiles thinly, letting go her breath.

ℋℋℋℋℋ

We end up winning the game. And my victory celebration begins with a kiss under the stands. As people straggle toward their cars, I engage myself in a slow trace of my tongue against Rachel's as we lean against the support rails. I feel the coolness of this last spring night on the backs of my legs, but the radiating heat from her body, the simple trace of her hands on my back, balms everything.

I hear a few familiar voices that melt into giggles when they see us, but it doesn't stop the motion of my mouth or *hers*. I'm very happy about that. She actually presses deeper, her fingers curling into my ponytail with directive. It's a very claiming motion, a show of ownership. It makes my stomach drop like a theme park ride as the charge of electricity bends through me in an arc.

I'm aware of the role reversal, the way I grab ungainly at the lapels of her jacket and struggle for purchase while she commands my kisses. She makes my knees weak, makes me feel like a teenager swept in a warm soup of first love. The feelings she elicits are so strong I don't remember anything but her hands and her lips and the way she touches me. It scares me, the power she has. I never actually let myself go. Not in the way she did, I was always in awe of it. I made her love me, made her succumb and submit to me, but there was always a part of me she couldn't touch. She had my heart and my soul, but she didn't have all of me. There was a small sliver I saved for myself because I didn't want to be at anyone's complete mercy.

It was because of my family, because of the way they emotionally manipulated and physically abused me. I just had to keep a small modicum of power and control. Even when I trusted her, loved her, died for her, she didn't get that piece. It made me confident that if her feelings ever *did* change, I could survive. It kept her from physically dominating me and on more than one occasion stopped my orgasms cold when they got too close, too real and emotional, and I felt that shard slipping away.

However, somewhere along the way in my new life I lost that part.

I don't know when it happened, if it was the night of the barbeque last month or in every moment since, but I can't find it. Without it, I'm open, vulnerable. It relegates my heart to the realm of nervous expectation and fragility. All the emotional development and self-actualization I've been through as an adult just falls away when she's with me because she *has* me. There isn't another person in the world who will ever be able to say they have everything I am, every fiber of my being, to do with whatever she wants. And when she kisses me like she is doing now, I become a very young girl, one full of hope, and love, and *fear*.

I'm so afraid that she won't love me, love me in the millions of ways I need her to. That she won't end up holding me in her arms singing me to sleep. I fear that her fingernails won't tousle my hair and her hand won't twist in mine. I'm desperately afraid hers will not be the eyes I stare into for the rest of my life. Because without her lips kissing mine, her heart protecting mine, and her arms sheltering me, I'm nothing. I'm lost.

It keeps me up at night. Alone in my bed I toss and turn. When I sleep over at her parents' house, it makes the weave of her sleeping arms around me burn.

Rachel ends the kiss. She's flushed when she comes back into focus. I banish my thoughts, giving her a smile. My eyes seek hers.

"You look amazing tonight." I compliment,

teasing her nose with mine. "Did you have fun?"

"Always...aside from your acrobatics making me feel like my heart was in my throat." She pecks my lips softly, drawing me closer into the warmth of her with firm hands on my lower back. "You better be careful, I like you not rolling in a wheelchair."

I laugh against her, taking her hand and entwining it with mine as we start toward the parking lot. "Me? I'll always be careful. I promise." I measure her with a look as she bumps her shoulder into mine. "Do you like me being a cheerleader?"

She shrugs playfully and nudges me again. "If I said you were super-hot as a cheerleader, would you hold it against me?"

"No," I tease.

"I think you're super-hot. Wanna hold all that hotness against me?"

I shake my head in mock scorn. "I was under the bleachers, you glutton." I wag my eyebrows at her before my expression grows serious again. "I have been thinking about quitting, just so you know."

That gets a very surprised look. One that for a moment makes me doubt if I'm attractive without the whole pomp and circumstance of 'Captain of the Cheer Squad' around me. I think she sees my face slip into a frown, because she scrambles for an explanation.

"No, don't frown like that. I don't mean my surprise in a bad way. I just thought it was something important to you, that's all."

I shrug, playing it off as I glance toward the car. "It is, but I was thinking about doing track instead. I missed the tryouts in January, but Coach Anderson saw me running the other day and mentioned they needed to fill a spot on the relay team." I pause. "He's willing to make an exception for me since I'm already conditioned from cheer. It's not gonna flip the team out cause I'm not a weak link, I guess."

Rachel nods, digesting. "Do you think people will get mad if you leave the squad?"

She's hesitant to look at me so I know what she is really asking is, are people going to pick on her again if I'm not head cheerleader. I wish I had an answer to her unspoken question, but it's all new territory for me. The only thing I know for certain is that if you're head cheerleader and you get pregnant your junior year, people treat you like shit and your life is never the same again.

"I honestly don't know, but I figure popularity is popularity and it carries with you no matter what sport you do." I glimmer a smile at her as we open the car. "Besides, if anyone can make track cool, it's me, whether you're my girlfriend or not."

"Don't you mean anchor?" Malina's voice literally puts a chill up my spine.

I turn, closing the door and putting my back against the side of the car. I cross my arms, fixing an angry glare on my face. "Well, hello. To what do we owe this pleasure?"

"Hi Malina," Rachel breezes tentatively, and when the Latina's eyes flick to my girlfriend's face, I feel my hackles rise.

"Yeah, don't talk to me. You aren't good enough to talk to me." She focuses back to where I'm standing.

"You aren't good enough to talk to *her*," I accost abruptly, angered by how dismissive she is. "If you have something you wanna say, say it to me. Rachel hasn't done anything to you, so do yourself a favor and have a little class."

"Oh like you the fucking traitorous bitch who would rather go slumming with some freaky troll? Tell me something. Is it true that your little Jew bitch tastes like iron from smuggling quarters in her pussy?"

It's amazing how quickly I see red. "You know Malina, I've put up with a lot of shit from you, but this is too damn far." I square myself before her. "First off, Rachel is incredible and totally off limits in this little fucking war we have. Second, I get you're pissed, but I'm pretty sure you're just jealous, so grow the fuck up."

"Jealous of you and…" she flicks those dismissive eyes at Rachel again, "that?"

"Yeah, jealous as fuck over the fact that you can't have with Lindsey what I have with Rachel." I laugh out loud just to drive the point home. "You are a sad pathetic excuse for a human being if you're too afraid to go after what you want."

I hear Rachel gasp at the revealed secret from behind me.

"Oh for fuck's sake, shut your damn mouth! And you, Blake." Malina pushes so close to my face it feels incredibly threatening. "I'm gonna fucking end you."

I grit my teeth and growl low in my throat. "How? You gonna try and start some shit here at a school event? Let me tell you something, and I really want you to listen. I'll say it slow so your dumb ass can understand it." I say the words so clear and definitively the consonants pop. "I don't care. I don't care about this *place*. I don't care about *you*. I don't care about *anything* you do here in this sad little corner of reality."

She laughs because she thinks I'm bluffing, but for the first time when it comes to my image and what really matters, I'm not.

"I have news for you. In a few years, this place and these people will be a distant memory. I'll be in New York with Rachel. She will be working toward her dream and I'll be going to med school. This place won't matter and if you don't figure out who your loyalty is with, you will fade into my distant memory, too."

"So, it's gonna be like that? Take years of friendship and flush it over *her*? I had your back. I was your girl. We owned this place, and now all people can do is talk about you fucking her and laugh their asses off."

"Let me just clear this up for you. We aren't fucking."

"Don't blame you, to be honest." She laughs boring her eyes into Rachel.

I see Rachel out of the corner of my eye as her face betrays her thoughts as her eyes shift to me.

Shit.

My brain scrambles for something to say. "You know, here is some friendly advice. If you spent less time chasing tail, you might have something worthwhile to offer Lindsey. Instead, all you have are booty calls, and from what I hear, even they get boring with you."

"Bitch, please. I have a trail of people lined up on their knees for a *chance* to have a shot at this. You hear no such shit from anyone because…here's some friendly advice for you…people are too busy talking shit about you. So cut your losses and drop the bullshit act."

I roll my eyes. "And when did you have a repeat taker in your trail of fucking? Oh, and by the way, I'm happy for *your* sake people are talking about Rachel and me. I suppose that is better conversation for you than Lindsey fucking...who was it again this week?"

She asked for it. Granted I didn't really have to give it to her, but I've already fired my warning shot and now she is practically begging for it. It's a low blow because I know Malina loves Lindsey, but if she is going to take pot shots at my girlfriend, then I'm going to come with a bulldozer of fucking agony for her.

"Shut the fuck up!" She rams me into the car and I'm surprised by it. So much so that I yelp in shock and my hands flail for hers.

And yes, I realize I asked for this too.

"Don't you dare touch her! Do you want me to call the cops?" It's Rachel, but I waive her off when Malina grabs the shoulders of my cheer outfit in her fists and holds me against the cold metal.

She spreads me back into a very vulnerable position, where I can't really move and I focus on breathing to keep my cool. "It's okay." I whisper softly for Rachel's benefit because I'm pretty sure Malina might be able to get a shot off before I can escape. "Mal knows that she can't hit me. If she does she's getting suspended and she'll miss the first round of our cheer competition where the California scouts will be watching."

I raise my eyebrow at her shocked expression. She looks like she forgot everything she wanted to do, I can tell she is thinking about how bad getting suspended would actually be.

I break Malina's concentration before she can rule in favor of punching me. My voice is icy and direct. "Your move, or are you just gonna stand here like you wanna screw me."

That shakes her up and she glares at me. "I fucking hate you Blake." She leans into me, digging her knuckles into the space between my chest and shoulder so deeply it hurts. I try to keep my face from showing it with a narrowing of my eyes. "I fucking hate you so bad."

I stare at her. In my peripheral I see Rachel slack-jawed, her cell phone in her hand and I'm pretty sure the number for the police is already typed. "You're really gonna hate me if you go toe-to-toe with me again. I have zero qualms about taking every single little thing I know about you and putting it out there for everyone to enjoy. How many skeletons are in your closet Malina? I bet you it's more than mine and Rachel's put together."

I feel her hands vibrate with rage.

"Think about it. If you go there I'll ruin you, and all the sad little ideas you have about your future will spin down the drain."

"Fuck you," she whispers, her face cold and emotionless.

I brush her hands off me and stare her down as I fix the wrinkles in my uniform. "You wish. Now, back the hell up and don't mess with either of us anymore." I move my hands so she doesn't see they're shaking. I don't actually like confrontation, so this...this scares me. I sometimes don't know the limits Malina will go to, so I'm grateful it didn't get crazier. I keep my eyes on her so she doesn't think about doing something stupid. "Rachel, get in the car."

Rachel doesn't say a word, as she follows my directive. When her door slams shut, I open mine.

"You're going to regret this Blake," Malina threatens, trying to get the last word.

I won't give her the satisfaction. No one gets the last word over me. "I guarantee if you start this war, I will end it." I clip the door shut and my trembling hands grab the wheel. I gun the engine and peel away. I don't slow down until I can't see her in the rearview mirror anymore.

We don't speak, not until we are on the highway back home.

"Are you okay Blake?" Rachel hesitates from the passenger's seat, her hand finding mine and squeezing. I glance over at her. "Did she hurt you? God, I wanted to rip her off you."

My chest hurts where she was digging into me, but other than that, remarkably, I feel okay. A little shaken, but it is mostly adrenaline, so I nod. "I'm okay."

"I'm so sorry. I wish I could have done something more."

I wave her off. "I'm glad you didn't. It would have just made it worse." I give her a meaningful look. "Besides, the last thing I want is to see you get hurt."

She nods, staring down at her lap. I reach over and tweak her nose before reclaiming her hand. After a bit she rolls down the windows and the cool air wraps me up. It ruffles the fringe of my cheer skirt and pushes the tendrils of my hair around. I steal glances at Rachel's hair whipping around her face as well. I love how dark and rich it is, thick and lightly curled. When she catches me looking at her, she opens her mouth to speak, but doesn't say anything.

"What?" I say over the sound of the wind railing around us.

"Can I ask you something?"

I arch my brow because we are way beyond her

asking if she can. It means it's something sensitive and I nod as I check my mirrors and change lanes.

"Would you ever really ruin her?"

Yes. I would grind her into little pieces if she ever hurt Rachel. I would absolutely annihilate her. I nod once, definitively. "It depends on the circumstances."

"What would those caveats be?" Rachel probes, her eyes sliding away from me. She twists her fingers in mine and it soothes the ache in my chest. God, I think I'm going to bruise.

I shrug, and swallow the physical pain it causes. "If she hurt you, then I would certainly make her pay. That's about it." I flash a smile. "She just has to learn to leave us alone. If she does that, she's fine."

"So," she draws the word in a long breath, "you would never tell anyone my skeletons, right?"

I glance at her to see if she is joking, but no, she is looking at me in all seriousness. "You would have to have juicy gossip-like skeletons in your closet first of all, and in the month we have been together have I ever betrayed your trust?"

"No."

"Then know that won't change even if you *did* have some terrible secret. No matter what happens, I would never ever tell people things you told me in confidence."

She bites her lip. "I do have secrets."

"We all do, but you're not one of *those* girls with *those* kind of secrets." I cock my head at her and with a serious expression I trace over her with my eyes. It's a split second, but the connection that shoots between us is enough to make my whole soul feel it. "And even if you were, nothing would ever shake my feelings for you."

Rachel tightens her fingers in mine, her body angling toward me in the car. "Here's a secret, but promise you won't laugh?"

I laugh then because I can't help it. "I can't promise that I won't giggle *with* you about something, but I won't laugh in a mean way. I promise."

"I'm kinda psychic."

This I knew. "Yeah?"

"Yeah, I just know things. I can tell that something is going to happen or already happened before anyone else sometimes."

I nod my understanding and the memory of her turning to me, announcing that our neighbor died, shoots across the synopsis of my brain. I can't help it. I still get the chills from it. And when Rachel sees it, she rolls the window up a little.

"I think that is an amazing gift," I whisper, now that it isn't as loud in my car.

"What is a secret of yours?"

I feel the tick in my eyebrow, and I focus hard on the road. I don't know what to say. I have a lot of really shitty secrets, things she discovered as an adult. Things she was shocked to find out about. I also have some funny secrets, sexy secrets. However, I'm afraid to tell her any now. I don't know if I can when so much is riding on her love for me. "Um, I don't know."

When she squeezes my hand, I glance down at her grip in mine. "You can trust me," she urges and breaks into a grin when I look at her.

I frown, wishing for that little piece of me back. That one little sliver, my insurance policy against this overwhelming doubt and possible heartbreak. "I-um." I wet my lips. "I-I have nightmares about a guy I saw die when I was like seven. We were driving home from a family trip and on the highway a car was pulled over." I glance at Rachel and squeeze her hand. "We pulled over and the driver was an older guy, he was choking on something, and he died right there on the road in front of me because we couldn't get whatever it was out of his throat."

"That is terrible. I'm so sorry." She shakes her head like she is clearing the image from her brain. "I can't imagine how scary that was."

"It was."

"I have one I'm really ashamed of," she admits softly next to me. "I did a musical when I was little and a friend gave me flowers and I took them and didn't say thank you. And because of all the people paying attention to me, I ignored her. She wasn't my friend after that."

"I'm sure she understood there was a lot of stuff going on."

"No, I shouldn't have done that. It wasn't very gracious of me. I think about that every time I sing." I watch her run her hand through her hair. "It bothers me because she was my first real friend."

"I think it says a lot that you still think about it." I nudge her arm to draw her attention to me. "I bet you think about it more than she does. And that says more about you and how out of character that was for you than anything else."

"I also have a panic attack before I go on stage every single time." She clears her throat. "I take medication to make it easier to deal with."

"Ah, so now I know why you disappear into the bathroom every night before bed." I already knew that too, but I give her a pleased smile that she shared it with me. "Now you don't have to hide it."

"Do you think it makes me weak that I can't do it on my own?"

As a doctor, I prescribed plenty of medications to people who I suspected might be scamming me. It was one of the hazards of my profession. I had people come to my door because of addiction or misguided 'easy road' beliefs. They were weak. In contrast, my wife wasn't weak. She was far from it. I had seen what happened when she wasn't taking the medication. I had held her hair back plenty of times when her nerves got the better of her and she was face first in a toilet. And even after vomiting her brains out, she still smacked a smile on her ashen face and took the stage.

She was the toughest person I knew.

She still is.

"No. I think you are incredibly strong because you still do it, because it's your dream. In my book, that makes you amazingly strong." It's something I have thought a million times, but I never actually said to her and now I'm glad I did with the way her smile literally illuminates the car.

It's like a weight slides off her shoulders. "I'm glad I told you then."

"I'm glad, too. I don't want any secrets between us." I swallow as I come to the interchange that should take us back to Danville. Instead I keep going, because there is something I want her to see. I notice Rachel's eyes travel to the signs, but when she sees I'm paying attention to the road, she doesn't question it. There is a glimmer of adventure in her eyes instead.

"So, tell me something else," she prods.

I really prefer the spotlight on her. It's comfortable to sit back and let her expose herself to me one fragment at a time. "I don't know Rachel, I just...there are enough to keep us busy for a while."

"Well, pick an easy one. One that doesn't bother you as much as the others 'cause your hand is sweating now."

I sigh. "I'm sorry." I brush my hand on the car seat before giving it back to her. *What the hell is wrong with me?* "Okay." I spread my free hand against the wheel to force the words out of my mouth. "I have abandonment issues. I don't let people get close to me 'cause I'm afraid they will leave." I swallow and wince when I realize I should probably say something more to explain myself. "I mean, well, with you it's different because–"

"You don't have to explain, I understand." She traces between my fingers, it's an even, smooth motion that makes me feel comforted as I whisper secrets to her.

I wait a beat then glance at her. "I sometimes don't think I'm worth more than a pretty face."

That gets her attention so swiftly I almost hit the break at the motion. "Blake, don't ever think that. You are so much more than that."

"Says you."

"Exactly." She looks away. "I wish I was pretty like you, or even Malina."

"You are drop dead gorgeous, Rachel." I laugh at how forceful I say it, softening the words that follow. "You have eyes that are deep and emotive. Your smile lights up the world. I seriously wait every day for that smile, whether I'm waking up to it, or coming to school for it."

"You have to say that as my girlfriend."

"No, I really don't. I really mean it. And we aren't even going to get into the rest of you because,"

I glance at her, running my eyes over her, "seriously you destroy me when I see you."

"Yeah?"

I nod. "Yeah, in a very good way. Always."

When she sighs, I brace myself for whatever is coming. "So, it isn't because I'm unattractive that you haven't have sex with me yet? Because I was thinking about what Malina said, and it seems like if we like each other we would want to explore. We have been together for over a month, and not once since the barbeque have you put your hands on me in that way."

Goddamn Malina.

I frown as I cut onto a different highway and start heading west. "Believe me Rachel, I do." I blow a breath and try to be honest about this. "It has nothing to do with you not being attractive. You are a very beautiful girl, so beautiful sometimes I think I might lose my mind because I want to touch you so badly, but we were going to wait."

"Is it a religious thing?" she asks suddenly. "If it is, I can respect that."

"No." I shake my head. "No, not that." I sigh.

"Then what? I'm much more comfortable now. I can give you what you want. I can do that stuff now. I want to."

So, I really don't have a good reason to answer with. I used to think that the reason I stopped that night at the family dinner was because she wasn't ready. That is a half-truth because as the days have worn on, I've realized...I wasn't ready.

I wasn't ready to be with her again.

And now, now that I love her like I love her, and now that I don't have my emotional insurance policy, I don't know what to do and it scares me to death.

Because she doesn't love me the way I love her, and the person who loves the least has the most power.

My gaze waivers and I firm my lips into a line before I say it. "I haven't had sex with you because I'm afraid."

"Afraid of what?"

"I don't know," I lie. I'm afraid I'll give her everything I have, a lifetime of love, and my heart and soul, and her hands will break me apart. I don't think she would do it maliciously, I just don't think she would understand what she has. And how could she, she has no idea about the extra years of history I carry and how much it means to me. She'll never know. She will never ever know the truth. It kills me that I have to keep that from her.

Rachel sighs and adjusts in her seat. "Tell you what," she announces, "since you can't do it yet, will you talk about it with me. So you can hear how confident I am in us?"

My eyebrows rise. "What do you mean?"

She moves closer then, her hand tightening in mine. She gets close enough that I can smell her shampoo. "You remember those things you said to me when we first kissed?"

"Yeah?"

"Tell me things like that again."

Everything gets caught in my throat and I clear it. "Um, why?"

She swallows and moves closer. Her lips brush my ear sending my body into a shudder that makes it hard to drive. "Because I want to hear those sexy words roll out of your mouth again now that I can appreciate them and feel what they do to me. I want to say sexy things to you too, because I know what it does to you."

"What does it do to me?" I have zero saliva left suddenly.

"It is something you need to get." She pauses. "Wet."

"Oh God." I wheeze past dry lips. I would give anything for something to drink right now, as all the fluid in my body gravitates southward, apparently under her command.

"So, say something to me."

But for the life of me, I just can't. "It has to be more organic than this. I can't just say it, I have to feel it."

"Did you feel that mysterious 'it' when you first kissed me?"

"Yes."

She is silent as she digests my words.

I feel my heart pick up a little and my hands start to perspire, for other reasons. I tighten my fingers around the steering wheel as I wait for her words to come.

"Blake, have you ever touched yourself while thinking about me?"

I glance at her out of the corner of my eye and she is staring right at me. There isn't a hint of blush on her face and that makes color scream into my cheeks. *Jesus.* It almost makes me lightheaded.

"Yeah. Have you while thinking about me?"

"Yes." She traces me with her eyes. It's devouring and makes me shiver. "How many times?"

Oh, Jesus. I couldn't count how many times in this life and the last. "A lot."

"How many times is a lot, exactly?"

I roll my eyes, as my cheeks heat further. "I don't

know, I didn't count. Maybe once every other day... twenty times?"

Her super shit-eating-grin maps across her face and I laugh despite how utterly exposed I feel. "I have that much too, just so you know."

I use my knee to steer for a moment as I hit a button and roll the window up. I don't want to miss a word when I ask my question. "When was the last time you did?"

"This morning before school."

"What were you thinking about?"

She laughs. "Nope, it's my turn to ask." She shakes her head and pauses, letting the silence stretch uncomfortably long. "What did I do to you in your most recent fantasy?"

I clear my throat. "Um, it's mostly about what I do to you, but you kiss me and touch me." She waits for more, but I can't give it to her. I shift in my seat. Already I can feel the tingle of desire in my abdomen.

"Go ahead, ask," I can feel her eyes on me, running over my body, memorizing me along their path.

"What were you thinking about this morning?" I catch the whisper of her smile in the flash of oncoming traffic as I navigate to the off ramp by the lake.

"Well, I want to set the scene for you first, okay?"

I swallow, nodding. God, I don't think it's ever been this hard to click on a turn signal. My hands feel like they're are made of lead.

"I was in the shower. I just got done washing my hair, and I was thinking about your smile. I really do think it's the best smile in the world." She grins. "So, I was soaping up, and ended up touching myself. I pictured that my hands were yours, tracing suds over my breasts and then over my stomach."

She bites her lip and I hear the roar of my heart in my ears.

"You were behind me, and I leaned on the tile, just letting you touch me. Then you slid your hand between my legs and circled my clit until I came."

"Oh God, Rachel." I can't even look at her. If I do I'm going to crash this damn car. The swirling inferno inside me feels like it is about to tear me apart.

"Did you like hearing that Blake?"

"Yes," I hiss. My voice is dark, lusty, heavy with desire. "God, tell me something else."

At this point I really don't give a fuck who has the power in our dynamic anymore. I'm pretty sure it isn't me because I'm so at her command I'm not going to pretend anymore. I don't know how I lost control, but I honestly don't care. I'm going to hang on every word she says because I love her. I love her and I need her. I need to hear her and feel her.

"What do you want to hear about?"

"Anything." I sound like I'm going to have a heart attack any second.

"Do you want to hear about how I felt when we first kissed?"

I nod because the words won't form.

"I was listening to you talk, and I kept feeling butterflies. Like just a silly amount of bounding and fluttering in my abdomen. Oh, and aching. And then when you kissed me," she mimes a shiver or shivers for real, I'm not sure which, "I just felt this wave of something come over me. I've never felt anything so intense, so desperate and deep."

"Yeah?" I focus on the road for a moment as I turn toward the lake. Once in the parking lot, I park in the darkest part overlooking the water, and cut off the engine.

When I turn to Rachel, her lips have a smile hovering on them. "Did you bring me here to make out?"

"No." I clear my throat. "I had absolutely honorable intentions." I flip the lights off and point out the windshield.

Before us, the neon spread of fireflies dot the area. They flash brilliantly, hectically, without rhyme or reason. I smile when she gapes at them and then turns to me. "How did you...did you have this planned all along?"

I nod slowly. "I did. I checked to see if there were any early sightings and last night someone posted they saw them here. So I wanted to bring you, to see the first sighting of summer."

"It's really beautiful Blake." She laughs and then glimmers a smile at me, "I honestly didn't think you could get any more romantic. But you have, you are."

"You make me romantic. You make me want to be. I want to give you romance every day for the rest of my life."

I don't even realize what I've said, until Rachel's eyes widen.

I redirect to take the implications out of my sentence. "Um, yeah, so, anyway...you were talking about feelings?"

She turns back to the view before us. "So yeah, I was really emotionally charged because I'd never felt so..." She lets her thought taper off, and I realize I've rung a bell I can't unsound. I can see her eyes churning, her thoughts whizzing past the dark in her eyes as quickly as the fireflies.

I go to speak, but she beats me to the punch. "Blake?"

The way she says my name carries so much gravity. It feels like that first kiss, full of expectation and hope. "Yeah?"

"Will you do me a favor?"

I nod, afraid to hear what it might be.

"Will you tell me how you would touch me *if* you loved me?"

All my functional processes scream to a halt. "What do you mean?"

She keeps staring out the windshield at the lightening bugs, her eyes follow the flitting embers of yellow. "If you loved me, if you made love to me, what would you do? I want to know what it would be like."

"Why?"

She blushes then, bright even in the sparse light. I can't believe how arousing it is to see that. "Because I want to imagine it and I want to feel it in my heart right now."

I fix my eyes on her hands and watch as they fiddle with my jacket absently.

"I would..." I clear my throat, thinking back to when I touched her, when I had the unfettered pleasure of just working my hands over her. "I would kiss you, slow and deep."

"I'd kiss back," she whispers, glancing at me for the briefest of moments.

"My hands would trail over your face and shoulder, feeling you, just soaking in how your skin feels."

"Would you be on top of me?"

"Kinda, like half on you and half on my side." I close my eyes, picturing it. "And I would pet over you, your arm, your shoulder, your side. I'd avoid everything sexual, just feel you."

She sighs and I hear the seat beside me creak as she shifts.

"I would pull you closer, kissing you deeper, while tracing your arms with my fingers. I have always liked the idea of dominating the other person, so I would slide my hand up under the nape of your neck and pull you into my mouth. I would roll with you, making sure to take full advantage of the bed. I'd want to feel you on me, feel you pressed against me, melting against my body."

"Just the idea of your skin on mine, it makes me really wet Blake. It makes me want you so badly. I would be dripping on your stomach, I would be moaning against your lips."

I chew my lip and peek an eye open to glance at her. She is looking at me and I watch as her breath deepens, and she smiles at me softly. "Rachel, you really are so beautiful." I whisper it, and reach out to caress her cheek.

She inclines her head into my touch and kisses my thumb. The love in that action is so undeniable, so true and honest and pure it renders me speechless. Her eyes are still closed when she begins again. "I would let you. Dominate me, I mean." Those thick lashes shade her eyes as she opens them and bores into my soul. "I'm not afraid, I'm not holding back. I trust you completely."

"I know. You have no idea how much I would treasure it. How much I treasure you."

"Would you let me? Would you let me learn you and dominate you when I wanted to?"

I clear my throat. She will never know the gravity

of my answer, but I think that is what makes it better. "Yes, I will."

The shift from hypothetical to *fact* is so apparent that her eyes snap wide. I smile, watching the shadows of emotion move over her face. It's the face of my wife. It's the same look, the same deeply burning fire for me. The same loving, caring, and acceptance that transformed me.

"Tell me more about how you would make love to me." She leans closer, and all at once she is pressed to me, her face resting against mine. "Tell me in my ear, whisper it to me. I want you to feel how hard it makes my heart race."

The center console and parking brake are in the way of most of her and I debate it, and finally surrender. "Let's move to the back seat."

"Oh?"

I press a kiss to her ear. "No, the first time will not be in a car, but I want to feel you, I want you to feel me."

She swallows and nods.

I feel her against me as she shifts, squeezing into the backseat. I follow her, not nearly as elegantly, but once I'm back there I smile at her disheveled image. "You already have that just-been-fucked hair and nothing has even happened," I tease.

"You are just that good I suppose." She smirks and then moves closer until her body is scorching against me.

When she grabs my shoulders and pushes me down onto the seat, I don't fight it. I lean back and feel her body cover mine. It's been so long. So long since this woman was against me. I close my eyes and remember. And she's doing it, the same way she always did. I can see it even without the use of my eyes. It's tattooed on my heart.

When she nuzzles down closer and I feel her whole body press to me, her words in my ear are like fuel on a fire. "Tell me more, Blake."

I heave a laugh. "I don't think I can."

"Sure you can." I feel her close her eyes against my face. "Please."

I nod trying to remember where I was. "I will pull you tighter, caress you, trace my fingers through the wetness you leave on my tummy."

"It won't bother you?"

"God, no," I whisper softly. "It will make me want you even more."

"How wet will you be?"

"I'll be dripping for you, Rachel."

"Oh wow, Blake." She sighs lightly and I feel her tremble.

It makes me clench so hard I arch and I become very aware of how wet I am right *now*. There isn't much to hide it, two layers of cotton and that is about it. I heave a breath.

"What then?"

I remember it. "I'll roll you over and kiss all over your body."

"Will you ever, um…" She swallows hard enough for me to feel it against my chest. "You know, lick me?"

I giggle because the way she says it is so unapologetically hopeful. "Yes, I will lick you and taste you and trail my tongue all over every inch of you."

"I will do that for you too, taste you." She smiles. "I like how that sounds better than 'eat you out'. That just sounds so, I don't know, trashy."

"Yeah, I know, I have always felt weird saying that."

Rachel inclines her head to look at me. "Can I use my mouth to make you come?"

I stare up at the top of the car and cough against how quickly I take a breath at her words. "I'm pretty sure you can."

Her heart is pounding. It feels like my own is double beating with how hard it's racing against me. "Will you do that to me?"

I push her a little further. "Why?"

She clears her throat and shrugs. "I have imagined you doing it to me. And I really want to look down and see your head between my thighs for real."

"Fuck, Rachel." I can't even believe she said that.

"Was that too dirty to say?" She says with a nervous laugh.

I incline my brow at how deliciously dirty I *want* her to be. "No, that is absolutely perfect." I close my eyes savoring the moment as a little of my nerves evaporate. "I like the way you feel on me."

"I like it too." She pulls closer, her hand fixing on my shoulder as her nose nuzzles me, "Blake?"

"Yes?"

"Tell me about how you will take my virginity."

I feel my blood boil through my veins. My hands tighten into fists. God, I should just take her home. I should just show her how gentle I want to touch her, how I want to make her climax in my arms and tell me she loves me. I stagger a breath as I place my hand on her back, tracing the jacket under my fingertips. "I will do it slowly. I will kiss you and caress you, and then I will slide my fingers into you."

"Which fingers?"

"My middle finger and ring finger. I will go slowly until they are all the way in. And then I'll hold them there, letting you stretch and get used to it."

"Then, once I'm used to you?"

I sigh, pulling her closer. "Then I will thrust slowly at first and then faster, kissing you and caressing you, until you climax."

She clears her throat and I smile when her hand leaves my shoulder to trail down to my free hand. I know where she is going, so I hold my two fingers together, letting her wrap around them, feel the thickness of them. It's erotic and beautiful and sweet as her fingers memorize softly. "I don't think it will take very long for that to happen."

"Then we can go for seconds and thirds."

We laugh easily.

"Hey Rachel?"

"Yes?"

"Are you wet now?"

She lifts her head a fraction, and then sets it back down beside me. "Yes. Very."

"Do you like this? Feeling like this with me?"

She smiles against my throat. "Yes. I don't think I could even imagine something as intimate as this."

"How does it make you feel?"

"Physically?"

"Sure."

"Um, like I'm gonna need a very cold shower tonight."

"Do you feel anything else?"

"Like emotionally?"

"Yes." I slide my hand under the bottom of the jacket and press lightly on her lower back, kneading her skin in slow circles. She groans into the motion and I deepen it, moving slower.

"It makes me feel cared for, like my heart is full and could burst any moment."

"Anything else?" If she says it, I'm taking her home. If she admits it, then I'm going to give her everything I have to give. I'm going to show her how much I love her.

"I feel powerful. I feel weak, too, at the same time." She lifts her head to catch my eyes. "What do you want me to say?"

I furrow my eyebrows. "Nothing. I just wanted to know how you feel."

"How do you feel?"

"The same, excited, full, warm, and totally under your spell."

"Nothing else?"

I swallow. "Like what?"

"Nothing." She quirks a smile and then puts her head down on my chest.

I listen to her breathe, and work up the courage to do what I should have done a lifetime ago. "Rachel?"

"Hmm?"

"I lied. I love you."

She shifts against me and squeezes my hand. Leaning over me her eyes are all I see in the dark of the car.

"I lied, too. I love you, Blake."

She kisses me, kisses me like she's never been out of my arms.

When she pulls back, her eyes trace my face. "Blake?"

I hug her tightly, my hand absently caressing up through her hair. I'm almost dizzy with how elated I feel, my heart thundering. I try to keep my voice even, warm, and soft even though every word wants to come out as a scream. "Yes, angel?"

Her eyes flutter closed and then her mouth slants into mine, her tongue coaxing until I take the initiative, and I'm exploring her mouth. I press her tighter, closer.

It will never be close enough.

When I feel her pulling on me, where she still has her fingers wrapped around mine, a whine builds in my throat because I know what she is doing. "Rachel."

She smothers my lips with hers. "I know you said not in a car, but I want it. I don't care."

I focus on my fingers, where I feel them brushing her shirt as they slide down. Her breath is coming quickly, and then stops when my fingertips slick over the soft skin of her stomach. Her body heaves under my touch as she whines urgently. When she leaves my fingers there, I look up at her as I thumb open the button of her jeans. "Once we start this, we can't ever go back."

I don't say it just for her, I say it for me too, to give voice to the fear I feel. Once we take this step nothing will ever be the same again.

"I know." She lifts up and shifts, giving me room to slide the zipper down.

I literally feel the nibble of every tooth in that zipper as it comes undone, it radiates through my hands. "I don't want things to be any different than they are now."

"I don't either. Except for this." She makes room for my touches and I map my way into her pants until I feel the warm softness of her lips, and her mouth drops open. "Oh, Blake."

I caress her, trace with as soft a hand as I've ever

touched her with. I think I'm biting my lip because when I finally gasp for a breath, my mouth hurts where my teeth were pinching. She leans over me further, giving me more clearance.

"Rachel, God, you feel so good."

She rolls her eyes closed as my fingertips dip between her lips and caress teasingly. "Oh, please, I want you to do all that stuff you just said you would."

"Yeah, me too."

She crashes our mouths together as I use every ounce of the fifteen years I've been her lover to combust her from the inside out. I kiss her, caress her, circle in just that rhythm. Stop when I know I need to, at just that point that she stalls at the edge. I drive her toward the peak over and over and to my sublime joy, drown in the animalistic sounds she makes against my mouth as she forgets how to kiss me under my motions. And when she's finally had enough teasing, when her hand covers mine and presses me deeper under her clothing, it's her plea that commits me to action.

"I'm so happy it's going to be you."

And God, I am too.

It's just like breathing for me, the motion, sure and steady. That is the only way I can explain it. I press my fingers forward and Rachel's teeth flash, her eyes close and when she presses her lips to mine in a moan, I have her.

I have *her*.

It surprises me when I feel her hand fumble against me, and wedge into my Spanx. "Blake." My name warps as she half moans it. "I want…" She doesn't finish her sentence because her tongue is in my mouth.

I take a sharp breath as her hand cups me. At

the silent command of her fingertips I part my thighs and with a confidence she shouldn't have yet, slide deep enough into me to bring tears to my eyes. It doesn't hurt, not physically, deep in my chest is where the tears come from. It is because the feelings are too much, and my heart is too full to hold it in.

She presses her forehead to mine, her fingers moving delicately as they learn me. "Are you okay, baby?"

I blink back my emotion and nod. "Yeah, you?"

She nods quickly, her eyes wide and overwhelmed. "You sure?"

"I just can't believe...I mean, God you're *in* me and I'm *in* you. It's incredible. I want to feel this every day." I swallow brokenly until she nudges me with her thumb and then I bolt under her, going from gut-wrenched to enflamed in the blink of an eye.

"Yes, everyday *just* like this." I hiss under my breath as I copy the motion, engulfed by the soft mew she breaks against my lips as they tangle with hers.

And we keep mimicking each other's touches until the windows are fogged and I've guiltily fulfilled one of my own fantasies.

I give myself over completely.

≈·≈·≈·≈

And after a weekend of lying in her arms, letting her learn me, and sharing something so intimate between us, I'm immune to anything the world can throw at me. I don't notice the plyometrics at practice, don't see Malina grinding her teeth, and I certainly don't hear the caustic words from my ignorant family.

All I notice is Rachel. All I see is her smile. All I hear is her voice.

And remember her note.

Even now, between classes, I stop in the bathroom and close the stall behind me. I seal myself away so that I can unfold it and read the words that mean more to me than anything in the world. I'm instantly emotional and I cup my hand over my mouth before I even start reading.

Blake,

You asked me something this weekend. If I was happy with you? If I always wanted to be with you? The answer is yes. I don't want to be with anyone but you. This weekend has meant more to me than anything in the world. I know that we are still in high school, but I know I want to be with you for the rest of my life. I know I want to make love with you forever. I love you. You are my soul mate.

Love always, Your Rachel

Chapter Ten

Without You
August 20, 2011

I have a confession.

When I opened this book and began this part of my and Rachel's life, I firmly believed I knew the end. That was why I gambled my heart and soul on it. I would be a liar if I said I thought the end of *my* life, *our* life, would come anywhere other than a wet grainy road in the future. I certainly never would have believed the end would come in the middle of her parents' kitchen, after a day of telling her how much I love her.

I'm utterly devastated by the magnitude of my entitlement and ignorance, because I bought into my own delusion–that I could foretell how the story would end. It was pure arrogance, blind self-preservation and selfishness on a level that I didn't think I was capable of. Living as an adult in a teenage world didn't give me the right to manipulate life like a magician. And I have now, only to reap my punishment.

Because, I've missed the story.

And I forgot that not every story has a happy ending.

I didn't see the writing on the wall, the inevitable end that was coming. It was whistling toward me with the acuity of an arrow's arc. And now that I'm pulling my head out of the fog, the damage I've done leaves a wreck around me. It leaves me bleeding, wounded, and pierced through to the very center.

I realize this, all of this, as I stand staring at the Stanford University early acceptance letter in my hand.

Rachel smiles at me. "Okay, so you look surprised. I have a reasonable explanation for applying."

I can't even speak because the rationale doesn't matter, it's the fact that the letter *exists* at all. It might as well be a barbed projectile in the space between my ribs.

"It's so you can apply to U.C. San Francisco. And you can congratulate me any time you're ready." She grins smugly before she takes a long gulp of water. I watch the liquid swirl in the glass when she pauses to breathe and then drink more. She empties the glass and sets it on the counter where her letter was sitting innocently a moment ago. "I'm only this thirsty in testament to your skill Blake." She gives me a lazy, sexy smile. It is a smile that would melt me if I wasn't shattering apart.

"What is this though?" I ask numbly, and the paper rattles in my hand. "You are going to music school in New York, not California."

She looks surprised, off guard, and leans on the counter sliding in close to me. Her fingertips worry the edge of the paper in my hand. "Well, I did some research and found that U.C.S.F. is the top school in the nation for General Practitioners, and they run huge studies in Alzheimer's treatment."

"So?" I hear myself say. "What does that have to do with you going to school in California?" I know I should be able to put it together, but my brain isn't working.

She stares at me, dumbfounded, but she presses on after a moment. "So I was thinking, since that is your dream–to be an amazing doctor and change people's lives–that you should go to the best place possible." She frowns.

I can tell it bothers her that she has to spell it out for me. We are normally so in tune.

"I was thinking about going to Stanford so we could be together. It's about forty minutes away."

"I don't think they have music there. Well, nothing like in New York." I set the letter aside and firm a smile on my face. "Congrats, but it doesn't matter because you have to go to college in New York so you are close to the Broadway scene."

She glances away from me then, tracing the bright airy kitchen with her eyes which eventually fasten to the paper on the counter. "I wasn't going to go to school for music. Remember earlier when we were talking about changing things up? You're doing track? I'm gonna quit music and focus on debate. See if I can hop onto the lawyer track."

"Law?"

I don't understand what she's saying. "Are you saying you want to go into law? Like take-the-bar-exam law?"

She shrugs. "Yeah. Singing is..." She glances away. "It's something childish, not secure, and I want to have a real adult life with you. I don't want to chase dreams and not make it, and have you go to N.Y.U. when you could go somewhere better."

Everything collides in my throat choking me silent. Love and pain, fear and horror twist my voice into a squeak. "But it's your dream." I don't have a better argument. I can't think of anything other than that. It's *her* dream. It is the thing she has spent every moment focused on since she was the little girl in baby-doll shoes singing at the mall. It is the dream she carelessly brandished in my face a lifetime ago, the skill and talent that will capture the attention of the world.

"Dreams change." She whispers it, fixing me with a loving stare and taking my hand. She knits our fingers together. "I have different dreams now. I have dreams of a real career and coming home to you in the evening." She moves in, her finger plucking at the front of the dress I'm wearing. She lifts to the balls of her feet as she kisses my ear. "I want to make you dinner, and make love to you, hold you, and build a future with you. I want a stable life, a routine, and a normal existence with you."

"But you can have that with singing."

She smiles in my ear. "I can sing to you instead. I'll sing to our children." She bites her lip. "It makes me so tingly happy thinking about that."

"But you *are* music. I mean it's in you. You have to share that."

She pulls back then, tracing the pained expression I know I have on my face. "Blake, it will always be a part of me, but it is just a part." She holds up her hand, miming a small space between her thumb and forefinger. "It's a small part. It isn't everything. It doesn't have to define me."

"But…"

She places her fingers over my lips then replaces them with her lips. "It's my choice and I love you for loving me enough to be distressed about it, but honestly," she rubs her nose against mine, "this is what I want."

"But–"

"Blake, today is our three month anniversary, and as much as I would love for us to talk more about this, let's shelve it for now. I just want to go back upstairs with you." She lowers her voice as her arms circle my shoulders. "And make love with you again."

"No."

I've never be able to tell her no. I don't think I have it in me to deny her anything. So when she begs to spend our three month anniversary playing in her pool, I grumble as I lather on sunblock so I can give her what she wants.

I'm kinda glad I did, to be honest. This is much more fun than the shopping, dinner and a movie I was going to do. The water is crisp and clear. I let it envelop me, crash over my head and lull me into it's grasp. Even though I probably shouldn't, I open my eyes. I watch the shimmering froth bound and circle up over my head as I sink. The sun pours down through it, the warm rays radiating and dancing as they come through the surface. They rain down on me and color me from the inside out.

The surface breaks again. Flashes of skin and bikini penetrate the silence around me in a spectacular whoosh. From down here, looking up, I see rainbows of color as my girlfriend arcs above me, passing over me just within arm's reach. I lift my hand in seemingly slow motion, feeling the tickle of millions of little bubbles and the final beautiful warmth of her body as it slicks past my fingertips.

I feel so blessed to be here, to be able to linger in her light. To steal so much of a life from my death is incredible. I memorize it, every iridescent sparkle that moves around her when she kicks, painting over the vibrant pink of her bikini and the deep tan of her sun kissed skin. God, the summer sun is kind to her, taking her already warm complexion and plunging it into a deep bronze.

I blink a few times to clear the burn from the chlorine as I follow her long strokes. I watch her twist. Watch the curves of her figure as she moves. She rolls over, dragging bubbles from her nose and mouth as she fixes on me. Her eyes are burnished copper in this light, ethereal. I let go a little of the air inside me at the sight of it, a big fat sphere tracing up to her. She catches it in her hands with a smile so large it crinkles the skin at her eyes.

Rachel's wild hair fans, drifts, and spins in a wave of black as she rights herself and curls her finger at me, silently drawing me toward her in this crystalline world. She wants me to follow her and I will, but I back paddle lower in the water. Her eyes sparkle at me as I play coy. Rachel hovers a moment longer, hanging in the cool water and then nods toward the edge of the pool, heading toward the surface.

I trace everything in her retreat as she rockets upward, the rise of her butt, the way the material gathers in tied bows at her hips, even the forced swells of her breasts because the top is pulling her tight. My favorite part though is the way I can see her muscles move. It's the flex in her body as it goes through the motions, so full of power and grace. The way her abdominals outline, her hips define, her thighs shift, it's poetry. It's a body I worship and in the back of my mind where my memories hold firm ground, I know it's a body that will carry my child.

I hang on that thought, even as the ache in my

chest forces me to the surface. I smile at her when I break through and she gives me a warm look. She's holding onto the edge of the pool now, hands fastened tightly as she kicks slowly to keep herself afloat.

"I was wondering if you were ever coming up for air," she says, followed with a wry chuckle.

I laugh too. "With how good you look, it was a tough call. I could certainly drown to that view."

She smirks and tips her head back, eyes closed under the sun.

I stare at her. I memorize her lips, her wet eyelashes, the sculpting of her neck and shoulders. She is beautiful, yes. I can't deny that. However, as I tumble back to my previous thought about our future, I realize that everything is compounded tenfold because I know. I know that everything I love, the dips and curves, the bone and muscle–everything beautiful to my eyes, will be a mother.

For me.

With me.

It makes the breath in my chest halt.

"Baby?" Rachel's voice pulls me from my thoughts.

"Yeah?" I swim over to her, planting a kiss on her arm before I slide into her. We twist together, knitting into one blur of darkness and light, blue and pink.

"What are you thinking about?" she whispers against my shoulder, one hand coming down to brush the dotting of water on my skin.

I watch her finger path a line, sending droplets to curve out of sight. "I was thinking about how much I love you."

She flicks her eyes up to me. From this close, I can see the expectation in her eyes. "How much?"

"With everything I am."

She grins. *"Now in math."*

I groan, stupid SATs that she won't let me escape. "I love you greater than or equal to the universe, plus or minus the function of infinity?"

She laughs, and the sound reverbs around the pool. "I love it."

"It's super geeky." I arch my eyebrow at her. "Now you, in music."

"Oh, God," she gushes and then looks up at me from beneath her thick lashes. "I love you like the major resolution at the end of a sad song. I would even take you in second transposition." Her eyes glimmer innuendo at me as her brows lift and then her face softens. "My life was a sad song until we found each other, Blake. You're the uplifting final movement in the composition of my life."

God, her words are masterpieces.

"Final?" I whisper, turning in the water onto my side, the same way I lay in bed beside her.

The confidence in her eyes lights me up inside. It is dwarfed only by the sureness of her touch when she presses the wet hair back from my cheek. "Yeah, this is it for me. I already know that." Her eyes grow distant. "I'm sixteen and it amazes me at how much clarity I have over the fact that I'm meant to be with you, until the day I die."

I'm not prepared for the wall of emotion that hits me when those words roll out of her mouth. It isn't what she's saying, well not only what's she's saying, it's that she still felt this way when she did die.

That she got that wish.

This beautiful human being that I love with all my heart felt this love when she was shattered into oblivion. Her heart beat for me and lived for me up until the moment it couldn't pump anymore. It hits me hard, a blazing rip of agony that shatters the warm summer day when I remember that she tried to hold on. That she died at the hospital.

I have tried not to think about it. I have almost blocked it from my mind. The living version of my wife has guarded against the bladed memories I cut myself on when I reach toward them. I remember that for five minutes this stunningly delicate beauty was in unspeakable pain. That the lungs that push notes that rend my soul apart were bleeding, that she was drowning in blood and fluid as she slowly slipped away. That the firm muscle and bone I drag my hands over in loving arcs had disintegrated into fragments. And even as her body gave up, I know in my heart she was probably hoping for me to get to her, just as I hoped on that not so long ago day.

I can't breathe when I remember the image of her broken, when the idea of it, of her pain, of her attempt to survive, tears a hole through me. My nose burns. I push a breath and my eyebrows furrow as tears dredge from my eyes.

"Blake?" Rachel whispers gently, turning toward me quickly as her eyes bound over mine. Her hand is soft when it traces the hot trails down my face and she pulls me against her shoulder with an excruciatingly loving look.

I cover the reality of where my emotion comes from with a truth just as real. "It's really beautiful to hear that. I love you like that too." I find comfort in her kiss then, and the water on her cheek dilutes my tears.

"Don't cry, I'm here." Warm words against my mouth cover me as she weaves that body against mine until we are a singularity.

"I know." I clear my throat. "I'm just broken."

"I'll be here to fix you, for always." She feathers touches on my back and it soothes everything away. Slowly, those dark memories fade, covered in smiles and sunlight as the living breathing angel before me mends wounds she doesn't know I carry.

"You are fixing me." She is. As long as she is breathing, my heart can beat another day.

I pepper kisses on her cheek and eyes, tracing my nose along her eyebrow. The muscles in her face form expressions under my touches. I can feel the adoration, the gentleness of it. "I love you." She whispers it as her skin moves over mine, cheek caressing my chin. I pull back and nudge her nose with mine before I make love to her lips, sensual and deep, poured with warmth and the millions of fragmented moments that hide in my heart. She matches me, reflecting and refracting with her own aura the love she has for me. I feel it and it warms me through.

Her hand claims the spot at the curve in my lower back, and when she slants her head, I'm lost. She's inside my heart, dizzying me with kisses that don't just mime, but force the visuals of love making into my mind. Even in the cool water, I feel the distinct shot of heat as it breaks over her skin. My eyelids flutter as I roll my eyes back.

"Okay enough of that, girls, we have neighbors!" Hiram yells from one of the upstairs windows and it breaks our moment apart.

I snap my face to the window, to where the new curtains Deborah picked are draping a very fidgety looking father. I feel thoroughly chastised and blush a little. I love him. But some things a parent shouldn't know about. I'm sure no one wants to see their child half naked and kissing like this.

"Sorry," I call.

"Dad!" *Rachel screams in mortification. It's ear piercingly loud from so close, illustrating how aroused she is and how uncomfortable she is with him catching us. I flinch away and she palms her hand over my ear to continue yelling.* "Nothing was happening!"

Yeah okay. I cock my brow at her. Hiram must see the glance because he gives her the same doubting look. "Then consider this me making up for all the times I've probably missed!"

I laugh. I can't help it, spoken like a true father.

He gives me a knowing look and then his tight lips shift into a smile. "Honey, are you joining us for dinner again tonight?"

"If that's okay," *I ask and he nods.*

"Sleeping over, too?"

"Yes."

He glances at Rachel. "Okay, sweethearts, I'll get stuff started."

We share a moment when his eyes fix on me again, one that speaks volumes in the split second before he leaves the window.

He knows.

He knows I'm in love with his daughter, but more than that, he knows we express it. I wonder what it means that he knows that and still allows me into her room all night. Is that silent approval? I flush at the thought and when I hear Rachel sigh from beside me, I look over at the matching blush on her cheeks.

"I'm sorry," *she grumbles.*

"Don't be, that was funny." *I try to alleviate the irritation I can see brooding in her eyes.*

"No, it was terrible." *She heaves a breath and*

pushes off the wall. When she rolls over to look back at me gliding toward the other edge, I can't tell what it is she is thinking but I follow in her wake.

She climbs out of the pool and I'm right behind her until I slip my arm around her side as we walk toward the patio chairs where our towels rest. I incline my head, angling words in her ear. "Don't be upset."

"It's embarrassing that he thought we were," she drops her voice, "having sex in the pool."

I roll my eyes at her as I reach down and fluff out her towel. She puts it around her shoulders while she chews her lip in thought.

"He didn't think that, per se. He just wanted to head anything off at the pass...you know. I mean he loves you. I'm sure it's awkward as hell to see your baby girl kissing like we do. I mean he obviously knows we are sleeping together." She looks like she may throw up for a moment, and I give her a light smile. Using my towel, I catch the drops of water beading on my shoulder. "Besides, you were kissing me really heavily, you know."

When she narrows her eyes at me, I smile teasingly.

"You were doing it first," she counters. It makes her smile despite herself and she starts patting the water from her skin. "And he's right anyway."

I question her with an arch of my eyebrow. "About?"

"All the times he has missed."

I roll my eyes when she laughs, then hugs me tightly. I wrap my arms around the lithe stretch of her body and kiss her. "Shower?"

"With you?" She laughs and adds with a sarcastic tilt in her lips, "I suppose I can willingly make any sacrifice for you."

She *really* meant it when she said she would make any sacrifice for me.

The thought catches and hangs heavily in the back of my mind. She will, and has, given me everything I have ever wanted. She gave up singing for me once, but not this time. I'll never let her do it, especially since she hasn't tasted the glory of singing to filled theaters and raised rafters with the silver tone of her angelic voice. No one should surrender pieces of themselves they haven't had time to realize. The loss of it, of her singular voice, is a trespass that I can't allow.

Rachel looks confused, then worried. "No?" She slips down from where she is pressing against me, circling me. She touches my abdomen, my hips, hands mapping as she rubs my back and her eyes run over me. She touches me like someone who loves me, someone who loves me more than I deserve. "Blake, I didn't hurt you upstairs, did I? I'm sorry baby, we don't have to go back upstairs and do anything." She ducks her head into my neck as she hugs me tenderly. "I would love to just snuggle with you."

I swallow thickly. "No, I'm not hurt. I want to talk about the school thing though. I don't want to shelve it Rachel. It's important."

She frowns up at me when I pull back to look at her. "Okay. What are you thinking?"

What am I supposed to tell her? How do I tell her that she is meant to take a stage and bring roaring crowds to their feet? That despite all her fears she will triumph and have everything, that she will have me. How can I tell her that I will be in every audience, screaming my pride and love to her? I can't think of anything, for God's sake. I scramble to speak while the scaffolding that holds reality at bay crumbles around me. "It would break my heart if you didn't go to Juilliard."

It's breaking already, because as I say it, I can see the determination in her eyes. I know it. It is the gauntlet being put down between us. I can see her spirit reflecting in her eyes as clear as a cat's eye at night. I would kill anyone to protect that spirit, but I know the boast of protection is just that. I've fought against it before and Rachel's fire doesn't need shelter. I know I'm outmatched before we even begin.

She will always be more headstrong than me, stronger, braver and certainly more noble.

"Baby, I've thought about this a lot." She sighs. "You're great at math, so let me put it to you like this. If you had two choices, one was ninety percent certain and the other was ten percent, which has the greater probability to occur?"

She picked the wrong subject to illustrate with.

"Theoretically, they both have the same odds, because every roll of the dice is a fresh attempt." I point to the letter. "This is you taking your ten and turning it into zero, and I won't let you do it. My dream, my goal, has no right to trump yours. I will do fine no matter where I go because it's flexible and attainable anywhere."

Rachel rolls her eyes. "Fine. Bad example." She sighs, again. "And I know you will do amazing, but why not give you a push–a head start. Also, where would you rather invest our money? Juilliard and Stanford are about comparable in price and I would rather go into debt knowing I'm gonna have a job on the other side, than go into debt and not know for sure."

I focus on her, trying to ease the pitter-patter in

my heart at hearing her say 'our money', like it's ours already.

Like we are one entity.

"My dream doesn't have a right to trump yours, either," she whispers.

"It's not. I know for sure you will be a success and I will be, too."

"How could you possibly know for sure that I'm going to be able to make it to Broadway?" I can tell my words are bothering her. The way she asks the question is laced with pain because she doesn't want to let her dream go.

But she will if it gives me a chance.

"Because I know you can do anything." I pull her closer to me, hugging her, trying to push my point with the crush of my arms. I press my words into her ear. "You have a beautiful gift and you have to do something with it. You have to give it to the world. That is your destiny and right now, even if it seems like there are other options or other things you want, you can't change that part. You have to sing, there is no other option."

Her hands clasp onto me as she presses her forehead to my shoulder and I think she understands me. I think I've won. But then she raises her head defiantly, and her words destroy me.

"I won't trade your future for a *chance* at those things. I love you, and I'm going to do what's in your best interest because of that love. Not my best interest. Yours. Because that is what people who love each other do."

That's when I realize that for these last months, I've kidded myself. I thought she was performing a form of CPR, fastening her lips over mine and blowing life back into me. That's what it felt like when she held me and kissed me. I thought she had put hands over my sternum and crushed life back into my chest. The way I ache for her when she's gone, and miss her just as much when she is close. It's a bone deep pain that manifests every time my heart beats. It's just like resuscitating someone, the depth of pressure and slow, even breathing that everyone needs to survive.

But no, it wasn't a spiritual resuscitation.

It was sacrifice.

Rachel has been trading her life for mine. She's giving me hers in the purest most beautiful way a person can give their life away and still live. She is doing that for me.

Because of me.

I've killed the woman I died for by loving her.

The take-no-prisoner, never compromising, spotlight stealing diva is dead. I've taken all the metal she had in her spine and melted it, showering her in a love so beyond her that she had no choice. I've entrapped and imprisoned her and given her only one way to go. And I can't watch her die again. No, I have to try and salvage her. Who she was. Who she needs to be. I swallow as a thought strikes me like a whip, branding the brittle shell holding me together. In another life, coldness pushed her toward her dreams and I have to somehow give her that again.

So I lie to her, for her, because it is the only thing that will stop her from destroying her life. And my words come unprovoked to crack her heart in half. "I don't love you enough to do this."

I've never been so in love, so perfectly in the moment with Rachel. And this is our moment, right here in the twilight with her. I think this might be our special hour, just after sunset, when the light is low and dying. Here amid the twinkling lights of her family's home, I lean into the easy touch of her hands and body and relish in the intermittent gusts of summer breeze.

She dances with me slowly, twirling me with a smile on her lips. I tumble into her eyes and her smile, the way the light hits her hair, and the soft brush of her hands. Rachel tries to dip me and I pull up short because I don't want to fall. We laugh into the growing darkness and I fall in love over and over with her heart, her soul, and the words she whispers against my neck. At the way her giggle rumbles through her whole body when I go to kiss her and we end up clicking our teeth together. "You should go right, always go right," I say as the music pours through me from the speaker on the wooden picnic table.

Rachel nods sarcastically, cocking her head left. "This way?"

I smirk. "Yeah, perfect." And I pepper her lips with kisses. When I smell the scent of dinner through the open door behind us, my stomach growls audibly.

"Hungry?" Rachel whispers. Her chin hits my shoulder then, hands tucking softly around my back and trailing lightly.

"Yes." I close my eyes as the rake of wind envelops me. I tilt my face into it, into the scent of nature and far off fields, a hint of barbeque from another person's home, and the ever present swirl of Rachel. My skin tingles, still sensitive from our afternoon in the pool and the positively scalding shower afterward. I can feel the air, the pleasant cool of it as it whips past us.

For a moment I imagine this is our house, and it's just me and her in the entire world. It makes me sigh with how much I yearn for it and when she spins me and pulls my back to her chest, I ease back into the arms that hold me so perfectly. I blink, when she rocks me slowly, comfortingly.

"This is so nice." She kisses my neck before nuzzling into it for a moment.

"It is." I lean back, pillowing my head against hers as I focus on the glitter of lights in the branches above. My eyes search their golden flickers as I smile at how safe I feel. I never would have been able to imagine something as blissfully perfect as this. It is more than the night, it is the way everything has propelled me to this place where I stand in her arms.

"Did you make your decision about track?" she asks, brushing her fingertips down to my pelvis. She traces over the line of my underwear and then follows it slowly down the crease of my hip.

"Yeah, I'm going to do it this coming year."

Her hand rakes slowly across my abdomen and reclaims her grip on my hips. I close my eyes as she shifts behind me to the rhythm of the music. "I think you will be amazing. I'll be able to come to your meets when they are after school. I'll cheer for you."

The thought makes me giddy. "Just not too loudly. I don't want you to hurt that voice of yours."

"Yeah, well," she scoffs lightly, "it's not that big of a deal. I was actually planning to use my voice for other things too, like the debate team."

I laugh. "Oh, no. I pity the poor person stacked up against you, poor bastard has no idea what kinda hell he walked into."

"So you think I would be good?"

I crinkle an eyebrow at the idea she could be bad at anything. "Rachel, you can do it all." I twist in her arms and steal a kiss as she blushes prettily under the glow around us. "You are incredible. I believe in you, I mean with your vocabulary alone you could probably send your opponent into a tailspin."

She sways with me, slow dancing in a moment of elation. "You like my words, don't you?"

I give her a knowing smile. "Yes, but that is our secret."

"Yes, ours." *Her hands sweep over my face and then glide all the way down my body.* "I love having an 'ours' to share and collective skeletons in our closet."

"Me, too."

"It makes me feel like I'm a part of something." *She twines her fingers with mine.* "I like being a part of you."

"Sweethearts, dinner's ready!" *Hiram calls.*

We fall still when we turn to the door. As Rachel starts toward it, I catch her hand.

She turns to me, hair tumbling in the breeze. It's the look she gave me in my office, the one that told me she loved me, that flickered with a drop of her depth of emotion for me. Her eyes are soft and warm—unfathomably deep with adoration. How I didn't see it before, how I let this love pass me by until I was twenty is beyond me. I tug her back, spinning her into my arms. The motion ends with her wrapped in me and I stare into her eyes. They reflect the glow of tea lights and drip with promise.

"You're more than just a part of me angel. You're the other half of me."

"Promise it?"

"I promise. Now, let's go eat, I'm starving."

I've promised her mountains and kingdoms of love. I've promised her unfaltering adoration and a safe place to land, always. I've given her arms that would break around her to keep her safe, and a heart that has loved her forever. I've loved her forever, for longer than I can remember. She was and is that one thing that matters, the only constant in the whirlwind of my existence.

She is the promise of my life and I'm breaking all my promises now, to her and myself.

And it feels like it will kill me.

I'm expecting Rachel to respond to my words and when she does I'm completely shocked. She laughs. It's forced, but it's still a laugh. She doesn't believe my words, she can't. Rachel has too much invested in me, pieces of her heart and soul have grown with mine, twisted together with me.

She loves me too much.

There is challenge in the way she looks at me, a defiant zealotry in her love for me. And why wouldn't there be? All the love I've put into her, all the love she has given, it forms an impenetrable shield around us.

I was building a relationship to last forever. That was my plan.

I loved her at sixteen the way I wanted to love her twenty years from now and then fifty. I built a foundation to a relationship that should have lasted a lifetime and now I'm trying to tear it down. Her soft brown eyes waiver when I don't laugh back and I realize I'm going to break her.

Oh God, I'm going to destroy her.

It is obvious when under that curt bitter laugh I see a flicker of pain so extreme it blinds me. It makes my stomach churn. To drown out the sound of my own heart shattering I move a step forward and say it again. "I don't love you."

"Blake." Her eyes fix on me hard, cooling slightly

to ease her temper. "I get you're mad, but don't say those things to me. It hurts."

"I mean it."

She taps a finger on the edge of the counter beside her, fingernail tracing the tile. "No you don't. I can hear in your voice that you love me. I can see it in your face that you do." She looks up at me then, smiling gently. "I know you baby, so talk to me. Tell me what's going on."

It horrifies me.

She does know me...she does...and it is the most beautiful thing in the world. Our collective intimacy, the life we are creating in tandem is the only thing that matters in the world. However, I know there cannot be an 'us' without a *her* and *I* first. My Rachel needs this. My wife needs this future.

And that is what I'm fighting for.

She can't give up New York for me. She can't do it so that I can go to a better medical school. I won't let her, because ultimately she will be incomplete. For all her boastful claims that music is only a little part of her, she is lying. It is everything she is. It's in her walk, her kiss, and the riptide of her eyes. Rachel is music in the way oxygen is air. She is meant to change people's lives through her song. She is meant to engender the love of millions.

I didn't realize how much her dreams were a part of me, too.

They are worth everything to me, and not just in lip service to seduce her. They represent a constant that is unalterable. "You can't go to California because if I *do* go to school out there I don't want you there."

Her eyes bore into mine, and I harden them as much as I can, burying the torch I've carried for her for more than half my life. I glare at her, channeling the young girl I once was. Her hand touches mine and I don't respond or tighten my fingers in hers when she squeezes.

"Blake, what do you mean?" She squeezes my hand again, repeatedly, like she will be able to pump love back into it.

Eventually, I pull it away and it makes her eyes gloss. I don't know how I'm going to say this, so I close my eyes and tell her I love her silently while I slice through her tenderness. "I want to try out other things, experience new things with different people." I shake my head. "I don't want to have some love sick puppy following me."

God, I feel like a love sick puppy, happy to follow her every command. Tucked into her bedroom after dinner she strips me down, body and soul, and makes love to me. Not even when she was my wife did she do these things to me. It's different, so different and amazing.

Rachel's father is missing another time.

I can't help but think it when I stare down into her eyes as I give her what she requests. I think poor Hiram would be horrified to see this look, the absolute sex she exudes as she thrusts into me. I don't even think I've seen this look before, so dark, so smoldering, possessed. She is growing into a different woman with me; one full of fire and confidence, brimming with adventure and excitement and willing to try anything. We have turned one another into our own private playgrounds. There are no off-limit signs posted, just an endless wild of anything we want that stretches to the horizon. For the first time in my life, I understand the empowerment of surrender.

"Keep going, God baby you feel so good," she whispers to me moving faster.

"Oh, God, Rachel." I grab for the pillow and cover my face with it as I cry out. It muffles me, and thank God, because I didn't know what a screamer I was going to be. As a grown woman, I didn't let her do this enough, and as a teen my body responds differently. Physiologically everything is just tighter and it makes her movements more pronounced.

She is just perfection for me as she hits everything just the way I need her to. She changes the angle, moving deeper and the pillow comes back to my face to smother the sound away. I hold it there, ride her as she touches me in ways I've never been touched. It's insane how different this feels–earthshattering. I'm at her mercy and I didn't know it would feel this good.

She pulls down on the pillow with a hushed request. "I want to see you." I drop the protective barrier beside us and palm over her.

"I can't not moan, Rachel. I don't think I can keep this quiet."

"Yes, you can. You will for me." She is so confident, so sure. Possessiveness looks good on her. I slam my eyes closed as she moves faster, and I bite my lip until I think I can taste blood. "Rachel." I strain as I feel a warble of my orgasm racing toward me.

She hushes me with a hiss and then pulls me down by the back of my neck into a kiss. I cling to her lips, opening to her in every way possible as she just owns me. There is no other way to put it, ownership.

I'm going to be so sore after this. It's going to feel so good lying beside her with the tingle of this feeling between my thighs while we kiss each other to sleep. It's my new favorite thing, this right here. This utter helplessness I feel as her knowing hands work over me and stretch me, tear me up, and set me on fire for her. She burns her hands on me, stamping a supernova with every touch.

When her parents are gone, she forces me to scream her name while she does crazy things to my body, and then at the next turn she tortures me with forced silence when they're here. She makes me do things I never would have done before, things that actually embarrass me when I'm not having sex with her. Things that fill walk-in closets full of secrets between the two of us, like a marriage.

Like a love that will last forever.

Just thinking about it, about how much I love her, makes everything tighten and as I do, her eyes get that much darker, that much more intense. And she forces another finger inside me. I cover my mouth with my hand as my eyes shoot open and I seesaw air through my nose. I don't ever think I've seen anything quite so satisfied as her face in this moment and it makes me just that much hotter, that much wetter, because I'm performing for her.

"Do you like that?" She growls it at me and I nod. "Good." Her face turns loving, melting into a myriad of emotions as she smiles at me. Her motions slow and her free hand twists with mine. "I want you to know you're mine and feel it, the same way I do when you make love to me."

I fall head over heels with her again, in love with her, and her words. It's a different woman before me than the wife I knew. Rachel was a love-maker, fiery in her own way, but this...this candid, emotional, open abandon is new. It makes me shiver.

She pulls me down onto her as she pushes harder.

I want to scream out, but instead I bury my nose into her hair and bite her shoulder. "Tell me something, anything, push me over the edge."

Her hand is in my hair then. "You want me to make you come?"

"Yes." I wince in pleasure as she goes that much harder and sharper. "Please, yes, please."

"Say it again."

I think I've unleashed a demon.

"No." I draw a line in the sand to see what she'll do.

She laughs silently beside me and then licks her lips when her eyes catch mine. "I'll talk dirty to you if you say it again."

I nip her ear as she grinds her fingers into me so deeply it makes my lungs tighten. I wrap my hands in the comforter around us and just tremble against her. I'm not going to give in. She twines her fingers in the hair at the back of my neck and strokes there while her fingers inside me stop. She's stalling me out. Jesus, she is so mean. "Oh Rachel, please don't, no, God I'm so close."

"Say it."

"No," I whisper.

"Say it, baby."

Her tone is so soft, so loving, I surrender. "Please make me come."

"How close are you?" She sighs against my ear, her touches soft and slow.

"So," I clear my throat, "so, close."

She grinds into me slowly, and I press back to get more motion into the movement. She cups her hand against the base of my head and, holding my cheek against her forehead, she moves inside me. Her motions *pick up, fast enough to propel me toward climax and I sigh, grateful. It touches something deep inside me, the comfort, the protectiveness in this touch. But I still need more. I open my mouth to tell her so, but she presses her lips to my ear and nudges me to my back gently. I splay out beneath her, letting her control everything as I give in and give over everything I have.*

"I love being inside you. Feeling you, touching you. I wonder if you feel what I feel when you do this to me. If you feel the tightness, the ache I feel, the way your fingers curve into me perfectly and fill me up."

I tremble, pulling her closer to stare into her angelic eyes. "Oh God, I hope so because this feels so good."

"Yeah?" she urges as I pant against her. I grab her shoulders, feeling them flex as she drives into me. Her lips quirk against mine and her teeth nibble.

When she returns to my ear, her breath is so hot it makes my skin race with chills. "Oh Blake, baby, think about it. Think about how it feels when your fingers are in me. How I grind into you, how I moan for you."

"Do it," I urge in a hushed whisper as she undoes me. "Close your eyes and imagine it and moan like I'm sliding into you."

She sucks in air and then hurriedly grabs the pillow, covering both of our faces. In this close of proximity when she moans in my ear, long and deep, it consumes everything. I know she is still imagining it when she keeps talking and moaning. "Baby, I love it when you press all the way into me. I love you, so much, you always feel so good inside me." She moans again.

"And what if I had a strap-on?"

Rachel's hand pulls out and then thrusts in hard between us. I arch up into her and mew against the damp skin of her neck.

"I would let you do anything you wanted to."

"Oh fuck." I pant harder into the pillow above me, ramping up. "Tell me."

"I'd let you take me missionary, my legs wrapped around your hips. I'd get on top of you, moving up and down so you could watch it disappear inside me. I'd let you take me doggy style, so you could scratch your nails down my back while I arched into you." I feel her neck shift as she swallows. "I'd give anything for your hands tugging my hair while I did that."

"Oh, God, Rachel."

"Oh you like that," she husks into my ear. "You like the idea a lot. I can tell. You just got so much tighter."

God, there really aren't any secrets between us. "Yes, tell me more."

I work my hand down, slipping through her wetness to claim her again. She arches down against me, thighs making space as I take her again. I feel the power between us shift, and I push the pillow away as I lift my head. I arch my eyebrow at her when she trembles.

"Tell me more about that."

She blushes and takes a broken breath as I ramp up my speed. "About you making love to me with a strap-on?" She clears her throat, dropping the volume of her voice. "How I'd want you sitting right here in my bed with me squirming in your lap while you pull me down onto it gently? I would cry out your name and moan. I'd have you cup my breasts and it would make me so wet I'd drip onto your legs. And then when you started thrusting—" She moans softly, dropping her head to my neck as I pound into her.

God, her moans sound strangled and needy and beautiful.

"When you started thrusting, just like this, I would hold your head against mine and rock with you."

It paints inside my mind, the image of her, dark and luscious before me. My breasts on hers and her hands in my hair as I nip her neck. "Yes. Oh God, yes."

"Yes, come for me baby." *She spreads over me, angling the words right in my ear. Her breath is hot and it prickles my skin down the side of my body.* "I'll lay you down and mount you, letting you just watch while I move up and down for you. And I'll come, it won't take long and you will be able to watch me orgasm for you."

"Why won't it take long?" *God, say it. Say it and I'll climax. I silently beg for it as she quivers deliciously and I feel her orgasm start with a tightening of every single muscle in her body.*

"Because, baby–I love you." *She whines as she arches, and I feel her tighten on my fingers, her words come breathlessly.* "And when I feel your love, I always want to give you everything I have to give."

That does it for both of us. I hold her eyes and we shatter apart together, panted breaths and soft mews the only evidence that our universe is exploding. Her lips press to my ear, littering a string of 'I love you's' and I drown in those words as she claims my heart and soul again.

"Love sick puppy?"

I don't think I've ever heard this sound. I've never heard her voice whistle with this much pain. I've never hurt her like this. In our other life, I had been cold on occasion, I had been angry. We had fought, but never had I lifted her so high, just to let her fall and shatter.

It's like putting a vase back in the cupboard only to have it slip out of my hands.

I don't miss that it takes a mockery of her feelings for me to eviscerate her. But when she says things like she is giving up her dream, it doesn't lift me to a higher peak, it breaks my heart instead. It makes me realize I've pushed too hard against her, and because she loves me, she will give in and give up the parts of her that define her. She gives away bits of her heart that I have no right to take. Mine are careless heavy hands that have handled her roughly, molding her into a quick-fire form of a woman that took thirty-five years to make. And even though I enjoyed it, enjoyed the things I made just like I wanted it to be, there is always a trade. There is always something that has to be swapped, because there is only so much of her soul to spread around. I built a perfect mold for me to fall into, but I left her music out.

It's not so perfect anymore when I realize that.

I try to think about it. I try to remember the last time I heard her sing. It's been months.

"Love sick," she says it again, mortally struck.

I firm my lips into a line as I watch it. I deserve this horror, this pain. And just as I watched her be buried in our other life, I will see this through to the end as well. "I'm sorry, Rachel, but this has been fun. I mean, right?" I force it, I force the words. They fit the situation like a square peg in a round hole because I don't mean them.

"Oh, God." Rachel puts a hand to her side and looks like she is about to cave to her knees. Instead she leans on the counter. "Don't do this. Not to us, not when we..."

She doesn't finish the sentence and I don't have

anything to say to that plea. I can't find words. I know what she is talking about. It is everything between us. It's not the sex, it's not the words, and it's not the looks. It's all of it in combination. It's the little things, the big things, how perfectly well we blur and wrap and tumble into one another. "Not when we, what?" I ask anyway, because the masochist in me wants to know what she is going to miss about me the most. I want to know what it is so that when I see it, when I feel that part, I can die over and over again.

"Nothing." She glances at me, wounded. Rachel has never begged, never pleaded, and never settled in her life. So when her lips crack and her voice rips through, I'm not expecting her words. "Please, Blake, please. Please don't do this to me, to us. Please, oh God, please. It will kill me, it will break my heart." She puts a hand on her chest, covering the wound I've inflicted.

I look away to cover the way my face slips. "I have to get my stuff."

Those words put motion in her steps and she grabs for me, holding my arms in her hands. "Please, look at me."

I can't, but I do.

She holds my eyes and I bite the inside of my cheek to keep the sob that hits the back of my throat at bay.

"We can never find this again, this right here, this magic."

It scares me because I think she may be right. I'm going to lose her. I'm going to lose this angelic beauty that smiles sunlight and draws hands in swirls on my heart. I'm never going to have her again.

But she was never mine in the first place.

Not this woman.

"Blake?"

"What!" My coarse tone is enough to finally make her cry.

It makes me cry too, makes big fat betraying drops spill down my face. She didn't do anything but love me and I'm hurting her. I'm hurting her so badly. Oh God, I think it may kill me first. Her hands soften and her thumbs are at my cheeks before I can catch my breath. I try to pull away, but my body fights against the fear that if I take one step back, she is going to be lost to me forever.

"You still love me." She says it over and over as the gentlest hands I've ever known wipe at my tears.

For a breathless moment, I almost say it.

I almost tell her everything.

I want to...my heart wants me to tell her the whole story. However the cold bitch I once was, stops loving words from coming. Because *she* knows what needs to be done, even if the rest of my heart forgets. "I just think this is so sad and pathetic." I pry her hands from my face. "You are so sad."

And with a snap, I turn away. I hear her fall to the kitchen floor and I run, I run as fast and as hard as I did the day she died. I run away afraid that I'll see her cold and broken again. I grab my bag, my clothes, my shoes and run out of her room. I'm afraid that when I turn the corner at the top of the stairs she will be there. But she isn't. She isn't on her feet fighting. It renews my tears, because I have, I've lost her. I'm leaving.

I take the stairs two at a time and I don't look back as I close the front door behind me. Outside, I stagger to my car, barefoot, wounded, but I can't find my keys. I can't breathe and I choke on air as I fumble in my bag for them. I've killed her.

I've killed her. This time it didn't take a car, it was me. My words, my actions, my heart that did this to her.

"Blake?"

I turn to Hiram's voice so quickly that it whips tears over my lips. Mr. Kaplan, I correct as I choke on my sob. He will never call me honey or kiddo again. It's more than Rachel, it's so much more. I'm giving up love in every possible way and going back to a cold dark world.

"What?"

He holds up my keys, but when I hold out my hand for them he shakes his head. "You can't drive like this kiddo."

He drives the stake that much deeper, until I might not be able to survive it.

I can't give into this, I can't. I pull a breath, and hold out my hand again. "Give them to me."

"No."

"I'm not your daughter! Give me my Goddamn keys!" I scream because I'm powerless.

He looks shaken. It takes a moment, but finally he narrows his eyes at me and hands them over. "I love you like it though." And surprisingly, he hugs me then–all warmth and goodness–just like his daughter. "Please be safe, and if you ever need anything... anything...I'm here...we're here."

"Don't be nice to me." I'm crying as I key the car open. "I don't deserve it."

"Yeah, you do, honey. I understand everything. I saw the letter, too." His eyes hold mine and I think he really does. But that moment, just like all the good things in my life, is gone in an instant. "I'll see you later, Blake."

I throw the bag across the interior, and as he turns away I make one last plea. "Please, please, make sure she is okay."

He doesn't look back. "She will be, eventually. She'll just have to get over you."

Get over me. That is what he said.

Get over me?

It is like a knife in my stomach, and it radiates up to where my heart used to be. The empty hammer of the car door matches the sound of the void in my chest. I gun the engine as I race out of Rachel's life. I'm doing what I have to, letting the universe reset her to a path she should have walked. One I never had the right to hold her hand on. She has to get over me. Move on so that she can do what she needs to do. I can't be her friend. I can't salvage anything. I have to let it rot. I have to watch everything I built die all over again.

My only hope, the only thing I can cling to is that in the future she will forgive me. She has to, right? She *has* to. I say it over and over in my head as I drive in a cold car when I could be in a warm bed with the love of my life. The juxtaposition makes me cry harder. I placate the pain in my heart by affirming that I have the worst of it. As long as I hurt more, then that is all that matters. And I do. I have to. There is nothing in this world that can be worse than the constricting agony I feel.

"She will get through this. She is brave, she will heal." I wipe my eyes. "All the wonderful things I know about her, the new things she has shared. All of that will still be here for me someday."

Someday.

"She is headstrong and proud. She will pick herself up and make a beautiful life."

That thought stops me cold, my foot lifting off the accelerator until I come to a stop down the street from my house. She's too proud to forgive me. I heave breaths as I stare at the visor above me, my hands clinging weakly to the steering column. That indomitable spirit I love, the one I would protect at all costs. The one I just shattered. That spirit will *never* forgive me for this.

I fix my eyes on my bag, clothing still warm from her touch. It smells like her, wraps me in the comforting scent of the only thing I need and want in the world. I reach out and touch the soft cotton and wonder fearfully what shadow of a life will we have *if* she were to ever love me again. I stop breathing, focus on the clothing, then turn and stare straight ahead. I will myself to keep going, but I can't depress the pedal because I've ruined everything.

Me. I did it. I put the tears in her eyes, stole her innocence, and broke her heart. One by one my trespasses slice the threads that reduce me to moaning sobs that I don't think will ever end. However it's this final horrid thought that bests the final string holding me upright.

Her trusting smile will *never* be the same again, because of what I've done.

Realizing that is enough of a sharp edge to sever me and I drop my head to the steering wheel to weep as the cover closes on my high school story with her.

Part Two

Chapter Eleven

My Clarity And Reasons
September 10th, 2011

I stare at my reflection.

I've done this for as long as I can remember, read my face and check that the cracks in my mask aren't showing. It's here, before the mirror in my room, that I have plastered over the wear and tear that comes with my life and hid from the world. There is a sense of peace in the knowledge that I can still do it so well. The reasons may have changed, but that doesn't really matter in the end.

Whereas once I did it because it was safe. It was easy. It was totally and utterly isolated. Now I do it so I can head fake myself into thinking I have the strength to do what I need to.

Maybe it *does* matter, come to think if it.

I've worn this look a lot in my life, probably more than I've worn anything. There is no piece of clothing, no hairstyle, no life choice I've worn longer than this look right here. I wore this face when my sister went away to college and left me to deal with the horror of my family, when everything in my life turned to shit the last two years of high school. It was my expression when I kissed Rachel goodbye in the morning and went to work, when I missed family time and holidays. This grim set of my lips and lackluster in my eyes is the very same as when I buried her, too.

It's my taking-care-of-business face, the one that makes it look like what I'm about to do isn't going to hurt me.

But it does hurt, every time.

My eyes grow thoughtful as I steal one last look. What I'm about to do is going to hurt me a lot. I grab my keys and head out the door. My parents don't look up as I leave, not that I blame them. They don't care about me; they don't care what I do to poison my life more. I pull my sweater around me tighter, to fight off the chill in the air.

It's cold tonight. It's been cold all summer since I let Rachel go. She was warming my world and I would do anything to have that warmth, the real version of her, back. That thought fuels my fire of determination as I open the car and turn over the engine.

Oddly, because I don't have her to focus on, I've come to a realization about her in the months since I let her go. I've realized that in our other life, when she talked about the paths that people walk, it was all true, that my presence here has led her down a different one. One that has changed the very center of her being. Perhaps enough that I'm going to lose the future I had with her. And I am afraid that I *do* know how to fix what I've broken, how to right the universe.

That is why I'm wearing this face right now.

Two weeks ago, I saw Rachel for the first time since our breakup and she wasn't the same person I knew. How could she be, after all?

She had been standing in the hall, looking for her locker. She didn't wear my jacket, didn't smile at me as I've felt her do so many times. Her eyes were the hardest I've ever seen them. Her lips tight and cold.

I could shoulder her animosity if I knew I had fixed things, but I don't think I have, yet.

She still talks about California. At least I think she does. I'm only privy now to the things I hear as I pass in the hallway. She couldn't be farther away from me if she were on the other side of the world. And yet, because I *know* her, I can see the tremble in her lip as she moves through the hallway like she carries a weight too heavy for her to bear. I notice the dark slash in her eyes when she looks past me. I've ruined her, physically, emotionally and for forever. So in a way, she and I will always have a horrible kind of closeness. A seemingly unmendable one that stamps us both to the core. It frightens me more than I can say. More than I'm willing to allow myself to think.

I don't want our sacrifices to be in vain.

Thinking about her now as I finish putting on my makeup for someone *else* at red lights while I drive, bothers me. I close the vanity mirror unsatisfied with the way I look, and the choices I have to make.

Choices. They really are a bitch.

I remember a conversation I had with her father once upon a time, as I silently pull into the driveway of Nick Cooper's house. Hiram always used to say to me that people aren't islands. I understand that now more than I ever thought I would. We don't sit idly away from one another; we don't stare across purple waters, deep and impassable. There isn't a space between us so much as there is a gathering place, the unavoidable mix of what we all share. I suppose we are like Rachel's trees in a forest. We twist and tangle and twine into one another. Everything we do cascades into one collective, into a forest, into humanity as we know it to be.

And in my mind, if the most natural and destined interaction changes everything, like loving Rachel too soon, then what about my path? What about the things I have neglected to do? The moments I might have been destined to endure?

Moments like the birth of my daughter Beth.

I swallow hard to clear the lump forming in my throat.

I had just turned seventeen when I had her. It was the most beautifully, terrifying experience in my life–to have lost my virginity and end up pregnant–yet have a role in creating another person.

She was nineteen when I died. Beth was a nationally ranked diver, All State Champion many times over. She had a full scholarship to Harvard and a shot for a place on the U.S. 2032 diving team. Her adoptive mother told me she had a penchant for Math just like me. Science, too. She wanted to be a veterinarian and save the world one puppy at a time. In the last picture I saw of her, Beth had my eyes and her father Nick's smile.

Surely if altering something as simple as loving someone four years *too* soon can create change for millions, then the birth of a human being must echo like a song across the face of civilization. I hang on to that, feel it as I slide out of my car.

Parked in front of Nick's house, I watch the figures move past the windows. And despite the fact that I know what it is I have to do, it takes everything in me to stay here, to not run away from it. I squeeze the car handle, half way between turning around and staying. I grab for any emotion, any thought, but nothing comes.

I'm numb.

I think there is a point in every person's life where they just shut down, where all the emotion and pain just vanishes. It's the breaking point. The wall you hit at eighty miles an hour and crush yourself to the point where you can't exist anymore. I'm there now. I've been there since I let Rachel collapse to the kitchen floor. What do a few more dark moments matter when I can't feel them anyway?

"Holy shit! Blake?"

I wave absently to a fellow cheerleader as I let go of the car and shoulder my purse. I dust my bangs to the side, make sure my long bob is falling perfectly around my shoulders. It's a new haircut for a new time in my life.

With a breath I set my expression again, and head to the house.

I'm halfway across the lawn when I see Malina look out from one of the windows. I catch the glint in her eyes and I sigh as she disappears. She's coming out, I know she is. Steeling myself for it, I loop my hand in the strap of my purse and plaster an angry tilt in my eyebrow. Just as I thought, she meets me on the porch.

"So, wow." She glances around mockingly. "No Kaplan? What the fuck has the world come to?"

I regard her evenly, not letting her words land. There is no vulnerability left.

"I had heard that you two weren't finger deep in each other anymore."

"No."

She narrows her eyes, her lips almost curling into a smile. "What a shame. Was it not deep enough?"

I hear what she is saying. I can literally see it in the dark flash of her eyes. She takes a very perverse pleasure in saying it to me. As if scrawling sexual innuendo on what's left of me is her most favorite thing in the world. Apparently, there is a little bit left of me that *can* be hurt. "Shut up, Malina."

She actually smiles then because she knows it struck a nerve. I hate that she can smell blood in the water like a shark. She moves one predatory step forward. "Did you finally wise up and break up with that dumb little midget?"

It's incredible how the party seems to hush on the other side of the door. I glance around at the people on the porch, they might not be looking, but they are listening. I chew the inside of my lip before I face Malina again and lie. "She broke up with me."

I think I actually hear someone gasp.

I shoot angry looks around, but I can't find the source. "What?" I say to no one in general, sending a few faces flinching in the opposite direction. "That's right, look the fuck away." It feels good to hear the dark edge in my voice. It's good that girl is still here, because she can handle the business that needs to be done. When I fix on Malina, she shifts on her feet.

I feel different suddenly, like everything good has been swallowed. I'm grateful for it. "Do you have anything else you wanna ask me, or do you wanna get the hell out of my way?"

"I think you should remember your place, little miss high and mighty. You aren't Blake Fortier anymore." She grabs my arm roughly, halting my progress up the porch. "You seem to forget that you are the closet lesbo whose fall from grace was expedited when you swan dived into Rachel Kaplan's pussy."

I stare at her hand, at the white of her nail beds until I feel my rage build. "Let me go."

"No."

"Let me go, or so help me God I'll–"

"You'll what?' She laughs. "Sex me up?"

"You wish." I pull my arm away and smooth my expression. "I'll get you kicked off the team."

"Oh, please. Your threats are so idle they stand still."

"Says you." I arch my brow at her.

"Damn right, says I."

I actually find this funny, in a very sick twisted way. "Oh, how I missed this." I say it sarcastically, but I did. The evil dark part of me that has reared her head missed this.

"Jesus Blake, go home. You might think there is something still here for you, but there isn't. Also, you stink of that little troll. I can literally smell the decay of her on your breath."

"That's coming from between your legs, you slut."

"Funny." Malina's hand comes out of nowhere, slapping me hard enough across the face that I almost lose my balance as I stumble toward the rail of the porch. I lift a hand to where I can feel the tingle, my cheek hot. I hear her angry yells, but don't process them.

"Get her out of here, seriously, before I have to get ghetto and cut her pretty little face."

I hadn't realized how large the crowd had gotten around us, until I feel hands push on my back, forcing me back into the fray with Malina. They circle us, three rows deep at least. Malina is turning away, going back into the house 'cause she thinks I'm done, and that just won't do, cause I'm nowhere near finished. I rush forward, rage rattling my hands. "Hey, Mal?"

She turns to me right as I backhand her across the jaw, the blow whipping her head away from me. All I can hear is the chorus of jeers around us and the thundering of my heart. "That's for everything you've said tonight and for thinking you could hit me and get away with it."

My Spanish is rusty, but when she comes at me, I think she is telling me to go fuck myself. The crowd intercepts her though, holding her by the shoulders, before she can do anyone of the number of things I can tell she is imagining. I give her a self-satisfied smile as I edge toward the doorway. "Now, shut your mouth, swallow your pride, and answer me. Do you want a drink, or not?"

She stares at me, absolutely and totally shocked. When her face cools, and the party goers release her, she almost seems to have a new found respect for me. She eyes me critically and then laughs. "Sure, a drink sounds good."

"Good." As I start inside, her words make me grin for the first time in over a month.

"You have always been a genius slapper."

And in some weird way, I feel like I'm back.

෴෴෴

However, it only lasts a moment because there isn't enough liquor in the house to do justice to how badly I need a drink. I realize this high school drunken bullshit of cheap beer and wine coolers is lame. Right about now, I'd give anything for a glass of rum and coke. Cherry coke preferably. Rachel and I used to get blitzed off that. It is probably not the best thing to think of as I get drunk on shitty liquor and prepare myself to fuck someone else.

Beside me on the sofa, Malina moans and I literally feel my stomach twist. I glance over at her, as the loud music and louder yelling makes my head start to pound. She is tongue fucking a hockey player and I'm pretty sure his fingers are *fuck* fucking her. I look the other way, chugging the warming watermelon wine cooler in my hand. It sours my stomach instantly, even more so when images of me and Rachel on a sofa doing that very same action ricochet around my brain. I busy myself with watching the milling people, the shadows as they come together in dark corners. I forgot how much I hated this life. Popularity sucks. Being a teenager sucks more. After spending an enchanted three months with Rachel, the wholesome heart-wrenching joy we had together mutes everything this life could offer. There is not a party or a hookup that could compete with summer sun and smiles, or dancing in her parent's backyard at twilight.

I'm heart wrecked as I realize she probably feels the same.

When I hear Malina's guttural groan beside me, I've had enough. I hunt for a coaster to set my bottle on and resort instead to putting it inside an empty cup. When I stand everything spins.

Oh, Jesus.

I swallow, putting my hands out a little to steady myself. Well, that did the trick. I don't know why I keep forgetting this body is young and half the liquor it takes for me to get tipsy as an adult is enough to knock me on my ass. I blink everything into focus. "Malina, I'm heading to find Nick."

Her reply is muffled and I stagger across the room, leaving her to her devices. I breathe heavily, grateful and yet a little nervous about how drunk I am.

I don't like being out of control. I don't like not being able to function. I think it comes from years spent tied to a pager at the hospital. I never knew when I was going to get a call, so I had to be ready at a moment's notice. It's hard to save someone's life eyeball deep in Sailor Jerry and cherry coke.

It was only when I disconnected from work and was with Rachel that I could get like this...that I could relax and know I was safe. And fuck, it tasted so good on her lips back then.

"Okay, just one more," Rachel says from the kitchen with a slur in her voice. I look at her as she peeks at me from around the wall. She holds up her finger belatedly, scrunching her nose up. "One."

I nod slowly, drunkenly. When she leaves I close my eyes, which is probably a mistake because everything spins.

"Rachel?"

"What?"

"No more one-mores."

"No, Blake, one more. Come on." I hear a bottle bang on the counter and I blink as I sit up thinking about checking. I just think about it though, because I'm too messed up to perform the action.

It feels like only an instant, but then Rachel is humming near me and I look over to see her bobble the glass in her hand. She spills drops on the carpet as she walks. "Not the carpet," I groan. She licks the side of the glass to stop the dripping, which only tips it in the other direction.

Though she is making a mess, it is a pretty nice view what with her in a tank top and sleep shorts that are just so deliciously short. I stare at her tongue dragging across the glass suggestively. "Thank you." I say as the cold glass makes it into my hand. I lick the rest of the spillage off the side.

Rachel drops onto the leather sofa beside me. "Welcome." She sips from her glass. "Hey, Blake?"

I incline my head toward her. "Hmmm?"

"Drink faster."

Her smoldering look propels the rim of the glass toward my lips. I take a healthy swig and then suddenly she's bouncing from the sofa, slamming her drink to the coffee table. I jump as she races past me.

"Where are you going?" I ask her departing figure as she vanishes out of the room.

"One sec."

I sit there staring at where she went. "Rachel?"

She doesn't answer.

"Hello?"

When she returns, she has her tablet and is flipping through screens. The pages map over her face in bright flashes of color. I nurse my drink. "Rachel? What are you doing?"

"Setting the mood."

"For?"

She smirks. "You'll see."

When the music starts, it reminds me of one of those slow grind hip-hop things. I know I've heard it before. I arch my brow at my new wife as she sets the tablet down and stares at me.

"Rachel?"

She laughs lightly. "Don't you just look overwhelmed."

I smooth my features. "I am not."

"Then get over here and dance with me."

I join her, standing a little wobbly. Her arms wrap around my back with warm hands pulling me into her. It feels good. And when she starts grinding around, laughing a little under her breath, it feels even better.

"Naughty little Rachel Fortier."

She nods. "Always your naughty little Rachel."

"Where you headed Blake?"

I turn slowly to Nick Cooper's voice, it's a nice voice. It's soft and deep and part of what I liked about him the first time I did this. I lean back against the doorjamb and bite my lip. I hope it looks sexy and not sloppy like I feel. "I was looking for you."

"You were? Why?"

"Because I wanted to talk to you." I lean toward him, ghosting my hand over the front of his T-shirt. I can feel the muscle there, the heat, the strength. That was the other part of him I liked. His arms wrapped me up and made me feel safe. In my own young naïve way, he made me feel special and wanted, and the bone crushing strength of his arms kept me away from anything that could hurt me.

Except myself.

"Where would you like to go to talk?"

"I think–"

"My bedroom?"

Well, that is mighty chivalrous and super easy. It doesn't disgust me as much as it amuses me at how willing he is to take a drunk girl to his room. I guess I shouldn't be surprised, high school stud that he thinks he is. I nod lightly and follow him down the hallway.

Malina's suddenly before me. I don't know where she came from. "Whoa. Where are you going?"

"I'm going with Coop to his room."

Her eyebrows shoot up and she takes my wrist in her hand. Her hands are like ice, where the hell have they been? On the hockey player? "No Blake, you got other shit to do."

"Like what, watch you mouth fuck some dumbass hockey player?" I sound as bitter as I feel.

Nick chimes in, the gentleman he is. "Malina, back off. None of your business what Blake and I do. We were just going to talk."

"Like hell you were." She cup checks him with the back of her hand. "Not with that. You don't talk with that."

I actually laugh. I don't even care. It is so good not to feel a damn thing.

When my unborn daughter's name races through my head it sobers me up enough to remember what I'm doing here. "Malina." I cup my hand over hers, patting it lightly. "Let me go. I'm gonna be okay."

She loosens her hold, but doesn't let me go. "You like girls. Don't do this to rebound, seriously. I'll kill Kaplan for hurting you later, but this is dumb."

Always my friend. Always. I could kiss her. I really could. I'm a sloppy drunk. I blink and focus. "It's okay."

"No, it's not. You are drunk."

I nod then roll my eyes. "Yeah, that is the point of drinking." Is it? No, it's not. What am I saying? "I want this."

I say it so convincingly I question myself. Do I? Do I want to have sex with him? No, I don't, but I will because I have to. I have a responsibility to bring Beth into this world. The world doesn't deserve her, but she deserves a chance. And maybe this will fix things, fix everything.

When she lets me go, it severs my thoughts. I feel Nick take up his place before me again and he eyes me dubiously. I arch my brow at him. At least I think

I do because I can't feel my face. "What?"

"Are you rebounding from being with Rachel?"

I close my eyes, everything is spinning and the closer he leans toward me the dizzier it makes me. "No, I don't rebound. You have to care to rebound."

"Okay, then."

I wonder what the hell that would matter. What would he care if I'm rebounding, if I'm broken hearted? All he really cares about is if my legs are spread under him. Right? He opens his bedroom door and I slide in under his arm.

Rachel drops onto the sofa and leans back with a dazzling smile on her lips. I try to follow her, a little out of breath from our dancing, but she blocks my attempt. "Nope."

I take a gulp of watered down rum. "Whatcha mean, nope?"

"Dance for me."

"Dance for you?" I take another swig and set the glass down. Her eyes on me make me feel so naked. "Stop undressing me with your eyes."

She grins wider, "Stop making me, with that cute nervous look."

"I'm not nervous," I whisper, trying to find my confidence. I come up empty. "I'm just not sexy like I used to be."

Rachel snorts a laugh as her eyes roll over me. "Yeah, right."

"I am right." I try sitting down again, but she grabs my hands, holding me at bay while I stand in front of her. "You have no idea just how sexy you are. I like it when you show it off."

"Show what off?"

"Everything."

I laugh. "Anything in particular?"

"Your legs."

I drop my voice. "What about them?"

"They're amazing."

"You want to see them?" I urge, holding her shoulder to keep my balance as I slide down my sweats.

"Stripper wife, my favorite." Rachel glides her hands around behind me and squeezes my butt as her lips brush skin by my navel. "God Blake, you are so sinfully sexy."

I slip away from her hands, giving her a smile as I turn the music up. Her words give me a false injection of confidence and I offer her a coy look over my shoulder. "Stripper wife, huh?" I ruffle my hair from its ponytail.

Rachel nods leaning back again getting comfortable as I start to feel the rhythm of the music move through me. And regardless of how embarrassed I might feel as I start dancing and shaking my ass for her, I get lost in her smile and the excitement in her eyes.

"Wow, you look so hot right now. Not gonna lie. I'm forgetting how to breathe."

I peel out of my shirt and tossed it beside her. "Don't ever tell anyone about this."

Rachel smiles. "Of course not."

"Cause I'm your stripper, no one else's," I reaffirm and pop the clasp on my bra.

"Nope, 'cause you're my baby, and I'll never share you with anyone."

His bed is plaid, it makes me dizzy and I sit down heavily on it, facing him as he closes the door. The music isn't as loud now and it makes my head stop pounding. I blink a few times as he nears me, petrified of what will come next. He surprisingly sits on the floor, smiling up at me with that shit eating grin of his. He is handsome, faux-hawk and all, with a strong jaw. Beth got that from him, chiseled features and endlessly deep hazel eyes.

"So, how are you Blake?"

I stare at him blankly. "We aren't talking. We are going to fuck."

He blinks at me and does a perfect eyebrow arch back at me. "You're funny. I don't doubt that I could make you straight again, but I can tell you're fucked up and I don't do the drunk girl thing."

You *mother fucker*.

"I'm not drunk." God, I sound drunk. I sound drunk enough that I bet he thinks I'm going to vomit and pass out any moment.

"Yeah, okay." He kicks his big foot at the rail on the edge of the bed. The pinging sound rages my headache again. "I've known you for a long time, Blake, like three years now, and I can tell you have some stuff going on." He nudges my foot gently. "So talk. What's up, babe?"

I roll my eyes and lick my lips. I got him to fuck me once, I can do it again. In the haze of my brain it all makes sense. This is what I have to do. I need to make this happen. So, what will tug at his oh-so-noble libido? "I thought another girl could make me feel beautiful." I fiddle with the tossed blanket, fingering it slowly between my words. "I realized I didn't need that. I needed something else."

He stares at me, his foot tapping lightly against mine. "You're a seriously hot girl, Blake."

I nod and catch my lip in my teeth for his benefit. "I like hearing that, but I wanna feel that."

"Feel what? That you're hot?"

"Maybe." I lean back and narrow my eyes at him.

From here on his bed, I regard the way his eyes travel over me. I bet he is thinking about it. His eyes hover on my legs. They are tan, tanner than they have been in a long time. "Do you like my legs?"

"Yeah."

"Do you wanna feel them?" I shift a little, hiking my dress just that much higher. His eyes pop, "Do you wanna feel them wrapped around you?"

"I-uh, I think you drank too much."

I snort a laugh. "Please." I wave his concerns off. "I can recite the alphabet backward which is proof I'm not drunk." I really hope he doesn't ask me to because I can't, not even when I'm sober. To ward off any displays of prowess I part my legs wider. "Now, do you want to feel them?"

"Yeah."

"Then get up here." I'm glad I don't have to tell him twice. It's too much work to do this. It feels fake like a movie with bad actors. A movie I don't want to watch.

I can feel his hands on my legs, big hands trailing calloused football strong palms over my thighs. I pull him down for a kiss, it's sloppy and foreign. His five o'clock shadow burns my lips and cheeks as he lashes his tongue against mine. It's nothing like the soft mewing kisses of Rachel's. It's nothing like her.

It's nothing.

His mouth tastes bitter like alcohol, but I kiss it anyway. I press into his lips, push every part of what I feel into a moan that rattles the air between us. I fake it. I force it and for those that don't know the difference, it's the sexual green light. Hands in hair too short to be hers I grapple for purchase, I hip my way into his lap, until he pins me. He's heavy on me. I breathe in short bursts as I dig into his sheets with my heels. "I want you to make me feel beautiful."

"I will." His hands are up my dress and they yank my underwear down.

Rachel wouldn't have said that to me. She would have kissed me softer. She would have trailed soft fingers over my face. She would have whispered I was the most beautiful thing in the world. I hang on it, even as my chest tightens and tears threaten my eyes.

She made love to my soul even when she was fucking my body.

I realize I was so wrong about my breaking point when he touches me. Right here as his fingers and body grind into me, this is where I can't feel anymore, because everything good about me is dead.

And yet, I still have so much more to destroy. That thought freezes the tears in my eyes and the cry on my lips.

Chapter Twelve

Reasons Enough
April 18th, 2012

Labor hurts, but you don't actually feel it. Not really. Well, I'm sure you feel it in the moment, you know when it feels like your vagina is being inverted. I'm sure I did, because God bless epidurals, but they really don't make everything as numb as you would like. I remember the hazy memories of thinking that.

But the moment Beth was born and I heard her cry, the rush of beta-endorphins and oxytocin carried it all away. I literally forgot the pain, forgot the misery. I had tears in my eyes and I didn't know why anymore, except because I knew that my baby girl was born and she was breathing.

Then I remembered she wasn't going to be mine. The tears were there for a different reason after that, and have yet to stop. As I sit in the dark of my hospital room, I hate that darkness is the recurring theme in my life. I sniff lightly to keep my nose from dripping as I stare down at the maroon blanket on my lap, what I can see of my lap anyway. I still look as pregnant as when I came in here and my hands slide over the hospital gown in memory. I know my baby isn't there anymore, but I'm still shocked when my hands press right *there* and she doesn't kick for me.

I can't seem to put it together in my mind that after nine months of getting to know my little girl, she is gone. All it took was nine hours of labor and several signed consent forms. I feel the tears starting again and I pluck at the blanket until it covers my stomach. Hiding it doesn't change it though; it doesn't change the reality that I'm ready now.

I'm so ready to have a daughter.

I ease a shaking breath and when I feel the hiccup of sobs at the back of my throat I grab my pillow and just wail into it. I hold it to my face and scream my agony into it, until my abdomen hurts. Until my voice is hoarse and no one will be able to hear me cry with or without my pillow.

I'll never be the same.

I know that this time is different and it makes me physically ill to remember signing my name to the consent for adoption paperwork. Before, I was able to use the justification that I was doing something good for my daughter as the excuse for giving her away. I was able to rationalize that her future was more important than my selfish desires.

This time though I'm not seventeen anymore.

I know I can be the mother she needs me to be. I can be warm and loving. I can hold her and comfort her, be her friend when she needs one and her mother when she needs that, too. I can manage her education, her needs, and her desire for attention. I can do all that and still be a doctor.

She isn't mine to have though, she never was.

It's so unfair.

She will always be a stranger I see in pictures and broken zoetropes, disjointed images that never solidify into real life. An arm's length and a heartbeat

away, she will be the child I never know but love all
the same. I blow out all the air in my lungs. I suppose
it's just as well. I don't even have a stable place to live
right now since my parents kicked me out. Anything
else I envision is just fantasy.

I uncover my face and when I see a figure beside
me I almost scream. I shift painfully away on instinct,
but halfway through the motion I realize it's Rachel.
She sees the panic in my expression and her hands
grab the handrail beside me. They miss my hand by
less than an inch. I fasten my gaze there, to where her
fingers grip so close to me I can feel their heat.

"I'm sorry. I didn't mean to scare you."

"What are you doing here?" I whisper angrily.

I don't know why she makes me so upset, so
bitter. Oh God, I feel a shot of pain from my abdomen.
I put a hand to the spot as I cover my face with the
other. The IV gets tangled on the bedrail, pulling
painfully and that is the last straw. I hiss at it, unable
to move, agonized and defeated, until everything
crumbles into a runny mess.

And I'm crying again.

Shoulders hunched and spirit broken I let it
all go because I can't hold it in anymore, not when
Rachel's here, even though she isn't mine to cry to
anymore. Her hand is on my arm then, gentle in its
motion as she pulls my wrist toward her a little and
unhooks where my IV is stuck. Finally free, I cover my
face and sob into my hands.

It is such a sweet gesture compared to what I've
dealt with in these last few months, compared to what
I did to her a year ago, I think it breaks me down even
more. I know I've hurt her tremendously. I have seen
the way her face has been contorted with misery over

the last nine months. It doesn't take a rocket scientist to understand that not two months out of her bed, I jumped into someone else's. Poor form on my part brought on by not sticking to my original life.

I can't even believe she is here.

I swallow and wipe my eyes. "I'm sorry. It's been a hard day." I clear my throat, mapping some semblance of collection to my features. "So, hello. How are you?"

She laughs a little, her brows furrowing as she gives me a meaningful look. "How are *you*? You don't look very good."

I make light of it. "Why thank you for noticing how crappy I look." I snicker. "I just pushed a watermelon out a hole the size of a lemon. Let's see how good you look after that."

"You know what I mean." She sighs, resting her chin on the bedrail. "I brought you some flowers." She glances over and I follow her gaze to where a small potted bunch of daisies announce themselves in white and yellow. "I hope you like them."

I smile darkly, mournfully. "I do. You know they are my favorite." I stare at them, and the intimate knowledge she has pulls a warm blanket around the cold hurt I feel. There is a card with them and when I reach out for it, I see Rachel wince.

"Wait."

I pause mid-motion regarding her.

"Wait until I leave before you read it."

"Okay." I return my hand to the place on my belly where it feels like I'm being peeled apart. I don't really know what to say to her. "So, what are you doing here?"

"Oh, um, I volunteer here now, and when I

found out you were in the maternity ward, I wanted to bring something by for you. No one should be alone, and I figured your parents wouldn't show."

"No, they didn't."

"I'm sorry, Blake." Her hand finds mine and squeezes gently.

"Don't be sorry. I deserve it."

She doesn't refute the statement. The void of her not defending me is deafening. I look away, to where the dark night sky is punctuating through my blinds. Her fingers leak away from mine slowly and I feel the loss of it deep in my chest. There is a question on the tip of my tongue and though I have a feeling it will hurt me, I ask it anyway.

"Why would you think I wouldn't like the daisies?"

Rachel licks her lips, her eyes narrowing as she thinks about her answer. "Because, I don't know if I know you anymore."

"I'm still the same person." I clear my throat. "Well, sorta."

"Yeah." Rachel looks down at her lap. "You aren't though. Not to me."

Those words scare me. "Hopefully someday we can talk about everything. I would appreciate the chance to explain."

Rachel nods. "Someday, when it doesn't hurt as much, okay?"

"Okay."

She heaves a breath and her voice trembles, betraying her. She's staring at her lap, and I watch the shimmer of teardrops fall. "I really can't think of when that will be."

"I'm sorry." I whisper it because I can't put tone

in my voice.

"Me too." She shifts then stands slowly.

I watch her. Watch the way she moves as she collects her purse and jacket. I have changed her so dramatically, piled years onto her through the vivisection of her heart.

"Blake?"

It's dark, but I hang on her outline in the light from the hallway. She fills up my view and it takes everything in me not to stretch out and beg for her to stay. "Yes?"

Her hands reach out and turn the small potted plant to where I can see a cluster of gold stars on the side of it. She taps it lightly, a perfect fingernail pinging against the glass. "I'm giving you these for the amazing job you did today bringing Beth into the world."

"Thank you." I firm my lips into a line to keep them from crumbling.

"Also, I'm really proud of you for making the right decision for her. Letting someone adopt her, it's selfless. You can be a good person when it matters the most."

I nod silently over and over, my eyes fix on my lap until the tears come. I just keep affirming Rachel's words until my heart overwhelms my common sense. "I wish you knew I was the good person when it mattered most to you."

"Blake?" Her words are choked tight in her throat. "God, you just don't get it…"

I hear how angry she is suddenly and when I look at her I can see the shimmer of more unshed tears in her eyes.

She forces a breath to steady herself, and wipes

her eyes clear. "I'm not giving you the satisfaction of one more tear. I can't do this. I can't keep finding room in my heart for you. It's killing me."

I swallow my words because it is jarring to hear I'm killing her, even if I already knew I was. "Sorry." I clear my throat, staving off my misery. "Go. Just go."

"I am. Goodbye, Blake."

The finality is overwhelming. I literally feel her seal up and block me out, a final wall cemented in place that will forever hold me at bay. I open my mouth to apologize, to beg for her to forgive me when I see her eyes harden. I try to think of the words to do it even as she walks away from me, swirling me in strawberries. There is something else there too, something under the current. It freezes my pleas in my throat. It's Chanel.

It's her in Chanel.

"Rachel." I whisper it too softly for her to hear it, but somehow she still does and turns to me with a hand on the doorway. She has no love for me now, no warmth, no compassion. If I told her to go to music school and we could be together again, it wouldn't even matter. "Chanel?"

She puzzles at me, looks over me, into me, and disregards what she finds there. "Yeah, I bought it for you, but figured you didn't need anything from me."

As much as this fire in her is nothing new, it's hard to take right now while my heart struggles to beat. The look in her eyes–the void–is worse than a lifetime ago when she feared me. Now she knows me, really knows me, and she doesn't care. I would have thought that with how brilliant she is, she would catch on to why I did what I did, why I broke up with her. That somehow I would be a hero to her even in light of what I've done.

Fantasies are dangerous that way, they never are the reality.

So as we stare at one another, I can feel my heart trying to beat, but every pump sprays blood into my chest. Rachel's words and looks have torn holes into me I don't think I'll ever recover from.

I don't think I deserve to recover from them.

When she has finally had enough, when she is done looking at what is left of me, she vanishes through the door, leaving the emptiness to echo and consume me.

⁂

And even when my parents give in and let me come back home, I know I don't belong anymore. I suppose belonging isn't the right word. I never really belonged here in this life, but I was able to make my peace with their ambivalent attention. It's different now that I have sullied their good name. They are downright cruel and it makes me very aware of just how wonderful and blessed I was to infiltrate Rachel's family for a little while.

I always knew when I gave up Rachel, that I surrendered more than a foothold in my own love story. I gave up so many other things, too. Things like dinners with people who didn't hate me, and warmth and love in a house that felt more like home and less like a prison. It's the little things, the little differences that stack on one another and make me feel even more alone than I thought was humanly possible.

It's the fact that I have the bent fork. I stare down at it. It's just as shiny as the rest of the silverware around the table. I know my mother has polished it to perfection as she's done with the other place settings. However, even with her great care, I still end up getting the fork with the twisted tines. It's intentional. It's a passive aggressive tactic because she just can't say to my face how much she hates me.

It's her way of saying that I disgust her.

I know she knew about Rachel. She knew that I cried at night for her and I know my mother can tell they are the heavy tears of someone who has been in love. With the pregnancy on top of it, it is too much for her to bear. When she glances to me I can see in her eyes that she doesn't know what to do with me, that the honest beautiful love I shared with Rachel is being vilified in her mind. I can see her twisting the way we held one another–the words of love and adoration we shared–into a spectacle.

It's a spectacle of my own making as well, because immediately after losing Rachel I had to get pregnant. That one action didn't just destroy what Rachel and I had, it destroyed the perception of what we were to everyone else as well. It's another burden I have to bear, just like I shoulder the coldness in my wife's eyes. I have destroyed something so unspeakable, that even silence is too much sound. I have ruined my family, and we were a beautiful family once: two perfect blonde daughters and my mother and father, rulers from their ivory tower.

Before Rachel, before this life, family dinners were symbolic of our unity–one group mind being indoctrinated by my father. He preached from his head-of-the-table pulpit, and I ate his every word as daintily as I ate everything else. I swore to uphold values of chastity and purity, swore to always be a good girl. I promised to keep my image as pristine as possible, to find a rich husband, vote republican, and uphold the conservative laws. I did all of that and in the next breath mocked people without money for clothing and education. Together we sat at the table and laughed about famine, unemployment, and social welfare. We all believed that glory was built on the backs of those who didn't deserve what we did.

In my youth, I truly believed that the path to a good life was littered in the wreckage of everyone else's dreams and opportunities. Now, I can't believe how wrong I was about everything. As I sit here amid the sparkle and glamor, the tingling of my father's Crown Royal and Coke gives cadence to the empty hollowness I feel. I remember the three months of dinners spent with Deborah, Hiram and Rachel. The way our laughter and chatting filled the house. I close my eyes, picturing the smiles, the warmth...and I miss it.

I miss it enough to speak., "School is good."

I don't get an answer. I don't even get a look when I open my eyes. The drag of forks and knifes against china is the response. I stare down at my plate and yearn for the dinnerware of the Kaplan's house and the way we all had a different fork. I never realized how beautiful it was to build a life of patchwork splendor, pieces of lives being brought together. Harmony extracted from randomness. And in their home, I never got the twisted fork. I never got the discontentment, the disenfranchising, the wall breaking coldness that strips me bone-bare through lack of affection.

I might be thirty five, but inside me there is a little girl sitting broken and she needs someone. I *need* someone. If not my wife then my mother or father, I need anyone to tell me it will be okay. "How was your day Dad?" I ask as he wipes the back end of his butter knife on the tablecloth. It leaves a swatch of brown fluid from stirring his drink.

He looks up at me catching my eyes, looks up like he is going to smile. I see it, I feel it. I miss it. Oh God, how I need it.

"Don't you dare talk to me."

It's so startlingly clipped I feel it shoot through my heart, or what's left of it, and it rocks the very foundation of my being. "Okay," I whisper as I stare at my plate. I swallow tightly until I realize I'm not going to win the fight and as the tears of surprise start, I clear my throat. My chair scrapes as I slide it back to get up. "Excuse me." I toss my napkin down and leave them to the bland food. I can feel their eyes on me, boring holes through my spine as I keep my back straight and make my way out of the dining room.

They don't even have the grace or decency to wait until I'm out of earshot to say evil caustic things. I lean against the wall at the base of the stairs and listen as, despite myself, I cry.

"First she's a filthy lesbian, then a whore? She shouldn't be in this house."

It must have taken everything my father had to say those words. I've never heard them in my life, not from his lips.

"We can send her to your Aunt Charlotte's in New Hampshire."

"I don't want anyone else to know about this debauchery."

"It's a little less than a year until her eighteenth birthday. We can look into something then."

I cover my mouth to keep from making a sound.

I never realized how disposable I was, how utterly unloved I had been. To hear those words come from my mother, the person who should love me always, pricks pain when I thought I couldn't feel anything more.

My father offers a heavy sigh as if he was debating it. As if my existence is debatable. "Well, at least we have Francine to make us proud."

"She's doing well. She might be pregnant."

"A grandson would be good."

"Yes, the perfect little boy for our perfect little girl. Not some bastard child with the punk kid down the street."

I slide down the wall when those words suck all the will out of me. I wait. I breathe. I circle my arms around my knees and hold myself tightly. Comforting arms that I pretend are someone else's. "Just one more year," I whisper it to myself as I stare at the front door. I focus on it until my tears fall.

I know what's coming though, my senior year and my final grand faux pas and the darkness of living alone in New York.

❧ ❧ ❧ ❧

And God, when you are afraid of something, it comes so quickly it might as well be on the back of a shaft of light. Is it possible that dread makes time move faster? It certainly feels that way as I race through the swelter of the end of summer on the football field. Coach is yelling at us to run faster. Well, she isn't yelling at me because I'm leading the pack, but she is yelling. Megaphone in hand she is chasing us with a cold uncaring voice.

"You need to slow the fuck down," Malina pants

behind me.

I look back at her, noting the sweat on her face and the pain in her dark eyes. "I have something to prove."

"What, that after being a baby momma you still got the speed? You have proved it, now simmer the hell down."

I break stride, slowing a little. She slides in beside me. Since the night of Nick's party, Malina and I have been closer. It isn't the same as it was, but it's better and more congruent with how I remember our friendship being. I assume the final piece of the puzzle is the last bit of me that hasn't been tarnished.

I stare down as my legs move under me, and sigh.

"I think you're faster than you used to be," Malina remarks.

"I spent all summer running."

"You should have run track this past spring."

I was going to. "Nah, not my thing."

"Stop talking and push it ladies or so help me God, you will lap this field until I'm tired! Blake, don't think for a moment that I can't tell that your hips are wider, your ass is huge, run faster 'cause you could use it!

"Charming." I arch an eyebrow at Malina.

"Yeah, your ass is amazing. I'd hit it if you could figure out what team you play for."

"What did I tell you?" I scowl.

"Not to talk about that thing with you and Coop, but girl seriously, I can't help it 'cause it was just so fucking dumb."

I roll my eyes as I speed up.

"Wait, Blake," Malina whisper yells at me. "I

hate you. Stop. Damn it!"

I pull away easily and leave her choking on my dust.

"Malina, I see Fatty pulling away. You get three more laps if you can't catch her in three seconds."

I laugh as I ramp up and open to full speed. The wind in my hair feels good as I clear half a lap ahead of everyone before Coach gives up and throws her equipment down with a squeal. I keep running. It's my last chance to really enjoy it. I streak past the goal post along the far side of the field and when I look back over the field I see Coach wave me in. Beyond her though, in the stands, I see Rachel. She takes a seat near the top and cracks a book in her lap.

It's odd that she is here just as she was before. With everything I have done to change things between us, the fact that she is here on this day makes me think that maybe my life is salvageable.

I finish my whole circuit before I join the team again. I walk slowly, stretching a little as I gather my breath. I shake out while everyone gets a verbal berating. "Never in my life have I seen such a sad bunch of pathetic losers. I mean, Jesus." She points at me and I arch an eyebrow at her. "Blake pushed another human being out from between her legs and they still work well enough that she can run circles around you, literally."

Well, that was a gross and uncomfortable reference. I shake my head.

"Okay, I really hope you have something better to show me when we go through our routines for the National Championship." She stares at us, measuring each panting girl in turn. "Well, don't just sit there like my time is free. Get up before I start charging you all personally what I get paid by the hour."

"You heard Coach," I drill loudly as they file slowly into a line. "Let's get moving." It puts a little more speed into their step and I look up at Rachel while I have a moment. She isn't looking at me, but I think she was a minute ago. It's uncanny how I can feel it.

We go through a few routines. They're easy. I use them to practice what I have to do wrong in order to break my knee. Every tumble I open a little earlier. The landings are still clean, maybe a slight wobble, but not enough to draw Coach's attention especially since she is angry at one of the newer girls.

When I'm set to do the routine where I end my athletic career, I lose all the resolve I've had all day. My throat chokes tightly around the words, "Pyramid to flips everyone."

A few people look at me confused and I realize they didn't hear me. I go to take a breath, but Malina takes the lead, beating me to the punch. "You heard her, Pyramid to flips! Stop dragging ass!"

"Thanks," I whisper to the Latin fireball beside me.

"Yeah, you know I got you."

I'm glad someone does. I focus on the stands, forcing a smile for show. "One! Two! Three!"

"We are the Titans, the mighty, mighty Titans!"

It's just like it was that night a year and a half ago, the night when Rachel fell in love with me. The memory burns so starkly in my mind that it makes my eyes sting. I move forward and high kick as I clap out the rhythm we all move to. When I move backward and drop, I have no doubt that Malina will clear me this time. There is no kicking anymore.

She is my friend again, because this is the way it had to be.

"Everywhere we go-o, people wanna kno-ow!"

I feel the breeze of her body whip over me and I spring up.

"Who we are!"

I hold out my hand and Lindsey smiles, reaching for me. I take it and she boosts me up. There is no tingle of excitement for me though, not this time. It's just dread.

"So we tell 'em!"

I plant at the top of the pyramid and we all scream in unison.

"We are the Titans, the mighty, mighty, Titans!"

Rachel had smiled at me then. She smiled dazzlingly because she loved me. I had that and I let it go. Stupidly or lovingly, I just let it go. This time she isn't looking at me, but I can see her hands are white knuckling around her book. She knows I'm going to do it, and the fact that she cares is *enough*.

I stare down at the ground and nod. I see the flash of motion out of the corner of my eye as the two girls take off into a run for their hand springs. I know I have to go. It's now or never. I swallow once and glance at Rachel one more time.

Her eyes meet mine and it startles me enough that I whoop in a breath. It reaffirms instantly why I'm doing this. It isn't just so that I fulfill my directive to become the doctor I was going to be. It isn't just so that Malina becomes Captain and gets a scholarship to California. It's for the brown eyed beauty staring at me from the stands. It's so that she can love me because of my imperfections, not in spite of them. Love me better and fuller than I could ever hope to be loved, and not all the cold aching rain in New York will change that. I wouldn't trade that love for a million backwoods runs, the ability to wear high heels for hours, or a full ride scholarship to the moon.

I buckle and drop forward.

I open early and when the bone crunching sound rips through my knee, it steals the air from my lungs. It hurts worse than the first time and it gives me something other than Rachel to cry about. I breathlessly howl in agony. Everything tunnels, and threatens to drop me into unconsciousness because... fuck, it's bad. It's really bad. Oh Christ, I think I broke everything.

"Blake! Oh fuck, Blake!" It's Malina and her hands are on my face and then my head is in her lap. "Oh God, don't move! Don't move!"

Everyone is screaming, but her voice is so close, it's all I hear. It's all I have to hold onto in this moment as my body moves of its own volition and I claw into the grass to escape.

"Don't move! Don't move!" Her hands are like vices on my arms. "Someone call someone! Yes, bring that here and put pressure on her knee!"

I soak in it, in the way she rocks me, and that stone cold bitch just melts. "God, honey, I'm so sorry, just don't move! I'm here! I've got you!"

"Oh God, Blake?"

I know that voice like my own. Between the swarm of my friends, Rachel is the last thing I see before I pass out. She came. I'm at peace with the darkness then as my best friend and my wife guard over me and keep me safe.

Chapter Thirteen

After All
September 8th, 2015

If fear makes time fly, then expectation makes it moves like an arthritic snail.

It's been three years since I saw Rachel last, but it feels like it's been a millennia. And that last time is bright in my memory regardless of how much time has passed. It was at graduation where she stood kitty corner to me. When I looked back to capture the image of her, she stared through me like I had never mattered to her at all. Like I didn't even exist, and in many ways, I don't feel like I do without her.

Literally, the only reason I've been able to get past the vacancy in her last look was by pinning all my hopes on *this* moment. I've waited, I've stayed away so she could grow into the woman she was supposed to. I've worked and studied, I've pushed toward my goals, dumping every shred of myself into school. I've bided my time and dreamed for this day. It's surreal that it's finally come.

Because here I am, exactly where I was in another life. It *feels* the same, I think. Just as I did before, I stand with a cab door in my hand. The misting of rain coming down around me as I feel Broadway Avenue under my heels.

And though my fears this time are different, I'm

still afraid. Because, well, this moment is the most important one in our lives together. It's the *original* moment where I fell in love with her. This is the night that started it all. And standing here in the drizzle, I don't really feel it because my heart is committed to feeling nothing but hope that I haven't wrecked everything between us.

I swallow nervously, taking in the massive glass structure before me. Did I completely ruin everything for us?

I clip the cab door shut and straighten my back despite that question being the thing I'm too afraid to ask. With a rock of dread in my stomach, I crunch over the asphalt and the shards of others broken dreams. I rush across the street, chasing the running rivers of light reflected on the wet ground. My breath plumes into the dazzling city lights swirling around me.

I push my way through bodies that crowd the sidewalk before Alice Tully's Music Hall. I don't know if they are the same people I had butt my shoulder against before, but that doesn't matter. What matters is that I know I'm following watery lights toward an impossible dream that has found a way to *not* shatter on the sidewalk. And just like I did a lifetime ago I stop before the glass doors, staring at the elegant frosted engravings on them.

They have the shimmer of promise that I couldn't see before because I had no way to know that my future laid on the other side.

But now I do and I pray it still does.

With familiar, yet shaking hands, I grab the silver handle and pull open the doors.

A firm hand takes the door from me chivalrously, and I slide inside quickly. "Thank y..." When I turn around, the man is holding the door for his family. I swallow my words, because he won't hear me anyway. I turn back to the entrance. A passing person jostles me, and I glare at her back as she keeps moving. I hate this city. I'll never get used to people treating me like I'm nothing.

I am something though. I'm Blake Fucking Fortier, and saying my name now, should give me the strength to keep moving, but it doesn't and it's not because my knee is sore as hell. It's because all I can do is gape at the enormity of the entrance, the sunken eating areas and raised planters that shoot over my head in cascades of greenery.

I can't even maneuver as I gawk like a child, more people pushing past me with muttered apologies. My heart starts pounding, my hands tingling with nerves.

What the hell am I doing here?

The ticket in my hand bites into my tacky palm and I stare down at it. Medley, it says. Even though, in the most literal of senses the ticket answers my unspoken question–I still don't get it. What the hell am I, doing here?

The answer is actually surprising. I'm lonely. I miss parts of the life I had before. I narrow my eyes at my own thoughts. Not that I miss Rachel Kaplan, but I miss familiarity. And I suppose the social pariah will have to do as the reminder of home.

I follow a guy in a suit on autopilot. My heels click over the hardwood floor and bur into carpeting nicer than I have at my dorm, which actually isn't saying much come to think of it.

I glance down at my ticket for the thousandth time and from the red swatch on it, I can tell I'm at the right door because everyone else's tickets look just like mine. In the crush of bodies, I look up at the glass, the light, the wood and steel, all of it melting together into a drunken mix of amazing.

I don't have better words just...drunk on amazing.

It makes me feel very shitty.

It is amazing that Rachel has this, finally. With the way she threw her talent in my face, in everyone's face, I was painfully aware of how gifted she was. And to be fair, she deserves this dream of hers for all the work that she put in to it. I'll never admit it out loud, but all of us in high school put together wouldn't have been able to compete with her talent. But, God, did she have to get everything she wanted? Why did life have to be so unfair to everyone else?

"Hello, miss," the usher holds out his hand and when I give him my ticket he glances at it quickly. "You're in row ten, seat H, it's to the left of this aisle."

"Thanks."

He slips a program in my hand as I pass him and I focus on finding my spot before I trip and fall. I don't know why my knees are shaking, but they are. Honestly, I'm crazy for coming here. I never would have imagined I would show up at a concert hall to watch Rachel Kaplan perform. Not willingly anyway, with how arrogant she always was.

I must be so fucking broken, because immediately after thinking that I'm wondering how I'm supposed to say hello to her if all I can do is lumber around like a moron? The thought breaks my stride and I slow. There is apparently a guy riding my ass, because he almost falls over me. I give him a look as he shuffles past.

Do I want to say hello to her?

I probe my feelings, and I'm surprised that I do. I want to at least congratulate her, it wouldn't be right if I didn't. I'm really fucking lonely, clearly, because I find the idea of talking to someone I used to know kind of comforting. I haven't seen my friends in a long time. It makes me miss Malina and Lindsey enough to twist my emotions.

I will have to call them soon.

I'm so caught up in my thoughts that I go one row too far and when the guy looks up at me expectantly from his end seat, I take a large comedic step backward. He laughs as he looks over his shoulder at me. "You can sit in this row if you want. My date ditched me so I've got an extra seat," he offers.

I roll my eyes at his really weak pass. "Yeah, I don't think so. I'm good." But I'm not good. I feel like I can't get enough air in my lungs and I'm shaking like a leaf. He says something else to me, but I don't hear his words because I'm too preoccupied with the same question I've asked myself all night.

What the hell am I doing here?

It was fate, that's why I was there.

Fate that I was about to fall in love for the first time in my life.

And with that lifetime of love behind me, I don't miss my row this time. I take my seat slowly, even though my hands rattle with the same nervous expectation.

"Hey there, I'm Tom." It's the young man in front of me. "Did you want to sit in this row? My date ditched me so I've got an extra seat."

I shift my coat in my arms a smile racing over my face. "I'm good, thanks Tom."

He nods and then clears his throat. "Do I get your name? Or are you gonna be that girl that I always wonder about?"

"Blake." I shake his hand awkwardly over the back of the seat. "Life's too short to wonder about things."

"Agreed. It's nice to meet you Blake." He smirks at me. "So, what are you doing here?"

I fix my eyes on the dark stage, tracing it for a moment. "I'm here to reclaim what I've lost."

Tom laughs lightly.

Now that blonde dude isn't trying to talk to me, I busy myself with the stage, how close it feels even from thirty feet away. It is hued in blue from sunken lights above my head. It makes it feel warm and inviting, like anyone could step up on it and perform. I know they can't, I know it is reserved only for gifted talented people, but yeah...it looks nice.

I run my hands over the plush seat beneath me. I really wish I had a pillow made of this material. The distraction only lasts for a few minutes, and then I go back to questioning my sanity. I ask myself the same question for the four-millionth time as people file into the seats around me. It makes me even more nervous, smelling and seeing all these stuffy over-the-top opulent outfits. I stare at the hem of my plain red dress and slide down in my seat, feeling a bit out classed.

The people sitting near me remind me of my parents. They have the same clothing and behavior, the way they carry themselves like they are entitled to everything in the world. I shift uncomfortably in my seat as more people stroll in. That's when my back starts itching where I think I left the little plastic thingy from the price tag on the dress. I glance around and reach for it, but the eyes of some guy across the aisle fix on my motions and I freeze, staring him down with an arch in my brow until he turns away.

This sucks.

I'm tired and I'm surrounded by asshats who pay too much attention to me. Tonight couldn't be worse if I tried, though in a way I did by coming here. I fiddle with my earring as I stare at the back of blonde dude's head, Tim or Tom...or something. I shake my vacant thoughts away.

I open the small folded program in my hand. I can see there are other names in it, other pictures, but my eyes move straight to Rachel's. There is a small biography printed beneath the image of her, and I can't help but snicker thinking it must have taken every ounce of her restraint to keep a biography of herself to five lines. The smile fades just as quickly as it came. I don't mean the frown that follows. At least, I don't think I do. I still feel a little bit of jealousy. I'm not gonna lie. When I used to pick on her, I always knew she would make it here. There isn't another person in the world that has as many gifts.

It's funny, but I might not have resented her had she not been as tone deaf in her arrogance as she was pitch perfect in her voice. It was infuriating, because she never understood that not everyone was destined for greatness like her. I both appreciated and hated her for that. She was so naive. It's what kept me from being her friend. No, that's a lie. I blow out a breath. I wasn't her friend because her vision of me was so much better than I could ever be. I would never be the person she believed I would become, and I just couldn't take any more failure in my life.

When the realization hits me, I twist my purse in my hands uncomfortably.

I really need to grow the fuck up and get over it. I'm twenty now for Christ sake, it's time to own my failings. It's time to not be so shitty, let those little things go, and stop being so jealous. So what if she got her dream and an article in the paper that said she was Juilliard's newest rising star and I didn't get any of that? What does it really matter now?

It's really stupid that I've felt this way for so long, but whatever. I'm here now and nothing is gonna change that. I resign myself to my spot, staring at the dark stage before me. I look down at the leaflet in my lap again. The almost smirk that beams from the page before me was the same one that I saw earlier today. It was right there in the newspaper stand. I don't know how I knew it was her smirk, but I did. I suppose there are just some things so arrogant they never change, even if they are correct in their arrogance. I trace the picture before me with a soft finger, and when the small smile threatens my lips, I pull my hand back quickly.

The lights dim and the audience quiets, the last of their footfalls echoing away as I adjust in my seat to better see the stage. I don't know why I get them, but I feel butterflies. The expectation builds exponentially as I see the curtain flutter for a moment, then it rises.

And when it does I see Rachel standing on the stage.

At least I think it's her, it's very dark and all I can really see is an outline. I swallow hard at the highlight of her arm and hip in the faint light from somewhere backstage. I can't pull my eyes from it and I trace that space over and over. When the lights finally come on, I'm expecting to see the girl I used to know. I'm convinced that she will look out over the audience and smile that huge smug grin that proved without a doubt that she was better than everyone in the room. I'm sure that she will just give me another reason to validate why I knew she was a bitch once upon a time.

I'm so convinced of it, that when the image coalesces into color and hue, I forget who she is, who it is I was expecting, who it was I had come to see. I almost don't recognize her, well, I mean, I do. I recognize Rachel, because it's Rachel Kaplan. However, the similarity ends there. It is her, but isn't her at the same time. The woman that stands on the stage, soaking in the light, is just so different. Instead of wild curled hair, hers is ironed flat and it pours like a ribbon of ink highlighted in gold. Her smile is so soft, so grown up. I sink in my seat under the enormity of just how much better she is than me.

There is something in her face I can't identify, some different thing that changes her whole appearance. And when the music strums through the darkened concert hall, and she tilts her head into the light, like it's caressing her, I forget more than who she is. I forget who it is I am, too. All I want is to know what thought passed through her mind in that moment because she looks so unfairly beautiful and at peace.

When my heart starts racing I clasp my hand to my chest. In my mind's eye, superimposed on the image of Rachel as an angel, I remember what I did to her years ago. I remember all the times she went to speak to me and I dismissed her. The looks and words that I used to carve into her.

And though I don't deserve it, for an instant I pray to a God that has deserted me for a long time. I pray that she can forgive me somehow, because I don't know why–but I don't think I can't not have her in my life. I touch my cheek and pull back my fingers. In the blurry mess of my vision I can see wetness. That's when I realize I'm crying, tears stripped from the very center of me. Emotion I don't think I've ever felt myself give before.

I'm staring at that space between her hip and the arch of her ribcage, the place where I would lean my head into and fall asleep when we watched a movie. It is the spot where I used to kiss and she would giggle ridiculously and in another life was reserved exclusively for my embrace.

The arms that would hold me and comfort me, hang limply by her side.

The spotlight pings through like a halo of dripping heaven in the next instant and my throat twists painfully. My fragile emotions just can't take how much it means to me to see her. Time loses its elasticity and breaks completely when I hyper focus on her with tears already starting.

I'll never run out of love for her.

Ever.

Rachel materializes from the darkness, like the dream I never had the right to envision. She's clad in a cream gown that drips off her shoulders, and mingles with the wave of darkness from her hair. Her warmly toned Mediterranean skin, just runs into everything as highlights and shadows draw beautiful lines all the way down her body.

It forces my lungs to seize until I think I wheeze and then my heart stops beating because I can feel it coming.

This moment, as she turns her face into the music and the light.

I asked her once, what she was thinking at this moment.

She told me it was love.

And I never told her I felt love, too, for the first

time in my life.

Seeing her vulnerability changed everything for me back then. This was the moment where I fell in love with her. Where I became the person who wasn't satisfied until I knew what she was thinking and felt. I wanted to be someone more than an adoring fan. I wanted to keep her safe, wanted to see behind the veil of perfection that hovered in her smile and eyes. I wanted to know her so completely, that she would forever be the pinnacle of poise on this stage, because I knew I could carry whatever damage and demons she could give me.

When the music starts, I lower my face into my hands and silently cry. Surrounded by an audience of people who don't know what a blessing they have in being here, I weep over the fragility of this perfect being and the perfect voice that follows a moment later. I hear the first note out of her lips, shot straight from heaven to my heart. It erupts in a perfect pitch that rings with familiarity, and yet more depth and breadth than I even remembered. It is the sound of success, of future fame and Tony awards spilling light. It is the sound of every tear I ever cried in losing her, and the affirmation that this is where her soul was supposed to be.

It is the voice that will draw me from bed to a chilly sound studio in our basement and will serenade me in every kitchen while making dinner.

I look up at her then as she moves across the stage. I realize, just as I had before, she is so much more than the rising star that the paper claimed, she has risen, and she shines more brightly than all the stars in the night. She might as well be a galaxy across heaven dimming everything in the universe.

But all too soon she is done and gone.

When her song ends, it leaves me breathless and rattled beyond anything I could have possibly imagined. For all my proclamations of constancy and coolness, my palms are tacky, my cheeks are stained. I shift in my seat and grab the arm rests to keep from chasing her. I watch as she backs into the darkness and I hang on where she was, leaning forward in my seat to glimpse just a moment more.

I let go a shaken breath as the lights turn color and Rachel vanishes in a thunderous applause. I can't tear my eyes away from the stage, can't even wipe my face. When I realize how terrible I must look, I glance around and then wipe at the dampness on my cheeks.

I don't pay attention to a single other singer that comes after. They are all boring, flat, and emotionless. They are all lacking in light compared to the most singular voice in the world.

Her voice. My God, her voice.

Her.

My Rachel.

I think that and it's absolutely primal, the bite of passion that whips me with its ferocity in that moment. It isn't in the sexual sense, but the desire to be near her. She is so riveting and soul shatteringly ethereal that it captures every part of my reality. And I need her. I need our futures to begin.

I can't wait another moment.

But I have to and by the time the performances are done, I can move, albeit on shaken knees. I stand, remembering where I was when she looked out over the crowd and saw me. I was right at the end of this row, just to my right. I look at it. I stare at the swatch of carpeting that is supposed to hold me until she commands me forward.

I gather my coat, slinging it over my arm. I walk there. I stand facing the stage and smile. I can hear my heart thundering in my chest. I don't hear anything else, just my heart and the whoosh of blood that follows it. My hands shake, sweat. I close my eyes, trying to focus, trying to keep myself from passing out with how rapid my breathing is.

I know in a matter of seconds everything in my life is going to change. Everything I've done, everything I've been, has led to this instant. So, I'm rooted in place when she comes back on stage. She is so soft and airy, so fluid she can't be real. Rachel has changed her clothing just as she had before, wearing sandals and jeans and a snug fitting top that just about screams at me to stare at it. So I do, I stare at her until I feel like my brain might explode with the image of it. I'm leering. I know I am and I just hope that no one is looking at me right now. I physically force myself to take a step forward, but even as I do time once again betrays me.

I can literally see Rachel's eyes drift, the way her eyelids open a little wider as she looks up. I'm so focused I can even see the pupils of her eyes constrict in the light from the stage. When her focus solidifies, it's surreal how her eyes are right on me. It's like she knew I was here the whole time, like we are connected. I see the flicker of recognition, it curves over her face, paints her in surprise.

Blake?

I watch my name form because I can't hear it. She doesn't move, doesn't breathe.

I give her a wry smile because it's been so long. So long since she whispered my name in the breathless way she just did.

"Rachel."

Her name on my lips somehow changes something between us. I watch her eyes light, watch that sparkle come over her and fill her. It's so beautiful to watch her shine from the inside out. Her honest smile hangs on her lips and it's one I will gladly lay my life down to protect forever, one that flickers hope into my heart. When she starts for the edge of the stage, I can't feel my coat in my arms, I can't feel anything. I jog forward unencumbered because seeing that smile on her face as she moves to the stairs mutes everything. I don't feel the stiffness in my knee, I don't feel the fact that I'm running in heels. All I can feel is her.

And I do feel her, deep down in places I won't ever be able to understand. In places that only she can touch, I feel her like a whisper because she is mine.

And I'm hers. Always.

When she hits the ground level, I let the coat fall to the seats beside me.

"Blake?"

Hearing my voice on her lips again rips me to pieces and I swallow hard to keep from falling to my knees at her feet and grabbing her. When we come to a stop near one another she doesn't hug me, not like she did before. I'm instantly aware of how she shifts before me, her eyes lilting on me. She's scared.

"You," my voice is shaking, "you were magnificent. I just didn't believe it was possible, but you are even better than I remember."

Rachel blushes lightly, running a nervous hand through her hair. It is the exact same motion she had in my office the morning I lost her. Arranging herself to be worthy of the compliment. "Thank you."

"You're welcome. You deserve all the praise they are giving you as Juilliard's newest star."

"You read that article?"

I smile. "Of course."

She winds up with excitement then, I laugh and extend my arms. Rachel swallows a little and moves in closer. Her arms encircle me. The hug is soft and delicate as she edges up on her toes. I can feel her warmth against me and I close my eyes, memorizing it.

"I can't believe you're here." She says it into my shoulder and I pull her tighter, pressing myself flush with her body.

"I wouldn't have missed this for the world."

We fit together in silence, heads pressed against one another. I breathe her in, tasting the scent of her in every facet of my being. When I feel her take a deeper breath, I ease the grip on her back and let her go. She pulls back with a smile, but slowly I see it fade.

"So, how are you?"

I shrug, nonchalantly. "Working too hard. You know. The usual."

"Yeah, you feel a little thin. You still skipping breakfast?"

It burns through me, the memories we have. The ones we share and the ones we don't. "I am. I've missed your pancakes."

I mean it as a joke, but she doesn't laugh. She glances away. "The secret ingredient is an eighth of a teaspoon of vanilla or almond extract. Now you can make them anytime you want."

Not exactly the response I was hoping for. "Oh, okay, thank you."

I don't know what to do when I feel the moment start to slip and slide away from me. This one moment had always been the most important to me. This was the night that would lead to her becoming my wife.

It is supposed to be markedly different from how it is becoming. We were supposed to go out to coffee. We were supposed to giggle and laugh together until dawn broke through the blinds of the diner. However, I realize, it's not to be as she shifts uncomfortably and takes a step back. Her eyes dart over my shoulder to someone else and she smiles at them. She smiles her warm heartfelt smile at someone else, not me.

"Rachel." I bring her gaze back. "I'm going to NYU, through their med school."

She nods a little, fixing a fake smile on her lips. I know it right away. "I'm happy. I'm glad you got to go where you wanted to."

I keep going even as the panic flares through every nerve in my body. "Well, I mention it because I'm living near here and I was hoping we could catch up sometime."

"Oh." She forces the politest curve of her lips I've ever seen. "I would like that." It's the same tone, same words she has used to rebuff would-be suitors when we were dating. Phone numbers she took to avoid confrontation and trashed at the first opportunity. I know exactly what she is going to ask, probably before she knows. "What is your number, Blake?"

I shudder a breath when I realize I have to say something...*anything* to salvage this moment. I say the first thing that comes to mind. "You said you wanted to know why I broke up with you. It's so that you could have this life."

When I say it, I know I've made a horrible

mistake. Her expression literally warps as her gaze razors to mine with an icy, bone deep pain.

"What?"

I can't believe I said it. I just can't believe it.

She swallows brokenly, crossing her arms over her chest. Her voice is very hushed. "You had no right to take that choice from me."

"You wouldn't listen to me."

"It was still *my* choice."

"I love you too much to let you throw away your life for me."

She presses her lips into a line.

"Loved."

If I never get the chance to talk to her again, then why should I hold back? I shake my head, steeling myself. "There is no past tense to it."

It rattles her when the words click. I can see the subtle shift. It makes her eyes glisten, her lips tighten, her shoulders shift forward under the weight of that knowledge. When her gaze lifts to mine finally, she is so twisted and conflicted I'm scared of what she is going to say.

"You don't break someone's heart if you love them."

"Don't you?"

"No. Goodbye, Blake."

Oh my God. She's leaving. I see the finality in her eyes, the wall she never had for me before, proud, strong, and holding me at bay now.

She turns away, and the words scramble from my throat at the same time as my hands go into my purse. "Rachel, wait."

I fish blindly in the pockets, pulling free the letter she wrote the night I gave birth to Beth. It is a note I have carried every day since, and has broken my heart over and over again. Her eyes are on my hands when I pull it free and hand it to her. I don't have to see the writing to know what it says.

Blake,
I heard you were gonna give Beth up for adoption. I just want you to know I'm really proud of you for doing the right thing. It means a lot that you're willing to do good things when it's important.
I wasn't, important to you, I mean. So I think it's best we just say goodbye right now. I know we'll be at school and stuff, but I think it's better this way if we don't talk. If we just pretend that nothing happened between us. Before we do that though, I need to clear the air about something. Please don't feel bad about what happened. You didn't break my heart or hurt me. It didn't mean anything to me either. It was fun, just like you said. So I don't want you to hang onto this, I want you to move on. I am, and it's gonna be okay.
Best wishes to you in the future,
Rachel K.

She reads it three times before she looks at me. "You kept it?"

"Of course I did."

"Why?"

"As a reminder that we are both guilty of hurting ourselves and the people we love, to save them from themselves. Isn't that what people who love each other do?"

She flinches like I hit her and then her gaze drops to the paper. She flips it over, fingers pressing the wrinkled edges flat. "Do you have a pen?"

I blink and stare down at my purse. It takes me a minute but eventually I hand one over to her. I watch her lean to the stage, scribbling on the back of the note with a sure hand. She doesn't look at me when she hands the pen and the paper back to me. So I look at her–stare at her like it will be the last time–because I'm afraid it will be.

And everything I know about her, all the love I have for her, will just cease to be.

She whispers a goodbye as she moves past me in true New Yorker fashion, on to the next fan, the next congratulations for a job well done. I feel vacant and empty as I stare after her. That's when I look down at the paper in my hands. And cry.

Yes, that's exactly what they do.
– Rachel
917-555-2856

Chapter Fourteen

The Climb
October 17th 2015

I'm putting stitches into the hand of a four year old boy when my phone chimes against my thigh. It probably isn't the best timing in the world, because the child is in a rather compromising position, but I literally forget everything I'm doing. It's probably only a second in reality, but for me it feels like an eternity, because there is only one person who would be texting me to the chime that I heard.

It chimes again, and I look up in chagrin. "I'm sorry." I direct my gaze to the mother staring at my coat. "I would turn it off, but I'd have to re-glove and I don't want your son to wait."

I try to make the best of it even as another message comes barreling through, because suddenly my heart is *that* much lighter. "Hey, Bailey." I direct my attention to the young boy staring at me. "How are you doing kiddo?" He is drowsy from sedatives, but he's alert enough to focus on me and smile. "I'm almost done here, I promise."

"Okay, it feels funny." He shakes his free hand.

I give him a bright smile, looping the needle. "It kinda tickles, doesn't it?" He nods as I tug another stitch into place. "You're very brave. Your mother told me all about how you saved Ruby."

"I love Ruby. The bad men were going to get her."

In truth, it was his toy soldiers that were the aggressors, but who am I to judge what limits of pretending people will go to in the name of love.

"Can you think of anyone who loves you as much as you love Ruby? Who wouldn't want to see you hurt?"

He looks over at his parents with what could possibly be the most confident expression I've ever seen. It isn't that look which catches and hooks my emotions, jangling my heart, while my phone lingers with a text from my wife. It's the look he is reciprocated with, the tender, honest, warm look in his mother's eyes.

I clear my throat, shaking the moment away.

"That's right, they do." I smile emotionally and tug the final stitch into place. "Now promise me," I say holding up three fingers as he mimes me with his uninjured hand, "no more G.I. Joes breaking through windows to save your dog." He nods and I laugh lightly.

"Thank you, Doctor Fortier."

I stand quickly, snapping my gloves off so I can shake the parent's hands.

Bailey's mother eyes my pocket where my phone must be illuminated through the light coat.

"It's my pleasure. We will get you released within the next thirty minutes or so. A nurse will be in to bandage his hand and give you the release papers and prescriptions." I wave goodbye and turn, letting the utter elation at having Rachel *actually* text me carry me through the curtain and into the break room down the hall. I'm grateful it's empty because I shut the door and lean against it as I pull my phone free. My breath is shaking as I stare down at the face.

Are you a resident at Saint James?

Please text me back, even though I don't deserve it.

Are you there?

I read them over and over as my throat chokes tight and I text back the answer, swimming in the euphoria of hearing from her. It sucks away the tiredness and ache in my bones from the forty hour shift. Drifting on my feet, I don't see the bland white walls around me. I only see her as the inexplicable fate we share wraps me in warmth.

I thought I had lost it...

It's been a day, one small, yet dauntingly long day since I saw Rachel. I think I've spent more of that day staring at my phone than I've spent doing anything else. Right now, the sliver of electronics is on my desk, and I pass it every thirty seconds or so, staring right at it until it's out of view.

When my fingers inch toward it, I pull away. How crazy would it be to call? I convince myself that it wouldn't be crazy at all, and as soon as I do it–the instant that I have worked up the nerve to call her–my fingers betray the confidence in my spine. It takes the better part of the day to actually get the phone in my hand and then once I've gone that far, I realize I might as well call.

It would be crazy not to.

I almost don't believe the line is trilling in my ear when I finally do it because I've imagined it so many times.

"Hello?"

Hearing her is like a sucker punch. It knocks the wind out of me.

"Hey."

"Who is this?"

I clear my throat. "It's me, Blake."

"Oh, hello." A beat passes. "How are you?"

"Good, you?"

"I'm well, thanks."

"Good."

Silence stretches like a hangman's noose around my neck. "So, did I tell you that your performance was amazing? I'm not sure if I did with how jumbled I was."

"Yes, you did."

"Great, I'm glad I told you."

"Yes, thank you."

Seriously, this is what it sounds like after we've been in a fight, one word answers or short phrases, a noncommittal commentary on nothing and no one. It's terrible and awkward.

"Did you want to go out?" I say it before I really have the chance to think about it and talk myself out of doing it. I'm both horrified and relieved that my mouth does what it wants to, regardless of my brain. Sometimes my brain thinks too much.

"Um, sure."

I worm my toes in the carpet staring blankly at the floor of my room. "Is there anywhere you would like to go?"

"Um, I don't know."

"We could always go to that coffee shop near Columbus Circle and sit by the golden globe." Please tell me it's a favorite place of hers still.

"Oh, yes. We could go there, but..."

"But?"

She sighs heavily. "I don't know, Blake."

I can hear it in her voice, the fear. I roll my eyes

up to the ceiling, staring at the bright swatch of sunlight that cuts through the blinds. Of course, she would be afraid. Who wouldn't be? I blow out a breath, knowing what I'm damning myself to. "Well, why don't you pick a place and call me when you've made a decision either way."

I can practically hear her decompress over the line. "That sounds good. I'll talk to you later, Blake."

To be honest, when I said those words, I was expecting a day maybe two at the most. I wasn't expecting a week to pass. It reminded me of how things were in high school after I kissed her, how I went through the motions, hanging on her whim and the hope that she would forgive me for my transgressions. The motions that filled my time then were going to school, to practice, and long runs through beautiful fields, but I don't have those anymore. My life now is a patchwork of swirling through curtains at Saint James, greeting patients, and assessing illness, with a long subway ride back to my dorm as reward.

But I do it. Armed with my stethoscope, a BP cuff, and a plethora of knowledge, I triage my little ass off in hope that I'll stop perseverating on Rachel. It rarely works. The nurses give me a hard time for being so regimented in my work, but it's okay, because I know where my future lies and I'm going to do everything I can to get to that place. At least, that is what I tell myself when I wear my brave face at work.

At home, it's different. Even though my sleep is precious, I lie awake countless nights in my tiny dorm room and wonder what path I'm on. I fear that my tree in the proverbial forest has grown so far away from Rachel's that it will never become entangled again. Other times, I think that maybe mine is the only tree still standing at all.

It's a week more before I talk to Rachel again. I call her because I can't take the waiting any longer.

I ask if she wants to hang out. And to my surprise she says yes.

⁂

I feel the hammer of the bass drum in my chest before I even get in the doors of the bar. The music is so loud I can't even hear myself think, which effectively takes talking with Rachel off the table. This certainly isn't the coffee date Rachel and I had the first time around.

Dragging my eyes from the signage outside, and the crowding of people on either side if the door, I pull out my phone. I've gotta be in the wrong place, right? This doesn't seem like a Rachel type of establishment. That thought is reaffirmed when I hear what sounds like a fight just inside the doors. I pull up Rachel's text, checking once more that I'm in the right place.

Yes, it's the address she texted to me.

Yuck.

It's been a really long time since I've been to a bar like this. In college I avoided places where leering eyes and brazen hands roamed, it was the last thing I wanted to deal with. Later in life, well...this is not the type of place that serves a good Cabernet, which is enough of a deterrent to me.

I direct a veiled glance at a clearly overdoing-it-fashionista being mauled by her date not six feet from me. This place certainly has a handsie type vibe which unsettles me 'cause I'm out of practice with the advances I remember from college guys.

And it's cosmic because as I think that, I feel the

brush of someone's hand on my ass.

"Excuse you?" I say defensively, turning, but the threat in my words dies in my throat when I see Rachel. She smiles at me smoothly.

"I'd know that butt anywhere." She laughs. "What are you doing out here?"

Did she just touch my butt?

I'm too caught up in that thought to formulate an actual response. "I just...um."

"Come on, drinks are waiting." She passes me with a definite swish in her walk. Looking back over her shoulder she flashes her ID to the bouncer. "You coming?"

Oh crap. I don't have a fake ID. I can't believe I forgot to get one, seeing as it's a staple of college life until you turn twenty-one. I had one once, but I haven't needed it in years, so it completely slipped my mind. I give her a look, trying to tell her as much without saying a word. I don't know if our secret language works anymore seeing as the woman that laughs lightly at my expression isn't the Rachel I remember. I certainly don't know what to think when she whispers something to the tattooed mountain of a man doubling as a bouncer. She kisses him on the cheek and points back at me. I can't hear her words, but he gives her a smile and a nod, then regards me silently.

When he slides aside and lets Rachel pass, I realize I have to follow her. And I do until the man blocks the door.

"ID?"

I blink at him. "What?"

"I need to see your ID."

I stare down at my purse. "Okay."

I fish it out with shaky hands. Maybe if I act like

nothing is wrong he won't notice.

"*Nice night tonight.*" *I make small talk and he snorts his reply. When he takes it from me, I stare inside the building. Rachel has slid up to a bar table and I watch as she hugs a few people before the bouncer beside me clears his throat.*

"*Blake, is it?*"

I nod lightly.

"*You aren't twenty-one.*"

I bite my lip to keep from telling him that I'm actually forty if you count all the years I've lived. "So? I don't think the police are gonna show up to raid this place if they haven't already."

"*Sorry, can't let you in.*"

I arch my brow at him. "Really? Half the people in there aren't twenty-one."

He looks back over his shoulder to where Rachel is staring at us. Her eyes meet mine, then his, and she beams a smile before turning away.

"*Yes, really.*"

I sigh. "Can I make it worth your while?"

He gives me a very cold look, sizing me up. "Doubt it."

And even though I didn't mean it that way, it's a little surprising to my ego. "Money," I correct, "I'm sure you can figure out a cover charge appropriate enough."

He debates it. I can see his dark eyes churning. "Fifty?"

"*Oh come on, really?*"

He crosses his arms. "Yeah, really, unless you got somewhere else you gotta be, doctor."

When he says that, it all comes together. My eyes go to Rachel and she isn't looking at me. She told him to screw with me. She is talking to a friend of hers clearly, with how they are leaned toward one another. When the girl's eyes shoot to me at the door, I realize Rachel is talking about me, but by the look on the girl's face it isn't nice.

"The girl I came with told you that didn't she?"

"Rachel?"

Seriously, how much does she come here? I direct my gaze from the icy glare I'm getting.

"No, you just have the look."

I don't know what look he is talking about, since I'm wearing pretty much the same thing as everyone else. Except I don't look like a whore. "What do you mean?"

"Snotty, little rich girl look, who I'm sure could afford to part with fifty bucks."

I feel my temper rise. I've never been extorted before, and I must say it's really not fun. I take a breath to keep from calling him half the things I think about. Instead, I decide it might be better to use my brains than the bitch instinct I feel vying to come loose. "Fifty bucks?"

"Sure." He brightens holding out his hand.

I pull out my phone and twist it in my hand. "Tell you what, how about I don't call the police and file a report, and in exchange I'm going to walk through this door and you aren't gonna stop me?"

He laughs in my face, before he waves me off. "You can get the fuck out of here now."

I scoff. "What are you going to do? Beat up on a girl?"

Okay. So I'm clearly out of practice at this, because then he gets downright pissed.

"I didn't want to have to get loud! But now I will! If you don't get off this property in ten seconds, I'm *calling the police!"*

When he takes a step toward me, I move back quickly, mortified at his behavior. I mask it as best as I can, smoothing my hair down, even though I feel my cheeks getting red. "Fine."

Rachel meets my gaze then, right before I turn from the door, and she laughs.

I swear I hear her satisfied voice call a very sing-song version of 'Goodbye, Blake' before I'm out of earshot. But her text is what haunts me, and that I have no ability to pretend I didn't hear right.

Better luck next time.

One thing I forgot is that as forgiving as Rachel can be, she can be equally as unforgiving if she chooses. And cunning. I had it coming, I know I did. After four years of stewing, I can only imagine what type of anger she must have been harboring. It doesn't make it any easier to deal with though.

I try to call her after that, not to yell, but to apologize. She might have been downright evil that night, but I know she isn't, not really. And apologies should be made if I can make someone so truly good hearted act that cold. So another call shoots through satellites from my phone to hers, brought forth by brazenly stupid fingers, and goes unanswered. After that, I drown in her apathy until I get the point she is driving home.

I should leave her alone.

And while my romantic life, or lack thereof, comes apart at the seams, I focus on my job because it is all I have left. It doesn't take long for my natural aptitude to be discovered and I'm 'promoted' to the ER rotation. I'm not flattered or proud because it's just code for working longer hours for the same pay. It also means I have the pleasure of following pompous doctors from one room to the other and being forced to listen to their evaluations. I take notes for them, interjecting my own words and my own understanding of pathology to make sure the patients get the most accurate treatment.

It saves me from killing someone while I listen to hours of talk about golfing and fantasy football. It saves them from killing someone, too.

And all the while, my phone hangs empty and lifeless, taunting me with its silence. It kills me little by little and stabs me every time I open my menu to the vacancy of her indifference.

And regardless of how painful this past month has been it makes me laugh now, now that her texts hang in the message screen of my phone. I'm so fixated on her message, I literally jump when someone knocks on the glass panel behind me.

"Blake?"

I turn quickly to Ryan's face, pocketing my phone in surprise. "Yeah?"

He presses open the door quickly. "There is this patient in room thirty-two. It's a funny one." He wags his brow at me as he takes up the space beside me heavily. We lean into one another. "Wanna look at it? Or is your shift over?" He wags the file at me.

When he says it, I yawn. "No, I've got to go home. I have class in the morning." I squeeze my phone in my pocket on reflex, but eventually my curiosity gets the better of me. "Give me the abridged version?"

He looks at the paperwork in his hands. "Outwardly healthy female, presenting with chest pain, no coughing, no wheeze. When we did a chest X-Ray, though, we found seriously gnarly pneumonia." He pulls free an image and hands it to me. "I mean check out the occlusion on that image, and she wasn't even coughing."

I do, tilting it into the light and then I realize…I know these lungs. The instant the memory clicks, my phone buzzes again and I pull it free in what feels like slow motion.

I'm here.

"Room thirty-two?"

"Yeah."

I grab the chart from Ryan's hands, and he yelps a little as I cut away from him. When I get to the door of room thirty-two, I push the curtain aside without so much as a courtesy knock.

Rachel's eyes widen and the nebulizer in her mouth drops to her lap with a dull thud. "Blake?"

"Rachel? What are you doing here?"

She puts a hand to her chest. "I don't feel very well."

"No, I'm sure. You have pneumonia."

"Oh."

I point at the Albuterol medication misting around where her hospital gown and the blankets are mingling. "That should be in your mouth so you can breathe it in."

She looks down at the plastic apparatus then replaces the mouthpiece. The gurgling sound of the pressurized oxygen and liquid fills the room around us. I close the curtain and flip open her chart, trying to read it even though I can see her in my peripheral vision.

"What are you doing?" she asks.

"Reading your chart."

"What does it say?'

"That you probably need to stay overnight."

She frowns. "I'm really sick, huh?"

I arch my eyebrow at the papers before me. "Yes, well...you will be fine once you cough everything up." I give her a look. "Does your mouth feel dry?'

She pulls the nebulizer out of her mouth again. "This thing is misting in it, so I'm not sure."

"You need fluids."

She makes an agreeing sound around the mouthpiece.

"We should get you an IV." I stare at the empty hooks beside her bed and it makes me mad. She should have one already. This is another example of why I opened my own practice, because generally medical people suck, and I just couldn't take seeing incompetence anymore. "I'll be right back."

"Where are you going?"

"To get an IV."

She goes to say something, but I give her a look. "It's my job, keep that in your mouth and take deep breaths."

When I return she is fiddling with the blankets, trying to tuck them under her feet. I set the IV start kit on the tray beside the bed and tuck the edges around her feet quickly. "Better?"

She nods.

I step up to the left side of the bed, and when I do, the shock has worn off enough for me to remember the last time I saw her in the hospital she was dead. I literally flinch at the flash of the memory. My voice is tight when I can finally speak. "Which arm do you get blood drawn from?"

I don't know why I ask. I already know. My brain won't work though because she is tucked into the hospital bed and her hair is wild from leaning back against the pillow, and she looks so fragile.

She points to her right one.

"I'm sorry Rachel," I say softly, even though the inflection I want to put into them would be deafening. I say it to the young woman before me, and I mean it to her ghost as well.

I tear open the kit and reach for the glove box on the wall. As I'm slipping them on, I glance at Rachel's wary expression. "I've been through phlebotomy, so don't worry, I can do IVs in my sleep."

She pulls the plastic from her lips. "I'm more worried you'll stick me in revenge."

I arch my brow at her words as I take her forearm in my hands and position it. "This is going to pinch a little." I tie the tourniquet tightly, tight enough that she winces. "I'm sorry, that is going to be the worst part, I promise." One alcohol swab later, I can see her vein, barely, and I press on it lightly to make sure it bounces back. "You have deep veins."

Rachel nods.

I smile. "Bet you're tired of people sticking you a million times."

"It's pretty hellish actually."

"In your mouth."

I hear the gurgling again and in one very quick motion, I apply traction to her skin just below where I'm gonna stick her, and tap the vein above my fingers. I don't have to look up to see her relief. I feel it in the muscles of her arm and the way her whole body unwinds. I take it as a silent message of thanks.

"Blake?"

I glance up. "Yeah?"

"I'm sorry."

My hands move automatically as I apply the

sealant tape and guard. "It's okay." I tape the rest of the IV into place. "I owe you an apology, too."

Rachel shakes her head. "I don't think I can talk about any of that yet."

She has that tone, when I know she is talking through a clenched jaw because the words are cutting her on their way out. When I look up at her, her eyes are rimmed in tears. She looks away, and I frown. "Hey, we don't have to talk at all."

I move away prepping the IV line and once I have it connected, I hang the bag beside her bed. Those dark eyes are on my motions and I look down at her with a light smile. It's hard, but I figure out a way to get enough distance between us to note her chart. I busy myself with fetching the remote for the TV from the locked cabinet. I dim the lights, fix the blankets and get heated ones. I do a million things, little things, anything to stay in the room but not make her feel like I'm staying unnecessarily. When I finally work up the nerve to ask her the question weighing on my mind, a totally different one comes out. "Why did you text me?"

Rachel is falling asleep, I can tell because her eyes are heavy when she looks at me. "Because, you're good at what you do."

Her nebulizer is empty now, so I pull it from her clumsy hand, setting it on the bed beside her as I turn down the oxygen. She reaches out slowly and her hand catches the edge of my coat.

"Was that the only reason?" I ask softly as I lean down toward her.

"No."

"Then tell me why."

Rachel tightens her grip. "Stay."

I nod. "I will."

"I'm sorry."

I hush her. "Sleep."

"Thank you."

"For?"

"Being you."

I can't hold it back anymore. "I love you."

"I know." Her eyes focus on my face. "Do you trust me?"

I give her a smirk. "After your little stunt at the bar, I'm not sure." I mean it as a joke, honestly I do, but her words help me realize the gravity of what I've done to her.

"Then maybe we are even, 'cause I don't know if I can trust you either."

It hurts to hear, but I understand. "Let's try to work that out together."

"Okay." An ungainly hand fastens on my collar, tugging me closer. "Stay."

"I will."

Closer. "Promise and don't break it, please."

"I never will again. I promise."

She is a breath away and when she patterns her eyes over me, I just want her to kiss me. I wish she would, but instead she lets me go. "I believe you."

And I stay all night so she never has misplaced belief in me again.

Chapter Fifteen

The Way It Could Have Been
December 7th, 2015

After spending the night in Rachel's hospital room, I was hoping things would be different. They have been, but not to the degree I was hoping for. It's dangerous to have fantasies, as I've said many times before.

My exact fantasy was this: in the morning she would open her eyes and look at me. I'd feel the tickle of her gaze on me and wake up. We would talk softly and I would kiss her forehead, glad to see she was feeling a little better. Then, she'd pull my face to her and tell me she loved me before she kissed me senseless.

Seriously, as adolescent as it may be, that is exactly what I imagined right before I fell asleep in her hospital room.

What actually happened was vastly different...

෴෴෴

I feel something cold against my face. Wet. When I blink my eyes open I'm able to see two things, the clock on the wall telling me it's 2:45 in the morning and Rachel's nebulizer leaking solution onto the bed sheet my face is on.

I see Rachel's hand, her finger twitching under

my gaze, and when I lift my head I confirm she is dreaming. Staring, I sit up slowly and watch shadows move over her face as her expressions changes. I wonder what she is dreaming about. I just soak in the image of it, the utter beauty of her face at peace. The way her lashes fan and her lips part with some secret, unspoken whisper. How the natural curl in her hair spools tendrils that circle the apples of her cheeks.

And for a breathless moment, everything falls away and I can pretend I'm lying beside her in our bed like I could a lifetime ago. But then I hear it, and I lean closer because I'm sure I heard the rattle in her chest. The hospital room coalesces around me again and yes, when she takes a breath, the congestion is literally audible.

Rachel coughs and I move back a little as she shifts in the bed, uncomfortable. My poor sweetheart is going to have a really long night and I know I should probably wake her, adjust her bed so she is sitting more upright, but I can't do it. She should have at least a few minutes more to sleep.

Two minutes later, she takes a deep breath and that's when I hear the sticky mucus literally web in her bronchus, and her body responds exactly how it should. Rachel coughs and the force of it pulls her into a sitting position. Her eyes are wild and unfocused as she literally coughs hard enough to make her red in the face.

"I'm sorry." I whisper it, and she shouldn't be able to hear it over the sound of her misery, but she does.

Her eyes fix on me, "Blake?"

"I'm here. It'll be okay."

"Oh God, uh..." She shakes her head, rolling into

another coughing fit. I feel the grimace on my face until she leans away from me over the opposite rail of the bed. I'm confused until she makes a gut churning sound.

Oh shit! I jump up and grab the cabinet handle blindly, pulling out the deepest basin I can find. I put it in her hand, and she gets it under her face, a microsecond before she throws up.

"Blake." She spits. "Please go outside."

"It's okay." I shrug even though she can't see me. "It doesn't bother me."

"I don't want you to see me like this."

"It's just me."

"Exactly."

More coughing, more throwing up. I'll be honest, it kinda unsettles my stomach from pure reflex. Rachel has always been a decently accommodating patient, but there is one thing she draws the line at. Vomiting. You can basically do anything else to her you want. Colonoscopy, okay. Endoscopy, not a problem. Surgery, she's ready to go. But put her in a situation where she's vomiting and even at home she'd cut fingers off with how fast she'd slam a door in your face. It literally took ten years of marriage before she was comfortable enough to let me help.

So, when she looks up at me, sweat on her forehead and tears in her eyes, I know exactly what she's gonna say. "Please don't watch me do this."

I smile ruefully, putting a hand on the curtain behind me. "But you still look so darn pretty, Rachel."

And she does the motion, wiping a shaky hand through her messy hair. "You're crazy." When her eyes go wide and her face goes back into the basin, I pull the curtain closed behind me and wince.

"Out." Her voice sounds watery and my stomach twists. "All the way out."

I slide out the door and rather than sit in the hallway, I sleep the rest of the morning away in the stockroom down the hall.

♫♫♫♫

And even though it's been two months, I can't help but feel like I broke my promise to her that morning. I wish I would have stayed, that she would have let me. However, the more I think about it, the more I realize, she seemed not to care *as* much as before about her personal boundaries. I assume that is because of what we have shared in this life.

When I connect the dots, it makes me wonder if maybe it wasn't that Rachel didn't want me there, but that she was in too vulnerable of a place to have me there. So I have to ask myself, what am I waiting for? I should be up and making things happen. I should be winning her love again, but I can't figure out how. My wishes for a resolution between us are tempered by the knowledge that if I push too hard, I think I'll break her and I can't ever do that again.

And again, like some hellish joke, I wait on her whim.

It's two weeks later that I'm staring at the phone when it rings. It isn't that uncanny, I stare at the phone a lot. The odds are in my favor, believe me.

"Hello?"

"Hello."

"Rachel?"

"Yeah, um." She pauses. "Did you have plans tonight?"

If I did, they aren't plans anymore. "No, why?"

"I want to talk to you."

I don't know how that makes me feel when she says it. It's all a mixture of elation and trepidation. "Um, okay." We are silent for a long time. I hear her breathing on the other end of the line and I obsess over what she is thinking. "You sound so much better."

"I feel better."

I clear my throat as the silence draws long and sharp against my nervousness. "What time did you want to get together?"

"Seven?"

"Sure, where?"

"My flat?"

I swallow hard. "Okay."

When the line disconnects, I stare at my cell phone and watch her number disappear from the screen. It's a ritual of mine because it's *her* number. The same number we had when we were together. The same number I dialed six years ago when I came back to this world.

I hold onto that, I cling to that one thing like it is the last line to my sanity every time my heart is broken by her.

♫♪♫♪

I arrive thirty minutes early to Rachel's. I wait in a cab down the street and stare at myself in my compact mirror. I blot my lipstick nervously until it's all gone and reapply with a shaking hand. Once I can't stand looking at myself and the fear in my eyes, I stare through the windshield at where the lights from her third floor flat glow.

As the snow gathers on the glass, I measure each window in turn and then pull the hood up over my head. I close my eyes with a steadying breath before I pay the guy, pop the door and hurry into the night. The cold makes me ache and I try to walk without limping, without looking as miserable as the winter makes me feel. I circle the flight of stairs and chase my destiny in a staggering step. When I get to the door of Rachel's place, regardless of the cold, I can't knock. I stand outside and agonize over what she is going to say to me.

The peephole and pristine numbers glint at me as I hold on to the belief that everything will be okay *somehow*, for one last moment.

When the door opens without prompting, I flinch as light pours out onto me. Rachel gives me a look and I open my mouth to justify why I was standing on her porch like a creeper, but she doesn't let me speak. She just brushes past me as she pulls the door closed behind her.

"Let's go."

"Go where?" I ask, turning as she starts down the stairs I just climbed.

"To my favorite restaurant. I'm hungry."

She doesn't turn to look at me, doesn't even say hello. As I follow, I'm shocked by how *not my wife* she is and how the small modicum of closeness we shared at the hospital is apparently gone. She further proves it when I realize she is making me walk on purpose. I'm pretty sure she intentionally chooses to go to a diner ten blocks away just to see if I can make it. I feel like she's testing just how committed I am to getting her back. As I make my way through the cold and follow in her footsteps I grit my teeth tightly, until I think I might splinter one.

I make it three blocks before we pass Oscars, the

restaurant where we had our first date, the restaurant that *really* is her favorite. In that moment, it is just too much to bear to walk another step in this bone deep cold with my life this different.

With the only person I love this distant.

When I stop beside the rail outside the restaurant and fight with the idea of begging that we get a cab, she says the first words she has said to me since announcing her hunger. "Your knee must be bothering you."

I shoot her a look, struggling to keep my emotions from tumbling over, as I ease myself away from the rail. It really does hurt, but not nearly as much as her devoid eyes that regard me. I shift under the intensity of her gaze and even though I don't want to answer her obvious rhetorical question, I do. "Yeah."

She frowns only for an instant and then her emotion is gone. Her gaze hovers over the jagged scaring that hides beneath my jeans. "I remember when you broke it." Her eyes are distant, remembering.

"Yeah, I remember you being the last face I saw and it made it better." I shift uncomfortably as she focuses on me. Rachel licks her lips, wetting them so she can speak. "I'm sorry. I don't think I can talk after all."

I feel my mouth drop a little, and I rush to get air into my lungs with how her words punch them empty. "Are you telling me that you changed your mind?" I almost want to add that she changed her mind three blocks too far, because now she is just adding insult to injury.

"I just don't think I can talk rationally, yet."

"Hey, wait a second." When she brushes past me, speeding back the way we came, I grab her wrist and she turns to me. "You can't keep doing this to me."

"I know."

She is close enough now for me to see the staining of tears on her cheeks and though I want to reach out to brush them away, I know I don't have the right to. There is nothing more painful than to know that my love destroyed my right to do what I want in the name of that love.

I let her go. "Okay, I'm sorry."

"Me, too. God, me too, so much," she whispers before rushing forward to hail a cab. The brakes scream between us, between the silent mosaic we make. I watch her open the door and then turn to me. "Get in."

I stagger forward, not even bothering to pretend that I'm not hurting in every way I can hurt. "Good night, Rachel."

"Good night, Blake." She frowns at me, at the way I know I just limped. And it's really difficult to see the mix of sorrow and pity in her face. I gather my tatters and stand straight, holding the door as I wait for her to walk away. I don't get into the car until I can't make out her form anymore as she disappears into a long stretch of darkness down the street.

It frightens me that she never looks back.

⁂ ⁂ ⁂ ⁂

Another week drags by me. I've stopped staring at my phone, because I don't think she is going to call. I have poured myself into work to keep me occupied. It's either that or cry, and just like Rachel said once upon a time, I have no more tears to give. So, imagine my surprise when I pull my phone free to check the time and find a text message from her. I read it with shaking hands and my breath goes ragged.

I don't know if you are working at the hospital

tonight, but if you aren't, I would like to talk to you. I'm not going to make you walk anywhere. I forgot about your knee and I'm sorry. If you still want to talk to me, can you come by at eight?

I type my message quickly and remember the nervous flood I felt the first time we did this. I can't believe it's been six years since I stood by the cross in the shadows of evening and hung on her every word.

I don't get off until midnight. Would it be okay if I came after or is that too late?

She doesn't message right away, as a matter of fact my phone doesn't vibrate against my hip until I've finished my rounds. I pause in the hallway between patients' rooms to read it.

Sure, come after.

Okay.

I want to say something more, but I can't. I read and reread her messages over and over every spare chance I get. And all the while the hours tick slowly past on the digital face of my phone. I've just about killed my battery when my shift finally ends.

Ryan is in the locker room as I gather my things. "You in a rush?"

My hands slow as I pull my purse free and close the metal door a moment later. "No, just going out." I don't know why I try to act nonchalant about it, but I do.

When I glance over at him, he is staring at me. "What?"

He shakes his head. "Nothing, just got a weird feeling of deja vu. You look like you're in a hurry. Got a date tonight?"

I frown because it couldn't be farther from the truth. "Why would you think that?"

"'Cause you are never in a hurry and you never date, so I figured maybe that was the correlation." He grins at me.

"I wish, but no."

He shrugs, laughing softly to himself as I shoulder my purse. "Well, whatever it is I hope it all works out."

"Yeah, me too."

But things rarely work out. I don't get to Rachel's until a quarter to one. The normal train I take, the Seventh Avenue Express, skipped my station and put me ten blocks out of my way. I got a cab, but it still made me much later than planned. I texted her exactly what happened, and she doesn't seem angry by it, but I still have a horrible feeling in my stomach.

Before I knock on her door, it opens. Rachel is dressed in pajamas. Her hair is twisted back into a bun, arms wrapped into an oversized blue sweatshirt. She looks like the little girl whose heart I shattered as she measures me silently.

"I'm sorry, I..." I freeze on the thoughts, unable to speak or move as the memories burn through me.

She gives me a look and I open my mouth to justify why I'm not walking in, why I am late, why I hurt her so long ago, but she doesn't let me answer. She just opens the door wider and I stumble into her home.

"It's cold out tonight."

I nod, and then push the hood back from my head littering snow on the wooden floor near the door. "I'm sorry. I was just about to knock."

She smiles thinly and nods. "Good, your coat?"

I strip it off and hand it to her, watching as she tosses it over the back of a chair. "I could have done that," I tease, more to erase my nervousness than hers.

"I suppose. Please come in." It all sounds very formal, and my nervousness explodes into full blown fear. I watch as Rachel looks at me, just *looks* at me without any readable expression. It's her actress face, the one that leaves me wondering what she is feeling.

I move away from the door and busy myself with looking at her place. I stare at the dark worn furniture, the vintage pieces she has picked up. I regard the items in turn, things I remember and things I don't. They ring very reminiscent of our home together. I never realized how much of the home I loved was built from her taste and not mine. Well, her taste before it became mine. "I like your place." It's hard to say, knowing that it might not ever be mine again.

She follows my gaze like she forgot what she was doing and where she was. "Thanks. Would you like a seat?" She leads a slow path to her old leather sofa and she gestures for me to sit. I do, unsure of what to do or say because it is so strange to have her entertain me. I haven't been her guest in a very long time.

"Thirsty?"

I lick my lips, wetting them enough to get words out. "No, I'm fine, thank you."

"All right." Finally she takes up the space on the sofa beside me. Her eyes focus on everything that isn't me in that moment, and I focus on breathing as I sit and wait for whatever it is she is going to say.

"I have a few things I need to say to you."

The sofa is very small suddenly as I feel the unease between us. "Okay."

"It's really hard to see you, Blake."

"I know."

"I'm still angry. I'm still hurt. What you did to

me was the worst thing that anyone has ever done to me."

"I know and I'm so sorry Rachel." I can't say it enough, and I try to put how heartfelt it is into my words. I hold her eyes until they waiver, until she can no longer look at me.

"What are you doing Blake?" She asks, her voice hushed with desperation. "Why are you here? What are you looking for from me?"

I can't tell her because what I want from her seems as impossible as anything in the world. It seems as impossible as me actually being here tucked into an apartment I shared with her a lifetime ago. All I can do is apologize, but I know she doesn't want that from me. She wants an answer I can't part with, so I play dumb. "What do you mean?"

Rachel leans back against the armrest, facing me fully. "You come to my concert, you tell me you still love me? Where do you get off thinking you can just waltz back into my life after you..." her voice fades out and she sighs, looking away.

"After I broke your heart?"

"Yeah, among other things. I mean, you must think I don't have an ounce of self-respect."

I don't know which comment to address first because the way she is looking at me is telling me exactly what I fear. She doesn't feel love for me anymore. I'm on the defensive and I have no leverage, no glimmering hope in the darkness of her eyes. I don't think there is anything I can say to fix this.

I don't know how I find my voice. "First, I know that you have self-respect. I wouldn't dare presume that you don't. That isn't what I meant when I told you that I still cared about you. I just wanted you to know that nothing has changed for me. I always loved you and I still do."

"So, I'm just supposed to be okay with that? That's supposed to miraculously fix everything? I'm just supposed to roll over like some *love sick puppy* and take your love when you care enough to offer it?" She literally snorts with fury as she quotes my exact words. "You had my love and you threw it away."

I know I did, and knowing I did it intentionally makes it *that* much worse. I wish she would just understand why I did it, understand and love me for it. "You know I didn't want to break up with you. You must know that I didn't want it, but you gave me no choice."

That was certainly not the right thing to say as she narrows her eyes at me in that silent fury Rachel seemingly reserves only for me. "How dare you. How dare you come to me and tell me that? I'm not some child, and I might have been young, but I *loved* you. I loved you enough that I was willing to give up everything so that we could be together."

"And do you really think that if I loved you I would just let you do that?" I stare at her hard, angry that she refuses to understand. "What kind of a person do you think I am? What good would it have done for you to sacrifice your dreams?"

"I would've had you."

God, she might as well just kill me with how beautiful that sounds in contrast with how her look resonates with hate. I want to tell her she can have me, have everything that she wants, but those words won't matter. Not now, not like this. I try to rationalize instead. "Tell me something." I lower my voice. "Let's pretend that you did. That you gave up singing here at Juilliard to become a lawyer out in California. Let's pretend that you never had the chance to see if you could make it as a singer. What then?"

"What then, what?" She terrorizes me with how furious she sounds.

"Well, would that have been better?" I gesture around at her apartment. At the apartment she and I once shared love and laughter in. It all feels so different and cold now. "Would it have been better to pass up this apartment, the smell of the stage, the roar of the crowd? Would it have been better to miss the sights and smells of the city, the cafe by Columbus Circle and the chance to make all your dreams come true?"

"That isn't the point Blake!"

"It *is* the point Rachel!" I return the same venomous tone with a pointed look of fury and it silences her. "It's the reason I've done everything I've done. It is the reason that I broke my own heart in the kitchen that day just as much as I broke yours. It's the reason I lied to you, saying that I didn't love you, that you were a love sick puppy–"

"I hate you for that."

And she means it.

"Fine, hate me. I don't care because you have it. Your music, your dreams, those are the reasons that I cried out the door, down the drive, all the way home, and every day after we broke up! You told me that music was only a little piece of you, but that isn't true. It is a part of everything you do, and the idea of you giving that up to keep me or have me was just silly. You could have had both."

I shouldn't have used past tense. Why did I use past tense? "You can have both."

She doesn't say anything and I don't know what

that means. I keep talking to fill the deafening silence between us. "I believed in your dreams. I believed in your dreams enough to give up the only person I could ever love, the only person I could be with, the only–"

"Then why the *fuck* did you have sex with Nick Cooper?"

And then there is that. I stare at the scratched wooden floor because I still have no justification for it, I can't think of a single thing to say that explains away that horrible trespass against her. "When I let you go, it was the final last horrible thing I could do to stamp out everything between us. Something as sacred to me as our love, our intimacy..." I can't even finish the lie. "It gave me something else to be destroyed over."

The statement skates dangerously close to the truth. When I can finally look at her, her hand is pressed to her chest. I stare at it until my eyes slide up to her face as it crumbles. She holds my gaze as tears glitter her lashes. Easing a shaking breath, she wipes at them as they fall.

Rachel shakes her head, banishing away her emotion and when she clears her throat, I feel the words she is going to say before she even says them. "I'm sorry, but I think you should leave."

"Oh, okay." That is all I can say as I realize I've lost her. Even as the thought hits my synapses–that she has slipped out of my hands–I feel myself standing. My feet push me past her as she covers her face. I can see the apartment moving before my gaze, but it's all automatic. I can't stop myself, can't control my own body as I gather my damp coat at the door. When I'm finally able to stop, I'm so close to the door it's pointless not to move through it...and let her go.

"Blake?"

I don't know if I really heard her say my name, but I turn to her anyway.

"Can you answer something for me?"

I swallow, shifting my feet. She looks amazing where she is. As untouchable as she is, with that framing wisp of hair that never *quite* makes it into her bun...a plaid pajama clad visage that represents everything I want in my life.

"Yeah."

She stares at me, deep into me and through me, deeper than she has ever done in her life. "Did you really love me?"

"You have no idea how much then," my voice cracks, "and how much I still do."

She nods. She keeps doing it, like the motion will sink the words into her mind. "Okay."

That's all she says. With my heart on the line, I stand with my coat in my hand at her door and watch the woman that was supposed to be my wife let me leave. Or maybe I let myself walk out of her life. I try to remind myself that there will be other times, other visits that will allow me to perhaps someday leverage myself back into her life, but even that comfort feels hollow to me.

I flip the lock and twist the knob in my hand.

"Blake?"

I stop with my hand on the door. "Yeah?"

"Don't go."

When I turn back to her, she is contemplative, regarding the coat in my hand. I'm scared to speak because I don't want her to change her mind.

She blinks a few times, then stands. Every step she gets closer my heart beats harder, until it's all I know in the world. It's like the thunder is the only thing that exists. Rachel stands before me and takes the coat away. It falls to the chair again with a careless hand. "Don't go away."

"I don't want to." I whisper because I can't get my voice to work.

When she locks the door, my heart stalls in my chest. Rachel takes my hand and pulls me behind her as she maneuvers into the darkness at the back of the apartment. It's her bedroom and I remember it well from when it was ours. It has the same dent in the aluminum blinds that I remember. Seeing that, seeing that little annoyance again with my own eyes, pushes my emotions just far enough to make me tear up.

I feel the bump of Rachel's dresser against my hip and I palm it when she turns to me and instead of kissing me like I desperately want her to, she drops to the floor. Her hands are on my injured knee as she peels me free of the boots I'm wearing. My tears start, because her touch is so gentle and knowing. She has always just known what I needed, even when I didn't know it myself.

"Sore?" Her fingers pry off my other shoe.

I sniff in the dark. "Always."

I don't have to see her to know her expression. "Come here."

It has been four years since I've been this close to her, four very long cold years. So when she wraps me up in her arms and pulls me into bed with her, I just want to hold on forever and never let go. "Rachel?"

"Hold me, Blake."

"Hold me, too."

We wrap into one another. Rachel pulls the blankets up around us and I feel the heat pour off her in waves. I don't care that I'm dressed, I don't care about anything. Nothing matters more than the fact that right now, she is in my arms. And I'm never letting her go again. "Please forgive me," I whisper.

"You're my *One*, Blake. I always will."

Her words hurt me in a different way, one I wasn't expecting. They make me cry harder and I stumble my apologies until Rachel covers my mouth with her hand.

She is staring at me, close enough that her eyes are the only thing I can see. "Stop." She pulls her hand back and I can finally breathe and I do so in a ragged rush of air. "You have apologized enough."

"It will never be enough."

"It will have to be, because I can't take hearing it anymore."

"Okay." I've never seen this hardness before, and that is my fault, too.

Then she softens. "You look tired." Her hand finds its way into my hair and traces softly.

I laugh, because she has no idea how long I've waited, how long I've dreamed of this. "I am."

"Let's go to sleep."

"I'd like that."

When she tucks her head into my neck, I marvel at the way she fills the space in my embrace. Her lips press to my throat and kiss softly. "I missed you."

"I missed you."

And despite the pain I have caused her, and the cracks I need to repair in our foundation, I find so much joy in the fact that she falls asleep in my arms like she always did.

"I love you angel."

And she whispers it back sleepily as her hands tighten and hold me just like they did so long ago.

Chapter Sixteen

The Color Of Fate
December 24th, 2015

Christmas Eve is the worst time to work at a hospital. Not because of the fact that you are missing out on your holiday fun, but because you have to watch peoples' lives come apart on the one day you really hope they wouldn't. It sucks, but I take comfort in the fact that I can at least make the night better for those unfortunate enough to be here.

After all, I have nowhere else to be.

Rachel is in Danville with her parents. It's the last night of Hanukkah, and I already called to wish her a happy celebration with her family, so truly I have nothing better to do than work.

And work I most certainly have done.

So far tonight the ER has been hopping. We've had three ladder falls from late night Christmas light fixes, an electrocution, too. A dog bite, four cases of frostbite, and sixteen people being treated for injuries related to fights. Oh, and a really mouthy drunk woman, who lovingly refers to me as 'blonde bitch'.

It is seriously turning out to be a marvelous Christmas.

When I finally have a moment to breathe, I stroll into the break room to get a snack and I see Ryan with his head in the fridge. I clear my throat. "Stealing more food?"

When he pulls back he is chewing on a chicken strip from Claudia's lunch and opening up a Red Bull. "What's it to ya, blonde bitch?"

His grin puts a smile on my face. I can tell that one is gonna follow me for a while.

"Claudia packs like eight meals everyday so she can spare a chicken strip, I'm sure."

I shake my head at him, moving to the vending machine. I pull free a dollar from the pocket of my scrubs and feed the machine.

"Whatcha getting?"

I stare at the choices. "I don't know."

"You should get Gummi Bears."

"I want something salty."

I can feel his expression heat the back of my neck. "Don't be a pervert," I warn, but before I make a selection, Ryan hits a button and I whip out to smack him. "You dick."

The machine spits out it's offering. "Damn it, really. Of all the shit in there." He just laughs as I bend over to get the little sugary morsels. "You are the reason that most of us have sworn not to have children."

Ryan scoffs. "I'm awesome and you all love it. I make sure you don't do your stupid girly indecisive thing." He gulps down his energy drink and then measures me silently. "Speaking of indecisive, what's up with you and that girl?"

I'm chewing on a bear, and it apparently wasn't a bad choice after all because I'm enjoying it. "Rachel?"

He laughs. "Yeah. Do you have five of them or something, player?"

"No." I wave him off with a grin. "No, just one.

Things are good."

Ryan grins lecherously. "How good?"

"None of your business."

He deflates. "Oh, come on. I'd tell you." Much to my chagrin, yes, he tells me *far* too much about his conquests.

"There is nothing to tell, we are taking it slow."

That gets him very confused apparently because he is staring at me with wide eyes. "You have got to be kidding me. It's been like a month. Aren't you lesbians supposed to bring a U-Haul on your second date or something?"

I grin because that is exactly how it was before. Date one was coffee, date two was sex and I pretty much didn't leave after that. "Cute, but no." I pocket my candy after folding over the top. "And it's only been three weeks."

"Three weeks, a month, a day...doesn't matter. Seriously, when she came by a couple weeks ago, I thought I was gonna stroke out with how fast the blood in my brain went to other places. Seriously, she is super-hot. If you don't hit it, I will in spades."

I glimmer a smile despite the fact he is insinuating having sex with my wife. His words are actually said from a place of love, because though it might not seem like it, Ryan will end up being one of our very best friends.

"Oh, I will." I arch my brow at him playfully. "Like I said, we are just going slow. No need to rush things."

He shakes his head. "I don't get it, but okay. Take your time and do your tantric lesbian foreplay."

That actually makes me laugh, which is a relief because it's been a hell of a night.

ALL PERSONNEL TO ER ENTRANCE TWO.

I glance up at the speaker in the ceiling. "Back to work," I state.

"Yep. How much you wanna bet it's another bar fight with a bunch of drunk and disorderly the police are dropping on us?"

I shrug. "Twenty bucks?"

"Pittance. I will not play with you for less than forty."

"Fine, forty dollars says it is something *other* than that."

He narrows his eyes and sets his voice in an accent I can't identify. "You are a minx and I accept your bet."

When he's within range with the cocky smirk on his face, I steal his Red Bull and take a sip. "I would like my forty bucks in crisp, clean, new bills, please."

He pulls the door open for me, it's all very chivalrous and charming to the casual observer, but he does it so that he can put words in my ear that leave me laughing.

"I'm gonna shit on them before I give them to you."

It's midnight when I finally ride the subway half asleep to Rachel's flat. Forty dollars richer, sans any type of shitting, I'm in a pretty good mood despite being alone on one of my favorite holidays. It's okay though. I won't be for long. Next year, Rachel and I will have a big celebration and since our holidays will overlap, it will be that much more special and fun. For now I'll have to content myself with watering Rachel's plant while she is out of town and using her cable to watch reality TV.

My phone chirps softly and I blink away the

sleep in my eyes as I shake it free of my pocket.

Merry Christmas, Blake.

I smile.

Merry Christmas, Rachel.

Have you been watering my plants?

No, they are all dead.

She doesn't rise to the bait of my sarcasm.

Shame. Have you already been over there today?

I arch my eyebrow at her words.

No, I'm on my way now. Long night.

I'm sorry. Despite it being a long night, when you get there will you throw out the plants. I don't want to see them dead when I get back.

I nod silently, even though she can't see me and the smile rising up on my face.

I suppose I can manage that. I'll make sure to get them out before tomorrow.

Perfect.

Swathed in the warmth of knowing I will see her face again in just a day, I balance myself against the handrail and fall asleep to the rattling chug of the subway. I dream of her, I dream of the fragments of life I'll have with her. There are clapboard houses and puppies and children. Hugs that wrap me so tightly I can't breathe, and arms that guard me while our laughter blends into sunlight. It's me and my best friend together. Finally, close enough we might as well be the same person.

It's exactly how it is supposed to be.

When the monotone voice announces my stop I think it's a dream because in my mind I'm leaning on Rachel's shoulder as we ride to Coney Island. It isn't until the attendant that knows me taps my shoulder that I realize what reality is.

"Blake, you getting out here?"

I lift bleary eyes to his smile and nod slowly as I drag my bone weary body to the crisp snow flecked festivities above ground. I make it to Rachel's flat on instinct alone, stumbling between happy couples who are laughing and dancing in the light. I don't feel alone though, not when I'm swirling in daydreams of her.

I take the stairs slowly, dragging a sore right leg with me. I shouldn't work so many shifts in a row. I know better than to skip my stretching exercises and work instead, but while I'm young, while my body can take it, I want to refresh myself with everything I haven't done in a while. Though, as the pain shoots up into my lower back, I think I might have overdone it.

With uncanny perfection, Rachel's spare key finds the lock and turns in my hand even though my eyes are closed. I don't take off my scrubs. I don't take off my sneakers. The white coat comes off in the entryway as I nudge the door closed. Thankfully, I salvage my phone from my pocket before I let the coat flutter to the floor and collapse to the sofa in a huff.

I don't brush my teeth, don't even turn on the TV like usual. Right now, I have to sleep or I'm gonna die. I begin to pull my ponytail halfway out before all my muscles quit mid-motion and I roll over. I smile sleepily in thoughts of Rachel before I'm unconscious.

It feels like only a minute when I suddenly feel something wrap around my ankle. I blink my eyes open and freeze, as the...it feels like fingers...tighten. I can't move, can't breathe. My shoe laces loosen and my sneaker slides from my foot.

"Rachel?"

I'm really hoping it's her, 'cause if it isn't, this is a really fucked up precursor to a robbery.

I roll over slowly so I can see the person removing my shoes. Rachel is bent over, her hair falling in a wave to block the inset lighting from the kitchen. Her tired eyes lift to my face with a smile. "Hi, Blake." She pulls the other shoe off, dropping it with a thud to the wood floor.

I smile, wondering if I should pinch myself to make sure it isn't a dream. "Hey."

It takes me a minute to realize it's still dark. I glance at the time on the cable box. It's two in the morning. I look back at her. "What are you doing here?" I rub my eyes sitting up. "You aren't supposed to be back until tomorrow."

She smiles a little, dropping to the cushions beside me. "Disappointed?"

I shake my head. "Not at all." I yawn and then watch her do it, too. "Sorry."

"I came back early." She leans back on the cushion beside me, her hand lightly tapping her jean clad thighs before moving over and taking mine casually. "You shouldn't be alone on Christmas."

Her hand feels good in mine and I stare down at it. It's only the second time in a month that she has put her hand in mine. When I told Ryan we were taking it slowly, he really only got half the story.

Glaciers move faster.

"Thank you," I whisper as she tightens her fingers in mine.

When I look up, Rachel inclines her face toward me. She looks so beautiful right now, mussed and sleepy, relaxed.

"You look beautiful."

She nibbles her lip and then eases toward me, slowly. Those churning coffee colored eyes of hers measure me as she gets closer. She stops a fraction of an inch from my lips and I hold my breath, hoping she will kiss me. Her gaze bounces back and forth. "You too, Blake." Her fingers slide over my cheek and find their way into my hair.

I lean into the touch, savoring it. When I open my eyes, I can see her debating. I think she wants to kiss me because she wets her lips, but yet it's almost like she can't. Like if she does, she will open the proverbial flood gates. She is probably right since her hand in my hair has my whole body trembling.

"I got you a gift," she whispers, her fingertips feather light as they map down my neck and slide achingly slow down my back. As much as I want to speak, I'm afraid that if I open my mouth, gibberish will come out. Her hands are too knowing, too perfect in their motion for me *not* to forget how to speak. I have missed her touches so much, and when those slow fingers reach the base of my scrubs, they fish slowly and then touch the skin on my lower back.

I shiver from the chill as her hand starts back up, under my shirt. I bite my lip under the intensity of her gaze.

"Did you hear me?"

I shake my head. "What?"

"I got you a gift."

I roll my eyes closed when her fingers splay over my shoulder blade and then map to the clasp of my bra. I don't even realize I'm arching until Rachel scoots forward and her lips press to my throat.

"Shouldn't sleep with a bra on." She traces her nose against the sensitive skin. "Don't you want to know what it is?"

I swallow, my eyes fluttering open for a moment

before I close them again, feeling her hand snap my bra loose. "Huh, what?"

"The gift."

"Uh huh." God, her fingers are delicious as they rub over the place where the tight material was just clasped a moment ago.

"You can unwrap it. It's in the kitchen."

I blink because I really thought she was going to say it was her.

She snorts a laugh. "Were you expecting something else? You just stopped breathing."

I arch my brow as I chew my lip again. "Honestly, yes, I was expecting something else."

"What were you expecting?"

I clear my throat and she nibbles my neck, making it that much harder to speak. "I was thinking you were going to say it was you."

She smiles against my skin. "Soon."

I murmur my appreciation as she goes back to kissing my throat.

"I just..." suddenly her voice is gruff as her other hand comes up and both of them pull me into a deep arch against her lips. I whine softly and her teeth graze in response. She continues, "Want to know..."

I drown in her touches, at the way her hands start a rhythm I know well, pulling me toward her over and over. She attacks my skin, and even though she is saying soon, her motions indicate *now*.

"Know what?" I drag my nails under the hair at the back of her neck and Rachel growls softly. It literally makes my insides turn to liquid at the thought of everything behind that passionate rumble being unleashed on me. God, I want it so badly.

"I just want to know that it will last."

I pant into her motions as they become firm and more insisting. "I love you Rachel. You know that. Please trust that I'll never hurt you again."

"I'm starting to."

I look down at her and she smiles before grabbing me tightly and falling backward. She pulls on me hard enough that I lose my balance and fall over her, catching myself on the armrest of the sofa.

She smolders up at me. "Don't let the sofa go."

I swallow hard. "Okay."

Her eyes consume me as she traces my whole body, she breathes even harder as she does it, her lips quirking into a sexy grin. "You know, Blake," her hands sweep over me, tantalizingly, "I can't deny that you have always turned me on. That I get so wet thinking about you." Her hands shift me a little and when I'm in her lap, she bucks her hips into me hard enough to lift me up.

My mouth drops open, eyes wide as I take in her motions.

"I get so aroused, imagining what we used to do."

"Oh, Rachel, me too," I whisper as she grinds into me again, her hands slicking down my sides and holding my hips firmly.

She does it again and I hear the desire in my own sounds as I moan at the contact.

I meet her eyes, burning embers in the dimness.

"I still think about it a lot. Even when I was hurt by you and then super pissed at you, I would have sex dreams about us and wake up ready for your fingers and tongue." With those words she slips her hands up the front of my shirt and palms my breasts.

Everywhere she touches sets me on fire. It is

excruciating to not be able to touch her. "I felt the same way."

She nods at me. "It's the emotions that matter though."

I struggle to breathe. "I know."

Rachel slows her motions, hands circling up around my back to pull me down toward her. "This is really easy for me because sex with you isn't the problem, Blake. Believe me, it's not. I'm so ready, I'm so wet. I could probably climax in five seconds after us teasing like this. And believe me, I want to have sex with you."

"I know." I swallow hard. "I want to, too."

Rachel sighs, pulling me even closer. "And Blake, I do love you. So that isn't the problem either."

It makes my heart stop. I go to speak, to reciprocate the words, but she puts a finger over my lips before I can say anything. "It's never been that I don't love you, or that I *ever* stopped, because I didn't. It's that I can't be *in* love with you until I know it will be forever. I can't give you what you want, things the way they were, until I'm one hundred percent sure that come hell or high water we are going to work everything out together. Until I know you aren't going to leave."

"I'm never gonna leave." I kiss her fingertip. "I don't want anyone but you. I want everything you have to give. I want you to have everything. I want to be accountable to you, and have you be to me. I want *us* back...our team. You and me against the world."

"That's the problem."

I kiss her forehead. "What is?"

"I'm still a little scared to go back to that place. If things were to change again, it would seriously wreck me."

"It won't change. I'm not going anywhere," I say again.

She pulls me closer, until I'm lying on her. She looks up at my hands. "You can let go of the sofa now." And she giggles softly at my bemused expression.

"It's hard not to challenge your resolve on this because sometimes I know I can't say what I feel. I can only show it to you." I twist my arm under her neck, sliding my free hand over her thigh and then up her side. "I want to show you, because I don't know how to make you understand with words that you're *my* One, Rachel. The one person I want to be with."

Rachel sighs as I do the motion again, feeling the heat and solidity of her. No matter how many times I imagined her and I together, there are so many things that separate the reality from the fantasy. I forget how warm her body gets, how her skin is softer than silk. How I can feel her heart racing against my chest, see the pulse point in her neck pound.

When she arches into the motion of my hand, I kiss her neck softly. Her mouth touches my ear and pushes words into my heart. "Just keep being you and give me a little more time. I promise you are well on your way to having all of me again."

"Rachel." I pull back so she can focus on me. She's blushing and I find it so charming and sweet.

"Yes?"

I caress her cheek and then find her hand in mine. I twine our fingers together, kissing her thumb lightly. "You can have all the time you need. I meant it when I said we were a team and even when we were apart we were a team then, too. A distant one, but a team nonetheless. I have thought about you every day of what feels like my whole life, so what's a little more time to make you feel perfect and wonderful."

Her fingers tighten in mine. "Thank you, Blake."

"So, I hope you believe me when I say it's forever. You know, in light of the fact that you just teased me to death and I'm saying take your time."

She laughs. "It works both ways. I'm not just driving you nuts, I'm driving me nuts too 'cause, yeah, I really want to touch you more." She pulls me closer again, wetting her lips. "Can you do something for me though, something I think will help me believe your promise of forever?"

"Anything."

"Kiss me." Rachel traces her fingers down my side and hooks her hand around my arm, holding me against her. "Kiss me like you used to, like I was the only thing in the world that mattered."

"You are the only thing that matters."

She tugs me closer, desperately. "Prove it."

I slide my hand into her hair and pull her to my mouth. I take it slow, dragging my lips over hers, and when she parts them, I kiss her fully. I pull back, making eye contact with her for a moment, and then lean back in. I tilt my head, deepening the kiss. I make love to her full lips, sucking them, licking them, nibbling on them until Rachel smiles.

"I love that," she whispers, breathlessly.

"Oh, baby, I know."

She laughs deeply and then swallows hard when I pull firmly on her leg and press my hip against the seam of her jeans. "And this, you liked this too."

She bites her lip lightly, as her leg circles my butt. "Yes."

And then I'm inside her mouth, tracing my

tongue over her teeth, playing with her as we spar for control. She lets me win and I press my body into hers, smoothing myself over her, as I do everything I can to make her want me and need me. But even more than that, I make sure she can feel that when it comes to her there is nothing else that matters in the world. We literally kiss for an hour, until my lips hurt, until Rachel hisses painfully under me.

"Ow, my hip! I've got a cramp in my hip!" She laughs as I scramble up. "I'm so out of practice, Blake."

I laugh, too, mostly because my knee is killing me. "I'll trade you the hip for this knee."

We sound like an old married couple.

"Ha. No, thank you." She stretches out, kicking her legs across my lap before relaxing into a reclining position. "Okay, so that was really nice. I mean really, super-hot, sexy nice." She taps her stomach lightly with her hands. "You hungry?"

I smile and then roll my eyes. "If you tell me to get up and make you a sandwich I'm gonna be super bitter about it."

She laughs, poking me with her toe in the side. "I only did it once and it was only a joke."

"Hey, Rachel?"

She smiles at me. "Yeah?"

"Go make me a sandwich."

I block the pillow she whips at me.

"I hate you, Blake Fortier."

I twinkle a smile. "No you don't, you wouldn't have given me a pillow if you hated me. I remember what we did with them."

Rachel literally blushes the color of the pillow I'm referencing before she hops up from the sofa. "Oh, God." She runs a hand over her face, mortified. "We can't talk about it!"

"Why not?" I tease, setting the pillow aside and following her to the kitchen.

"Because, it's so embarrassing."

I lean on the counter, soaking in the joy of being able to play with her like this. I missed it, missed the camaraderie, the amazing connection we shared. Rachel glances at me with a grin, her blush fading now that I'm not teasing her anymore. She goes into the cupboard and pulls down two plates. "Did you eat dinner?"

I smile at her as I try to remember, but my thoughts are lost to me. When I try to go back to a memory from earlier today my mind starts playing from the point where Rachel woke me up. "I don't know."

Rachel just shakes her head. "Which means, no."

She opens the refrigerator and I grin so wide my cheeks hurt when she starts humming. I close my eyes and listen to her, letting the warmth fill me.

"What are you thinking about Blake?"

"You."

I open my eyes to her looking over her shoulder at me. She catches her lip as her eyes work me over before going back to the take out carton from the Thai place down the street. I trace her with my eyes and lean further on the counter. My elbow nudges something, and I focus my eyes on the sparkly red wrapping paper before me. I blink at it. "Did you put this here?"

Rachel looks back again. "Yeah, it's your gift from me. Well, obviously from me."

I run a finger over the glitter. "Thank you."

"You're welcome." Rachel pops dinner in the microwave and leans back on the opposite counter from me. The machine rumbles softly in the content quiet between us. Well, maybe not content, because Rachel is staring at the package. "Aren't you going to open it?"

I shrug lightly. "I don't know. Maybe, after we eat."

I can tell it drives her crazy when I say that, because she starts shifting from one foot to the other impatiently. "Okay."

There is an edge not taped down tightly and I pop the tape on that portion before her rapt gaze. "Or maybe I can open it now." I pull a little more, and the more I get loose on the fairly large, oddly shaped package, the more curious I become. Rachel laughs when I finally stop playing coy and use both hands to unwrap the gift. It's a small art kit–paint, brushes, and a spiral of matte paper. I pull free a detail brush and hold it in my hand. It's been a long time since I picked up a brush. It makes me feel so strange to hold the implement in my hand again. I can feel Rachel's eyes on me, so I struggle to say something. "Thank you. It's been a long time since I painted."

"Well, now you can whenever you like." She pulls the food from the microwave and then slides in beside me. "I always thought you were happiest when you were painting." I look up at her and she brushes a lock of hair from her face. I know I must be smiling because she looks at my lips and then smiles, too. "Well," she drawls after a moment, "there were other times that I think you were at least *equally* as happy."

"Yeah?" I trace a finger over her cheek. "When was that?'

Rachel smirks. "I'll give you a hint. There were pillows involved." She winks at me as she grabs the plates and carries them into the living room.

With my art supplies in tow I follow on her heels. "Guess I'll just have to paint in the meantime."

Rachel scoffs as she hands me my plate and a fork. "We are grown women now, pillows are no longer necessary."

I smile over at her. "True."

She turns on the TV, but leaves it muted. I don't really look at it as I munch on the most delicious smelling pad Thai in the world, next to my favorite person in the universe.

"You should paint something for right there." Rachel points at the wall beside us with her fork.

I look at the picture on the wall, "You already have something there."

Rachel swallows her food. "Yeah, but when I walk in that is the first thing I see and I would rather have a Fortier original instead."

It pings off my emotions because *original* Rachel wasn't nearly as interested in my art. Certainly not enough for me to put something up in our house. "Okay, I'd love to." I think about her words while we eat and talk about nothing important. We just laugh, we laugh more in the span of a reheated dinner than I remember laughing in fifteen years of marriage. It's absolutely magical.

"So, put your plate down and come here." Rachel stands and holds out her hand. I slide my plate to the coffee table and take her hand but she stops me. "Paintbrush."

I arch my brow at her. "You want one?"

"Yep, the medium one."

I hand it to her.

"Perfect, now paper."

I give it over as I gather the sleeve of paints in my hand. "Okay, so what are we doing?"

She saunters over to her desk and grabs the scotch tape. "We, my darling, are going to paint a masterpiece."

Her words make me feel butterflies and I actually giggle over it, like I'm twenty for real and caught between being an adult and being a girl in love. "Okay."

Rachel tears a piece of paper out of the spiral and tapes it to the wall. She pulls it free and then takes a step back making sure it's straight. Once she's satisfied she looks at me. "Okay. So, now what?"

I shrug. "I have no idea. What do you want to paint?"

"I have no idea." She brushes her hair back. "But I gotta get this hair under control." She drops back onto the sofa and grabs the ponytail holder I had in my hair earlier, swirling her hair into an unruly bun.

I smile at her as I lean on the back of the sofa. "What colors do you want it to be?"

"Don't we need to have the subject first?" Rachel stares hard at the paper. "Focus on it, all great artists stare at the page and it talks to them."

I wrinkle my nose at her words. "Who told you that?"

"I don't know, some jackass at a bar trying to get my number."

"Sounds like a jackass for thinking he *could* get your number." I bite off a smirk. "I've got your number, Rachel Kaplan."

She rolls her eyes with a laugh. "Yes, you do."

I stare at the paper.

"I know what I want, Blake. A tree." Rachel

glances over after a full minute of me staring at her.

I raise my eyebrow as I look over at the paper again. "A tree?"

"Yeah." She narrows her eyes as she climbs to her feet, her fingers move over the paper taped to the wall. "With long branches that stretch out like paths."

I turn to her hesitantly. "Like paths?"

"Yeah, it will remind me of the paths we take and the choices we make."

"You sure you want to look at a constant reminder of life and fate?" I remember that she didn't, once upon a time.

"Absolutely." Rachel shifts close to me and kisses my lips. "I can't see any reason why I wouldn't want to be reminded of where I am, and where I'm going."

She pulls back, nipping the tip of my nose cutely. "Let's do this, Picasso."

And we do, or start to. It's all very serious as we mix the blue and gray paint together and apply the first strokes. It's only when Rachel tries to twirl her paintbrush and instead gets paint all over her hand that things degrade into silliness. When I laugh at her, I get a strip of paint down my cheek from her next intentional accident. It becomes all-out war then, as I dot acrylic paint down her arm and she gets some in my hair.

We laugh late into Christmas morning, and over coffee at the kitchen table marvel at our work.

"I love it," Rachel says softly, her foot caressing against my calf.

I turn to her and lean my head against her shoulder.

"I do, too." My lips find her shoulder and kiss right beside a splash of white paint.

She tips her head against mine. "Blake?"

"Yeah?" I say sleepily, finally exhausted from all the laughing and fun we've had. I really can't wait for the coffee to kick in because I don't ever want this moment to end.

"Best Christmas ever," she whispers into my hair before pecking a soft kiss there.

I close my eyes briefly, nuzzling closer as her motions make everything right. "Best Christmas ever...so far," I add.

She toasts her mug against mine before setting it aside and pulling my face up to hers. "I can't wait for more." And with a rake of her fingers through my mussed and painted hair, she seals my lips with her kiss.

Chapter Seventeen

Her New Year's Resolution
December 31st, 2015

In another world, I didn't have this night with Rachel.

I didn't realize it until now, until I started stealing back more time from the rip of the universe, but we really fought a lot. I don't remember what it was about, I never did remember the reasons we tore into one another, but we had gone our own ways for New Year's Eve.

The car pulls up to the curb outside her apartment and I look out at the warm glow of the windows. Smiling up at them, I can't help but hope that I'll get to see her graduation as well, since another fight had stolen that from me too.

I can't believe how many milestones I missed. It blows my mind.

When the driver opens the door for me, I tighten my coat warding away the chill as I step out into the snow. It stopped falling, so it feels colder as I fish into my purse and pull my phone free. For some reason I feel warmer in the light from the street lamp, so I stand in its halo, as I get my phone in my hand.

I really am sappy, because I touch the screen, and a picture of Rachel laughing pops up. It makes a smile tug my lips and I swipe the image away only to replace it with her contact listing. Everything Rachel, and I wouldn't have it any other way.

The line rings, and when it connects I glance up at her apartment again.

"Hi, sweetheart." I can hear her smile through the phone.

"Hi, angel. I'm outside."

"Okay, be down in a minute."

"See you."

My breath blossoms in the night as I wait, only to have it whisked away by the air a moment later. I stare at the stairwell she will walk down, until my eyes play tricks on me, until I swear I can see her. She doesn't appear from the shadows though, so I know it's just my imagination. She will be down any minute and my stomach knots in anticipation, hoping that she is surprised.

Hoping that she is happy.

I said we were going out to dinner before meeting up with our friends at a bar downtown, but I really hope that the limousine behind me gives a clue that this isn't any ordinary date. Nope. This is the start to something I want to be magical. When I think that, I don't mind that I'll be eating Ramen for the next month to afford it, nor do I even feel the brisk rake of winter even though it pulls my hair around my face and into my eyes. I swipe the strands back and when I do, I see Rachel coming down the stairs. She slows at the bottom as she looks out at me and then trades the mottled shadow on the side of the building for the amber glow of the street light as she comes toward me.

I lose my breath, because she really is the most excruciatingly beautiful creature on the earth.

She comes toward me putting one foot in front

of the other in a model walk I showed her for fun years ago. I grin when I see it, and her lips form a secret smile because she knows *I know*. I follow the swank black high heel boots up as they move, as her legs shift under the matte leather pants she wears.

Okay, leather pants. Seriously, she must be trying to kill me. They make her legs look so long, pliant, and toned as the light outlines every sinew, every cut of her dancer's muscles and her lithe gate that seems set to music. I drag my eyes further, to where her peacoat is wrapping around her like a lover. The lover I wish I was for her. It shifts with the gentle curves of her hips and breasts.

She prowls like a panther, dark and sexy with a whisper of danger in her advance. I've never seen this burning confidence anywhere other than the stage. It makes her look like a totally different person or at least it seems like it, until her ruby red lips part with the beaming smile owned by my best friend.

I reach out when she's close enough and touch the red ribbon tied in her hair gently. My fingers feel numb and I don't think it has anything to do with the cold. "You are stunning," I whisper in awe, my hand falling to her cheek in a caress.

She blushes prettily. "And you got us a limo?"

I lick my lips, because I can feel them cracking with how hard I'm breathing at the image of her. I almost forget what I planned.

Almost.

I reach back, popping the door to the sleek black car and offer it to her. "For you, angel." I think I see her lashes flutter when I call her that.

"Thank you." She grins at me, before I follow her into the interior.

In the dim light I reach for the bottle of champagne, rolling the window down a little. "Champagne?" I smile at her frown. "Don't worry, this is a pink moscato, so it's sickly sweet."

She's still working on enjoying the taste of wines, sparkling or not, so she smiles now that it's confirmed she can actually enjoy it. "And it's pink."

Her favorite color.

I nod as I work loose the cork and then angle it out the window as it bursts, shooting out into the night. I love that it makes her jump and then melt into giggles. "Pretty slick, Blake." She pats my leg. "Do you do this a lot?"

"Just for you." It's the truth. She is the only person I've ever shared champagne with. The thought catches me in surprise, because it's true. I catalogue through my life in the blink of an eye and realize, I've never had champagne with anyone else.

Apparently it's *our* thing.

I pour a glass and when I glance at her, she is looking out the window in the direction of the cork. I head her thoughts off at the pass. "I don't think a cork is gonna cause near as much damage as the tons of confetti being released in Times Square tonight."

She seems at peace with that thought.

When I pass the glass to her, she touches my hand and then looks up at me from beneath thick lashes. It spreads warmth through me, and I marvel at how she has always been able to touch my hand and reach my heart.

"So what are we toasting?"

The engine turns over and I pour myself a glass as the driver pulls away slowly from the curb. I lean back into the seat beside her, shifting as close as I can get before my knees touch hers. She makes space for me to get closer, and when the streetlights flash over her, I can see her smile right before her legs squeeze my good knee softly.

I lift the glass. "First your birthday a couple of weeks ago. Happy twenty-first."

"Thank you."

"And mine, too. So you can't ditch me in front of a bar."

Rachel laughs as she clinks her glass against mine and takes a sip. She shivers and I'm not sure if it's from the window or the bite of the drink. I roll up the window just to be safe. "Will I ever get to live that down?"

I regard her before I mock roll my eyes. "I suppose someday." Rachel leans toward me with a very apologetic face and I peck a kiss to her pouting lips. "I'll let you live it down in like twenty years, okay?"

She grins so vividly with that lipstick as bright red as it is. "Okay, deal."

I clear my throat, lifting my glass again and Rachel mimes the motion. "We also need to say goodbye to the year." Her hand finds mine in the darkness. "It was a very good year." She takes another sip and then smacks her lips, twisting her drink in her fingers. "Come to think of it, so is this," she notes.

I lean against the warm leather and remember the times we nestled into the back of a car and drove to the airport. None of those times can compare to this, because it was never for fun. It wasn't like we ever got a town car or a limo and just went out. It was always something functional, to avoid leaving our cars somewhere or to escape the hassles of parking. I never just let her enjoy things, or myself come to think of it.

I was always too structured and it was *such* a waste of money.

What it really equated to was a waste of the time we had together.

"What are you thinking, Blake?"

"I was thinking that I like taking a pretty girl like you out on the town in a limousine."

Rachel laughs softly. "I like to be taken out in a limousine."

I edge a tad bit closer, tightening my hand in hers. "I have no doubt that someday you will get shuttled in one all over the place."

"That would be fun, though I'm sure it would lose the appeal if done too much."

"There are some things that don't lose appeal no matter how much you do them." I feel my eyebrow raise, feel the blush starting on my cheeks, because, yes, I meant it like *that*.

Apparently there is enough innuendo and blood to go around for both of us, because Rachel blushes too. "There is only one thing I've found that doesn't lose appeal, no matter how many times I get the chance to enjoy it."

I wet my lips as her eyes fasten there. I don't know if it was her gaze on my mouth that made me have to wet them or if it was the other way around, but it feels rather surreal as she leans toward me in slow motion. I watch her come to me, all dark tumbling curls and an innocent red bow, and she closes her eyes at the very last moment. I smile into her kiss and I feel her lips pull tight into a grin.

It's so funny that now, even though I have been greedily kissing Rachel over the last two weeks, now I feel the crush of emotion that silences my thoughts. I feel it in my heart. It must be the night, the thievery of this moment that plays with my feelings. It's so very thrilling, because in this moment it feels like she is kissing me differently, like I'm kissing her back differently, too.

It feels like I'm kissing my wife.

When I feel that, it's like Rachel knows, because her fingers thread into my hair. It's one of my favorite things, a motion that will forever be reserved for her, and it winds me even more. Her tongue traces my bottom lip and I press closer, reveling in the insistent touch and finally I soften my lips. The tickle of her fingers in the hair on the back of my neck is spellbinding and when she tilts her head and that soft tongue is everywhere against mine, I'm lost.

I think my eyes flutter open, because for the briefest of moments I can see her eyelashes, long and soft, and the curve of her cheek, then I'm in the darkness again hanging on her lips like I'm drowning.

And in many ways I am.

I have been drowning for years, for a whole lifetime before, but never as deeply as I have this time around. In the past two weeks I have literally fallen in love so much harder and deeper that I feel like I must not have loved her before. There is no way I could have, because it shouldn't be able to get deeper than *that*.

But Rachel is different now. Somehow she is better, wiser, more dynamic. She is less focused on herself and more on other people. She's had me painting almost every day with her and I can't really say how much it means to me. She *cares*, and that isn't to say she didn't before, but that blindingly bright arrogance and the streak of self-centered drive is somehow subdued. And for the first time, I feel like the room I make for her to grow isn't at my expense.

I didn't think it was possible, but she is a better version of herself and I truly hope I am too.

I think I am.

Rachel's hand cups my cheek as she pulls back, touching her nose to mine. "I love you, Blake."

Her words never cease to make my heart skip a beat. Literally, it does a hiccup in my chest. I smile. "I love you too, angel."

I think we kissed for twenty minutes, because it should have taken that long to get to the restaurant, and now I can see it out the window as the car comes to a stop.

I don't know how I'm supposed to walk out, or scoot out, or even move because her touches have made my legs jelly. I know I need to get out of the car, that I have a highly sought after reservation waiting inside, but seriously I want to be driven around for the rest of the night while I make love to her lips.

Rachel brushes a hand through her hair and smiles back at me before the door pops open and the interior lights highlight the flush in her cheeks. It makes me feel better that I'm not the only one being betrayed by physiology. She takes my hand as she moves out. I don't let it go, though I might have put a little bit too much direct weight on my knee because of it.

The Blue Hill Restaurant is one of the most beautiful, well reviewed restaurants in the city. I put in my reservation a month ago, it's *that* in demand. And on a night where couples all across the city want to flock to the romantic ambiance, I knew I had to get in early. I gotta say, I almost feel bad for passing the line of people waiting to get in. That is until I realize that many of them are looking at Rachel and then our hands twined together. Then I'm in love with the idea of passing them, falling under their watchful gaze. I'm in love with the image they must see, and the sheer fact that it is *my* hand in hers. No one else's.

Mine.

Her fingers tighten reflexively, and just because I can, I lift her hand and graze my lips over her knuckles before I open the door for her. Yes, I'm *that* ridiculously lame and in love. I'm proud to own up to it, especially when she gives me a very loving look and blushes a little more.

Not all the eyes in the world could ever compare to hers.

When we make it to our table, a half curve booth in the back, Rachel takes up the place near me. Looking at her now is difficult because I think she intentionally wore a shirt that would test my ability to keep my eyes above her neck. It's unfair actually, because she has a long crystal necklace and it tumbles ever so delicately between the swells of her breasts. It keeps winking at me with every breath she takes. It's like being in church and trying not to laugh, the more you tell yourself not to do it, it just makes you do it more.

I think I can hear the host rattling off menu options, but I'm stuck on that necklace and the way the candlelight sparkles right where I wish I could kiss.

"Um, a red wine." Rachel reaches for the wine list, and the view is *that* much better. "A cabernet."

"And for you miss?"

I blink, because I realize my eyes are on her cleavage and the host is waiting on me. "Um, I'm sorry?"

"Would you like something to drink?"

"An ice tea, please."

I fill my hands with the menu but all I really want to do is get back into the limo and fill my hands with her. I find it very hard to focus on the food choices, because across from me the candle is flickering and it makes Rachel look ethereal. I glance at her over the top of my menu, watching for a moment as her expressive eyes map over the pages. Okay, so it's more than a glance, because I watch her swallow, watch the skin at her neck pull, watch her lips move as she reads.

"What?" Rachel asks softly before looking up at my rapt gaze on her.

"I was just thinking about the little things you do that I like so much."

"What are those things?" Rachel sets her menu down and reaches for her wine to take a sip. She doesn't actually drink anything, she just pulls it closer.

I arch my brow. "Are you reaching for compliments from me?"

"Maybe." Rachel shrugs lightly. "Or maybe I want to know so I can do it more for you."

She tilts her chin a little defiantly in challenge. It makes my throat tighten, because it is the same look when she refused to believe that I didn't love her four years ago. It's a tiny motion, yet it speaks volumes. I don't even think she knows she is doing it, but that makes it all the more beautiful to me.

I clear my throat. "It isn't stuff that you know you do, and I'm pretty sure if I told you, you would become aware of it and the cuteness would be ruined."

Rachel laughs. "You must be studying your clinical psychology segment right now."

I swallow a sip of my ice tea and roll my eyes. "Maybe." However, more than that, I know from previous experience that if I tell Rachel about her lip-synched reading, it will eventually disappear.

I don't want to lose it, not this time around.

When the waiter comes back around Rachel orders something, and I ask for the same thing. It's less that I want to eat what she's eating and more like I don't know what's on the menu. I'm too absorbed in her.

Eventually she works up the desire to drink her wine, I giggle before the glass even hits her lips because she's already making a face.

"Making fun of me isn't nice," she warns, taking barely a sip. She scowls.

"Just cause you are twenty-one doesn't mean you have to drink. I can tell you don't like it." My hands work across the table and corral the flute of the wine glass moving it away from her.

Rachel eyes me and brings the glass back toward her. "Wine is an acquired taste and I'm working on acquiring it." Her face grows somber after a moment and she fixes her eyes on the stem while her fingers twist around it. "Can I ask you something?"

It's gotta be serious if she is asking permission. "Sure."

"Are you happy?" Rachel asks softly.

I don't really know how to answer her question. She has a tone in the asking, one that makes me hyper aware that she is probing for something specific in the rather innocuous words she uttered. "What do you mean?"

"I don't know, are you happy, you know, happy here with me?"

"*Of course* I'm happy here with you." I put enough inflection into it that she smiles. "What is there not to be happy about?"

"Are you sad that things are different than they were before?"

I really can't explain how double entendre that sentence is to me. I know what she is referencing, that we aren't the same as we were four years ago, but yet I feel very strange suddenly. The restaurant seems to hush around us, as if everyone is listening with baited breath.

"I miss some parts."

Rachel nods. "I miss some things too."

I really want to say that she is the only one that can change our current stalemate, but without a caveat and a conversation about it, it will just make me sound like a jerk. So I drink my tea instead.

"Is there anything you aren't happy about?"

I stare at the table top, again unsure of what to say. As much as I do enjoy the thrill of new moments between us, it's unsettling when I feel like anything I say will mess things up. "You know Rachel, I could just answer your direct question. Just ask me what you want to know."

"Are you content to keep things how they are between us?"

I shake my head. "No. I want a lot more."

Rachel looks away, and I don't know what it means when her gaze gets lost on other people. "How much more?"

"How much more are you willing to give me?"

Rachel traces a perfectly manicured nail over the tablecloth, her eyes coming back to firmly glue on the wine glass. "Do you remember the car?"

I'm confused. "The limo?" Is she talking about our kiss?

"No, the car where we..." She gives me a look.

Oh, *that* car, by the lake with the fireflies. She is talking about *a lot* more than a kiss. "Yes, I remember. I could never forget."

"That night," she glances up at me, "wow, well, that night was amazing. It wasn't just because of the obvious though, you know?" She drops her voice. "It wasn't because of what we did."

I lean on my hand, staring at her in the low light. "What was it about then?"

"It was about the fact you went first. That you told me you loved me. That you opened up." She shrugs. "I'm gonna tell you something, and it's really weird, but you'll just have to go with it."

Her words put a nervous tingle up my back. "Okay."

"That night was the first time that I felt there weren't any secrets between us. It was hard in the beginning to trust you, because I've always had this feeling that there is something else going on with you. That you were hiding something from me."

I swallow slowly. "I don't have any secrets. I've told you everything." I remind myself that I've told her everything I *can* and it makes me feel like I'm *not* lying.

Rachel fake sips her wine again. "I know. I told you it was crazy. I suppose I just need you to put yourself out there again."

"Put myself out there?" I pause, looking down, mostly because it's desperately difficult to hold her eyes when her sixth sense observations are proof that we are closer than we used to be. "I'm pretty sure I put myself out there when I told you I loved you again at the concert. I don't think I can put myself out any further."

"And I remember I asked you what you wanted from me, and you couldn't tell me. Have you figured it out yet?" She arches her eyebrow at me as she grabs her napkin. I realize the waiter must be here with the food. I can't take my eyes off her, not even when white plates interrupt the view of her taking a gulp of wine.

She doesn't look at me when we are alone again.

I stare at my Fettuccine Alfredo and push it around with my fork. I'm not really a pasta person, so this is probably the least desirable thing I could have chosen. I glance at Rachel and her eyes are on me as she chews. She tilts her head in question. "Not what you wanted after all?"

I set my fork down. "I know exactly what it is I want."

"We aren't talking about food anymore, are we?"

"No, with you. I know what I want." I take a very long pull from the straw of my iced tea. "I just don't say it because I worry it will mess everything up."

"I remember I knew a young girl who was in love with a super confident, head cheerleader." She smirks. "I probably never told you, but my favorite thing about you was that you had no fear when it came to us."

If only she knew. "Are you telling me to just say it?"

She stabs absently at a piece of food. "I'm telling you to give me the answer to my question, and we will see how things go from there."

I lick my lips, I'm sure by now there is no lipstick left. "I want you Rachel. I want to know you're exclusively mine. That we are together. I want to touch you, kiss you, and lie in bed beside you every night. And I'm not talking about for a month, or a year; I'm talking about for always."

She sets her fork down. "And?"

I don't know how she can be so blasé after I just said what I said. I really don't know what more I can say to impress upon her how serious I am. "And, what?"

Her phone makes a twinkling sound, and she actually turns to her clutch, leaving me hanging on the words between us.

"And you're going to *actually* answer your phone." I roll my eyes as I go back to poking my food.

"I'm buying time."

"For what?"

"For you."

I shake my head. "I have no idea what you are talking about."

She just smiles and slides her phone away. "So you were saying something about me being your permanent booty call."

My eyes shoot wide. "I didn't say that. That isn't what I meant at all."

"Then tell me what you meant because if I take away the flowery language in that sentence, that's exactly what you said."

I frown. "I really hope you're messing with me, because I know you know that wasn't what I was saying."

Rachel maps her hand across the table and takes mine as she moves closer. "Maybe a little, but I also know you aren't being totally truthful, so it seems fair."

"I *am* telling the truth."

"But, not all of it." She's pushing me to say things I don't know if I should, things I don't know if I can. I want our future, my past, back. She's so close to me now that I can feel the warmth of her thigh against mine. The tumble of Chanel pours over me, and under that the whisper of wine adds the finish as we breathe the same air.

"Tell me, Blake." She begs with her eyes, in a way that makes it impossible to resist when we are this close to one another. "You were always the one with a plan when it came to us."

"You want to know..." the motion of her hand capturing the span of my thigh just above my knee, halts my voice.

Her words ghost over me. "*Everything* you want from me, in plain English."

I swallow as the wave of hopes and memories melt together. "I want to date you, build a life with you. I want to watch you graduate, propose to you, marry you. You have no idea how desperately I want that, to buy a house with you, build it into a home. I want to have children with you. Live with you, love with you, be your wife, hear you say it every day."

Rachel's eyes consume me. "That you're my wife?"

I take a breath. "Yes."

"Is that all?"

I can't think of anything else. Except this, and it makes the tightness in my chest that much sharper when I say it. It takes me back to our living room floor, and the lonely death I had. "I never want to live a day without you because I don't think I can."

Her fingers tighten on my skin and she let's go of the breath she was holding.

"Is that everything?"

"Yes, everything. That's what I want, what I've always wanted."

"Okay."

❧❧❧❧

And on the back of such profound confessions, her whispered okay is incredibly underwhelming. In the limo, as we race off to O'Malley's bar, I stare out the window in silence. She hasn't said anything to me. I can't even look at her. I can feel her eyes on me every now and then, lilting on me as I watch the snow come down from the warmth of the car.

When I focus on the windowpane, I see her ghostly image. She looks deep in thought, her expression churning as much as the darkness in her eyes. When the limo slows and pulls to the curb, it's uncanny that my eyes focus on a cork, half buried in the snow. That's when I realize we are back at Rachel's place. I turn to her so quickly it makes me a little dizzy.

"The bar?" I can't get any more words out than that.

"I told you I was buying you time."

"I thought it was so I could answer your question."

"No, I had other motives."

"What other motives?"

"You'll see." She pops the door. "Wait here."

I nod, waiting, watching as she tightens her coat and circles the car. She casually traces a heart into the frost on my window with her nail before moving on. I touch the looping lines and before it disappears from the heat of my fingers, I pull out my phone and take a picture.

It feels like forever, long enough for her frost heart to be coated in snow, before she pulls the door open again. The frozen snow-swept wind that comes in, literally steals my breath. It litters her dark hair in glitter.

"You ready?"

I shiver, clutching my coat tighter. "Yes."

She gives me her hand and I slide outside. The cold shoots into my knee immediately, making it feel like the joint is made of blades. I try to ignore it as Rachel's hand twines over mine. We get halfway up the stairs when I remember I have to authorize the charge on my debit card. "Wait, I have to go back and pay."

Rachel holds my hand firm. "Already done." She flashes her Platinum Visa before sliding it away into the back pocket of her pants. She hijacked my date.

"Rachel."

Her laugh is self-satisfied. "I can be very persuasive when I want to be. Besides, it's my parents account. They won't mind me using it this once."

"You sure?"

She smiles over her shoulder at me. "I don't really care to be honest." She opens her mouth to say something, but nothing comes as we move up the last few steps.

"What?" I finally ask, as her keys slide into the first bolt and then the second and her door groans open. She shakes the keys free before meeting my gaze on the landing. "They won't care once I tell them it was with you."

I follow her inside, dazed. "Really?"

"Yes." Rachel drops her purse to the chair by the door. "When I had break ups with other people, they would always say, such-and-such never cared about you like Blake did."

I stare at the brass doorknob in my hand.

"Lock the door, please."

"Did you date a lot?" I really don't know why I asked the question, I don't want to know.

"I'm not talking about it right now. I have something else I want to say." Rachel says it from behind me as I lock the door. I turn to her slowly, because she has that tone, and it makes my heart flutter. I'd be a liar if I said I wasn't hoping for a reciprocation of all the things I've said.

I hold her gaze as she slides her hands over the front of her coat, plucking at the buttons. She parts it wide. The necklace that has been taunting me all night catches the light, refracting bursts of color over the swells of her breasts. She lets the coat fall to the floor. It makes my knees weak and I press my back to the door as I'm swallowed by the image of it.

"I owe you something." In the sparse glow from the nightlight in the living room and the arc of inset lighting in the kitchen, she bites her lip as her eyes move over me. I don't need to be psychic to know what she is thinking with that predatory look. I go to say as much, but when she takes up the space before me and blocks the light, all the air is sucked from my lungs. I can barely manage the words on the tip of my tongue.

"What do you owe me?"

"My New Year's resolution."

"What's your resolution?"

Her voice is very dark and the heat of her breath covers the exposed skin at my throat as she gets even closer. "It's something I'm going to do a lot this coming year."

"Yeah?" I sound almost as breathless as I feel.

"Yeah," she husks, her fingers snaking out in the blackness. I shiver as they trace sharply along my pants as she uses her nails to path a line from my thigh to my ribs. "Something I plan to absolutely wreck for years to come."

I shift into the motion of her fingers on me as they move back down, out from under my coat and slink to my leg. "What's that?"

I can only make out the shape of her lips, but I can tell she's smiling. "It's something I'm absolutely in love with."

I wet my lips 'cause I can feel them cracking with how fast I'm rushing breath into my lungs. "Oh, yeah?"

"Uh, huh." Rachel's hands stop at the waist of my pants and she curls her finger into the top hem, twisting the material in her grip. "It's something that I think really needs my attention."

I laugh. "I have a feeling your generosity is selfish."

She ghosts her lips over my throat and I shudder a breath. In her heels she is eye to eye with me, and I gasp as she tightens her hand in my pants. "Very selfish."

"So, what's this resolution?" I wrap my hand in her hair, inclining her face to me.

"You."

Our mouths slant, tongues meet, and my reality is swallowed by her kiss. She kisses me so well, she knows everything I like, and she uses it to her advantage as she robs me of all reason with her incredible lips.

"Maybe I don't want to be your resolution, how about that?" I tease as her lips trail down my chin and firmly fasten on my neck.

"Oh, you want to be." She growls between the motions of her mouth as her hands start a kneading motion on my butt.

Yes, I really do.

She removes one hand and twists it in my hair with a tug as her tongue maps my ear. "Come to bed with me."

She says it with a tone that *clearly* implies it's not for sleep especially with how she is touching me, but I continue teasing her anyway. "You want to go to sleep already?"

Rachel smirks against my ear. "Fuck, no."

And then she's on me. It happens so fast and with such force, the front door rattles with the impact. I grunt as I submit to her ravenous lips along my neck. Her hands clawing hungrily over my jacket, fisting the material to graze the skin two layers deep.

"You won't be sleeping for a while."

I shiver as I arch into her. "Promises, promises."

She laughs. "Nope, fact."

Her lips fasten to mine, and I kiss her, hands roaming, pulling her toward me. She brazenly nudges my legs apart and then presses her hip into me. With the extra height and leverage, she pulls my hips to her, grinding into me until I drop my head back against the door and moan softly. "Do you like this?"

I can't answer as she does it again, while her mouth moves over my skin. I slide my hands down to cup the pliant leather covering her butt. I pull her into me over and over, until my legs start to shake. "God, Rachel." I swallow the smoke in my voice. "We keep this up you might get me to come without taking my clothes off."

She smiles and then grinds harder. "Wouldn't be the first time."

I hike my brow at her satisfied grin. "You're right."

"But I want your clothes off."

She squeezes my hips, making me ache. I toss my coat.

"Now your sweater and shirt."

She looks so confident, as she stares at me. It makes my hands tremble, which makes the removing of my sweater harder. I shrug out of it, and after four very exaggerated attempts, slide it off.

Her eyes breeze over me as I pull my shirt off. "You are so beautiful, Blake."

"Thank you, now yours."

"In a minute."

I get my disappointed whine halfway out of my mouth and then Rachel jerks on my hips and unclasps my pants. I blow out a breath as she slides to her knees wrestling with the zipper. "I want to taste you," she hisses.

At this point she could fucking rip my pants, I don't even care. She doesn't, she gets them undone somehow, and I roll my eyes closed as the material slides down and her hands pet over me.

"I've thought about this for a long time," she whispers. "I always loved the taste of you on my tongue."

Her eyes meet mine, and she looks so innocent with that bow in her hair it puts a blush on my cheeks. "That bow makes it seem doubly dirty when you say that."

She laughs. "Then pull it out, because I'm gonna say a lot dirtier things."

"No, I like having a tanned version of Snow White between my legs."

Rachel's laugh turns into a soft moan as my hands twist in her hair a moment later. She moves in and I arch in anticipation, but when I feel her lips, her *tongue*, I'm not ready for it. There is no way I could ever be.

Her groan travels the length of my body, hands caressing up the back of my thighs to grab my butt while she circles with her tongue. "Just like I remember."

And she's sucking.

"Oh, Jesus." I spasm against the wood finding the doorknob to keep myself upright. "Oh, God, I love your mouth, baby."

She pulls back, and when I see her lick me off her lips with that smile, it's *on*.

I'm most certainly a romantic type of person in a lot of respects, but right now, not so much. "Put your mouth back on my clit."

"With pleasure." Rachel laughs until her mouth becomes otherwise engaged and my fingers tighten in her dark mane.

My knee groans in protest as she pats down my pants in an attempt to get them off, but they are completely twisted in my shoes. I feel like I'm going to lose my balance and the door rattles in my hand. "Not gonna happen, they're too…" I choke on the rush of air in my throat and when she grazes me with her teeth, I squeak, "Tight."

I can feel her smile before her tongue flicks softly. Her hand lopes up the inside of my leg and I stare down at her, at the tumble of her dark hair as her head moves, and then her fingertips are pushing into me. The tremor that follows takes over my whole body, because those beautiful fingers that I held earlier are inside me.

Oh my God.

"I have to kiss you." She stands, smoothing herself against me, her kiss twisting against mine.

I can taste myself on her lips, on her tongue when she explores my mouth. I moan against her as she shifts her wrist and presses as deep as she can go. Her palm grinds, fingers hooking to press right *there*, and I see stars.

"I need you naked, I need to taste you, lick you, fuck you," I rush between her kisses, my hand grazing under her shirt and cupping her breast.

"Oh, you *will be* fucking me all night. You have a lot of missed time to make up for." She flicks her fingers inside me and I can't take it anymore. I grab her arms and shuffle forward, pushing her toward her bedroom. She's giggling. "I'm still inside you." Her voice is very sing-song and proud.

"Not for long." I push her backward, her hand slipping free as she falls to the mattress. I lean on her dresser and shake loose my shoes, stripping free my pants with a hurried hand. When I can pop my bra off, Rachel is arching on the bed, working her leather pants off. It's probably the hottest thing I've ever seen. She slides them down her legs and then kicks them backward over her head to smack the closet door. Her shirt and bra follow a moment later, and she rolls over brushing them off her bedspread. Okay, I stand corrected...she's wearing a lacy black thong.

That is the hottest thing I've ever seen.

I slide my hands to her lower back, pinning her in place on her stomach. I crawl over her, pressing my body to hers, grinding into her butt. "So sexy," I purr in her ear, feeling chills race down her body. I tug her underwear off.

"Can't wear pants that tight without a really awesome pair of underwear."

She rolls over and I slide back into her, feeling her heat press everywhere against me. I don't waste a moment, I duck my head and kiss a line straight down the center of her and finally stretch her open to my tongue.

"Oh, Blake." She presses her hips into my face, until my nose is teasing her clit with each thrust of my tongue. It's so hard, she's so wet. I claw my nails into her skin until she hisses, until she moans my name in the darkness. Then I circle her clit with my lips and pull it into my mouth with enough suction she strangles the comforter in her hands, whining desperately.

"Oh, angel." I lick teasingly, my hand trailing up her thighs, over her stomach to brush her nipples. She circles me with her leg, caressing her calf over my shoulder blade, pulling me closer.

I don't know if she meant for me to hear it, but after a few moments of my attention, her voice breaks over her words. "I missed you." It's just above a whisper, but it fills my ears and I slow my motions, sliding my mouth up to kiss the crease in her pelvis.

"I missed you, too."

Her fingers trail into my hair, and I rest my head against her thigh. When I look up at her, past where her chest is heaving breaths, her lips hover with a fragile smile. She catches my hand, and tugs gently. "Come up here."

I arch my brow at her, debating whether I want to stop doing what I'm doing, but she pulls again and I shift until I'm lying against her. She wraps her arms around me, pulling me down until we are nose to nose. I thread under her neck, until her hair is tumbling over my arm. "This is what I want. I want to be in your arms."

I caress her side. "Well, now you are."

Her eyes map over my face, and she traces my cheek with her finger. "I missed you so much. I was serious when I said it was always you, that you are my soul mate Blake."

Her words make my whole body buzz and I regard her expression. "You too, you're mine."

She cups the back of my head as she pulls me down for a kiss. It's soft, the fury of our passion ebbing like the tide, leaving a frothing flood of warmth between us. I feel like I'm in a free fall as her lips connect with mine over and over. I circle her tighter as she pushes me onto my back, her hair falling over us. I stamp my hands over her back, feeling the warmth and softness, drowning in the scent of shampoo and Chanel.

Rachel breaks our kisses after a moment, pulling back to straddle me. "Dry mouth, one second."

I watch her slide away with a whisper of a smile on her lips. It's all I can make out in the soupy light from outside. "Sorry my fault," I tease.

She catches herself on the doorjamb halfway out of the room and I see the shadow of her form take up the doorway again. "Totally your fault."

Alone in her bed, I stare up at the ceiling, until I realize I'm in her bed. I valiantly suppress my emotions as they roll over me like waves. I work my hands over my face, holding tight and telling myself not to cry. It doesn't help, because I can smell her all over me, and it makes reality that much more beautiful, that much more real. My eyes feel hot and when I hear the cap break on a bottle of water, I realize Rachel is back in the room. I pull my hands back, and notice the light is on in the hallway. I sit up slowly, squinting as the tears pooling in my eyes come down my cheeks.

She looks like her angelic namesake, like the young woman I saw onstage three months ago, with light pouring over her shoulder. This time though, her hair is wild and tousled from me, by me. I can't see her face, but I know she can see mine, she can see I'm in tears. There is something very exposing about it and I wipe at my face, ready to make my excuses, ready to disavow how deeply I feel right in this moment, until I see the wetness on Rachel's face when she sets the bottle aside.

"Hey, come here," I whisper. She shifts on her feet like she is going to sit beside me and then climbs into my lap instead. I sit up meeting her body. Our everything mixes in that moment as we kiss–skin, atoms, tears, arousal, emotion. Everything she is, I am, and she is, too, again.

"I never thought I'd have you again." Kisses pepper over my cheeks and into the hair at my temples. "I can't believe it. I can't explain what it means to me."

"You don't have to, because I feel it to."

When our mouths meet again, it feels different and in the back of my mind I wonder if this is how Rachel felt that night she cried as I made love to her. Every touch of her sends shimmers through me, until we are arching into one another and I swear I'm a ball of stardust, a swirling galaxy in her hands.

"You feel so good," I whisper, brushing her hair off her shoulder to catch the soft skin of her neck.

Rachel arches against me, sliding her warm hands over me. "You, too." Her fingers keep moving down and I slide to my back under her. My hands take the same path, and she shifts over me when I slip between her legs. "Yes, Blake, right there." I caress until the brush of her fingertips against my clit splinters a jolt through me. Then I pull her down into a kiss as I press into her.

"Oh, honey," Rachel moans against my lips, fingers following my motion a moment later to claim me for herself.

"I love feeling you inside me."

"I do, too."

And when those sculpted fingers start a slow thrust into me, I follow her motions, keeping time with her. She drops to her elbow over me, her breath tumbling over me and into me as I whisper her name over and over. I lean into her hand as her fingers thread into my hair and her thumb caresses my cheek.

"For the rest of my life."

"What?" I tremble as her motions pick up

"You and me, Blake."

Her words make me feel like everything in my life has come down to this moment between us. It feels like this was always supposed to be, that she was supposed to be here in this moment with me. My heart thunders as the passion stretches between us, our bodies grinding in a well ingrained rhythm. Everything is aligned, and for the first time I can see how my world weaves together with hers.

She feels like the sun and I'm captured in her gravity as I spin my own path. I may have gone in a circle chasing myself across the universe. However, I know it will always be to her, around her, with her.

We will dance across the stars for eternity. I know it.

It renews me, invigorates my soul.

And when she finally arches desperately against me, her sounds in my ear letting me know she is there, I blow stardust behind my eyes as my orgasm rips my soul in half. It makes me cry because I can't hold in the power of my love for her. Because the force of it shatters me to glittering pieces and there will never be another moment like this to show her what she does to me.

I tremble in her arms to the same pulsating shudders that echo from her. I feel like I'm being buffeted by a storm, like I'm hurling into the void with her.

And in a way we are...always and forever.

Overwhelmed, Rachel collapses against me sniffling, reaching to pull me tighter. "Don't slide out. Don't let me go."

I peck the top of her head shakily and my arm corrals back, squeezing. "Never."

"Never, ever?" She smiles up at me and I measure the damp mahogany eyes holding mine.

I grin and shake my head. "Never, ever."

Rachel sniffs again and then pushes herself up, my fingers sliding *that* much deeper. I feel my eyes go wide, as the blinds map tiger stripes across her. Between the image and the feelings, it's enough to push another loping shuddering orgasm through me.

"Jesus, Rachel," I gasp as her body mirrors the contractions I just felt. "God, angel..." I can't even form a coherent thought, watching her climax over me. Rachel grinds down with intent and then even my words fail me.

She fills in the blanks for me, as everything crackles again between us. "All night, I want you all night. I don't care if I can't walk for a week. I want it, you, everything until I can't anymore. I want you to own me like I *am* your wife."

"Oh, God," I moan, grappling for her and pressing her to the bed beneath me. And though she doesn't know it, she pushes boundaries for something I'm very willing to give, if only for tonight. "I'm going to absolutely devour you because I love you so much."

"Blake?"

I slow my motions. "Yeah?"

"Prove it."

"Oh, I will." And I do as I make her my wife over and over again until the shimmer of morning races through those eyes I love.

Chapter Eighteen

Always
May 16th, 2016

I'm not sure where we are going, but as the laughter and screams of happy graduates fades behind us, I settle into the idea of Rachel leading the way. The world blurs around us, fuzzy at the edge of my vision. Rachel smiles at me, and when her hand tightens in mine, I relish in the contentment we share.

It feels like another movie moment, the way her red gown flutters, how her hair spirals in auburn highlights and makes her eyes sparkle almost burgundy. The cap she refused to throw has a tassel that shimmers as she turns to me and kisses my lips. I hold to her tightly, laughing into her kiss, and she is laughing too. I can't put into words how happy I am and how breathless I feel in every moment between us.

But no moment as much as this.

This moment where the lighting is perfect and it tangles in the brown of her eyes and crashes against the white of her teeth as she pulls back and laughs in my arms. It splashes against the tan of her throat, rushes the blush on her cheeks, and blows stardust into my heart. She is a crescendo of navy blue dress and the shimmer of diamond earrings.

And when it seems like it can't get better, it does.

I hold her close, wrangling the sunlight imprinted

beauty in my arms. "I'm so proud of you." My fingers find the ropes on her shoulders, the symbols of graduating with honors. I twist the silken cords in my fingers, blue and gold burnished proudly.

Rachel is breathing hard. "I love you, too." She giggles, pulling me back into a kiss that shatters time, and the world drops away because it is undeserving of this moment between us. The moment where she slides her arm over my shoulder and the dangling tassel sways in the breeze while I hold her to me by a gold and blue tether.

While I hold her with my lips.

Always.

"I didn't say that, but I *do* love you," I tease, breaking the kiss to trace her nose with mine.

She shakes her head, giggling at herself. "I mean I'm proud of you, too." At my eyebrow arch she blinks and rolls her eyes, letting go a breath. "I mean, thank you." Rachel pulls me behind her again, fingers twining hypnotically as I giggle at how utterly adorable and confused she is. The riptide of Chanel falls over me as I move, making every step a litany of here again and never been before. I capture another moment and reclaim it as *mine*.

When we get to a nondescript doorway, she stops, her hand sliding toward the bright silver handle. "I want to show you something."

I push back a lock of hair and nod. "Okay."

She opens the door, and though she would have had a meltdown over scuffing her first and only pair of Jimmy Choo's in another world, in this one she uses the heel to wedge the door open and hold it for me. I glance up at her, at the warm smile that reaches up into her eyes and softens them. "After you, my love."

I can't help that I swoon a little, slipping into the darkness. "You're allowed to be in here, right?"

Rachel presses her hand to the curve in my back and guides me forward. I pass a large rack of clothing and sequins tickle my skin, balmed by the soft rub of cotton after. "Alumni have open access to the stages and practice rooms." She touches her lips to my neck and in the darkness it's so sensitive.

My breath falters because the flash of Rachel's lips on mine, her fingers in my hair, whips through my mind. "Have you ever wanted..."

Her hand firms around the front of me, pulling me to a stop. She twists me in her arms. "Yes." My heart starts pounding as she brushes into me, pressing her body against mine. I shift backward, finding cool brick against my back. It creates a tempest within me, the shock of her heat and the stone's chill against my exposed skin beneath my open back dress. "I've wanted to kiss you here." Her lips feather softly and finally lock when her fingers do the same in mine. "I want to kiss you everywhere I go."

All I know is that every place is home to me, because she is with me.

As her lips draw against me in the dark, I soar with joy over our story. Over the fact that I'm done with four years of school, that Rachel's a graduate, that my little ingénue from Illinois had the chance to make it. That the newspaper clippings that litter a small notebook under the bed are the start of boxes worth.

That I get to stand beside her once more on this journey. Our journey.

She coils a long strand of my hair around her fingers. At her request, I've grown it out. "I love your hair." She pets me lovingly and I close my eyes.

"I love yours," I hum into her lips coyly, before claiming them in a scorching tangle.

And at my request, she stopped straightening hers and I grab the wave of it. It's of dual benefit, because I get to watch the natural curls bounce with her footsteps and be the recipient of her ministrations as my lover since she has less to do in the mornings.

"Blake?"

I stretch for her lips, and steal one last kiss. "Yeah, angel?"

"I still have something I want to show you."

I nod, tracing slowly from her jaw to her shoulder, down the arm of her robe. I take her hand. "Lead the way."

Frazzled by her touches, I straighten my hair absently, swallowing repeatedly to get my throat working because my voice is warm, the kind of warm I don't want anyone but Rachel to hear. The kind of warm that whispers of hungry kisses in our bedroom, secrets shared and echoes of a future that will come to pass.

Rachel turns suddenly, cutting left as she slips into an alcove. "Steps."

I'm glad she said it because I would have very gracelessly fallen. Like a proper gentleman, she holds my hand, guiding me up. When we get to the top, Rachel slides aside, circling my waist with a casual hand, turning me toward the endless wave of dark seats. I blink when I realize where we are, when I can see the dark wood stage and the race of red plush upholstery in the low light.

I turn to her. "Your concert."

She smiles. "Where we met again." Her kisses

break over me, swallow me whole as we stand at the place where, in my heart, it began a lifetime ago. I feel a twist of Dèjà vu, like we've kissed here before, like I've stood in this concert hall and crumbled under the molten burn of her love. And then I remember I have. I *did*.

As a twenty year old girl, I fell in love right here.

Rachel pulls back, her eyes tracing over me. "Wait right here." She shifts me a little.

I laugh softly, bemused as she retreats. And like a love sick puppy, I obey and hold the spot on the stage. It surprises me constantly how much Rachel has grown. How much we both have. It makes me wonder if the flaws Rachel had before were my doing. If I held her back, or not challenged her enough. I would feel remorse for it, if I wasn't overcome with the perfection before me. And the image of my beautiful Rachel how she is now, blacks out the fading memories of who she was.

Our life together will *always* be paramount, the pinnacle I will always climb toward, but I do it hand in hand with the brave woman that stands before me here and now. I'm not pushing her forward, being pulled behind, but at her side. Her equal.

It dawns on me that this is the first time I feel like I deserve her love. That I've earned it. I'm still reclaiming my life with her, but the work that I've poured into it, the tears and love, the heartbreak and hope, is erasing the terrible mistakes I've made in my lives. I'm finding absolution through paving new moments and memories over the broken glass of my past.

Like today.

Rachel and I had broken up a week ago in

another world because I mortified her at a family lunch. Because I exploited her love in revenge against my family. That was my growing, the better me I had to find. I still marvel at how much easier it is just to love someone, really love them without regard to fear. I thought it was a sliver I had held onto, guarded with my life, but it was a whole me, a whole person that I kept captive.

The Rachel that stood beside me and died deserved it. And now, God now, she has more than earned it.

"You still in the same place?" Her voice comes over the speaker system, from everywhere at once, startling me from my thoughts.

"Why are you pulling a trap door on me or something!" I yell it, because I have no idea where she is.

"Maybe." This time it's soft and I see Rachel by the rigging rack. I watch her hands move over the labels affixed to the triggers and pulleys. They are strong, sure hands. I held them when she died. I kissed them goodbye.

It almost feels like it happened to someone else, because so many things are different about them. They move with a command I can't explain, fingers trailing through literal and proverbial dust, they wipe away the weight of the world. When Rachel smiles over at me, in that spark I know she has the strength to survive anything.

Me and the world alike.

"You ready?" she asks.

"Always."

She begins flipping switches and it races the curtain closed beside me. I jump a little. I spin to my left as a hiss puffs fake fog from a small hole in the wall near me. Rachel flips another switch and a backdrop of a forest and glittering water rolls onto the stage slowly. I stare at it as it lumbers past her and obscures her. A tire swing lowers from a beam overhead and I stare up at it dazed.

I wrap my arms around myself as the image around me develops like a polaroid of another time. The fog covers the stage, pushing against the forest and the glittering lake. It's just like back home by the lake. I think it right as Rachel clicks something and the sound echoes around me. A dusting of orange L.E.D. lights bob from the scaffolding above me and twinkle in the fog banks. I stare at it, remember it, let it fill me.

When the warmth of Rachel fills the space beside me, and her hand fills mine, I lean into her. "This is amazing." I glance at her, overwhelmed. "Really."

"Come with me." She walks me toward the tire swing. "They just did a play about the bayou, so I figured I'd steal their set." She grins as she lets me go, and runs her hands over the rubber tread, fingers working over it and holding it steady. "Want to swing?"

"Don't you?"

"You first."

She offers it toward me, and I duck my head, climbing in. I lean back against Rachel once I'm sitting, and her arms wrap me in a hug. I press my face to her neck. "What is this for?"

"Just because."

Her hands press to the tire swing around me after that and she starts pushing me forward. I'll be honest, my heart shoots into my throat as she starts jogging, but it's less about me getting hurt and more about her twisting an ankle in her heels. I'm not exactly the lightest thing in the world, so when she finally grunts a little under her breath and I slip out of her hands, I go flying across the stage.

I don't even realize I'm screaming until I see Rachel laughing but can't hear it over the high pitched wail igniting the air. Her fingertips brush my back again, keeping me going.

Always keeping me going.

Always.

My momentum starts to slow and we just stare at one another in a moment between the moments. When I finally come to a stop, she takes up her position from before, strong hands holding the tire swing still while I lean back into her. I look up at her. Rachel leans over me and the hiss of the fog machine covers the incendiary sound of our lips meeting as we kiss. We stay like that long enough for me to get a head rush, for everything to get dizzy and warm and perfect. I slide free of the tire swing, hands finding the soft silk of her navy dress to keep place for the fact that my lips can't hold her. Her palms fasten to my back, fingers tucking under the material of my dress to touch my shoulder blade.

It puts butterflies in my stomach, the good kind, the kind that flutter hard enough to make up for lost times.

"I love you, Blake." Her eyes hold mine as her thoughts whirl. "I felt you, you know? Here."

"Felt me?"

She blushes in the low light, so very much like the young girl that handed her heart and her everything to me in this place. "I can't explain it, but when I stepped out on the stage and felt the music start, I just felt something. A wave of love." She licks her lips. "I think it was you. I *know* it was you. I've spent a lot of time thinking about the future and the past these last few months. And I have something I need to tell you." She glances up at me, pulling back from my arms. "It's all good, so don't frown." Her fingers rub the creases in my forehead I didn't even know I was making.

"Okay." I take a steadying breath, because I can feel a charge of something moving between us.

"It's graduation time, so I think it's pretty normal to catalogue your life, figure out what you want in it, figure out what path you want to walk."

"Did you figure it out yet, because you don't have to. You have so much time to make those big decisions."

Rachel shakes her head and then places her fingers over my lips. "Let me talk. Don't say anything yet, Blake."

She looks so serious, a small furrow above her brows making its first appearance. I had forgotten it and how it shows when she gets her determined face. Her fingers leave my lips and she slides them under the high cut neck of her dress and the shimmer of a golden necklace slides over her fingers. She cups it in her hand as she plays with the latch. "As I was saying, I've been thinking about what I want from my life. What path I want to walk." She shakes her hair into place and holds the chain in her hand. "I know what I want and I never told you."

"Never told me what?" I sound breathless. I am breathless. My gaze fastens to the innocent gold chain hanging from her fingers.

"That I want you." She tips her head and nudges my jaw softly, drawing my eyes to her. "Don't look so surprised. I have said those words many times."

I feel the tug of a smile. "But not like this."

"No, never like this."

No, not at all. I've never heard this tone, this clear and precise love bared for me.

"I think back to the things in my life, my dreams. Things that propelled me forward when I was younger, my dreams of Broadway, and they seem so muted now in comparison."

"Comparison to what?"

"To my dreams with you. To the future I want *now*."

My mouth goes dry instantly as she fiddles with the chain in her hand. "You make me happy, happier than a stage, than a curtain call, than a standing ovation. And I've done what you said. I've enjoyed those things, tasted those things."

I shudder a breath under the weight of her words, fearful that she is going to give it up again.

"You taught me I could have both, and I have it. Well..." she gestures at the dreamscape around us, "I will have it." She glances behind her, to where I can see the tree stump over her shoulder. She nods toward it. "Come with me."

My knees feel weak, but I follow.

"Please sit."

And I do.

She faces me, her fingers worrying over the item in her grip. "I've gone through this speech a million times in my mind. I recite it when I'm riding the subway, when I'm in the shower, when I'm falling asleep."

She hands me the chain in her hand. I look down at it, brushing it with my thumb. And then she slides to her knees on the faux grass at my feet. Everything crashes together in that moment, my throat tightening to the point where I feel like my vocal chords might snap. I can't speak, can't breathe as I stare at her.

"Sarah Blake Fortier, I knew you were it for me when I was sixteen years old. I knew you were the one when you kissed me that first time in the practice room, when you became my best friend and my only love, when you taught me that love was just as much about me as it was you, and forced me to realize that anyone who would steal away my future wasn't the right person for me."

"Rachel." It's all I can manage as the emotion in my chest forces a burn into my eyes.

"Blake, you were the one when I came out here, when the days were hard and the nights were long. It was you I missed every day." The surface tension breaks in her eyes and a tear rakes her cheek. "Always you, always. It has been, and will be, always you, *always.*"

I think I say something, but my words are lost to me when she smiles.

"So..." she brushes the tear off her cheek, "so... make me the happiest person in the world. Say that it will always be you. Always."

The ring she brandishes is antique, glittering in the light, and it clicks in that moment that she got it from her mother and father. This was why she wanted to go alone to the airport to get them, why they smiled at me the way they did last night over dinner.

Her hopeful eyes glisten at me. "Be my wife."

"Yes." I would scream it if I could, if my voice would work. Instead I push the words from my heart and achingly stretch my fingers toward her. The rake of the ring sliding up my finger explodes everything within me. And I can't get to her lips fast enough. I can't kiss her hard enough, hold her tight enough to waylay the inexhaustible tears I have for her.

Always.

She's hugging me, holding me tight. I'm doing the same, closer to her than I have ever been in my life.

This is who Rachel was supposed to be. I can't stop thinking it, as her cheek presses to mine and then she pulls back with that smile. I press my forehead to hers. "Will you still take my name even though you beat me to the punch?"

She clears her throat. "Aurais-je faire une bonne Fortier?"

I trace her lips with mine, a glutton for the soft lilting tones of her voice when she whispers in French to me. God, it's beautiful. "Yes, you will make an amazing Fortier."

"Then, yes." She pulls back again, smirking. "I like it, Rachel Fortier. It has a ring to it."

"It sounds like the name of my wife."

"It is."

And I pull her into my arms kissing her like I have my whole life, like I did years ago on a misty night by a lake covered in the dottings of fireflies.

And I have her.

Always.

Part Three

Chapter Nineteen

Promises
August 12th, 2016
(14 years left)

The night air is balmy and heavy with salt. I breathe it in, long steadying breaths that seem to be my only link to reality. I pace back and forth through an unfamiliar, long dining room. Its billowing curtains, French doors, and dark wood floor, elegantly stream past my view in the meager light around me. It feels like a dream as I weave in and out of the long races of white material, waiting. I stare at my feet, at the sandals that wrap in a crisscross up the top of them and peek out from my under my dress with every step.

Far away, just over the sound of the tide and the twinkle of a wind chime, I can hear the musicians tuning their instruments. It makes me stop, and I hazard a look outside, my gaze racing past the veranda of the beach house and further to where I can see people milling around on the sand in lantern light. There's an archway with white flowers backlit by hurricane lamps, and for a moment I get dizzy thinking about the fact that all those people will be watching as Rachel and I say our vows beneath it.

My hands hold me upright in the middle of one set of doors as my eyes catalogue the image and memory of it. It makes me feel very exposed, because before...well, before was very different. I had married Rachel at a ceremony at the civic center on the fly. It was the very cold December of 2020, and taxes were really gonna hurt that year if I didn't have a write off. So we went on a whim, held up our hands and attested that we were who we said we were, and tied the knot in front of a Justice of the Peace.

It saved me twenty thousand dollars in taxes, but it wasn't the priceless moment that every girl dreams of, and after waiting eight years to get married, four years more than even *now*, it certainly wasn't what we deserved. To be honest, it was probably the most unromantic moment of our lives together and the second biggest mistake I've ever made aside from letting her leave my office our last day together.

I stare across the room at my reflection, at the cream dress that loops at my shoulders and spills in shimmers down the length of my body. Even under my withering inspection, I like what I see, the curves and dips, the long lines of my body honed through Rachel's galvanizing touches. I look more like the woman I thought I would become, than I actually was. I can see it in my eyes, where the hazel burns brighter than I've ever seen before. Though it feels like I carry more responsibility and weight than I ever did before, it doesn't touch the depth of the green that sparkles back at me from my reflection.

I look back outside, at the countless figures shifting in the light. It's more Rachel's thing to have hundreds of eyes on her, but I can't really find complaint in exposing myself because I love her and she loves me.

I'm okay, sharing that with everyone.

I hear a loan violin's tremulous voice in the shifting shadows, and I close my eyes as it makes my heart race.

"Blake?" I flinch when Hiram opens the door behind me. "I've got it. All proper wedding superstitions are now accounted for." He comes in, and then stops short when his eyes fix on me. "What's wrong?"

"I'm just happy." I put a hand to my stomach when I turn to him. "I'm just nervous, too."

He smiles easily. "You *should* be nervous. It's your wedding." He unwraps his handkerchief wrapped package. "Here. This is your something borrowed. It also counts for something blue. You already have old and new, so I think we have it all."

I was so preoccupied with making sure Rachel's traditions were covered, that I forgot about mine. I didn't think it was important to me until today.

I stare down at a winking sapphire and diamond littered barrette. It puts starbursts of color over the white cloth and it's so amazing I'm scared to touch it. It takes a frozen minute for me to get the words out of my mouth. "It's beautiful."

"Rachel wanted you to wear it, it's my sister Margaret's from London." I look up at Hiram then and he smiles. "She wasn't fooled by your whole shtick, Rachel had Margaret bring it especially for you."

He says it with a smile and I swallow. "Tell her Aunt Margaret, thank you."

"She's your Aunt Margaret too, so you can tell her yourself."

Before the words hit my emotions, Hiram takes my hand and turns me around. "Now, we just need to get this into your hair." I feel him squirreling with the tendrils that have been tucked and styled into a cascade with Baby's Breath woven in. "I should get Deborah to do this, she's better. She did Rachel's hair when she was little."

"No." I reach back and catch his hand, holding it, soaking in the way he tweaks my fingers softly. "It's okay. I want you to do it." I stare out through the dusting of candlelight at the dark water at the horizon.

"Alright, kiddo. I'll do my best."

His words pour into me and I sigh. I love him so much. I missed him almost as much as I missed Rachel all those years. He grounds me in a way I can't explain and knowing that I have Hiram back is a gift I can't express. It warms me to have a family again, parents who care about me. It doesn't matter how old I am, how accomplished, I'll always feel like a little girl lost.

However, when Hiram is here, and to a lesser extent Deborah, I know it will be okay because they will make it better. It's how I hope my children feel someday about me. "I'm glad you're here with me." I whisper it because I didn't actually mean to verbalize the thought.

"Me, too." I feel the barrette slide across my scalp as he affixes it into place. He pats me on the shoulder. "I *was* gonna say this at dinner in a toast, cause I have to speak if there is an open mic, you know I can't not." He laughs and I laugh too. He turns me slowly facing into the mirror, and I see him behind me in the reflection I was looking at earlier, his hands squeezing my shoulders.

"I look at the woman before me, and you are a mitzvah in our lives, in the life of my little Rachel's. I always knew it was going to be you Blake, for her. I knew it the moment I met you and that horrible night when you guys broke up. After I tucked Rachel into bed that night, I went to Deborah and said, 'we haven't seen the last of that girl,' and I was right." He smirks when I turn to him, "It's good to be right about something once in a while, am I right?"

I nod. "It is."

"Ha. I'm right again. This really is a good day."

I laugh.

He studies my hair, reaches out to fix something out of place. And just like Rachel does, he opens his mouth to speak, but doesn't actually say anything, not on the first attempt anyway.

"Blake, I owe you an apology."

"For?"

"It probably wasn't good that I enabled you two to get as serious as you did. You were both very young. You're still young for God's sake. I don't think it was fair for me to make what happened possible."

I shrug lightly. "It's okay, I think it was pretty serious from the start and there wasn't much you would have been able to do to stop it. Rachel and I are both of a singular purpose when we get going on something."

He nods, narrowing his eyes at me. "I figured it was, but I also saw what happened coming from a mile away. When Rachel loves, she does it with everything she has and would give up everything to make another person happy. Exactly what I feared would happen, did happen, and a far lesser person would have let her abandon her dreams."

I swallow haltingly. "It would have destroyed her."

Hiram nods. "It would have eventually, once all the passion had run its course and real life set in, but it would have been years later." He thins a smile at me. "Hence I knew it wasn't over between the two of you. You were thinking twenty years ahead when you left that night and not even Rachel in all her stubbornness could walk away from that."

"I'm glad she didn't."

He laughs nudging me. "I did a lot of talking to her about it, to make sure of it. You can't let someone who cares that much go. It was real love and we all knew it. Talking to her on your behalf was the least I could do because I'll never be able to thank you enough for not letting my little girl ruin her future."

He hugs me tightly then, and I lean my head on his shoulder. Big hands and soft shoulders anchor me.

"Thank you, too, then for everything you said."

"Speaking of things needing to be said, I have to tell you, you had more spine at sixteen than I think I have now, because I can't honestly say that I could have made the choice you did had I been in your shoes. I'm glad you're finally my daughter, too."

His words warm me, cracking the brittle places where I will forever carry wounds from my parents, for their lack of love and affection. When I pull back from his shoulder and sniffle to still the watering in my eyes, he gives me a reprimanding look.

"Don't get all mushy on me, yet. Even though I love you like you're my own, that doesn't mean I was necessarily *okay* with what was going on between the two of you. As a parent you learn that there are never right answers, only the best possible option," he chuckles, "which had it gone on much longer might have been to soundproof her room to spare Deborah's and my sanity."

Okay, so that makes me blush the color of a

tomato and makes me forget my personal pains. Which when I survey the grin on his face, was probably his intention.

I tease him back. "As a parent I don't think I could ever be as," I'm not sure how to describe it, "understanding."

He sighs, "I don't know if I was understanding per se, Rachel is my daughter after all and there are some things a parent *actually* doesn't want to know; however, because she *is* my girl, I know better than to try and stop her from getting what she wants, too."

"Or you." He tweaks my nose softly. "You have always been a stand-up act Blake."

My throat chokes tight at the expression on his face. "Hiram?"

"Yes, kiddo?" He is fiddling with his suit and I help square his bowtie absently. It makes my words easier to say.

"Will you dance with me?"

He ducks his head and looks at me over the rim of his glasses. "At the reception?"

"Yeah," I find it very hard to get the words out of my mouth with how important they are to me. I don't like feeling this much, not like this. "Traditionally a father dances with their daughter at her wedding. Will you dance with me, too?" I don't want to look up from where my eyes have fallen, because I had a woman spend the better part of an hour putting on my make-up and if I look at him I'm going to cry and wreck my mascara. So I stare at his hands as they take mine.

"As your father, I will be proud to."

☙ ☙ ❧ ❧

I linger on the figurative warmth in those words

as I hold the literal warmth from a tea light candle in my hand. The glass holder shimmers in my palms, and I look at it, memorize it and remember it. I don't see the eyes of *our* family anymore as the orchestral music swirls over me and the breeze ruffles the gown I wear.

All I see is her as she moves toward me.

I stand beneath an arbor of white camellias and roses, my heart in my throat at the image, the image of the slow walk she makes with a matching candle cupped in her hands. It radiates over her, lighting her like the star in the center of my universe. I know there is a whole world beyond her, an ocean, a beach, a wedding full of people, but my vision and my memories will always begin and end with her. My angel in the darkness with a smile that has saved me a million times over. The beauty whose arms shelter me when I'm lost and push me forward when I've found my way. The woman who can't steal blankets anymore, because we sleep in the middle of the bed twisted in one another. Whose poorly folded blankets and slippers punctuate my existence with a reality more real and beautiful than any life I've lived.

A life I would lay down my own to protect. I vow it to the darkness between us that *nothing* will ever steal away what's standing in front of me. She mouths a silent 'hi' to me as she brushes into the place beside me, and it has my heart plunging off the face of the earth because it's so precious. We turn to the small stand before us and carefully I place my candle on it, followed by Rachel. She takes my hands in the sputtering candlelight and commits her life to me, and I to her. My favorite moment is made then, when I'm saying my vows, Rachel mimes the words back to me silently, because I know they are so important to her that she wants to remember them.

Every word for the rest of her life.

༄ ༄ ༄ ༄

We dance late into the night, the D.J. putting together an amazing mix of fast and slow, treble and bass. As promised Hiram not only danced a slow dance with me, but got his boogie on and showed me a very horrendous version of "The Electric Slide." I don't think I've ever laughed as hard as I have tonight.

Hand in hand with my *wife*, I'm still laughing as we head to the beach house, our sandals dangling from my fingers. She is still dancing and humming as she spins in my arms, and I keep her doing twirls until she dizzily catches me and holds on tight.

"Blake, I love you."

"I love you, Mrs. Fortier."

Rachel giggles. "Can't wait to see it in lights."

"You will."

We take the steps slowly and when we get to our room she opens the door and slicks her hand over me as I pass through. "So..." Rachel presses the door closed. "Here we are."

I arch my brow at her with a smile. "Yes, here we are."

"I can't say I love you enough."

"Me either."

"I think we should have a drink, just you and me together. Don't worry about the glasses. I'll be drinking this from you." She rattles the bottle in her hand and I feel my brows blur into my hairline.

"Pretty kinky, Mrs. Fortier. I'm impressed. Are you going to make good on all your promises over the years if I give you this?" I whisper, as I slide to the edge of the puffy white bed.

"As your wife, I'll make good on all my promises."

I slink out of my dress an inch at a time. "Good, so come over here and let me love you."

She watches me bare myself to her and then locks the door with intent, sealing us away from the world. Flashing a sexy smile, her words make me laugh. "I'm very curious to see what *new* things we can do to each other."

"Well, we can start with a toast," I tease, beckoning her toward me silently as I lean back. She's got that fire in her eyes, and I let it burn over and through me as she lets her dress pool at her feet before joining me.

And Rachel keeps me giggling and playing with her all night, coaxing touches and soothing kisses pave the way until we make room for more skeletons in our closet, like a marriage.

Like a love that will last a lifetime.

Chapter Twenty

Tripping Through The Rifts
February 16th, 2017
(13 years left)

It's raining and I watch the lines it makes along the plate glass window here at the top floor of Saint James Hospital. It's thick enough to obscure the skyline in the distance. Somehow though, as if it is my very unfortunate gift, my eyes find the building where my practice once was. It is surreal seeing it, silver and gray in the gathering storm. Up until now, I've avoided looking at this part of the skyline because I didn't think I could face it.

I measure the windows that were once my office, twenty-five stories up, and it fills me with a dread that I can't fully comprehend. It's a place where Rachel and I kissed countless times in the fold of stormy clouds and where I regarded a world from my complacent tower that I never imagined in a million years would change.

But it did, in the blink of an eye.

When I can't look at the building anymore, I stare at the steps beside me, where my lunch tray sits at my feet uneaten. I can't compel myself to find my appetite, not even for strawberry Jell-O. I have a bad feeling about today, and that bad feeling is something I can't seem to shake. It's also what has brought me here to linger in the things I seem to forget when I'm assuaged by all the wonderful in my life.

It doesn't help that today I'm especially sensitive to everything I remember about this place, both Saint James and New York City. My eyes find my old building again and I palm the glass, an outline growing where the heat of my skin finds the cold pane.

I must have really bad PMS, because it's almost beyond me to cope with today. I step back from the window, leaving my handprint as a reminder of my passing and fall to a seated position on the empty stairs beside me. Behind me, the corridor is cordoned off due to endless budgetary restraints that keep the new wing of Saint James from being completed. It leaves me alone aside from the occasional wandering person in the tier below me, and thank God for it, because I'm tired enough to feel weak today.

The edge of the concrete cuts into my thigh and I palm my face in my hands. I remember standing on these very stairs, talking to Ryan after Rachel died. It was where I asked him to prescribe me the medication I needed to end my life. It was raining like this too, but instead of construction tape, there had been residents moving around, surgeons, nurses buzzing to and from the new wing of the hospital.

I watch it rain as a world I once understood feels alien around me. People pass me, and then move on. Frozen in this purgatory the world keeps turning even though I am rooted in place.

"Blake?" Ryan's voice sounds absolutely shocked as he does a double take at the peripheral of my vision.

I don't want him to see me, but I need him to at the same time.

"What are you doing here, baby?" Now he sounds

worried, and that word, that term of endearment on his lips is hard to hear. He puts a hand on my arm, pulling me into a hug. His arms are warm and solid and make me feel so small in comparison to when I was able to hug Rachel. My throat tightens at the thought, and I lift my head from his shoulder as I realize again that she's gone. I don't know when I'll ever remember to forget it.

I pull away from Ryan's embrace.

"Hey, hey, talk to me."

I shake my head, because I can't. If I surrender to the emotion I feel, I will be swallowed whole. I might just lay down right here and died. That's what it feels like anyway.

"How are you doing, Blake?"

I glance around at the busy hall and my eyes fix on the plate glass window behind him. The sky weeps for me. "I'm doing." I firm my arms around me, holding tightly. "I need your help."

Ryan frowns and takes a step toward me before deciding to give me the space I need. He resumes his position. "Anything, babe."

I don't take my eyes off the sky. "I need help getting my anxiety under control. I was hoping that you could write me a script for something."

He moves toward the window, getting us out of the thoroughfare and giving us a modicum of privacy as people blur past. "Aren't you seeing someone? A doctor for that? If you don't like the one you've been talking to, I'm sure I can find someone."

"I am," I lie, tightening my grip on myself. "I'm just asking as a friend because I don't want to go spill my guts out. Not right now, and that seems to be the arrangement. I get into the office and have to vomit my feelings before I can get something as simple as

Valium."

"*Nothing like an emotional enema, huh?*"

I force a laugh, fake it until I actually believe I'm laughing. "*Yeah, it's really shitty.*"

Ryan grins, honestly happy for a moment in our wordplay. I watch his eyes rake over me slowly then the smile slips from his face. The way he is looking at me makes my spine tingle with nervousness. I don't need a mirror to know how terrible I look. I can see it in my hands when I run fingers through my hair and it comes out in dull clumps, in my body when my clothing hangs and bags where it never did before. Where I don't even bother putting on a bra anymore, because I don't need it, which isn't saying all that *much, but enough, because I was at least adequately stocked in the breast department.*

Rachel never complained, and just thinking that now, makes me sick.

"*Blake?*"

I snap my gaze back to his face from where my eyes had fallen to his name stitched on his coat. I don't know how long I must've stood staring. "*Yeah, sorry.*"

"*What can I do to help you? Please tell me what I can do.*"

The humorlessness of his tone confirms he sees the dark circles under my eyes and recognizes them as literal physiological markers of severe depression...and his voice so soft and worried really honestly hurts. It hurts me even more that he only sees me, his friend, and not a woman who should be locked up as a 927 right about now.

Bless him.

"*I need a script for Flunitrazepam.*"

Ryan screws up his face. "*What do you need*

Rohypnol for? It's not like you're gonna roofie some pretty..." He doesn't finish his sentence, and I'm glad for it. He lowers his voice as a group of nurses walk by on their way to the cafeteria. "That is off the market for a reason, Blake."

When I look over my shoulder at the women passing, they give me soft, pitying looks, and hurry away. I wrangle my hair, combing order into it. I see more looks, and realize that everyone knows. There probably isn't a single person that doesn't know the tragic story of Blake and Rachel Fortier.

I've about had enough when I see Dr. Hall, the most disgustingly myopic right wing extremist I have ever known, and he passes me with a soft apology. It just about kills what's left of me because I know just a year ago he was probably wishing that something terrible would happen.

"Blake?"

I focus back on Ryan. "What?"

"Have you exhausted everything else? I mean really, have you tried?"

"Yeah." I stare down at my shoes, moving my toes under the canvas of my Vans. I feels so disjointed standing in the hospital wearing tennis shoes and jeans, instead of my skirt and pumps. It takes a long time for Ryan's words to sink in, another testament to how fucked up I am because my synapses aren't firing correctly anymore. "I didn't have to come to you to ask for it. I'm sure I could have done it myself, but I wanted to be on the up and up about it." I don't really know when I got to be such a good liar, but I'm grateful for it. My mouth keeps moving, keeps spouting lies and even if I wanted to stop, I'm not sure I could. "Look, I came to you as a friend, and I don't want people thinking

I'm abusing my ability to self-medicate. It would be a career killer when I come back."

"Understandable." *He scratches the beard on his chin. It's new. A change brought on by his wife Sandra, no doubt.* "Fine. Anything. I just want you back, Blake. I love you so much. I loved Rachel too, and it's killed all of us being here without her, but without you especially. You're the rock of this place, your training and guidance are invaluable to the new doctors. We need you, I need you. You are invaluable to me."

"I know."

"I want you to take as much time as you need to get back on your feet. We all know it will be a while, but we're here for you and we want you back."

I nod silently because I will never be able to get back on my feet. Every single breath is a struggle I can't fight anymore. And fuck this place, and him, for asking me to! If I wasn't as vain as I am, I would've already done it a dirtier way. However, I really don't want to live through an amateur attempt on my life with ligature burns, disfiguring gunshot wounds, or a broken neck.

Medicine is all I know, and it is time to use it for something that benefits me.

Before the silence stretches too long, I know I have to say something. It takes everything in me to keep my voice level. "Thank you, Ryan. That is what I want, too."

"Good." *He glances around at the empty hall.* "I do need to go honey, but call me. I don't want you doing this alone."

For a moment, I think he's telling me to call him when I do it, so he can be there with me. It's not possible though, not with how selfish he is of my time, of how he wants me at his beck and call to consult. Without me, he will actually have to stand on his own two feet and stop being such a piss poor doctor and human being.

The motherfucker.

I give him a thin smile as he scribbles on his prescription pad, and force home the last words I'm going to say to him. "Thank you for everything. You mean the world to me."

He does, I don't know what I was thinking before.

I'm losing my mind.

When his blue eyes lift to me, his hospital issued phone goes off. He silences it automatically and pulls me into a hug that crushes the pain away for a fleeting instant. That is, until I remember that I used to silence my phone automatically. I used to be that person with Rachel. In our last years together though, I stopped. It didn't matter if we were at lunch, or on the phone, or what the topic was. I had forgotten what was important.

His lips touch my head at the same instant my tears hit my cheeks. I wrap my hands, holding, clinging, dying right here in his arms. And he has to save me, he has to. If he does, I'll keep going. Please, God, someone give me a reason!

"I'll see you later, Blake."

But God doesn't answer.

I nod silently. "Yep." I say, tightening my grip around the prescription in my hand.

I shake my head and hug myself as I blink away the memories. Because of my selfish actions, Ryan probably lost his license. I feel my brows furrow thinking about that, wondering if the world kept moving without me. I wonder what happened after the paramedics found me dead, if there was an investigation, if they buried me beside Rachel.

When I hear my phone ringing, I'm not sure if it's my imagination or not. I grab it from my coat and shake my head clear of my pitiful memories before accepting the call. "Hey honey, how did your audition go for Cabaret?"

"First, what's wrong?"

I blink, my voice doesn't sound any different to me. "Nothing."

"You have that tone."

I smile. "No I don't, *you* have a tone, missy. Tell me about the audition."

Rachel harumphs into the phone, but lets it go. "It went well." A pause. "I think I got it, but I don't want to jinx it."

"I'm sure you did. If you didn't, give me his name and I'll make sure someone amputates a leg instead of giving him an IV next time he needs the ER"

Rachel laughs and I smile as I listen.

She does get it. It's the first Off Broadway production she stars in and it's also the start of what we eventually refer to as 'musicals in the key of C'. Because in order she will do, Cabaret, Cats, Chicago, Come Summer and Cougar before moving on to Les Miserable, Funny Girl, Rent, Mary Poppins, Hello Dolly, and Wicked. I'm impressed I still remember, though it is hard to forget a list she had me repeating every day to pander to her ego.

"Did they say anything to you?"

She sighs. "No, just thank you, but it was a good thank you. We'll see." I hear her padding around the apartment. "How is the rain treating you?"

I look out the window above my head and watch the clouds whip by. "It's cold."

She stops walking. "How's your knee, baby?"

I can't get over how much she asks. It's so wonderful. "It's fine, nothing a bath won't fix."

Rachel hums into the phone. "How is work going?"

"Busy 'cause of the rain." I reach down and unwrap my sandwich. I don't know why I do it because there is no way I'm going to be able to eat it. I drop it to the tray and rest my head in my palm. "It's been a long day. I wish I was home with you."

"You're always home, *to* me." Rachel soothes and I smile even though it pinches my chest.

"Cheesy romantic," I whisper.

"Only for you."

I roll my eyes with a genuine grin.

"Blake. If I get this role, not that I will because I don't want to jinx it, but if I *do* get it, I'll have to work like sixteen hour days for a while. Which means I probably won't see you much."

"I know." It's something I'm prepared for, but not. I thought about it on our honeymoon, while we traveled through eleven countries in Europe and enjoyed our time together. I knew that when we got back, that when life started again, that things would change. That we would be spending our time like two ships passing in the night, at least for a little bit, until I get promoted from night shift, which won't be for another year.

"It makes me sad."

I frown. "Don't be sad, angel. This is all good stuff. I'll write you notes, and you can always give me kisses and wake me up. I don't mind."

"Same here, but it isn't..." She sighs in frustration. "It's not how I wanted it to be."

"It won't be like this for long, I promise. I could

always do something fantastic and request a shift trade."

"If they know what's good for them, they would just give it to you." Rachel thuds her head against a window, I hear it through the phone. "I'm looking at the rain outside. It's colder when you aren't here."

"I'll be home soon," I confirm, feeling the exact same way.

"In like..."

I hear her lean to look at the clock.

"Six hours," she grumbles. "Will you wake me when you get home?"

"With kisses?"

"With anything you want, baby." There is flirtation in that voice of hers and it puts a smirk on my face.

"No dirty innuendo on the phone while I'm at work, it makes it hard to stay here and focus."

"Okay, I'm sorry." Behind her voice I hear water running and for a moment I'm convinced that she is outside my building. I hop up from where I'm sitting and look out at the street below, hoping like hell I'll see her rushing up to the entrance. "What are you doing?"

"Hold on." Rachel drops the phone and I strain to identify the rustling I hear. She comes back a moment later, breathless. "Sorry."

"Where did you go?" I hear her suck in a sharp breath and it gets my mind wandering. "What are you doing?" I can see my reflection in the glass, and I look like an idiot with this stupid grin on my face.

"You gave me an idea, so I'm sitting in the bathtub to take the chill off."

"Oh, really?" I inquire as my brow arches in the image I see of myself.

"And I'm drinking a glass of wine."

"Oh, yeah?" It arches further. "What else?" I prod, glancing around to make sure I'm alone before resuming my seat. Rachel, plus water and wine, is a sexual powder keg. I clear my throat casually as out of the peripheral of my vision I can see people moving around the floor below me. "What else?"

"Well..." Rachel begins, but when I see my supervisor passing beneath where I'm sitting, I instantly feel like a kid caught with my hand in the cookie jar. "We ran a chest x-ray and a C panel to confirm, all came back normal." I rattle it off when he glances at me.

"Someone just walk by?" Rachel purrs sexily in my ear.

"Yeah." I wait anxiously for his figure to turn the corner. When he does, I'm back in our steamy bathroom with Rachel. "What else?"

"Are you asking if I'm touching anything or if we should get another procedure done?" Rachel laughs. "Now, now, naughty thing. No talk of this at work, remember?"

I think I hear my teeth grinding as I think about it. "I miss my Rachel time. We didn't do anything today. That is probably why my day has been such shit."

"Breaking the routine, I know."

I hear water slosh.

"Twice last night should have made up for it."

"Two thousand times wouldn't be enough." I snicker. "Though all that would be left would be dust after that much..." I make sure I'm alone, "Sex."

"I thought use was the best way to prevent dust."

I smirk as I cup my hand over the phone. "Then

you probably own the shiniest vajayjay in the world."

Rachel chokes. I didn't realize she was drinking. She coughs into the phone. "So evil, but hilarious. I can just picture my next pap smear. Doctor Mackinnon, please don't mind that my vagina sparkles, it's *all* the rage these days."

I giggle, and when the sound finally dies, I go back to my previous thoughts. "So, don't play with me, were you doing anything?"

Rachel clears her throat a little. "No, but I can if you want."

I swallow. "If you want to."

"I always want to, which is why we have a six month streak going." She laughs softly as I hear a gentle slosh of warm water. "I really love being a newlywed."

I smile into the phone almost able to see steam curling around her shoulders while she stares at me. "Me too."

"It doesn't hurt that I'm married to a total whore either."

I roll my eyes. "Whatever...Sparkles."

Rachel rushes a breath. "You can't call me that *ever* because yours gets just as much use as mine."

"Should I have Ryan call you that instead, since it's off limits for me?"

Rachel snorts. "You tell him anything and I'll make sure you have a six month dry spell instead."

"Well, I wouldn't want that."

"I know something you do want."

"What's that?"

I hear her move in the water and she whines into the phone softly. I take a very deep, very unsteady breath when she does it, and absolutely forget where I am. In my mind all I see is her arching with her head pressed back to the tile.

"Oh baby." The sound of my own heated response bounces around the hallway and the white hot trickle of panic slides down my spine. I clamp my hand over my mouth, looking around, and I can hear her burst into laughter in my ear.

"You're gonna get me *so* fired someday." I chew my lip, wishing away the furious blush on my face.

"Probably, but you know deep down inside you like it."

"My feelings on this are actually pretty superficial and incredibly obvious. The entire building probably knows how I feel right about now."

"Well." Her voice is a growl, low and slow. "I like it deep down inside."

When the wave of her moan splashes against my eardrums, I bite my lip to keep the needy whine at the back of my throat caged. I listen, closing my eyes as she keeps going, as her soft cries keep tempo. "Keep going, but faster." When I hear the rush of her breath in a steady, even rhythm, intermixed with longing moans, I'm very aware of what she is doing that elicits those sounds. It has me moving around, pacing aimlessly from one side of the area to the other because I can't sit still, not when she sounds like this, not when all I want is to toss on my coat and head home at a thousand miles per hour and replace her fingers with mine.

"I want you in me."

"I wanna be."

"Do you want to hear more?" She's out of breath.

I cup my hand over my face. "I want you to get what I'm thinking about, and use that."

She laughs. "I'm not stupid, I already have it. This was exactly what I had planned and I'm not leaving this water for anything."

I try to find moisture to speak, but it's all gravitated south. "I want to hear that."

She goes silent and I wait with baited breath, knowing she is going to penetrate herself with one of our toys. It doesn't disappoint, as her sharp gasp breaks the air between us and I have to sit down or I might pass out.

"Oh, my God," I rush.

"Tell me what you want. I like when you tell me what to do."

"I can't." I look around nervously. "You already know what I want."

"Fast or slow."

"Fast."

"Shallow or deep?"

"All the way." I actually wheeze because of what she is doing to me. "Hard."

"Is it that kind of day, baby?" Her whisper is somehow transcendent of what we are doing. "How hard?"

"As hard as you would let me, knowing that it's that kind of day."

She moistens her lips and I swear it's right against my ear. "Sometimes a little pain can really make you feel alive."

"Yes, exactly." It's amazing how clearly I can imagine everything even though we are ten miles away from each other. I can see her adjust in the tub, see the water drip off her shoulders and her knees as she spreads them. I hang on the image of it, focusing primarily on the way she lolls her head to the side and her eyes smolder. I feel the first thrust like she is doing it to me, as the motion and her throaty groan warps through the phone. I close my eyes and breathe. My words are soft, daring and whispered. "Right against your G spot."

Her sounds change, becoming sharper and more desperate. When she goes quiet, winding up, I can hear the swish of bath water, and her head thudding softly against the tile.

"How is it?" I ignore the fact I think someone just looked at me and waved.

"It's so good I've got tears in my eyes."

That makes me smile and I sigh wistfully. "If only I was there."

"Yeah? What would you do?"

I quirk my brow at the image that melts in my mind. "Well, I wouldn't have stopped, I didn't say stop."

"Oh, really, little miss bossy pants?'"

"Yeah, but I'd be a little faster and I would kiss your eyes."

Rachel starts again and I revel in her.

"Tell me how it is."

"So good, baby. Oh, Blake, oh baby. Oh, God. When you drive into me like this, and I hold you, fuck. I wanna come so badly around you."

I love it when she talks dirty with that ragged desperate edge in her voice. *Jesus.*

"How bad?"

"So fucking bad. Tonight I want you to come home, get undressed, put on the strap-on and fuck me. No warm up. No pretense. No foreplay. Just kiss me then bend me over the side of the bed, or the dresser, or the kitchen counter and *wreck* me."

Oh holy shit. "My pleasure."

She slows her motions. I can tell because her breaths are full and not broken and crushed from her motions. I hear a dull thud on the floor of the bathroom and I start laughing. "Did you just–"

"Toss it on the floor? Yes." She sighs softly with a tired single laugh. "I have to stop 'cause I'm getting sore, and I don't want to be sore for you. I have a revelation, bathwater washes everything away and isn't nearly as sexy as one would imagine."

"I think it's pretty awesome right about now."

"You would. Besides, I think I've been trained only to orgasm with you 'cause this just doesn't do it anymore. Not without your help anyway, your voice in my ear."

I look around again. "I don't think I can say what I want to without someone hearing."

"Well, I don't want to share you, so I'll just have to wait I suppose." She shudders a broken breath. "So damn torturous."

"You have no idea." My phone goes off in a litany of high pitched tones and I silence it. "After we are done tonight I'm gonna make you do laundry, Rachel Fortier."

"Cause you're super wet, I know. Sorry, I totally will." She laughs, until she clears her throat. "Was that your phone?"

I blink and stare down at it mutely. "Yeah, I think so."

Rachel shifts in the water and I hear her take a drink from her glass. "Go to work, save some lives." She lowers her voice. "I'll be here when you're done and you can finish the job just as I instructed."

I actually whine a little. "It certainly isn't a job,

until the fourth or fifth, then you take too long."

Rachel scoffs. "I'm gonna pretend you didn't say that because I'm sure there are people out there that would like to get just one out of me. And here you are, bitching about number four."

I have no doubt there are.

"Go," she spurs. "I love you."

"I love you, too."

≈≈≈≈≈

She gets the part as I knew she would.

This time around though, things are different and much easier to bear. It's funny how people make the best of it when they're forced to, when there is enough love to make it worth the little sacrifices. I nap at work between rounds so I can spend the daylight with Rachel instead of rest. She buys energy drinks to keep herself up and alert after spending the early morning hours with me. And I've now found a laundry room no one uses to reciprocate the sexy sounds she offers over the line.

I feel better, more steady, because even though we are living real life now, it's still a dream. That isn't to say we don't work to make that happen, because we do, but instead of fighting the tide, I'm holding her as we go over the falls.

And I'm head over heels falling every moment, perpetually.

"Tell your dad thank you." I'm on the phone again, eating my dinner.

"You should call him. He hasn't talked to you in a week and is giving me serious crap for it."

I nod, spooning halfway decent pudding into my mouth. "Good, it is your fault. I was going to call two days ago, but then we had to go get Italian Ice at eight in the morning in March."

"I had to have it, sue me."

I smile. "When you're pregnant I can only imagine the weird cravings you'll have." I actually don't want to imagine it because they were kinda gross.

"Blake?"

I finish my pudding. "Yeah?"

"Did you want to have a baby again?"

I make a weird strangled sound I've never made before. "Like give birth again?"

"Yeah? Did you want to carry, or should I? Did you want to get pregnant again at all?"

I clear my throat, a little confused about the random shift in topic. "I don't know if I want to talk about this while I'm at work. This seems like a face-to-face conversation."

She goes silent and I open my mouth to say something more, but Rachel cuts me off. "You're right, I'm sorry."

"I'm sorry. This is just really important, and I want to talk to you, not to my phone."

She sighs. "We just have to get you away from that place."

I frown. "I know, and while I'm a resident I don't have much of a choice, but once I graduate things will be different."

I don't know why, but Ryan chooses that moment to slam open the door of the break room. His eyes are wild and when they focus on my face, I feel a charge of adrenalin shoot through me. "Where the fuck have you been?"

"This is why I can't talk at work about things that are important, because Ryan is a pain in my ass.

Hold on, Rachel." I glare at him as I move the phone from my mouth. "I've been right fucking here."

"You always swear like a sailor with him," Rachel burrs teasingly.

"I had them page you twice. We have an MCI and I need you to lead triage because I fucking well can't."

"Okay." He shuts the door and I shift my phone against my ear. "Jesus fucking Christ. Rachel I have to go, there is a mass casualty incident that apparently needs my attention and Ryan is in full meltdown mode. Can we talk when I get home in the morning?"

"Sure."

"Okay, love you."

"You too."

I'm out the door then, rushing to the entrance of the emergency room. Everyone is congregated there and I give them all a cursory look before I tie my hair back in a ponytail. "What do we have?"

It's Ryan who answers. "Shooting on 55th and Lex. Twelve inbound, three already called at the scene."

My eyes drift to the television screen on the wall behind Ryan's head, I see a flash of a newscast and an aerial shot of a downtown storefront. The caption reads, *Shooter Targets Passersby.* I hear the sirens coming, like a whisper of darkness as I pull gloves on my hand and rack my stethoscope around my neck.

"Okay." I nod as my mind catalogues the situation and orders rush from my mouth. "Lucy, call PR and tell them to get someone down here to field reporters. James, I'm gonna need at least another ten people, call a few from pediatrics just in case there are children." I turn to Ryan and lower my voice. "Call

Dr. Bell and tell him we need someone with authority down here, but don't tell him I said that, okay?"

"Got it."

I'm by no means an adrenalin junkie. So when I see the flashing lights, the whisk of the doors sliding open, my guts check themselves against my larynx. I literally feel my sympathetic nervous system kick into overdrive, feel my eyes focus, my hands vibrate from the rush of endorphins through me.

I'd gotten soft when I had my own practice. Sally Millman and the plethora of tennis elbows and acid reflux cases had seriously made me lose my edge. In the back of my mind, as I move toward the wall of paramedics entering, I wonder if I had had these quick automatic responses if I would have been able to save Rachel. I stop the thoughts before they totally form, because I can't think like that anymore. I'm not going to lose her again so there can be no more regrets.

I grab the corner of the gurney. "Go."

"Mr. Hernandez, forty-three-year-old male, hypotensive. Blood pressure is ninety-eight over forty-six. Gunshot wound to the left shoulder and right upper quadrant abdominal. Respirations good bilaterally."

I move my stethoscope over his stomach, where bandages hold back the blood. "But not good enough." I turn to the waiting staff. "Take Mr. Hernandez to trauma two, critical. Start a CT scan and chest radiography to rule out penetrating wounds to the chest cavity. IV with Ringers full open, type his blood, oxygen full open. Go."

I turn back to the man as he reaches out to me. I grab his hand. "We've got you, hang in there. Okay, Mr. Hernandez?"

He nods.

And they rush him away.

I take the next and a gray haired paramedic regards me warily. "Can we get a real doctor?" he states coldly.

I have to remind myself constantly that all people see is a twenty-two-year old resident, and not the forty-two-year old woman I actually am. This man before me is no different and remembering that eases my fury.

"I am, so speak," I order unceremoniously.

"This is Officer Phillips. He was injured in the shooting."

I look at the tourniquet around the officer's thigh and he waves to me. I smile at him, loosening it to make sure he doesn't lose his leg. "Congratulations for your soon to be paid vacation my friend, but you look well enough to hold the wall for a bit."

"Okay." His eyes widen at me. "But I'm family."

He's referencing the fact that all medical and safety professionals are afforded better treatment than everyone else. I'm all for it, but not when lives hang in the balance, and not when this is my ER "I'll get you the best morphine, I promise."

I bark orders. "Cut the tourniquet, get his leg elevated and bandaged. Get him the good stuff until I've figured out what else we have!"

I tap his shoulder and move on to the next.

And the next.

And the next, until I have a sea of gauze and blood and have to get someone to call facilities because it looks like a war zone. By the time I'm done, I have five critical cases including Mr. Hernandez, two stable, four walking wounded including Officer Phillips and one person who didn't make the trip.

My nervous system is still revved, still going strong as it carries me from room to room, my memory so sharp, I know what's happening before anyone can open their mouth. I forgot how good I was at this, how this was my calling.

Ryan hands me the phone in his hand between the hospital charts I'm juggling, and I have it at my cheek before I know what I'm doing. "Yes?"

"Dr. Fortier?"

It's my supervisor, Dr. Bell. "Yes, sir."

"I hear everything is fine and you have it under control."

"Yes, I do."

"Good. Starting next week, I need you leading on day shift. Thank you."

"Thank you."

He hangs up the phone and I drop Ryan's cell in my pocket. I don't have time to get happy though, because there is a first year resident asking questions about her patient's chart and the code alarm goes off. I scribble my name ordering a complete pharmacotherapeutic drug regimen to start on the patient in room twelve. Room twelve, Hilary Morris, twenty-five-year old female, respiratory distress and penetrating chest wound, starting on immune boosters and anxiolytics. Got it. I put it away for later in the file cabinet of my mind in the blink of an eye.

"Who is coding?" I ask, moving toward the nurse's station.

"Trauma two."

"Mr. Hernandez? Shit." I slide into the room. "Get me the crash cart right now." I point at Ryan. "Intubate him."

He hops to the command and for a really odd moment, I feel completely at ease because I know Mr. Hernandez will be fine. It has nothing to do with the fact that I've lived this moment before, because I didn't. It has everything to do with the fact that I'm here and fuck all if I'm gonna let him die.

Rachel's right, I swear a lot when Ryan is around.

I point at one of the younger medical interns beside me. "Go."

"Go?"

"Save his life." I pull the cart toward me and hand her the paddles. "Start at 200 Joules." I squeeze conductive gel on them. "Place the paddles anterior and posterior to the heart and proximal to the midline." I help her get them in the right spot as the machine hums to life.

"Everyone. What's the magic word?"

"Clear?"

"Exactly. So say it." I let her hands go and get my distance.

"Clear!" She glances around, her eyes wild and when she looks at me for confirmation, I'm right back where I was. The teacher, the mentor, the rock of the intern program that will eventually make three-hundred voraciously intelligent doctors in the ten years I lead it.

I give her a nod and she crushes the triggers on the paddles, and eventually brings him back to life under my watchful eyes.

Chapter Twenty-one

All I Asked For
November 8th, 2017
(13 years left)

The days move, they speed past me as I blur through our first year together. There is a rapidity in the footfalls of nature, but its lingering moments are superimposed on the mosaic of us together. The whole year is a reminder of what we have, a calendar of keepsakes I hold close to my heart while she loves me.

Spring is the pink of cherry blossoms framing her face as we walk hand in hand through the Brooklyn Botanical Gardens where magnificent trees gnarl and twist in a dark brown the same color as Rachel's hair, and litter the ground in careless color. They blanket our world as carefree as we laugh through theirs and steal kisses to the rustle of leaves.

Summer echoes the long slow dying light of sunset as we sit on blankets and listen to arpeggiated guitars in Central Park, singing songs with no real lyrics while enjoying a few glasses of wine. Good friends and hot sparklers lead the way in glittering trails as we visit empty beaches and scream our delirium to the stars. It's the season where Rachel learns to perfect her handwritten 'F' in light against the dark of the ocean, and though she lives and breathes the role every day, she can finally sign that she is my wife as gracefully as she embodies it.

Fall becomes the crunch of leaves, the brisk rail of the wind that strips them from the trees in a shattering rainbow. It morphs into the crunch of breakfast over the morning paper and the sweetness of sugar cookies in the kitchen before bedtime. The nights turn crisp and clear, as crisp and clear as standing ovations when my wife brings the house down one enamored crowd at a time. It's the thunder of my heart and the soaring of my soul because I'm living it. It's the wash of her unabashed tears from good and bad reviews alike and the way she holds me in those moments, when the cold of New York breathes in on her dream and we keep it warm together.

And Winter. It's the sound of jingle bells a month too early, Rachel's voice humming to the tempo of the rain, and running into restaurants laughing as we steal warmth from their fireplaces. It's crunching snow as we window shop, the sound of the heater kicking on and then dying. It is the trace of pruning fingers and toes from holding each other in the bathtub for hours to stay warm. Winter is the popping open of my birthday present and finding a storybook written in her hand. A story about *our* story and what it felt like to wear her skin as she walked through the world. Her feelings, her dreams and hopes around it.

Winter is the sound of her whispering it to me as I lie in her arms and read along until the tears blur the pages.

And Winter is *this*, the sound of my promise to her.

The heater cycles on and rattles softly. I shift closer to Rachel, holding her middle as I snuggle myself into her shoulder. She kisses the top of my head, and her hand goes back to caressing my back languidly.

She pauses, glancing down at me and I up at her. "You really want me to read this?"

I nod. "Do you not want to?"

She blinks blankly at me and then finally smiles. "I don't mind."

Rachel clears her throat as her book splays between fingers, propped against her thigh.

The dedication reads, *To my little Devil, from your little Angel. Always.*

"Always." I trace her side, worming closer.

"Yes, for you my wife, always."

She says it on purpose with a squeeze, because she knows how much that title means to me. I don't think that word will ever stop making my heart kick-start in my chest.

I skim the words on the pages while Rachel turns them, her arm pulling me closer as her voice runs a narrative through my heart. She laughs through our youth together, recounting her feelings from when I kissed her the first time to when we fell in love.

Well, when she fell in love with me.

I revel in the fun of our time then, how easy and simple it was. Until the end.

When we get to that part, it catches on her emotions and makes her voice foggy. It brings tears to my eyes, as I listen to her breaths beneath my ear and the steady beat of her heart. The emotional twinge is *that* much sharper, because I can hear the heart I broke beating, at the same time I hear the words that describe its vivisection.

I kiss under her chin, fingers sliding over her

soft sweater and caressing the place where I know her heart is. And when I lift my gaze past the writing and her knee, I see our painted tree with its branches spreading in the watery glow of dawn. I don't know how long I stay like that, eyes fixed as my brain works over the image, until another image replaces it. It's drawn through Rachel's words as she reads.

"It was the first thing I thought of after we were married. The idea that we can have a family, a home and children together. It is what drives me to be the best me I can be."

I look up at her lips as she speaks, where they catch in her teeth and falter over the words, because I don't think she had the intention of reading this to me.

"I imagine it every day, baby carriages and back to school nights, sleepovers with *real* little angels curled in the living room of the house we will have someday. I want to create a legacy with you that will mean more than any shiny award could ever hope to."

I put my hand on the page she's reading and her eyes waiver before fixing on me.

"Rachel." I look up at her from where I'm pillowed against her.

She runs her hand through my hair and cradles my head closer. "What is it, honey?" She sets her book aside, letting it fall closed.

I stare at it, at the innocuous cover and the words 'Our Story' until I squeeze her softly. "Is that what you really want? To have a family now?" I watch her face. She glances at the book, clearly nervous as her eyes land everywhere but on me.

"Yes, those are my dreams, Blake." And really she doesn't have to say more than that. She runs her hand over mine slowly and then rubs her thumb over my arm. "There isn't any rush though. When you're ready, I'm ready. I know it's hard."

"It is hard." I haven't forgotten what it felt like to let Beth go. I haven't forgotten the pain of holding her in my arms and then giving her away. How my signature had never been as dark and heavy and horrible as it was when those papers raced under my hands. I remember it every time I sign my name, every time I see a child at the store, every time I feel the cyclical pinch when I ovulate.

And worse yet, was losing the baby Rachel and I had when she died. Our little miracle. *Our* perfection.

And though I thought time would cure those moments of remorse, it hasn't fixed it or desensitized me to it like I had hoped. Beth and Emily did as much damage as I thought they would, if not more.

But still, looking into Rachel's clear loving eyes now, I know I can't let those fears stop me and rob her of the joy that she wants.

Of the completeness I think I will find.

I *know* I will find.

"What are you thinking?" she asks softly.

"That I want us to try."

Rachel doesn't speak, doesn't move. I don't even think she breathes. Not until her body forces it and even then it's thin, like we are on a mountain top and there isn't enough oxygen for both of us. "Are you sure?"

"Yes."

It's so easy to say, this time around. She's so much more domesticated, so much more into creating a home and a life together. Even though she is going to be *only* twenty-three in a month, she does things she did at twenty-seven and at thirty-five before. She worries about money, worries about a down payment on a house. Where I was the one that put up budget restraints, laid down limits on fun, and was the general party pooper in our previous life, now I find myself wondering where all this coupon litter is coming from and why on earth her closet rack hasn't broken under the weight of clothing.

Because it did before.

It literally tore out of the wall in the middle of the night under the weight of her stuff in our other life and thoroughly scared the shit out if us.

Where once she was lost in her image, in her dream, she isn't now. Her desires for a family were fickle at best. The next week she would be refocused and pushing forward, running at the speed of light toward her goals. Then family, and even I, didn't matter.

I admired that about her, actually. I really didn't know any better because I was as driven too.

I know better now, as even my goals have realigned. Those things we desired in our other life on a whim are now the standard that defines every cadence of our day. In light of all these new things, it makes this moment easier. It makes this conversation and the thousands more along this path infinitely more beautiful because this time, I know it *is* all she wants.

A family with me.

It's all I want too.

It makes my heart race when Rachel smiles, her hand squeezing mine tightly. "Really?" her voice breaks upon repeat. "Really?"

"Yes, really." I reach out and hold her cheek.

"Come spring I promise, we will start down this road together."

And when spring comes, I keep my word.

It becomes the season of doctor visits, of bland walls and invasive tests. It is the blue and white of my hospital gown, and the dark red of vials of blood. It's the tired high five Rachel gives as we pass one another in the hall on our way to different radiography tests and the dissection of the microscopic pieces of us. It's the silent pensive look in her eyes and the jarring questions that hang unanswered between us. Spring is the season of revelation as we discover more about each other than we ever thought possible in every possible fundamental way.

And it's this–the deafening silence of waiting.

It's cruel to put a clock in a waiting room. I learned that early on in my own practice, before I knew how to manage my time. I stare at it, watch the hands turn slowly, like torture. Behind the counter, the nurses talk in hushed tones that make me think they are talking about us. I glance at them and though they aren't looking over, I'm pretty sure it's only because Rachel is staring, and has probably been doing so for a lot longer than my glance.

I take her hand in mine and she jumps a little, before sliding her other hand over the top.

"Hey?"

She turns to me and shakes her head. "I'm really nervous."

"It's going to be okay. Dara is my friend, and she is the best."

She gives me a thin smile. "Okay."

I let her go and she corrals another magazine, the same one she's read at every doctor's office we've been to. She flips pages with nervous hands and stares blankly, unseeing. It's the same look she's had for three months. That look where the churning thoughts in her mind never touch her face.

I know what she is thinking. She's worried that she won't be able to have a baby. I already know different, but my words don't touch the well of worry she's drawing from. I think everyone, when they get serious about it, feels like this, feels the crush of fear. It's a test you can't study for but will define your life regardless. It's like taking a dry run at a bar exam, or the final for your capstone class in college. And it's something she never thought about until now.

"Ladies?" Both our heads turn at the same time to the woman holding the door open. I give Rachel a nervous squeeze and stand, letting the nurse escort us silently toward our future.

My friend Dr Darajit Kootarappali is what some would call a miracle worker. I would be part of that group. She holds a double doctorate in genetic engineering and fertility, making her one of the very few "Designer Baby" doctors in the world. And while there might be ridiculous amounts of controversy, you don't see it in her. She isn't jaded by the press, or enamored by it either. She isn't what one would expect from a doctor that literally plays God, and makes more money than Him. She looks more like a middle aged soccer mom with a white coat, and she is the miracle worker who gives Rachel and I a child.

"Blake." She catches me in a hug before I'm totally in her office. "So good to see you, and this must be your wife, Rachel."

Dara hugs her, too, and it seems to suck all the nervous energy right out of her because her face relaxes. "Nice to meet you, Doctor."

"Dara," she waves politely. "There are no titles here, not when we are talking about making a baby together. Sit, please."

After we sit, Rachel, in her silent way, pleads for me to ask the questions she is dying to, but can't. I take the hint.

"Dara, is it good news? I don't think Rachel or I can take much more."

"Yes, all good news, a little strange news, and a lot of decisions today. You can breathe, the hard part is over."

It's Rachel that audibly releases her breath and when the fifty megaton weight she's been carrying on her shoulders slides off she is bubbly and smiling again. "I'm glad to hear it. I didn't want to face anything worse than the dye test."

Dara nods and winces in sympathy. "Not very much fun at all, I know. I'm sorry. I don't think I've ever met a woman who's a fan of the hysterosalpingogram." She shuffles the papers on her desk and slides a thick manila folder to the middle of it. "We will go over all of the results, but most people, once they know everything is fine would prefer to get to the good part." Dara wags her brow. "Would you like to know how your genetic typing went?

I turn to Rachel.

"Of course," Rachel answers, leaning forward a little.

Dara literally beams. "This is my favorite part, so pardon the inappropriately large smile I have." She turns her folder. "This right column is you, Rachel, and this left one is you, Blake."

I was on the right the first time we did this, and

I feel a lump slide into my throat, because it isn't the same. It's also twelve years earlier this time. When I reach for Rachel's hand and catch it, I'm shaking as badly as she is, because it's different.

"As you remember we pulled a few vials of blood from each of you and had an egg retrieval procedure done. We used all of this genetic material to type and split your genetic code, essentially finding all the things that make you, you." She points at the page and I scoot closer. "This percentage here is the accuracy of the data we gathered, and here the standard deviation allowable for using the code. As you can see, we have about eighty-five percent complete gene codes for you, Blake, and eighty-two percent for you, Rachel. Both are really good numbers."

Rachel swallows so hard I see it. "Does that mean the baby will only have part of the genes they need?"

Dara smiles. "No, nothing like that. It just means that your sequences were incomplete. In some cases we have to use filler DNA from an anonymous male donor, or re-sequence again, but here is where the strange news comes in, because I've never had this happen before."

Rachel's hand has been progressively tightening on mine, particularly on the words *anonymous male donor*, and it now feels like my fingers are going to break any moment.

"Your sequences broke at two different polar caps." She draws a diagram, hashing through one X at the bottom and one at the top. "To make it simple, if yours degraded up here, Rachel, then yours was down here, Blake. And it happened in every chromosome, every allele. So I actually have a complete genetic code from just the two of you."

Now I'm squeezing her hand, and she taps me with her thumb. I loosen my strangle hold on her fingers. "So you're saying you don't need filler DNA, that our baby will be one hundred percent our genetic code." My voice is strained with how tight my throat is because it wasn't this good before. It wasn't.

I nearly don't hear Dara's words over the frantic rush of blood in my ears.

"Correct." Dara pats the paperwork. "It will obviously mean that there are some guaranteed traits exclusive to each of you, things that we will just have to take with a grain of salt, but it's quite remarkable."

"Wow." It's Rachel that says it, but it steals the word right out of my mind.

"So what traits do you want to pick?" Dara flips the page, and I almost turn away from it because I don't want to see what options there are. I don't know why. It's totally illogical.

Dara continues unabashed by my flinching. "I think the goal would be to take the best of each of you, speaking in regard to heredity. We would want your daughter, which obviously the gender is a given, to have the best possible health."

Rachel nods slightly.

"For instance, Blake, you have a genetic predisposition to Asthma. It's recessive which is why you don't have it, but we would want to use Rachel's allele there to make sure your baby doesn't develop it. It goes on from there, heart disease, stroke, anything where one of you has a predisposition that is more favorable than the other."

The list of possible illnesses has my heart thudding. "What are the givens? Are they congenital things? You said, take it with a grain of salt, what does that mean?" I clear my throat, because I sound much more emotional than I mean to.

Dara thumbs through the chart as she pulls it back. "No. It's small things, Rachel's hair color, your eye color, your height." She turns another page. "Rachel's body structure and bone density, your hair texture. It's a lot of macro physical characteristics, which is good because the finer points are things we can engineer to be as perfect as the two of you are together."

"Can we pick all her physical characteristics aside from those givens?" Rachel's hands move over the file when Dara puts it back on the desk. "Like her smile and her legs? She already has Blake's eyes, right?"

It plucks my emotions that Rachel listed the features she loves the best about me.

"Yes, she will have Blake's eyes and yes, absolutely you can designate anything else you want."

"But..." I wrangle in my feelings. "We talked about it and we would like to get as close to the old fashioned way as it can be. Is it possible to just mix everything up and whatever happens, happens?"

Dara blinks at me. "I'm sure I can do that through an algorithm and apply it to your daughter's gene sequencing."

"I think I've changed my mind about that." Rachel runs a shaky hand through her hair, and the dread knots in my stomach. She doesn't look at me. She's staring out the window when the words come. "If that's the case, if we can pick anything we want, I want our daughter to be beautiful like Blake, not me."

When she says the words I'm so utterly shocked, I don't even know what to think. I look at her, stare at the side of her face until I must be boring holes into it.

I don't understand. She never said this before, never breathed a word of any of this to Dara or me, ever.

"Rachel, that's crazy," I finally say.

I can feel Dara's eyes on me and I swallow past the tightness in my throat. When I look at her, my friend and colleague, I don't know what to say. "Can you give us a moment?"

"Of course." She stands, but instead of leaving leans over her desk. "Rachel."

My wife looks up at her, and in the light from outside I can see her swallowing over and over to keep her emotions in check.

"I don't know if it matters that I say this, and I'm sure I'm speaking out of turn when I do, but," she pats the file, "there is nothing but good in here, from *both* of you. In all of your bits and pieces, you have the beautiful gift of creating a life, and I would no more want to subtract you from this, than I would want to subtract Blake."

"Okay."

Dara smiles softly and looks over to me. "I'll give you two a moment."

When she leaves I feel like the room has been sucked empty of all air and sound. The only thing I hear is Rachel's words over and over in my mind. I stare at the folder on the table. "You can't change the plan without telling me Rachel. We had decided to just let her shake up the mixture and give us a child."

"Okay."

I purse my lips and frown at the same time. I haven't felt this kind of unease in a long time. "Okay is your way of placating me."

"I don't know what you want me to say, Blake." She wipes at her eyes when I glance at her. "We have the chance to give our child a gift, give her confidence and charisma, elegance and refinement."

"By excluding you?"

"Yes."

"You are elegant and refined."

"Not like you."

"I don't understand why you are thinking like this. Where is this coming from?" I turn to her in our separate chairs and strangle the arm rest. "You are so beautiful, you *know* you are."

Rachel laughs bitterly. "It's in the fine print of our contract that you tell me that."

"It's the truth."

"It wasn't always."

I sigh. "No one is beautiful all the time, baby. You've seen me in the morning, I look like hell. When I'm looking my best it's thanks to a lot of make-up, amazing hair products, and hours at the gym. There is no magic or science to it."

"But when she's little, before she can wear make-up or put stuff in her hair, I want her to be happy and healthy and confident. You don't get that, that feeling that you're unstoppable, by being made fun of and picked on."

"Who picked on you?" I ask, before I really think about the question I'm asking.

She turns and looks right at me. "You did."

Rachel lets the words hang before she continues. "Because I wasn't pretty, or popular. Because I had a big nose and dark hair and I was fashion dumb and awkward. Because I wasn't like you."

She shreds me to the bone with those sentences.

"And you may tell me that you picked on me because you liked me. And you may lie to my *face* about that to try and make it better, but the truth is if I was beautiful in the millions of ways that you are, you never would have been able to let me go back then. You would have followed me to the end of the world, like I was willing to do for you."

I breathe raggedly, my lasting damage bared to me. And I was blind to it. I figured that everything I'd done in the past was erased by the present, but I was wrong. I was wrong about so many things. I didn't have any idea what she was thinking all these months. And maybe, the things I love about her domestication are more because I ruined her confidence, and less because she loves me more.

That thought makes me truly and utterly sick to my stomach. I put a hand to it, in effort to still its churning.

"Is that really what you believe?" And I pray she says no, because if she doesn't I won't know what to do.

"Yes." She runs a hand over her face and into her hair. "Maybe...sometimes...I don't know."

"It's not the truth."

"Okay."

"It's not."

"Fine."

I know better than to push more when she says fine, especially with the tone she just used. That word is the line in the sand, a line that if I cross will begin a battle royale, but perhaps it's a war we *need* to have.

I must open my mouth a hundred times, ready to say something, but no sound comes. I run through a million conversations, outcomes, ways to start it, and things I want to say. When I actually speak, I'm surprised by the words I've somehow picked in the jumble of my mind.

"I think you're a liar."

The answer comes very quietly. "What did you say to me?"

I stare hard at the folder on the table. "I think you're doing your thing, where you put emotion into something else because you don't want to tell the truth." In a testament to the magnificent actress my wife is, she can actually do this, this twisting of her own feelings and displacement of her anger from one thing to another. It's the same way I can cry for who I lost in another life, but tell her it's for her. It's a real pain, just not *the real* pain. And Rachel is better at it than anyone else I know.

She doesn't look at me and to be honest I can't look at her either.

"This is how I feel."

"Are you really sure?" I touch the folder, sliding my hand over it. "Think very carefully about what you say before you answer me."

Silence.

"Yes, I'm sure."

I push the folder sharply, and it slides to the far side of Dara's desk. "Fine." I stare hard at it. "If that is how you feel, then I can't do this."

"How can you say that?"

Her words make me angry, perhaps illogically, but she doesn't understand how hard this has been for me, staring into this fear, unblinking. How afraid I am to have a baby for the normal reasons, fear that I won't be a good mother, fear that I won't make the right decisions. Then there is the compounded fear, that the moment she gets pregnant, I'm afraid she will be crushed out of my world again.

The only saving grace has been the idea that *we* would have a baby, that the person I love the most in the world would give pieces of herself with me to make that happen. That God, in the form of a random selection, would reduce us both to puzzle pieces and fit it all together to make our miracle. I've told her all this. She knows how important it is to me.

So, now, I'm angry and hurt because she is taking it away.

"How can *you*?" I counter. "How can you sit here beside me and take away the things that matter most to me? You are the reason I'm doing this, because it's *with* you. If you aren't in it, it might as well be me again in high school, and I can't do it again." I shake my head. "I can't."

"I know you can't do that."

"I thought you cared more." I didn't quite mean it like that, but I do.

Rachel doesn't speak for a long time, her face turned from me. "Maybe you're right." Her voice is very small. "I think I'm afraid and I'm saying things that will throw up roadblocks." She turns to me.

I meet her gaze warily.

"Will you do it?"

My heart isn't pounding anymore and has stopped instead. "Do what?"

"Carry our baby?" Rachel searches my face beseechingly. "That's what I'm afraid of. That I'll lose her, that something will happen. It's too important, too precious to risk. My mother, she lost her first, I don't think I could survive it."

When she smiles hopefully at me, like all the fear is gone, I can't seem to breathe under the pressure of this decision and the way Rachel is staring at me like all the hopes in the world are pinned on me. "Of course, I could do it, but..." I don't know how to feel. "What if *I* lose her?"

Rachel threads her hand into mine. "You won't."

It's so easy for her to say, but so hard to hear. I say the only thing I can say. "I love you."

"I love you, too."

I thin a smile, trying to use it to force away my fear. "Next time it's your turn."

"Yes, I'll go next. You're older, you should go first."

I roll my eyes. "By only three weeks."

"Still older."

There is a tap on the door behind us. "Can I come in?" It's Dara, and I really want to say no, but I can't. I feel like I'm in a car sliding on ice, out of control and unable to stop.

"Yes, Blake and I want to discuss a change of plans with you."

I squeeze Rachel's hand like it's the only thing I have in the world.

≫ ≫ ≤ ≤

Summer becomes white, the color of the ceiling I stare at. It's the color of the sheet over my thighs and the plastic stirrups. It's the muting of Dara's voice as she whispers to me, and the punctuated 'I love you's' Rachel presses into my ear, like I'll never hear her voice again. It's the pinch and the burn, the promise that it will only be a second, but I feel it for three hours. It's telling myself to breathe, because everything is colliding inside me. It's the tears I spill in the bathroom, as I face my demons and hopes alike to the broken watery reflection before me until Rachel sweeps in to hold me.

And it's this, a pregnancy test in my hand and a ghosted pink plus sign. Then summer is tears, and kisses, and hands that touch me like they want to set me on fire, that move in worship not consumption. It's the nine month path spreading out before me, and baby clothes months too early because Rachel can't help herself. It's waking up to my wife's head on my stomach, her face shadowing a smile while she sleeps, and her voice lulling me into dreams with whispers I can't understand to our child. And her voice singing to us every moment between.

Summer is the secret I carry, as I listen to the melody on Rachel's lips. It's the knowing smile at Rachel's first *On* Broadway performance, where the box seats vibrate with the thunderous applause. Summer is the silver bell perfection of her voice as it sweeps all of New York City and changes everyone it touches. Summer is smoothing my hands over the flatness of my stomach and knowing there will someday be two heroically angelic stars that shine so bright they dwarf the galaxy.

Knowing that when my wife opens her mouth it's the voice our daughter Emily will have.

Because it was the only thing I asked Dara for.

Chapter Twenty-two

Nothing I Wouldn't Do
March 1st, 2019
(11 years left)

*I*t's night and the darkness is all around me, choking me like smoke, sliding into my mouth and nose and burning my lungs. The impact of my steps jostle through my whole body and I feel the ground move under me as I run. It races in a river of cement, on and on forever in trails of lights. I can't see anything other than color, as my tears drag everything into a melting pool. I claw at the air, pulling myself forward, racing like I did when I was young, like I spent my whole life to get to this moment.

I don't remember why I'm running, but the pain in my chest is a memory I will never forget. It winds me when I finally put it together, when my heart reminds me what it feels like to be broken. That I'm running to her. It tears me apart, and I breathlessly collapse against the wet pavement. My fingers wedge into the cracks of the slabs and I cling to them. If I let go I feel like I may slide off the face of the earth into Hell.

I know I'm supposed to still be running, so I lift my head. The first thing I see is a blur of red light and when I blink, it says words in a block print that is branded on my soul.

EMERGENCY ENTRANCE

I wheeze a breath, struggling to find enough power to put motion to my body. It takes a moment, but I get my knees under me and push myself to my feet, onto shaking legs, to stumble toward Saint James' Emergency Room.

It's light inside, sterile lifeless white, I see it through the doors as I approach. They pneumatically hiss open when I'm near enough that they feel me, blasting me in air. It's a bone chilling wind; it rips the warmth from my body, evacuating the blood in my veins, to refill them with ice instead.

The E.R. is empty of people and my footsteps echo eerily. Long crystalline strands of I.V. tubing hang like vines from their stands, grabbing at me as I pass them, as I search for something I don't think I want to find. Down the hall an incandescent light flickers to the same rapid beat of my heart.

"Blake."

I turn in a circle to the whisper of my name. I don't know where it came from, it moves in an echo from everywhere at once. It somehow makes my blood colder, the room colder, until my every joint is frozen under the wave of fright it spreads.

I head to the nurse's station, the only point of reference I can find in the jungle of menacing medical equipment and harsh shadows. Though it is ten feet from me it takes an eternity to get there. I walk forever, space stretching to accommodate the endless count of my steps. Again, I hear my name, and it compels me forward. I run toward it blindly. My hands slide over the counter of the station rattling aside charts and equipment, gauze and pens. For a moment, behind the counter, I see a computer monitor and the flat lined EKG that skitters across it.

When I turn the corner, heading toward the trauma rooms, I slip in something. I brace myself, covering my head with my hands as I slam to the ground. I hear a crunch, but I don't feel it, not at first. All I feel is numbness where I jammed my shoulder. It's when I go to move that the warp of pain stops me. I think my clavicle is broken and I roll over to my back slowly. With shaking hands I reach for it and ease a jittery breath at the jagged bone that meets my fingers under my skin.

I see blood out of the peripheral of my vision. I loll my head to the side, staring at it. It's what I'm lying in, what I slipped in. It spreads forever down the hallway beside me, smudged and streaked like something was dragged through it. No...like something broken moved through it. I sit up painfully, cradling my arm in my hand. When my eyes fall to a perfect footprint, the outline of which I know so well, I forget my arm and it falls limply beside me. I smell the whisper of Chanel, and it puts the tears back in my eyes. It's all Rachel's blood, I know it is. I've never seen a color so stark.

Red had never been as red as it was the day she died.

And though I don't want to, my body pulls me upright, pushes me inexorably toward the room at the end of the hall. The room where I know I'll see her broken again.

I follow the trail. My shoes are gone now, and I can feel her blood gushing between my toes, imprinting my footprints to the places where hers are. I can feel her life drying on the cold tiles and on my skin, as I march on. The only sound I hear is my own inner monologue that tells me over and over that it's too much blood. It's too much. Unendingly I repeat it as I get closer and closer to where the trail leads.

When I pass into the trauma room, the sickly sweet smell of gore, of death, that I know so well from years in medicine, overwhelms me. I gag on it, putting a bloody hand over my mouth to quell the churn of my stomach. And then I see her. She is leaning on her hospital bed, untouched, staring at the ground. It looks like she's waiting for me; waiting for me like the million times she has waited so we could go somewhere.

"Rachel."

She's so beautiful, so perfect. My sweet angelic wife is safe.

"I missed you, Blake." She says it with a smile in her voice.

It all goes wrong when she turns to me. Right before my eyes an invisible force drawn straight from the maw of Hell, wipes over the side of her like an etch-a-sketch.

And she comes apart.

I stare in dumbstruck horror as the point of impact, right at her middle thigh, sends a shockwave through her, collapsing her body in an arch. Her eyes go wide and she screams, but the sound does nothing to dampen the crackle of bones breaking, of her right leg shattering to pieces.

"Rachel!" I scream her name like it is the last word I will ever say. I push forward to save her from the damage I can see occurring with every passing second, but the horrible IV tubing that has been ghosting over me, binds me up. It strangles me silent, choking my voice off, holding me still as I pull toward her until my shoulder separates and my broken clavicle seesaws under the skin.

My eyes move up and follow the arc of chaos

where her pelvis twists as some form of force overcomes the inertia of her bones and they splinter like kindling. I see it under her clothing, the way the curve of her hip disappears, and then her ribcage caves an instant later.

She takes a sharp strangled breath, and her coffee colored eyes meet mine with grim understanding before she's ripped off her feet. It doesn't make sense, because there is nothing there, but after crumpling she suddenly reverses direction like she's bouncing off something. In that moment, I literally feel the sharp crack as her jaw breaks sending her face at a horrific angle, and the whiplash of it turns her spine into a broken zipper.

Everything goes black.

And then she's on the bed, blood leaking everywhere as invisible shears cut perfect lines in her clothing, baring her paling skin to me. Where the sharp stab of an intubation tube garrote's her throat and I realize in horror her voice is destroyed by the motion. Watching as her bruising flesh is cut by the surgeon's hands, and she is opened for me to see. For me to remember that the places where I touch and firm bone meets my fingertips will be nothing but shards of white and cream in a mottled void. That every last organ and vital system will be punctured and shredded beyond salvaging, and the hollow of her pelvis, where our baby was, will become a wash of matter and bone.

My eyes rise from the horrific wrongness of seeing into her, and to my horror, she's staring at me.

Rachel.

I have no voice, so her name forms on my lips soundlessly. Her hand reaches out to me and I struggle against the tubing again, pulling myself almost parallel with the floor before I sink to my knees, unable to get farther. My empty hands strain.

"Blake, where are you?" I hear her voice clear even though the skin of her face stretches where the tape holding the tubing in her mouth pulls.

I can't let her down again I think as the adrenaline hits my synapses, and I stand yanking hard enough against the shackles to break my wrist. I don't even feel it and I don't even care. I scream for her so she knows I'm here, but nothing comes from my mouth. My wail is silent even though it is crushed from my chest until my lungs are empty.

She reaches for me like she heard me though, her lips attempting to move, but she can't speak. The sound of her bloody gurgle resounds in my ears instead. When her hand comes up to her face, those beautiful fingers skinned to the bone from being dragged across an invisible road, I can't look away. I stare into her fearful eyes while she claws at the tape on her mouth and rips the intubation tube out of her throat in a ribbon of carnage. I feel my stomach twist again and bile hits the back of my throat as the contraption falls to the floor in a plastic rattle followed by what I think is part of her larynx.

"I know you're here, I can feel you," she wheezes from her torn lips. "I waited for you to get here."

I try to soothe her, to comfort her, but the air rushes soundlessly between us.

It doesn't matter how terrifying it is to see her like this, I love her more.

I will always love her more.

Her eyes survey me, where I'm frozen in my place. They light with understanding. "I'll come to you." Because she will always come to me, to help me, and protect me instead.

She groans as she moves from the bed, impossibly

stable with the extent of the damage, with how she is literally pouring from where her body has been cut open. In the empty space between us, her broken body and pulverized bones finally betray her, spilling her to the floor in so much blood and carnage it's hard to believe that it's my wife. It's hard to believe that this is what she looked like in the hospital so long ago, that this is what she looks like as she dies in front of me.

I scream to her until I must be blue in the face, pulling on the clear ropes that hold me until the bone of my clavicle cuts a hole wide enough that my own blood comes down my side. I pull until I can't anymore, until my feet are sliding through the slick of her life as it slips away. I fall to my knees once more beside her as my blood mixes with hers.

She's so close, so very close, and yet my hands can't touch her.

"Blake?" Her fingers slick over my knee and grab my scrubs before she closes her eyes. "I'm sorry I couldn't wait longer."

I scream.

I wake to the sound of my wail of agony. I can't breathe, can't move my arms. I thrash against the twisted restraints around me.

"Blake?"

I can't breathe. Oh my God, I can't breathe.

"Baby, I'm here."

I know that voice, but the realization of who it is, is muted. Slowly, everything becomes clearer. I'm in our bedroom, with Rachel, but that doesn't make it any better. When I'm able to free myself from the sweaty wrap of blankets around me, I claw my way to the edge of the bed, stagger to my feet, and into the closet door with a bang loud enough to wake the dead.

"Honey, what's wrong? Blake! Baby, are you okay? Are you having contractions?"

My stomach rebels against the images I can still see and when I glance back at the bed and see Rachel, her hair disheveled and eyes wide with concern, I feel vomit hit my tonsils. It all bleeds together in that moment, as a bloody angel, in a blue lace negligee, reaches out to me.

"Come here to me, baby."

"Oh, God." I lunge for the bathroom and I can hear her startled outcry, the blankets being tossed aside by her hurried hand. I collapse to my knees on the tile, hard enough to make my teeth rattle and shove my head into the toilet a moment before I throw up.

"Baby, oh baby. I'm sorry." Rachel's hand touches my back for a moment and then she vanishes, leaving me alone so I can literally purge every last ounce of everything from my stomach in peace.

I don't know how long I stay there, how long my hands strain on the porcelain as I dry heave and spit into the water. It doesn't seem to stop until after my knee starts throbbing and my nose is running, until Emily kicks me hard enough in the kidney to bring realization back to me.

It was just a dream.

And even as I say that to myself, I know it was but *wasn't* at the same time. It's what I've forgotten happens to her. When the thought lands home, I'm reduced to a quivering mess and I reach blindly for the toilet paper roll. I find Rachel's hand full of tissue instead.

I flinch when I touch her. Afraid that if I look at her she will be destroyed. I shudder a breath and blow my nose. It takes everything in me to meet her eyes as

442 *Stephanie E. Kusiak*

I finish wiping my face.

She is sitting on the floor, hands corralling a glass of water. She offers it to me. "You okay?" Rachel tilts her head, her bleary eyes regarding me as she scoots closer, slowly. "Can I get you crackers or something?"

I shake my head numbly, and toss the paper in the toilet. "No." I reach up and flush it. The sucking swirl is so loud it makes my head hurt. I stare at her, and she frowns at me. She straightens her hair, yawning and when her wedding rings flash in the light in the hall, it twists me up inside.

"Do you want to get up from the floor?" She reaches for me.

I shake my head because I don't think I can. I cup a hand under Emily and use it to relieve the ache I feel in my back as I sit on the edge of the tub. I lean against the wall, jittery and tired.

Rachel frowns again as her eyes map from my hand to my face. "I'm sorry you don't feel well baby. I thought by now it had stopped. You haven't thrown up in months." She stands slowly and pets my head. "I'll change the sheets, get you new sleepy-clothes." Her hand moves down my shoulder and plucks at the tacky material clinging to me. "Oh, Blake." Her fingers twist in the cotton. "You are drenched. We have got to get you out of these."

"I know." I press my forehead to the wall tile and soak up the coolness.

Her fingers brush back the strands sticking to me. "Let me help you." She feels my neck. "You don't have a fever do you?" She holds her palm there, waiting, then touches my forehead with the back of her hand. "No, you don't."

"No."

"Which part are you saying no to, the helping or the fever."

"The fever."

"Okay, come on then."

Rachel wraps her arms around me, and with her help I stumble to my feet weakly. I cling to her, feel her, feel that she is alive as her warmth presses to my side. It makes it better and worse at the same time.

She coos softly in my ear, holding me tightly as I limp into the dark bedroom. "It's okay, I'm here. I've got my girls."

Her hands work expertly, stripping off my T-shirt and sweatpants. I cross my arms against the cold of the air as she drags a damp towel over my skin. I don't know where it came from. She hums softly in the darkness, working over every inch of me. Runs her hands over my skin soothingly, until she presses her hand in that one spot where Emily can feel it, then she bends to kiss my stomach as our daughter responds.

"Why are you giving your mom a hard time, Em?" Her whisper tickles my skin as her thumb feathers over where I can feel Emily's heel pushing.

"She isn't." I clear my throat. "It's fine. I'm fine."

"Then what is it?"

And my emotions break under the weight of my misery. "Nothing."

I don't realize how chilled I am until Rachel pulls me close and her arms wrap me in warmth. She presses her forehead to my bare shoulder, lips moving softly over my skin. "Let's get you something to wear. Something warm, okay?" Her fingers map over my back before she pulls away. She returns quickly with a sweatshirt and sweatpants.

"Here." She is smiling. I can hear it in her voice.

"An old cheer sweatshirt will make it better. Nothing could be as rough as those days."

I wish.

And though I know she's trying to make me feel better, it isn't working as she playfully tugs the red and black cotton over my head. It's tight around Emily, and Rachel's hands smooth the material awkwardly. "Guess this was a bad choice. Did you put on weight, Blake Fortier?" She pokes me gently, and Emily kicks in response.

It's two weeks to my due date, and I realize Emily has dropped, which is why she could kick me in the kidney earlier. It's also why I was able to bend over far enough to not puke on the wall. I blow a thin stream of air between pursed lips. "I'm going to have her soon."

Rachel nods, her breath brushing my neck as she says, "Just breathe." I think she's saying it for her own benefit, because she does that.

She drops to the floor to feed the pants over one foot and then the other, pulling them up my legs as she stands. "Is that what's going on? I'm scared, too."

I almost think about telling her yes, lying about it. "No."

"Baby." Her gaze catches mine and she pulls me into a hug. "What is it then?"

"Just a dream."

Rachel narrows her eyes at me as she takes my hand, leading me into the living room. She flips on the light, and I watch her pad away in a scantily clad little nighty. She returns from the kitchen with a piece of banana bread. "Come here and sit with me." She falls into the sofa, tucking her legs up under her, as she takes a bite. She chews with a smile and pats the cushion beside her. "I know how much you *cannot* stay away from my banana bread. So come here for the bread, if you can't do it for me."

"I can come over for you." I shiver as the cool of the leather sofa leaks through my sweats. I pull the raspberry throw around my shoulders, under her watchful gaze. I don't know how she isn't freezing her ass off. She's barely dressed by comparison in her new sexy little thing.

"Blake?"

I wipe my hand over my face before I turn to her. "Yeah?"

She leans back against the sofa, her eyes holding me as she offers a piece of bread. I hold up my hand, declining it. I still don't trust my stomach. "You've been having nightmares on and off for the last three months, you know. Stop telling me it's nothing."

"It's nothing, Rachel."

Her hand worms under the blanket and rubs up my back as she shifts closer. When her head leans on my shoulder, I tip mine against it.

"Tell me."

"No, baby." I collect myself. "I'm fine."

After a few soothing caresses, she laughs through a mouthful of food. "I wish you would just tell me." She takes my hand and then slides her fingers over the front of the ill-fitting sweatshirt. "We need to do everything together. We are stronger and better together. And even this, we should share." When she's done eating, her arms wrap protectively around me and Emily. "Aren't you supposed to tell people your nightmares so they don't come true?"

I glance at her. "Nice try, but that's not true."

She sighs, her head resting against the blanket on my back. I hear her yawn softly. "I wish you would just tell me because you love me, then. I'm here, I'm up with you, I care, just tell me."

Her touches are so gentle they implore me to speak despite my better judgment. "I dreamed you were dead."

She tightens her hands and I feel her head move, her chin resting softly against my shoulder blade. "But I'm not." She squeezes softly, confirming reality. "I'm right here, baby. I'm not going anywhere."

She pulls me closer, easing the ache in my lower abdomen when I recline back against her. I wish it was that easy. For her to just say it and it would be so. That her words could wipe away the terrible things I've seen. When I close my eyes, I see it again and the image pricks tears and rattles my breath.

I don't know what I'm thinking when I open my mouth. "But you will be." When I say those words and turn into her arms, everything comes apart. I sob once sharply, and then everything just strips out of me. "You will and I can't stop it. I am supposed to be able to fix people, but you are too broken for me to save. Of all the things in my life that I need to save, I can't save you."

Rachel pulls me against her, holding tightly. My head pounds as insane words purge from my heart. "No matter what I know or what I do, I can't. How can I not save you? How can you be just out of my reach?"

Rachel coos nonsensical words as she pecks kisses against my hair with quiet understanding. She inclines her head to meet my face as I look up at her. "You better than anyone know that no matter what, people we love leave us." She smudges her thumb through the tears on my cheek.

I didn't even know I was crying.

"Do you think I want to imagine a life without you?"

"Can you?" I whisper getting my breathing under control.

"Of course not. I wouldn't even want to picture it." She leans over, and I hear her knuckles rap against the coffee table. "God forbid it ever happens, but I also know, and you taught me this...I know I could lose you any moment of any day, and eventually, someday, I'll lose you no matter what, but that can't stop me from loving you and being with you."

"And what if you lost me tomorrow?" I question seriously, even though the weight of the words is actually more than Rachel could ever understand. "What if I," I force my words past the lump in my throat, "stepped out into the middle of the road and got killed by a car?"

Rachel looks away, thoughtful, her bright eyes glancing around while she contemplates it. When she answers, her face shows a grim understanding. "It would hurt me more than you could ever imagine, but I would find solace in knowing that I did everything I could to make you happy." Rachel sighs heavily as her fingers work through my hair. "I have, haven't I?"

"Have what?" I ask softly, pressing my head into her tan shoulder and smelling her hair where it tickles the side of my face. I know all too well the pain Rachel is talking about, but the solace of knowing I had given her my best is something I've never had before.

"Made you happy?"

"Yes, you are the only good thing in my life." I immediately open my mouth to correct that statement with the little angel I can feel within me, but Rachel smiles thinly when I pull back.

"I know. I'm just one of them."

The way she looks at me then, literally tears down all my restraints and I roll my eyes to the ceiling to stave off the hot tears I can feel. It's too late, and they come crashing down on me. "Oh, God, these hormones are just too much. *Jesus.*"

Rachel squeezes my hand firmly.

In the quiet moment that follows my deluge of tears, I stare at her fingers in mine. I think about what it will be like to remember this moment in the future, to remember her hand in mine when I've lost her again, and her warmth, her fingers in mine, are *only* a memory. I cover my face, and fight valiantly against the unwinding of my emotions until Rachel's arms come around me. Then I'm hysterically crying, crying like I haven't cried in years–not since I sat in the driver's seat of my car, and wept for letting her go.

"Let's go to bed. I'll hold you. It's okay. I'm here and I'm never leaving you." Her protective embrace carries me to our room, where Rachel peels the sheet and comforter off the bed and lays me down. "I'll be right back."

It feels like only a second. The breeze of the sheet fluffing over me lets me know she is back. It's followed by the crinkle of a faux down comforter and it falls heavily on me. I'm still wiping away my tears when Rachel slides into bed and spoons me.

"It's okay." She pets my head, and kisses it over and over. Her touches help alleviate the pain I feel. "Will you promise me something, Blake?"

I nod silently, pulling her arm around me.

"Promise me that you will always be with me. That if I ever lose you, you will haunt me, so we can always be together." She snickers in the dark. "Or whatever naughty Christians do while waiting to go to heaven."

I force myself to be playful, to forget. "Even naughty ones go straight to heaven. It's you Jews that take forever straggling around."

I feel Rachel laugh good naturedly behind me. She rolls me to my back, and her body shifts to fit against me. "Whatever, I'll take my sweet ass time then, but I promise to haunt you if you haunt me."

She kisses me then, all sweetness and warmth. When she pulls back, I can see her eyes skim over me. "That was supposed to make you laugh, honey."

"Rachel?" I touch her face, letting her body anchor me in our bed while I think about spiritual dualities. "If I *did* die and you had a chance to do everything again, what would you do differently?"

Rachel rests her forehead against my temple, her eyelashes fluttering softly. She holds me for a long time, long enough that I think she might have fallen asleep. "Rachel?" I whisper hesitantly, because if she is asleep I don't want to wake her.

"I can't imagine I would change anything. I can't think of anything better than the life we've had, than the love I have with you." She makes a small sound before she kisses my cheek. "I take it back. The only things I would have done was save you from breaking your knee, and I never would have filled out that application to Stanford." She sighs. "Actually, no. There is something else I would do. If I knew you were going to die, get hit by a car or whatever, I would be there. I would be there on that street that day and I would do whatever it took to protect you. There is *nothing* I wouldn't do for you."

"Nothing?"

"No." She pats the bed beside my head to accent the word. "I would maim, shoot, kill anyone that got in my way. I would gladly throw myself in the way even. I would lay down my life for you, Blake Fortier." She kisses my lips. "Don't ever forget it."

"I won't."

"I love you too much." Rachel brushes her lips against my cheek and then presses her face to my neck. "I love you too much not to fight for you with my very last breath."

"I would fight for you too."

Rachel sighs heavily, her hands pulling me close. "Good. Now hold me and I'll keep the nightmares away."

I do. And she does.

For a time.

Chapter Twenty-three

The Things I've Learned
September 17th 2022
(8 years left)

I've learned that the apple doesn't fall far from
the tree.

There has always been a part of me that wanted
to know what Rachel was like as a child. Hiram and
Deborah used to tell me stories about how mischievous
she was. Apparently, there was a day where she spread
Vaseline over the entire bathroom floor and screamed
bloody murder until Hiram came running, the end of
which I'm sure was jarring as he flew across the room
skidding out of control. She also colored a white silk
shirt blue with dye from the bluer in the toilet. And
as the story goes, called the police saying she was left
home alone, while Deborah was in the kitchen cooking.
The outcome being she was unceremoniously barged
in on by the Sheriff's Department.

Did I mention this was just one day?

It was just *one* day.

It all seemed pretty funny at the time, but I've
had a revelation in the last three years since giving
birth to Emily. It's only funny if it's someone else's
child, and I now know firsthand what Rachel was like
because Emily is just like her. I think that as I watch
her play on the floor, where I can keep tabs on her

and negate her subterfuge while I attempt to text Ryan my opinion on a case. I really hope she turns out to be a singer, or she's going to end up being a criminal mastermind. Even now, as I turn away for a moment to reference my notes, out of the corner of my eye I can see she is trying to scoot toward the kitchen nonchalantly.

"Emily."

That's all I have to say. It's not what I say, it's *how* I say it. I could probably say *bagel* the same way and she would still respond by giggling maniacally and coming back to her toys. 'Cause she knows she's been caught. It's very much like the giggle Rachel has when she's doing something she shouldn't be.

It doesn't just end with the temperament and the personality. She is Rachel through and through, from the long spiraling dark hair, to the tan skin and pretty little pouty lips. She has my eyes though, and the contrast is very extreme, incredibly breathtaking. Every time I look at her, especially when she's angry because it's so darn cute, I'm spellbound by it.

Which isn't probably the best thing, since it makes standing my ground against her whims difficult.

And though I'm okay with her being three and strikingly adorable, I'm *not* okay with the idea of her growing up into the stunningly beautiful woman I'm sure she will be. I cannot wield a baseball bat as well as I will *need* to in order to keep the boys away.

Or girls for that matter.

Whatever makes her happy.

"What are you doing?" She stares at me, hazel into matching hazel. This is something else she picked up from me both genetically and environmentally–the eyebrow raise. She's using it on me now.

"I was thinking about you, sweetheart." I shuffle my papers to the side, giving her a tickle.

"Play with me?"

"What do we say?" I prompt.

"Please."

"Okay, let's play." I slide to the floor, stretching my legs out to get comfortable.

Emily blocks the toys when I reach for them. "No, you have to sit like this." She points at her lap, how she's on her knees with her legs tucked under her. "You have to ask for the toy you want, too."

I grin. "Em, you know I can't sit like that. Mommy's knee is broken." Broken is an easy concept for her, because she's broken enough windows and vases to redecorate the house. She might end up playing softball with the arm she has.

Emily seems to contemplate it, mull it over and weigh whether it is an acceptable response. "I think I want to see the scar."

Okay, so this is another thing she is super into, which gives me nightmares about who she might end up dating someday. She's very interested in scars. It all happened when she scraped her knee playing in the yard. Ever since it healed and she got *her* little scar, I think she considers us twins. It's *our* commonality.

I love it, kinda. Until she comes home with a badass, scar-riddled biker, and then *I'm* going to have a freak out.

"Okay, but only once and then we'll play, okay?"

"Okay, mommy."

I pull my pant leg up. I still get a little nervous when she reaches out to touch it. Rachel is the only one I've been comfortable with, but Emily has gotten better at not poking things, like puppies and bunnies and my knee. Her little fingers trace slowly and when her big green eyes come up to me, I smile to take the ache away from the expression on her face.

"I'm sorry, Mommy." She reaches over and hands me her favorite toy.

This right here is probably the only reason I haven't killed her yet, that and her angelic little face. It's because when she wants to be, she can be the most emotive and wonderful little girl in the world. It's these moments when she truly shines like Rachel, when I can watch emotion move over her face and display such a depth of love and understanding.

And though she won't ever remember these moments shared between us, I'm sure I'll cling to them and love them when she's a rebellious teen. And it will probably save her life, yet again.

"It's okay, baby."

"It's a big ouch." She worms her way around, to put her legs out and pokes her own knee. "Mine's little. It doesn't hurt."

"I'm glad, buttercup."

"You don't hurt either, right mommy?"

"No, not when I have you to make me happy."

"Then you can be the princess."

"I would love to be the princess."

I've learned that validation isn't in awards or stipends, it's in the words of your child.

Since we bought our house in Rye Brook, going to work has been hard. Thank God I only have to do it four times a week, I don't think I could do it more. I don't know how I *did* it more. There is nothing I want other than to be at home with Rachel and Emily. I was so compelled by it, I used to go back to the apartment between patients and at lunch, but I can't steal away to see Emily anymore, or Rachel for that matter.

It's about an hour commute each way from the house to the practice I'm working at, hellish sprawling downtown traffic that makes me sincerely wish I didn't have to do this to myself. However, having Emily early came with a price. That price being long commutes and time away from the two girls that mean the most to me in the world.

The money we would have used to put down on our house was used on the procedures to bring Emily into the world, so the mortgage payment is a little steeper and a lot more demanding than I'm entirely comfortable with. That isn't to say we are living beyond our means, but it does mean that I have to endure this commute a lot longer than I want to. And we both had to buy cars, which is weird, because I haven't owned a car in almost ten years. Boy does that make me feel old, again.

My only solace is the phone call I get every morning at 7:45 a.m. It's always over breakfast, right after Emily's fruit has been cut up and she's tucked into her booster chair.

Rachel is amazing at running a household. Really. I couldn't do it better if I tried.

The clock on my dash turns and the speakers announce the incoming call. I punch the button. "Hi, girls."

"Hi mommy!" Emily's voice is followed by a horrendous crash that makes me jump.

"Sorry, she dropped the phone."

"It's okay. If only everyone was so thrilled to talk to me." I smirk as I stop in traffic.

"Are you coming home?" It's Emily again, her mouth is full, I can tell.

"Eat your peaches, baby. Mommy is going to work so we can talk for a bit, but not with food in your mouth." Rachel's voice gets nearer. "How's traffic?"

"Like usual."

Rachel sighs. "I'm sure there are practices out here that are hiring."

"I'm looking." I decided not to strike out on my own this time. It makes it easier, less work, and certainly less expensive. I certainly don't need the accolades, because they're worth nothing in comparison to this.

"When will you be home Mommy?" It's Emily, sans food in her mouth. Her lips must be in the phone with how loud she is with her subsequent words. "We miss you."

Her voice warps through my car and I feel that twinge in my heart over it. "I miss you both, too, buttercup. I'll be home tonight."

"Why?"

"Because, I have to go to work."

"Why?"

I smile as I stare at the back of the car in front of me. I have to make my answer good, so it stops the 'why train' from getting too far out of the station. "Because, mommy has to make sure other mommies and daddies and their babies are healthy like we are. We don't want anything to happen to other people, right?"

"No."

"So, that's why."

"Oh." She moves around, I can hear it. "You're a good mommy. Go be good."

Okay, those words really get me. And I take a moment to clear my throat of the emotion in it. "Thank you, Emily, you go be good too."

"Hold on Blake, I've gotta let her down before she falls." I hear the phone set on the table and I steady myself by clearing the lump in my throat.

After a moment I hear Rachel speaking. "What do we say to Mommy when we hang up the phone?"

It picks up a moment later. I'm ready for the 'I love you' and kisses, it is how we end every call. What I'm not ready for...what makes it so hard to stay on this highway and not turn around...are the words my daughter says.

"I wanna be like you Mommy."

I've learned that the price of empathy is the cost of an extra McDonald's meal, and one sleepless night.

"There it is!" Emily squeals from the backseat as I make a right-hand turn into McDonalds parking lot.

"Yep, there it is." I glance in the rearview mirror at her cheeky grin. Okay, so I'm not above bribing for good behavior with her favorite treats. Besides, how bad can apple slices, yogurt, and orange juice actually be? Not to mention my coffee and breakfast sandwich. I'm sure it has done more good than harm some mornings.

I pull into the drive-thru and study the menu, which is probably a mistake because Emily sees her new favorite obsession. "Buttons! Mommy, it's Buttons!"

I really hate how lovable Disney characters are and how my daughter is as susceptible to them as everyone else.

"Yes, but you already have a Buttons toy at home." I turn back to look at her. She's pointing out the window at him, at his super happy, grinning visage. For all the money I've pumped into Disney over the last three years, I'd punch Buttons in his face if I didn't think I'd go *straight* to hell.

That and probably irreparably damage my daughter.

"But I want him!"

"No."

"Yes!"

"No yelling," I scold. "Emily, what have I told you about yelling?"

She measures the sternness of my expression and gets her determined face instead, the one her mother Rachel has right before *she* throws a tantrum.

I head it off at the pass. "Don't even do it, young lady. I'm not kidding."

"Pleeeease." She drags the word out until she is red in the face and then burst into tears.

Like I said, face punching of Disney characters sounds good right about now. She cries all the way around the bend, all through the huge order the car in front of me places, but stops the instant I pull up to the speaker. There she waits, sniffling.

I stare at her in the mirror as she ever so casually fiddles with the strap of her car seat. I can't believe it, but I know she's listening to me. It's incredible to see, to watch her intelligence and personality unveil to me.

"Hi, welcome to McDonalds, can I take your order?"

I sigh. "Do you have the new t-o-y available?"

I literally watch Emily's brows shift because she knows what I spelled. The little smarty-pants.

"Yes, we do."

"Can I get that–"

"In a happy meal?" I look at the clock. It's ten in the morning. I really hope she's joking.

"Um, no, just alone please. And an order of apple slices, an orange juice, a croissant breakfast sandwich, and a coffee."

"What size coffee would you like, ma'am?"

I glance at the expectant face in the backseat. "The largest you have."

"Okay, your total will be nineteen-fifty-six at the first window."

I dig in my purse for my wallet as I contemplate the inflation on the cost of McDonalds' toys. I get the bag and the tray of drinks, give over a twenty, and drop the change into the collection box for their charity.

"Mommy, I want my juice."

"What do we say?"

"Please."

I pull over, grab the sippy cup I keep in the glove box for just this occasion, and pour some in. I once gave her the glass with the straw. Once. I think I still have dried orange pulp ground into the seams of my backseat. And on the floorboard.

Oh, and the roof.

"Here you go sweetheart." I hand it back to her, and she takes it, pausing to stare at the bag on the center console. I follow her gaze. "Did you want your apples?"

"No."

"Okay." I feint disinterest because she isn't asking for the toy like I expected her to. I pull away from the turnout I pulled into and start toward the house. When I look back in the mirror Emily is leaned over with her hands against the window.

"Where is your drink, Em?" I'm really glad I gave her the cup I did, because I think she dropped it. When I realize she is ignoring me, I turn to look at what it is that has her so captivated.

That's when I see the homeless man. I have to

say, I think it's terrible I didn't see him before. He's right next to the car. It goes to show how desensitized I am compared to my little girl. I read his sign quickly, averting my eyes because I don't have any money to give him, and speed off as soon as the light turns.

"Mommy?"

I hazard a look at her. "Yeah?"

"Why was that man all dirty?"

I stop at another red. "Because he is homeless." I say it like it answers all the questions, because I don't know how to explain to her that sometimes horrible things happen to good people. That we are all one stroke of bad luck away from losing everything we have. And sometimes, in those worst cases, homelessness is brought on by illness that could be treated if people gave a damn.

"What does homeless mean?"

"It means he doesn't have a home to live in."

I tap on my steering wheel anxiously, introspectively, staring at the red light. And to stave off the guilt I feel, I reach into the bag and pull out the Buttons toy for Emily. She squeals happily and I tear it open and hand it to her.

Her little hands grab for it and she greedily tears it out of my grip. I listen happily as she warbles a few notes from the movie we saw, prancing with it over her little jumper covered knees. We are almost home when she goes quiet. I know quiet isn't a good thing.

When I make the right turn into our subdivision and clapboard houses with manicured lawns flank our way, I see she's crying out of the corner of my eye. "Emily?"

When she looks at my reflection, she throws her toy down and wails hysterically for no reason at all.

The only thing I can think is that she's hurt. It's her hurt cry. "Emily. What's wrong baby?" I pull over and unbuckle my belt so I can reach her. "What's wrong? Emily, are you hurt?"

"No, mommy, no!"

I don't understand what's wrong. I check her hands, that her belts aren't too tight, that her car seat isn't poking her. I even take off her shoes and check there isn't anything in them. I arch rather far over so I can get her juice and wipe the spout of the cup before giving it back. "Emily, did you want your juice?"

"No!"

God, it is so hard to see her in agony. I think about calling Rachel and asking if she's ever seen Emily do this before, because I haven't. It's so extreme, so gut wrenchingly painful, I don't know what to do.

"Emily, honey, tell mommy what's wrong." And then it clicks. "Are you upset about the man?"

It stops her dead in her place. She nods desperately, all bouncing curls and big watery green eyes. My nose burns and I press my lips into a line to still the tremble I feel. "Do you want to go back and help the man?"

She nods again.

"Okay."

I buckle my belt again, blinking a few times before turning around and doing what I should have done in the first place.

And that night, when Emily can't sleep because she is afraid to lose her home, and Rachel and I take turns trying to console her, I realize something very powerful.

We should all care as much.

I've learned that the parents' curse is actually real.

"So I was thinking that we might be able to have some grown up time tonight?"

I smile into the phone as I sign my name to the medical chart I just finished reviewing. "Oh really?" I hand it back to the nurse and head toward my office. I pass a wall with all seven doctors' doctoral degrees and in habit, I click my fingernail against mine as I turn the corner.

"Yeah, you, me, a chance to break in our bathtub." Rachel laughs. "We bought this house because it had a nice neighborhood and schools, but also because of the master bathroom. You remember that?"

I nod, sliding into my desk chair and gliding my hands over the first file in the stack before me. "I do remember, and that sexy see-through shower door," I purr at her and she smirks, I hear it.

"Yes, that bathroom."

I breeze through the notes quickly and sign my name ordering an evaluation of the patient. "So how are we going to manage a whole evening?"

"I have my ways."

I arch my brow at her through the phone. "Should I be worried?"

"Not at all, there is a really great babysitter right up the street, and she will do it at her house." I hear Rachel pull out a dining room chair and sit.

"So, we are talking about a one night staycation then? I'm game." I lean back a little and twirl the pen in my hand. "I think I forgot everything you like it's been so long."

"Yeah, it doesn't take either of us forty-five minutes to shave our legs in the shower."

"I knew you had other reasons for getting the massage head in the shower." I laugh, sitting up.

"Shameful, you should have told me. I wouldn't have been so religious about turning it from pulse to gentle rain."

"Pulse *is* pretty amazing."

"Not as amazing as you." I pull another chart and wait for her response, but nothing comes. "Speaking of you, where did you go?" I wait, "hello?"

I hear Rachel groan. "Blake," She pauses. "I swear to God I'm gonna kill that little girl."

I laugh at her because at least once every phone call she swears she will. "What happened?"

"Remember the magical disappearing vegetables?"

I do. Emily finished her broccoli last night, or apparently didn't. "Yes? I take it you found them."

"Yes, under the seat cushion I just sat on." She blows a breath.

"Enjoy that one," I deadpan.

"Why do I always get the messes?"

"Your parents cursed you, that's why. They wanted you to have a child just like you."

"You weren't perfect either."

"Does the word Vaseline ring any bells?" I laugh.

"Okay enough, I don't want to hear another word out of you."

I grin. "Perfect, we weren't going to be talking tonight anyway."

"Aren't you cute." She sighs.

I smile. "I really am, I know this."

"Yeah, if cute is spelled b-i-t-c-h."

"Sorry, I didn't catch that. Can you spell it again?"

She laughs. "Hold on."

I close out a few more charts, glancing at the horizontal lines of the sunlight coming through the small window beside me. I look at it, tracing my fingers through the rays. Almost time to go home. It makes me grin.

"Back."

"Did you kill our daughter?"

"No, but I did trip on a roll of floss strung like a tripwire in the bathroom."

"Uh, huh." I pause. "She's more slick than I thought."

"Yeah."

"Seriously, I hope she ends up being a singer cause if not, she'll be a diabolical mastermind, I'm telling you."

"Well, if she's going evil, she's getting it from you."

I finish my last chart. "I remember a nasty text outside a bar from once upon a time. You have a streak, too."

"Well, then she is genetically screwed."

I pack up my briefcase. "Yep, pretty much." I shut off the lights. "Though, she is absolutely beautiful like her mom, so she has a saving grace."

Rachel ruffles her hair, I hear it, hear that endearing motion. "We did good in that department."

I nod as I move out into the glowing golden afternoon. "Yes, we did. Though I'm not amused that I married a woman who was so naughty as a kid."

"You should see me as a grown up."

"Mommy, I did something bad! Come see!" I hear Emily distantly and rather proud sounding. I can't resist the words that follow.

"It's a trap Rachel. Don't go."

"Don't I know it. If I don't call you back in twenty, I'm dead and Emily has the conch."

"Reaching all the way back into high school for that Lord of the Flies reference. Your life is already flashing before your eyes." I tease.

"Don't enjoy this so much Blake. You still have to come home to the aftermath."

"But she'll be a saint, like always."

"I'm hanging up now because I hate you."

"So does that mean the bathtub is on hold?"

"It means that tonight I'm gonna be too busy getting un-hexed by parents to attend to your needs."

"We could always do both. You used to be able to keep you voice pretty level on the phone when we had sex."

"And now I'm *really* hanging up. Drive safe. Love you."

"Love you too, Oh, and Rachel?"

"Yeah?"

"Just remember this is all your fault."

She laughs and it is my companion as I make my way to my car in the warmth of the afternoon.

And I've learned that no matter what, keep the recording on.

I hold Rachel on the sofa as we try and watch TV. It's something I don't quite understand, it looks like a children's show, but it's not. I don't really get kid's shows anymore, and what's worse is that Emily isn't even watching anymore, but we still are.

Rachel's head lolls back on my shoulder and she sighs deeply. "Do you know where the remote is?"

"No." I pat around next to me. "I'm too tired to look for it."

"Me, too." Rachel shifts, her hand sliding around my side and squeezing me softly. "I'm too tired to get up and change it." She groans and it melts into a laugh.

"What is this anyway?"

I narrow my eyes at the screen. "I think that little dog is friends with that computer looking thing."

"Is that a dog? I thought it was a horse this whole time."

I kiss her forehead. "At least you're pretty."

She playfully digs her nails in my side and I squirm. "No, none of that, I'm too tired."

We fall still, and it's so rare in our crazy lives that I can't help but exploit it. I catch the back of her head and pull her into my lips, devouring her mouth. Rachel pushes closer, holding to me with a smile tugging. It's slow, long, breathlessly perfect in our home, with it full of our family. It's true what they say, that absence makes the heart grow fonder, because I miss kissing her for hours. It makes my heart race again like I'm sixteen. I'm pretty sure if I was standing, my foot would pop behind me.

When Rachel pulls her lips from mine, instead of mapping her eyes over me like she always does, she turns away. "Did you hear that?"

"Emily is asleep." I say it not because I'm sure, but because I'm hoping so.

"I thought I heard her."

I sigh. "We should check then."

Rachel inches off me, and I untangle from the warmth of her. She eases a smile at the expression I must be wearing. "Oh, Blake. Don't worry, we'll just check and then go to bed." She grins clarifying. "Go to bed in a not sleep way."

"Okay."

I take her hand as she leads me through the darkness. When we get to Emily's bedroom door, kitty corner from ours, we slow. There is light under the door and in the dimness I see Rachel put a finger over her mouth.

I hear something soft and silly sounding. I can't explain it. I know it's Emily, but it sounds like a warble or a whine. I'm not sure which. Rachel puts her hand on the knob and turns it so slowly, I'm not sure if she is turning it at all. We both peek in, Rachel ducking a little so I can see too.

What I see isn't what I was expecting at all. Emily has her little Buttons recorder and is standing on her bed, singing into the microphone.

Rachel's hand strangles mine as I make out a few words here and there, and I realize she is singing "The Sun Will Come Out Tomorrow." I watch her dance around dreamily, and I can't help but wonder if this is what it was like when Rachel started. If she was once a onesie-clad little sweetheart with a recorder and her dreams, dancing on bedsheets.

Rachel pushes the door open all the way and Emily turns to her, dropping her microphone. I'm almost sad for it, *almost.* That emotion lasts only for a moment, then Rachel picks Emily up and kisses her face. And Emily kisses her back, laughing. "Did you like my song, Mommy?"

Rachel nods, pressing her forehead to our daughter's, mixing all their burnished chestnut hair together into streams of shimmering curls. "Do you want to sing more?"

Emily nods.

And even though I know *our* fun is coming to an end, I'm perfectly okay with it. Rachel gives me a kiss on the lips as she breezes past me with Emily in her arms.

"Wait." It's Emily and Rachel backs up so she

can kiss me, too, with a dizzying giggle.

I beam, following as Rachel goes to the basement door and pulls free the key she keeps on top of it.

"We can't go down there." Emily, looks at me with wide eyes.

"It's okay with Mommy," I reassure.

"Only with your mommies, Emily. Promise me," Rachel adds.

"Okay."

It's Rachel's sound studio, and I take up my place at the soundboard as Rachel puts Emily down for a second. Emily is immediately in the cords, and I watch her as Rachel flips a few switches. My heart starts pounding as I hear the warble of music pour through the speakers inside the sound booth. It's the song Emily was singing. When I look at Rachel, she smiles.

"Like I wouldn't have all the classics. Please." She holds out her hand to Emily and she takes it. "You ready?"

"Yes."

But I'm not ready. I'm not ready for this. I'm not ready as Rachel lifts her in her arms and moves the microphone closer. My hands shake as I pop the record button. I watch the digital feed race across the computer screen beside me, as it spikes when Rachel takes a breath.

"Do you know the words, Em?"

"Da, da, will come out da-morrow."

"The sun will come out tomorrow."

Rachel sings it when the chorus strums through the speakers. I cover my mouth, grinning so wide it hurts because Emily has wider eyes than I've ever seen before. Rachel doesn't sing like this with her. She baby sings, playful sings, but this...this is real singing.

Emily copies her.

And maybe we are bad parents, but Rachel and Emily say and sing the same words over and over all night into a microphone that captures every single breath.

Every moment.

Every note.

It also captures the moment where Emily not only says the right words, but does it perfectly in tune, on pitch. I catch Rachel's eyes when she turns to me, and it's Emily's hands, not mine, that wipe at Rachel's cheeks.

"Emily you did it. It was so beautiful baby." The digital feed captures the emotion in my wife's voice. "Blake." She turns to me, smiling at me through the glass. "Come in here."

I do, and we capture, forever, the three of us singing the same line over and over, together.

Chapter Twenty-four

Signs Of The Times
August 12th, 2027
(3 years left)

It's our ten year anniversary today.

It's the first thought in my mind when I open my eyes to the hazy predawn light leaking into our bedroom. I blink at the ceiling, at the blurred shadows that pattern from the trees outside. It still isn't bright enough to make the image of branches and leaves solidify, so I have no idea why I'm awake. And not just awake, but *wide* awake.

It drives me crazy because it happens more and more. At least once a week now, I'm up before dawn for no reason. Well, that isn't necessarily true. I have phantoms of dreams that still linger, but I can't make them out. The instant I try to focus on what I was envisioning, it's gone. And the harder I try, the faster they go. It's infuriating, because not only am I left with this vacant foreboding feeling, but I feel like they are important, that these dreams *matter*.

They taunt me whether I'm awake or asleep. But I really wish it wasn't today that I woke up with this gnawing feeling in my stomach and a nervous itch in my bones. I try in vain to force it away as I roll over slowly so I don't wake Rachel. My eyes map over her, over her sleeping face and the way her lips pull into a smile while she dreams. Watching her now, seeing the peaceful warmth in her face is a salute to no matter how much time passes, she will always be the most beautiful thing in the world to me.

This is where I find my consolation in my early rising and these dreams that liquefy upon waking. It's stealing these quiet moments where I can watch the sunrise come over her like it's doing now, and brush a golden glitter to her skin. I gently twist a short strand of her hair around my fingers before raking my nails through the wave of it. It rouses her, and I watch her back lift with a deep breath, before her eyebrows shift and her eyes open. It's very brief. I can hardly see her irises before she's asleep again with that same smile.

I trace her lips lightly with my finger, watching her lashes move as she drifts into wakefulness from the motion. I caress her bottom lip with my thumb, until it parts from its partner and her teeth move to nip my digit softly.

"I love you, angel," I whisper, feeling her mouth quirk a smile against my fingertip.

"I love you." She kisses my finger softly. "Happy anniversary."

"Happy anniversary."

"What time is it?" She clears her throat.

I glance at the clock over her shoulder. "Ten minutes after six."

She shifts, opening her arms to draw me in to her, but that nervous tingle returns and I stay where I am. I force a smile, even though she can't see me. "Come back to sleep with me."

My smile fades. "I can't." I don't know if she heard me because she's already fading back into oblivion, I can tell by the way her lips relax and her expression falls neutral. "Give me twenty more minutes then."

"Okay." I press a kiss to her forehead, lingering there to breathe her in before rolling from bed. As I leave the bedroom, I look back over my shoulder so I can memorize the image of her poured into the sheets. I open my mouth to say something, to tell her how beautiful she is, but I can't.

I leave instead.

Once I'm away from Rachel, the feeling is even more pervasive. That nervous jitter sweeps in and makes a mockery of the calm I just found. I busy myself in the kitchen, making coffee, checking the fruit in the bowl on the counter to see if it's ready to eat.

It's difficult to put a finger on where this anxiety comes from, but I think it's over the fact that I've conned myself into believing that I have the power to ignore fate and dismiss time. For instance, it's Wednesday, but I'm profoundly aware that it's a Wednesday that never existed. Not to me, not in the memories I have clung to for so long to guide my life. I don't know how to feel about that to be honest, because it just recently occurred to me that I cannot predict anything in my future past with certainty anymore. It leaves me feeling naked, off balance, and budding with dread over no longer having any semblance of an idea where my life is going.

It would be nice to have hope instead, but I'm not an idiot. I might be an opportunist and most certainly self-deluded, but I'm not dumb. Just thinking about my life in this moment, puts a knot of apprehension so heavy in my stomach that even though I've found a pear that looks good, I can't eat it. I put it back and stare at it mutely.

I've lived in a world of suspended animation

where the sun rises just as it's doing now, but it never had an effect on my world. Everything was always the beautiful, perfect sameness. I have gotten up, gone to work, come home, and had dinner. I've watched TV, played board games, tucked Emily into bed, and made love to my wife. And because I'm *really* lucky I have been able to wake up and do it every day in an unending string of amazing.

It's harrowing to note how foolish I feel that even though I've watched Emily grow, I've always felt that *I* wasn't changing, that *Rachel* wasn't changing and that the perfection of our lives would last forever. But that's not how it is. And that scares me more than I can put into words. Those marching sunrises *do* have an effect. They have made us older, better, but yet not. As much as I want to pretend it is just a sunrise, that it's just another day. It isn't. It's a sign of how quickly times running thin on the both of us. I lean heavily on the counter, hiding my face in my hands as I recount the change that has eroded my life.

"*Your daughter is so naughty.*"

"*My daughter? How does that work?*" I love how Rachel keeps trying to pin her evil on me. "*What did she do?*"

"*She cut her hair.*"

I roll my eyes. "*How bad?*"

"*Bad.*" Rachel sighs. "*So bad I had to call Raul and schedule an appointment this evening to fix it because I can't, and she won't leave the bathroom.*"

I laugh. "*Will she be bald when you two get home?*"

"*No, but you can say goodbye to the length, that's for sure. I'm not sure what she was going for, but it didn't work out.*"

"You're going to send me a picture, right?"

"I'll send you a picture in a second." Her voice gets distant. *"So you can see what I'm talking about."*

I hear knocking on the bathroom door and then Emily screams angrily in the background when the hinges squeak open. *"No, don't take a picture, Mom! Stop it!"* The door slams shut.

"She has buyer's remorse on this look for sure." I hear Rachel open the bathroom door again. *"If you didn't do it, I wouldn't have to take a picture. Just to show Mommy, I promise."*

I raise my brow. *"You better be crossing your fingers, because you have to keep it."*

"Of course I will." Her voice directs away from the phone. *"Emily, take that towel off your head. We are going to get it fixed, I promise, but you have to let me take a picture for your mommy or she's going to be sad."*

"No!"

"Come on."

"No, stop being mean! Don't laugh. No! No, picture! Damn!"

I laugh.

"Don't you say damn, young lady, or you'll go straight to your room," Rachel chastises. *"Besides, I'm not being mean, this is what family is all about."* Rachel smacks a kiss to what sounds like Emily's head, as our daughter growls a little in the background. *"Got it, picture coming to you."*

My phone twinkles at me. Okay, so if a picture is worth a thousand words, then all of them would probably be profanities with the angry glare Emily has. And Rachel's right, half her head is short choppy strands, and the other side long spirals. I lift the phone back to my ear. "Yeah, I don't know what she was going for either. Is it as short as I think it is?"

"I think so. I'm just gonna have Raul fix it."

"What time are you going?"

"Five, so you're on your own for dinner. I can pick up something on the way home if you want."

"Sure. See you then. I love you."

"I love you too. Hey Blake," she interjects. "I'm going to color my hair tonight, I think."

I arch my brow at the wall of my office. "What color? Please don't say blonde. I really don't think that would go well for anyone."

"Oh, God no." She hesitates for a second. "The same color as my natural. Dark brown."

I don't know why she announces her natural color, it isn't like I don't know what it is. "Thank you for stating the obvious." I snicker, and her silence drags on. "Why are you coloring it then?"

She sighs. "Don't laugh, but I found three white hairs yesterday and I refuse to succumb to my thirties like this."

"But you just turned thirty." I don't know why I say it, it's not like that matters.

"I know, it's like everything is programmed to break down. I'm so over waking up sore. We need a new bed." The silence drags out again between us. "So, nothing nice to say to me in light of my getting decrepit? As if getting old isn't hard enough."

I laugh, correcting myself in light of my stunned silence. "You're always gonna be beautiful, regardless."

"Thank you, but not with a head of white hair, hence I'm getting it done from now on every six weeks. I don't even wanna know when more comes in. You don't think it makes me less sexy, right?"

I blink. "No, not at all. I love everything about you."

"Good, that's the right answer."

I raise my brow. "I'll even do a cursory check down below to make sure you aren't going gray anywhere else."

She snickers. "I hate you so much right now. I can't even tell you."

"You can tell me about it tonight while I'm investigating."

"Oh stop." *She laughs.* "Seriously, you're gonna make me self-conscious."

I smile. "I can give you other things to think about."

"I have no doubt that you will."

But *I* can't think about other things. Not anymore, because it didn't end with that. It seldom ever does.

"Mother?"

I start in my place and open my eyes to Emily's worried expression. I'm not mommy anymore, unless she's upset, and though I'll never admit it, it makes me sad. It makes me feel like the young girl I look at isn't the same little baby I once held. Especially in the last year, since she's grown so much.

She's on the other side of the counter, and her hands tighten as she hangs off the raised countertop. "Don't hang on that Em, I don't want it to break."

"It won't break, I'm not that big." She pulls herself up again, in direct contrast to what I just told her. Her burnished gold and green eyes peer at me. "I don't wanna go to school today."

"Seriously, get down. And you *are* going."

She complies. "But I don't feel good. I think I'm sick."

When she comes around into the kitchen, she's a totally different child than the one that was just hanging like a monkey off the counter. Her head is bent, face drawn, and she has her hands wrapped around her stomach.

This is one of the greatest disadvantages to having a mother who *is* a doctor. I don't fall for her feint illnesses at all. There are some days, where I can tell she's saying she isn't feeling well because she's upset about something, and those times I *do* let her stay home. I'm not a total jerk about it. I remember what it was like.

I think today is one of those days for her.

"What's wrong, Em?" I ask as I reach into the cupboard, pulling free three bowls. I grab the paring knife and a couple bananas, setting to work cutting them up as I wait for her response.

"I have a tummy ache. Maybe a fever." She squeezes her middle and frowns when she looks back up at me.

I'd almost believe her with the pitiful noise she makes afterward, if her stomach didn't growl and her eyes weren't on the banana I'm cutting.

"So how about you tell me what's going on at school?" I pause, counting the slices in each bowl. "Does this have to do with your tryout in music today?"

She let's go of her stomach. "No, I'm not afraid."

"It's okay if you are," I offer, regarding her solemn expression. "I was always nervous when I had a tryout. I had tingling in my stomach and my hands got shaky, too." I put the knife in the sink and rinse my hands. When I point toward the bedrooms at the back of the house, Emily's gaze moves that direction. "You should talk to your mom about it. She's been through some pretty crazy auditions."

"I'm not afraid."

"Okay." I shrug. "You're not afraid."

In contrast to her comment though, she comes over and while I'm reaching for the cereal on the refrigerator, she wraps her arms around my waist and buries her face in my chest.

I look down at her wild wispy hair and smooth the strands down softly. "It's gonna be okay. Whatever it is, whatever you're upset about. It's going to be fine."

She nods, but yet doesn't seem wholly convinced.

I regard her, at the way she burrows as tightly to me as she can. I hold her in my arms. "You wanna talk about it?"

"Remember when you fell in the shower?"

I wince. "Yes."

"I had a dream that your knee broke again."

I wet my lips, dried by the sharp breath I take in memory of it. "That's not going to happen." I pull her face up to mine and bend down far enough I can kiss her forehead. "Everything is fixed. It's all fixed. I'm okay."

"I don't want you to leave."

"It's just two days. Mom and I will be home soon. You will see your friends at school and get to hang out with Savannah down the street. You'll have a lot of fun and won't miss us at all."

Emily frowns. "I'm afraid something will happen."

It strikes me in that moment that *maybe* she has Rachel's gifts. That maybe she knows something that I don't, and without my guide of already living, perhaps I shouldn't be quite so dismissive. It gives me the chills, makes my heart pick up as I regard her. "What are you afraid of, specifically?"

"That something bad will happen to you."

I nod and force a smile for her benefit. "Your mom isn't letting me out of her sight. So you don't have to worry."

I feel bad I've done this to her, that she had to witness yet another telltale sign that time *is* passing. "I love you for worrying about me. I love you so much, Em."

"I love you, too."

The faucet squeaks when I turn it off and I listen to the water spiral down the drain. I grab my towel off the shower door and pat my face and shoulders dry before wrapping it around me tightly. Rachel has me doing this routine now, because the biggest downside to having a massive shower is, well, cleaning it. So I set to spraying God knows what on the tile. Which, I probably should have done after I opened the small slide window at the top of the shower. Yes, it's so big it has a window in it. Rachel and I thought it would be sexy to shower together, hence the stupid huge shower. And for the record, that activity has happened all of twice since we bought the house two years ago.

I sigh at the window high above my head and stare dubiously at the tile seat built into the corner of the shower. I measure the distance between the two; it's not far. Just to be doubly careful though, I take off my towel again and wipe down the tile I'm thinking about standing on. When I go to put it back on I realize it has that anti-mildew shower spray on it, so I drop it with a grumble and reach for Rachel's towel, but it isn't there.

"Jesus Christ. Really?" *My irritation echoes around me as I regard my nakedness.* "Fine."

I wonder idly if the universe is trying to tell me something. If I should just give up while I'm ahead, and before I get a head rush over the fumes I'm no doubt breathing in. Maybe that is what is making me so dumb right now.

I look at the closed window again and it taunts me.

"Stupid, fucking, high ass, window." I curse as I shift Emily's toys off the tile seat and climb onto it. The window is actually much closer than I thought, which is great. It pops open in my hands, and the blast of cold air puts a chill up my whole body. I really should have dried off more.

I survey where I'm standing, holding the tile sill tightly. When I look down I realize the floor of the entire shower is wet, and my towel is bunched near the door. How I'm going to get down is beyond me. It's really cold, too, but at least I can breathe. I glare up at the window nonetheless.

I try stepping down, try turning around to hold the wall and back down. I even try sitting, but my knee gets a little weak on me and I get an image of impaling myself on a shampoo bottle so I stand back up. "That would really suck," I whisper to myself. That is not a trip to the ER I would want to take. In full confession, I've seen things like that, or at least kinky things gone wrong that were blamed on a slip and fall. I'm not a fan either way...well...of the going to the ER part, the kink on the other hand, is fine by me.

"I can't believe I'm stuck in my own shower." The surprise and defeat in my own voice irritates me. When in the hell did this happen to me? I mean, I'm still Blake Fortier, right? I'm still the same badass I once was. I stare at the towel again. I could just jump for it.

It makes perfect sense. It's not that far, just like the window wasn't.

Right?

I mean, Jesus, I was a cheerleader. This is nothing at all. The pep talk makes it a little better, a little easier. So I do it. I take an exaggeratedly large step and make it to the towel. What I didn't think about, is that the towel had soaked up water while I was building my courage. I feel how slick it is the second my foot connects with it and though I'm landing on my good knee I realize I'm going to fall if I don't stabilize myself with my bad one.

I grit my teeth and flail my arms, my hands sliding over the moist walls and as soon as I plant my right leg, I know I've hurt myself. As a matter of fact, the whipping crack that reverbs around the enclosure and the warp of pain that moves up my body is so dramatic, it actually puts dots that swim before my eyes.

I hear it. I feel it. I know I broke it.

And I collapse to the tile.

I would like to say it was artful. That I was graceful about the fall. I was not. I'm not seventeen anymore. I hit the floor with enough force to numb my side. And then everything goes black. I can't move. I can't lift my head. When I open my eyes, I can see my hand by my face. I focus on it, telling my fingers to move. When they do I breathe a sigh of relief. As soon as the panic of being paralyzed vacates my system, the screaming agony of my knee announces itself followed by an ache in my head. I scramble to pull myself up into a sitting position, but I crumple against the tile because my arms are weak and shaky.

I don't want to look down. I don't want to see it. The drip of the faucet is somehow back, and I realize I must have tried to grab for the handles. The water patters down over me, washing a slow trickle of red down the drain. I'm bleeding.

It's all very delayed.

I'm bleeding.

I touch the back of my head and my fingers are covered with red. I'm bleeding from the back of my head. I make a strangled sound of panic, and it petrifies me more.

Oh, shit.

"*Mother?*"

Oh, shit! When I hear Emily's voice I hold my breath, cutting off the whine I hear in my throat. Oh God, she can't see me like this.

"*Mother!*"

I clamp my hand over my mouth when I move and the pain makes it hard to breathe.

When she passes the shower door and I see her clearly, I'm torn between calling for her and praying she doesn't turn to look in. I also see my knee, in the peripheral of my vision and it's destroyed. Seeing it scares me even more.

It scares me enough to speak. "*Emily?*"

I didn't mean to say her name, but I need help. When she turns toward the shower door, I have no doubt what she's thinking. Her face is absolutely horrified.

She's instantly in tears. "*Mommy!*" *She grabs the shower door and tears it open.*

I suck in a breath, wrangling whatever reserves of composure I have. It's amazing how much more I have now as a mother, especially when my baby is upset. I surprise myself. "*I'm okay, Em. I need you to get the phone for me.*"

"*Okay.*" *She stares at me, shocked.* "*Mommy, you're bleeding! You have to fix it!*"

"*I will, but I need the phone sweetheart. I can't get up because my knee is broken. Please get the phone.*"

She races off.

My head is throbbing so much it makes me sick. By the time Emily returns, I don't think I can open my eyes. I force them open as she comes crying into the shower.

"Shh, baby it's okay. Please don't cry." I try to soothe her. I take the phone. "Can you get mommy a towel? Do you know where they are?"

She's crying still, hyperventilating. "What?"

"A towel? To cover up before the firemen get here."

She covers her face with her hands. "Firemen!"

Oh, my God. She is not nearly as composed as I was at her age, or Rachel for that matter.

"Emily!" I have never yelled at her before. I've certainly raised my voice, but not yelled. It shocks her in her place, and her tears fall silently. "I need you baby. Please, breathe slower, but I need a towel. Go get it now."

She takes off again now that I'm commanding her and not asking.

I place the call to emergency services. Emily still isn't back when I dial Rachel.

The line trills.

Please pick up.

She does. "Hey."

I don't have composure anymore. "Rachel, oh God, come home right now."

Her voice is instantly whipped in panic. "What's wrong?"

"I fell. Oh shit, my knee is broken. I'm hurt. Please hurry."

"I'm coming. Call the paramedics. Where's Emily?"

"Getting a towel. It hurts so much." I wipe at my

tears.

"*Getting a towel?*"

"*I fell in the shower.*" *And when I shift, I'm sorry for it.*

"*Don't fucking move. Just stay right there until the paramedics arrive.*"

"*Okay.*"

"*Don't hang up.*"

"*I won't.*"

I hear her hurrying, her breath coming in rapid pants. The car engine turns over. I hear the sirens. Emily is still gone. I'm still naked. "*I don't know where Emily is.*"

"*I'll find her. I stopped at the store. I'm ten minutes away.*"

I hear a knock on the door downstairs. I drop the phone. "*Emily! Open the door for the firemen!*"

Another bang, this time harder. Rachel's voice drifts from the phone. I lift it. "*... out of her mind.*"

"*What?*"

"*I said, I'm sure she is scared out of her mind. Just like I am.*"

"*I am too.*" *I hear wood splinter.* "*I think they are breaking down the front door.*" *I don't know why, but it makes me cry harder.*

"*It's okay,*" *Rachel soothes.* "*It's okay. No big deal. We'll buy a new one. Don't worry about it. Just stay still.*"

"*I am.*"

"*It's gonna be okay baby, I promise. I know it hurts, but we'll fix everything.*"

"*I believe you.*"

And I absolutely did.

And she absolutely fixed everything. I didn't

contribute much aside from keeping a brave face.

The news wasn't what I was expecting. I thought I had stepped back wrong and had given myself a torsion fracture, which happens when you plant and twist at the same time. In the scatters of my memory that is what seems to have happened as I replay it.

It wasn't.

It was because my bones had degraded enough from my surgery in 2012 that the pins holding everything in place shattered the head of my tibia. To sum it up, it happened because I'm getting old, or rather my broken knee was getting old. The pins were getting old and by extension *I* was getting old.

Everything else is just noise and pandering doctor bullshit.

So I got a new knee. Well, Rachel insisted that I get a new knee, and a new tibia, I was pretty much in and out of consciousness when the decision was made. Not that I minded, because I really didn't want to be awake anyway. The only time I *did* mind was when I came out of surgery and realized the agony I had felt in the shower was only the cusp of what I was going to feel when the medication wore off.

But Rachel helped me fix that too, somehow.

I wish all things were so easy to fix. Like Emily and her nightmares. She's probably going to remember that day as long as I will remember the day I lost Rachel. Oh, and the reason Emily didn't get me a towel? She was hiding in the bottom of our closet because she was so afraid. I don't think I'll ever forgive myself for being such an idiot and scaring her so much.

The door was a breeze, Rachel called the order in and had our neighbor put it up when Home Depot delivered it. I didn't even know they delivered. As a matter of fact, I still don't know our next door neighbors number. I think about that as I slide from the car, pushing forward without a limp on my new knee. It doesn't matter how many years I've outlived her. She's still better than me.

At everything.

The door, the situation, my knee.

I pause my thoughts as I cross the street toward the Winter Garden Theatre. I stare down at the hem of my skirt. She even requested a plastic surgeon redo the work the orthopedic doctor did, replacing the butchery that had previously been done with a small sliver of a scar. Somehow, she's made me feel whole again in a way I didn't even know I was lacking. In ways I didn't think we're possible to correct. So why I feel so shitty about everything is beyond me. I should be grateful. I used to be grateful. I used to have this feeling of blessedness around me. But not anymore.

Once inside the theatre doors I head toward the stage. Rachel has somehow coordinated to have Emily picked up from here, then she and I are heading upstate for our two day mini vacation. Again, I'm reminded of how good she is at everything while I wedge the door open.

From the doorway, I stare out over the empty seats, tracing them as they race across the floor of the theater. Everything is wrapped in gold, and as the most beautiful and landmark stages in all of Broadway, it takes me aback. It will always take me aback that Rachel stands on stages like this as if it's the most natural thing in the world.

Because to me, it will always be such a triumph.

I was expecting Rachel to still be practicing, but when I see Emily sitting on the empty stage, I realize it must have cut out early. I move forward a few steps, but slow music permeates the room, rushing through the sea of shadows to pour over me.

It stops me cold in my place.

Rachel appears from behind the curtain then, and I watch as Emily turns to her folding her legs Indian style. "Tomorrow," she says it with a smile in her voice, from years old memories that warm all of us.

"Yes it is." I watch as my wife slides down to the floor. She corrals Emily in her arms "da-morrow," she teases softly, tickling our daughter until they are laughing together.

Rachel ends up holding her in her arms, as the music swells. I almost don't hear Emily state, with the same succinctness Rachel had when she was young, "I love this stage. Someday I'll sing here, too." It leaves no doubt to the validity of the statement.

I watch my wife pull her closer, pressing kisses to the top of her head. I love it when their hair spills together, and I swallow the emotion I feel seeing it on the stage.

On this stage.

In this world.

"Why don't you sing now?" Rachel offers.

Emily leans back in her arms, looking up. "Can we sing it together?"

Rachel pecks a kiss to her forehead. "Of course. You go high, I'll go low."

"I like going high."

"Okay, then sing it to the stars, baby girl." Rachel pulls herself up and starts the music again. I wait with baited breath until Emily starts singing.

Then I have no breath at all, because my sweet

little eight-year-old daughter isn't just singing, she is filling a professional theatre full of a voice that rivals her mother's.

And it makes me afraid.

Rachel laughs softly, tugging on my pants as she worms around on the end of the bed. "Before I forget, parent and teacher conferences are next Monday. You have to meet Emily's music teacher, he's hilarious."

I nod, staring at the ceiling. "Okay, I'll take off early next Monday."

Rachel grins in triumph as she pulls my slacks free. She pushes herself up, and drops them off the edge of the bed in a crumple. "Make sure you put it on your calendar."

"I won't forget."

"Hey, Blake." *She smacks my leg and I peer down at her, where she's smiling at me.* "What?"

"You seem distracted." *She bends over and grazes her teeth over my hip bone.* "Are you distracted?"

I jump when she does it again. "I'm distracted now."

"Good, the proper kind of distracted." *I smile at her, feeling an odd heaviness in my chest.*

I watch as her smile melts and she catches her teeth in her lip. "So, I lost the bet."

"Yes, you did." *Though I'm pretty sure she did it on purpose to get me in bed with her. Who in their right mind would bet they could beat their doctor wife in the medical category on Jeopardy? Seriously.*

She bends over me, her hair tickling my stomach as her tongue licks playfully from my navel to my underwear.

I shudder. And though my body is alive and well, it just feels so forced. I shift under her, under the contrived motions, trying to get out of my own head.

"I love this right here." Her nose nuzzles the outline of my pelvis against my abdomen. "What muscle is this?"

I glance down at her, at her spooling of chocolate, copper and auburn highlights. It's her new hairstyle, the new color. Not her original brown at all. I move it aside so I can see her face and those eyes I know.

"Where that dip is?"

She nips my skin softly. "Yes."

"It's the inguinal ligament that makes that ridge."

She pauses her kisses as she traces it lower. "Oh, well I love your inguinal ligament." Another kiss. "And where it's leading me."

"Oh?"

"Oh, yes." I close my eyes, forcing myself to relax as she hooks the waistband of my underwear in her teeth and pulls on them. They come down a little and I swallow tightly fixing my eyes to the ceiling. "I really like where it's leading me."

Her lips move over my skin and I feel her index fingers hook in the cotton panties and slide them further. Rachel's kisses are wet and warm, moving over the skin she is exposing. I reflexively back away from her mouth when she kisses the crease between my thigh and my pelvis.

"Tickles."

"I know." Her teeth graze lightly and when I glance down at her, her eyes are smiling at me. She tugs on the material in her grip, baring me to her exploration, as I lift my hips. I hold her eyes as they smolder at me, while her hands caress up the insides of my legs and press them apart for her. "Did I ever tell you I love your scar?"

I glance at my knee. "He did a really good job."

"Not that one."

I arch my brow at her. "What scar?"

"You have a scar." She glances down suggestively.

My jaw falls open. "I do not."

"Yes, you do." Rachel laughs and then peers down. She narrows her eyes and ducks closer.

I press my legs closed. "Seriously, I feel like I'm at the gynecologist. You can never look at me with that kind of intensity again unless you have a speculum in your hand."

She grins. "That can be arranged, but seriously, hold on a second. Let me find it."

I glare at her. "No, what is this? I'm not letting you go hunting for something that isn't there."

"If it isn't there, then you wouldn't care if I looked."

"I care that you are staring at my...stuff like that."

"Prude," she teases. Her hands brush aside her mussed hair. "What's wrong? Blake Fortier can't say vagina? What kind of doctor are you? Not to mention I'm your wife, can't take my eyes off your..." she bites her lip seductively, "pussy?"

I roll my eyes. "There is no scar there. I'm not humoring this."

Rachel presses my legs apart again and crawls between them. "Blake?"

"Hmm?"

"It's right around here." Her finger caresses over my opening. I jump because I wasn't expecting it.

"No, it isn't," I defend. "Believe me, I would have known after I gave birth to Emily."

Rachel shakes her head, leaning over me. "Don't

you remember those times we were making love and you complained about getting super sore superfast? It was a month or so after we had Emily."

I do, in a hazy kind of way. Everything during that time was so amazing and exciting and scary that I don't think I could fully process anything. "Maybe."

"You were still healing. That's why." Rachel crawls up my body and presses her lips to mine. "It's my favorite scar ever."

I break the kiss with a genuine laugh. "That is so weird."

Rachel rolls her eyes. "It's just ours. No one is going to ever see it. No one is ever going to know. It reminds me we have a child together every time I see it. And not to mention, when I see it I'm making love to you. So, yeah, call me weird, but it's the best scar ever."

Her candid confessions breathe a little bit of happy silliness into me and I hold her close. "I'm calling you weird, but I love it."

"Good because I love you, Blake." Rachel draws her head back so she can see me. "I love everything about you."

"I love everything about you, too."

"And now I have a debt I have to pay."

I realize she is pushing against my arms, and it isn't because she's trying to escape so she can slide down my body. It's because she is putting clearance between us. I glance down at the arch she is making. "What's wrong? Why are you trying to get away from me?"

Rachel scoffs. "I'm not trying to get away at all."

"Yes you are." I pull her closer, and the space between us shores up. "Why are you so far away from me?"

"It's just easier to see you from here." She presses

herself up on her elbows.

That's when I remember she used to do this when her eyesight was getting worse before she had her glasses. And when I think that, I distinctly remember keeping them on her nightstand by the bed after she died. I remember holding them when I cried. It makes me realize how close to the end we are, and any arousal I had drains out of me instantly.

Rachel smiles and rakes her nails through my hair. "Now, you just lay back and let me play with you."

As she slides away, I think about how many times those glasses stabbed me at night in those final years. How much I hated it, but missed it, and loved it when it was gone. I don't think I'm going to be able to live through this again.

I don't want to.

When that thought cuts my mind Rachel's mouth is hot on me and I arch under her touch in reflex. It almost hurts because her motions are so perfectly sharp and I'm not turned on anymore. I can't do this. I can't. Oh God, I can't make it through this again.

"Rachel."

She pulls back. "What's wrong honey? Are you okay? I was just teasing you earlier. Don't be upset."

I can feel my heart fluttering and my chest tightening. "No, it's okay." I sit up slowly, sliding my legs off the edge of the bed. "I just, um, I just got really stressed out about nothing. I'll be right back."

"Blake?" She's sitting on the end of the bed staring at me. "Baby, I'm sorry. Don't be stressed."

I nod, grabbing my pajama pants and a T-shirt on the chair. "I know. I'm sorry. I just...I need a minute." And I close the door on her wounded expression.

I don't know why I did it, but I slept on the sofa

that night. As if the idea of getting close to her was going to burn me.

And just thinking about it now has me brooding. I can feel it in the pull of the lines on my face. It's very rare that I've turned Rachel down for sex. Once was because I was feeling sick, three times while I was pregnant, and one other time when I was drunk and didn't want to throw up on her. In ten years I can count them on one hand, because when it comes to Rachel, I really am kinda whorish.

It's become much more frequent now, enough that even I feel weird about it. I feel like there is a question that hangs between us that she wants to ask, but can't put into words. That is part of what I think this weekend is about. She's taking me somewhere romantic to rekindle something. What she doesn't understand is that the thing that is killing my libido can't be escaped.

The sunlight is coming horizontally through the canopy of trees as Rachel drives. She takes the twisted road smoothly, holding the middle line like a lover as we bank our way through the scenery. I stare at her hands on the wheel. They look like a mother's hands. It's strange how that thought strikes me, how I classify them as such. I don't know why I think that, because it isn't that they are old, or marked in some way. There is a speck or two of permanent marker on them from helping Emily with her schoolwork, but she has had that before, back when she was doing her own assignments for school.

I think it's because those hands hold our lives together, mine, Emily's, and hers. They do it seemingly effortlessly, and I wish I could still find as much comfort in her touch as I'm sure our daughter does.

When Rachel glances at me with a smile on her lips in the golden light, I smile back at her briefly, pulling my eyes away from the plastic frames she wore in another world too. They sit on her nose, cutely, and are a burnished reminder of what I could lose. What I'm losing even as I sit here.

I stare at her hands again. I can't stop thinking about them, about how in another world they never had the chance to do all those things that mothers do. Give the angry point, take a tiny hand for a walk or rub a child's back until they fall asleep. Her hands in *this* world are the manifestation of that title, that moniker that so many want, and so few achieve.

It's easy to have a baby. It's hard to be a mother. And like I said, she makes it effortless. It's no wonder that she wants to have another baby.

I stare out the window, and after a minute I punch the button, rolling it down to the point that air tears around the car and Rachel laughs softly.

"Feel good?"

I nod, leaning on the armrest while the wind rips through my hair. I breathe it in, hoping it will wash away the terrible agonizing slow death I'm dying now.

Rachel's hand takes mine after a minute and twines our fingers together. I stare down at it.

"Are you okay?"

I nod, unable to lift my eyes. Because I'm not and it's hard to lie to her.

"You sure?"

"Yeah." I swallow. "Just melancholy."

"Why?"

"I don't know." But I do know. It's because I'm watching my life unravel a strand at a time.

"I'm sure you have some idea." She traces her

hand up my arm and caresses my cheek with her thumb. She glances at me briefly when I lift my eyes. "You can talk to me, you know."

I wish I could. I wish I could tell her everything. I know I should say something, but I don't know what words to use. When she regards me for an instant, I see so much sorrow in her eyes. She goes back to the road, chewing her lip. "Did I do something?"

"No." I sigh heavily. "It has nothing to do with you."

"Is it Emily?" She rolls up my window from the console beside her. Her hand comes back to mine.

"No."

Rachel frowns. "It sounds to me like you actually have a pretty good idea of what it is that is upsetting you, since you're so sure it isn't the two of us."

I don't like it when Rachel reads me so well. I also don't like it when she can pick out such irritating tells in my diction.

"It's fine," I say, taking a deep breath and blowing it out. "I'm just in a funk. It's nothing."

"It's certainly something." She lets me go, running her hand through her hair. "Is it about the baby?" Her voice is very scared, very hesitant to bring it up.

"No." Yes. It's that and everything else all packaged together in a huge red ribbon of bullshit.

"Are you sure because–"

"It isn't that. Let's just try to have fun, okay?" Why I do what I do next is beyond me. Right as she goes to speak, I clip on the radio. "Enough. Time for fun."

She doesn't look at me then, and to be honest, I wouldn't be able to look at myself either.

"Blake, are you awake?"

I blink in the darkness. "Yeah."

I feel Rachel shift, rolling toward me from her side of the bed. "Things going okay at work?"

I feel my brow arching. "Yeah, things are fine."

"How is the volume?"

My teeth catch my lip, and I worry it between them. "Busy, why?"

She shrugs. I can feel it. "I'm thinking of taking some time off next year. I have one more show lined up and then I was going to slow down a little. Do you think that would be a problem? Financially?"

Okay, so, Rachel slowing down is about as possible as breathing water. Which means that she isn't slowing down her life, she's just thinking of putting something in place of the time she would be spending doing music.

"Why?"

"I'm just curious."

I roll toward her then. "Why?" She doesn't meet my gaze and I stare at the clock behind her, noting the ungodly hour. "And why do we have to have discussions at one in the morning?"

Her teeth flash in the dimness, grinning despite how caustic I sound. Why do I sound so annoyed?

"Because this is the only time I feel like a grown adult and not the best friend of an eight-year-old. That's why."

The silence stretches between us. "You know, Blake. There was a time when you loved talking to me at all hours of the night. Do you remember that?"

I do, and the mention of it puts a burn in my eyes. The woman in the dark beside me is still Rachel, still my best friend. I don't know why it is that for small moments, I forget that. "I'm sorry." I soften the hard edge in my tone. "*I do love talking to you. I'm just worn thin from the plethora of stupidity I have to deal with every day at work.*"

She tsks. "*Shouldn't talk about your patients like that.*"

"*I'm not. It's the other doctors and sometimes the residents at Saint James. I would kill them if I thought I could get away with it some days.*"

Her hand touches my side and I jump. "*Sorry.*" *She shifts closer, pressing her head to the niche in my shoulder.* "*So, back to what I was asking. Could I take a hiatus without breaking the bank?*"

I nod. "*Do you not look at the banking statements?*"

"*Not anymore, no. I trust that you will tell me if I need to work more or I'll get an instant message that there's an overdraft on the bank account when the bills autopay.*"

I scoff. "*Next time one comes in the mail, I want you to open it and read it. You could retire if you wanted to and we would still be okay.*"

"*Could I?*"

She says it with a tone that sounds a little too eager and a lot contemplative.

"*Um, do you want to tell me what you're thinking about?*"

She's silent for an uncomfortable amount of time. "*I think I want to do it.*"

I must have missed something. I'm really tired. "*What?*"

"*Have another baby.*" *She lifts up a little to look at me.* "*My turn though.*"

Her words turn my blood to ice and I frown under the cover of darkness. "*Oh?*"

"*Yeah. I mean, we talked about it a while ago and*

I thought it was time to revisit it because things seem good."

"Just the perfect time to throw a wrench in the works?" I laugh haltingly. Why did I say that?

Rachel forces a laugh of her own. "I don't know if that is how I would describe it, but okay. I suppose." She jerks on my arms and I gasp as she heaves herself over me smothering me in the tickle of her hair and her kisses. "I think we will be fine." Her lips pepper over mine. "I know we will be, look at how awesome we have been so far."

I kiss her back, trying to let her happiness leak into me. "True. Besides, I don't like odd numbers."

"Four is a better number."

"Yeah. Four is good."

"Perfect for rides at theme parks."

I smile genuinely. "And sitting at a square table."

"Or a four seater car."

I press my hand through her hair, brushing it back. "I sincerely hope that four people is the correct number for a four seater car."

Rachel giggles. "So, is that a yes? Are you okay with it?"

I nod, because if she gets pregnant next year, there is no way she could be pregnant like she was before. I won't lose her and the baby, so it's safe. As I rationalize it, I can feel my chest loosening, my concern fading away. "Yes."

"Yes?"

"Yes." I pull her to my mouth so I can kiss her fully.

Her soft laughter slows as she pulls back to stare down at me. She is nothing but shadows of darkness and light, but I can make out those eyes. They shift back and forth over mine. "I love you."

"I love you."

"I'm not afraid at all."

I hesitate my subsequent words because I'm unsure if it's the truth or not. "I'm not either."

"I can't wait to feel our baby inside me, growing."

I edge a smile. "It's amazing."

"Hey Blake, can you do me a favor?"

"Sure."

Her lips touch my forehead. "Will you make love to me? Please?"

My mouth touches the stray strands of hair by her cheek. I brush them aside as I press a kiss to her skin there and then further, to her ear. "Only if you say please again."

Rachel smirks. "Please?"

I roll with her, smoothing her beneath me. "Ask again."

"Please make love to me baby?"

Blessedly, I feel the hammer of desire splinter through me. I stretch her hands over her head and pin them down with fingers twisted in hers. Rachel's breath is already erratic and it makes the way she looks up innocently at her hands that much sexier. "Rachel?"

She arches into me from her prone position. "Yes, love."

"How much do you want me?"

She tightens her hands in mine. "Desperately."

"Yeah?"

"Yes."

"How desperately?"

She surges up and I pull back before she can kiss me. Her soft needy whine presses a shudder through me. "So desperately."

"Say something sexy to me."

"I want you to make love to me like we can defy biology and you can get me pregnant."

I wasn't expecting that and it chokes me up instantly. "Yeah?"

"Yes."

"Okay."

I lean down into her lips and it's like she's pulling me in, sucking me into the warmth of her body. She draws me in with her words even more, as if another syllable out of her lips will drown me completely. "I want to feel you, touch you, surrender to you. I need you, Blake, I need you inside me and your lips on mine. I want you, always you. Always. Let's see if we can do it, let's see if we can love each other hard enough to make it possible."

I brush her lips with mine, hovering just out of reach as she stretches to me. "Maybe we can make it possible."

"I believe in magic. Let's try."

I believe in magic, too. Even if it lasts only for tonight in her arms.

And it *was* only a night, because magic isn't real, not anymore, and certainly not as I slowly watch my life slip out of my hands a second at a time.

Chapter Twenty-five

Absolution
December 15th, 2027
(3 years left)

I pull the car into the driveway and stomp on the brake with a heavy foot. My eyes trace the snow covered awnings of our house and the antique Christmakkah lights that glitter in the frost. They are warm, charming, and cast a shimmer of light over the snow laden bushes in the yard.

I turn the key in the ignition and listen to the slow tick of the engine in the silence. I know I should get out of the car, but I just can't do it, not when I look to my right and see the spread of the front yard and the tire swing dusted in snow.

I stare at it, until my tears fall.

It isn't just the tire swing, it's that I promised Rachel I would swing her in it and I haven't. It's that I've somehow become the woman I hated so much, the woman that died so long ago. My secrets and sacrifices used to feel like an homage to love, and now it feels like the poison of it.

It kills me one tiny lie at a time.

And now that I stand at a crossroad in my life, I wish I had my love to keep me strong. I wish I had my wife to keep me upright. I wipe my face, eyes fixed on the snowdrift near the tire swing. There is another reason I'm crying here in the car over that tire swing. It's because of my dream, the nightmare I couldn't remember that has been chasing me for five very long years. I can hold onto it now.

And it starts right here.

I pop the car door, letting the cold wind rush in on me. Instead of heading inside, I walk across the yard, my boots crunching over snow, as I trace my way to the swing. Once there, I crouch down until I'm eye level with the top of it.

I'm staring into bright hazel eyes. They are framed with a curtain of curls that sway in the breeze. The little girl is plucking at her pant leg, sitting alone. Waiting. She has my eyes and Rachel's chestnut hair. She's our baby. I know it like I know my own name. She looks so much like Emily used to when she was little with her angelic little face. The girl's expectant face lifts to focus on something behind me. When I turn, I see a car pulling into the driveway. It's not mine or Rachel's, it's another car. The back door pops open and a garbled voice pours from it.

I can't understand the words, and I've tried so hard to hear them.

Our daughter slides free of the tire swing and walks into the car. Every time I dream this, I try to tell her to stop, to not get into a car with someone, but she doesn't listen. She can't hear.

She just goes.

And I follow, moving faster than I've ever run. The ground speeds beneath me, and I keep with the car as it blurs over the street. I follow it until New York City as all its monochrome glory juts into the sky like the teeth of a hungry animal.

Ready to eat me up and tear me to pieces.

Then, I trip and fall because I know where I'm going and what day it is.

The street is hard against my hands, palms scorched by skinning them in my fall.

It takes a moment, but the jerk of reality shifts me somewhere else. I'm standing in midtown. I know it well, the congestion of other cars humming with purpose. The vehicles blow past me, unaware of my presence, and I spin searching for the vehicle that holds our daughter. It passes right by me, within range of my touch and I pound on the window, but my fist bounces off it soundlessly.

It stops at a light.

The little girl in the backseat has a phone in her lap. She drops it in the purse at her feet. She's staring out the window then, unmovable and unchanging in her place. Though she doesn't know it, her eyes are staring into mine, matching mine with the same color and inscrutability. We are the same in that moment, a life beginning and one ending.

Seeing that, feeling that divide between us, I can't express the flood of absolute and utter love I feel. It is the love only a parent can have for their child, undefinable, because it doesn't come from our world. It's from somewhere else, much better.

The car accelerates into the intersection when the light turns green, and turns right.

No matter how many times I see this street, I'll never get over the agony of standing on it again. I've avoided driving it for thirteen years. I've gone out of my way not to go near it, because it's something I can't face. But I'm facing it now. Frozen in this moment, in the absolute horror of benign buildings and a street that once bore the blood of my only love.

I chase the vehicle, tracing the places my feet fell in another life. The same pulse of agony punctuates me as it did then, a drip of pain I'll never forget hurries my steps.

And I see it.

The car that stole the light out of my life.

I scream soundlessly, in panic, in terror. And it keeps coming, rocketing forward. The two vehicles connect, and it's so slow that I can see the shock waves travel through the car that carries my baby. There is an eruption of sound and color. Plastic and glass blossom like a twisted flower over the lanes. Like the daisies Rachel held for me. The air lights with the refracted rain of blue and red, glitters of a shattered life streak across my view. Twisting, whipping metal slices past me, burning me they're so close.

I run forward.

I scream soundlessly, choked to tears with fear and pain.

My hands tear at the handle on the door, but I can't open it. Through the window all I can see is my daughter's phone, screen shattered on the floorboard. She's not there, she's in the front seat crushed against the dash.

And I can't look, I can't do it.

I collapse to my knees and beg for someone to help me.

But I'm not there, not really. I'm somewhere far away.

Before my eyes, everything melts and becomes my home once again. My dream swirls me into the quiet warmth of a world that isn't violently coming apart. It's our bedroom and Rachel is smiling in my arms, snuggled close on our freshly made bed. Her bare toes trace the top of mine languidly. My hand is on her hip, holding her to me, while I kiss her. We lay together unaware that our life has been torn apart on a road where it ended in another life. Her hand is on my face, fingers tracing slowly when she pulls back.

And I close my eyes.

It's a choice I can't make.

A future I seemingly can't escape.

And a fate that will destroy me one way or another.

My daughter or my wife.

It pains me so desperately because if I had to make a choice, I know what it would be. I love Rachel, but I love my daughters more. The guilt I feel in the admittance of that is deep. I'm comforted only because I know that is how it should be. A mother should be willing to sacrifice anything for their child.

Regardless of the misery.

The branches of my tree feel like they have been trimmed by a heavy hand, because though I will continue to live beyond her death this time, I know it won't be as long as it could have been.

I lift my eyes to the windows of my home with Rachel, a home that shelters people that I love more than anything in the world. I stand straight in the snow as it comes down on me from the clouded dark sky. Resolute in my path.

Until she opens the door, and spills a path of light across the darkness.

Rachel. *My* Rachel. My love, and my life.

I stare at her, at the coat she is slipping on over a pair of bubble gum pink pajama pants and my shirt from cheerleading. The endearing mismatched image puts tears in my eyes again. Her hair tumbles in the light as she moves it aside. Boots untied, laces hanging, she steps forward.

She doesn't say anything, as her dark eyes measure me from the porch.

And then she slowly moves toward me.

I follow her motions as she walks through the snow. Her gate is different, more careful and a little less lithe because she's pregnant. As I think it, her hand firms protectively over the place our child is.

Celeste Marie Fortier.

We picked her first name because it means heavenly, and how could it not be the name of the child that comes from the woman walking toward me? The angel that has stood beside me, who I've walked with hand in hand. Whose soul is nothing but heaven's light.

When she stops, her fingers find mine and their warmth covers my cold.

"Baby, you're so cold."

"Not anymore." Not when she's near, not when I can feel her like the sun radiating across my world. I pull her into my arms, pressing a cold cheek to her forehead. The motion knocks her glasses askew and I pull back just long enough for her to remove them with a soft laugh.

I hold her in the yard. In *our* yard, before the home we've built, and the twinkle of holiday lights. I capture her forever in this moment, memorize it, until the patterning of my thoughts drag tears down my face to fall against her skin. She brushes them without moving, her knowledge of me so intimate and precise, she doesn't need eyes to see me. She just knows me.

"Where have you been?"

I know she can feel that I *feel* different, that I've

reached the end of my rope and I have nothing but slipping air in my grasp. And I return to her, like I always have and always will.

"I've been falling apart."

She pulls me tighter. "You don't have to fall apart alone. You're never alone, Blake. Ever."

And maybe she is right. Maybe with her by my side I'll be able to do everything I have to. Maybe that was the whole story to begin with. That I had to learn to really love by surrendering all the pieces I couldn't before. And with her help, I can salvage my life. "I know that."

She wraps a strong arm around my waist, and leads me back to the house. Once there, once the door closes, her hands are in my hair. They smooth away the dusting of snow, and twist wet strands around her fingers. She pulls me into her lips. "I've missed you."

Her words tug a sob from the deepest part of my chest. "I'm sorry, I'm so sorry."

Those ever expansive hands, the ones that hold everything together, free me from my coat and slide over me. They balm me from the outside in, holding me close.

"Tell me."

I press my lips to her forehead, closing my eyes. "I don't know if I *can*. What it would mean if I did. It isn't that I don't want to."

Rachel nods, and then pulls back to look into my eyes. With her glasses back on, she looks both like the woman she was and who she has become. A perfect marriage of everything that was *supposed* to be.

She is so many things and I see them all now as I hold her gaze.

That untouchable star, the formidable Rachel

Fortier with a voice that is shot straight from another world. The gracious woman who thanks every person that gives her flowers because of old regrets. The loving mother, the dutiful daughter. The wife...that part is all for me. The woman that wears pink pajama pants and fifteen year old T-shirts. Whose hair is going gray and whose eyesight is worse than she will admit. The perfection in my life, who loves me for all of my imperfections. The woman that honors me when I'm at my best, and silently witnesses my worst.

I'm tired of being my worst. I'm tired of being anything less than the best for her.

"Rachel." I say her name with a break in my voice. And the words I've been afraid to speak pour out with my tears. "I lost you in another life."

She frowns, running her fingers through my hair. "What do you mean?"

"There's something I have to tell you. Something I've been afraid to, but I can't hold onto the secret anymore."

"Okay." She holds me tightly.

"You aren't going to believe me when I tell you this, but I need you to." I fist my hands in her jacket. "You *have* to believe me, because it's all the truth, I swear to God."

"Okay," she hushes softly. "I believe you. I believe *in* you. Tell me everything."

"I don't know where to begin."

"At the beginning."

I open my mouth, but nothing comes out. Not until she smiles at me do I have the strength to do it.

My heart pounds, my throat runs dry. "It all started when I went to your first concert, but it wasn't in this life. I lived another life before this. I fell in love with you there."

Her eyes waiver. "But, we fell in love in high school. How could it be at my concert?"

"Because I came back and I couldn't stay away from you this time around." I glance at the sofa. "You should take a seat, because at the very least, this is going to be a long story."

Once she's shed her coat and slowly slid to the cushions, once her eyes are on me with that open, honest, warmth, and infinite understanding, then...

Then, I tell her everything.

And she believes me.

And we cry all night long together.

⊰⊱⊰⊱⊰⊱

When sunrise breaks the clouds and unchains color, Rachel is staring at me. Her eyes are red, cheeks pink with rawness from wiping at them. She's never looked so beautiful to me, in the unfiltered clarity of what we share. Of the fate that pulls us together by the fibers in our soul. Rachel's gaze patterns over me, over and over me. She moves a little, patting down her pillow to better see me.

I keep feathering my fingers over hers, untwining and twining them together in a dance.

"You are incredible." She whispers it and her breath runs ragged as more tears rush her eyes. They fall. "I don't deserve you."

"You always did and always will."

She takes a steadying pull of air through pursed lips and her hand tightens in mine. "I didn't think I could love you more than I did last night. I was wrong. I love you more than I can put into words."

"I love you, too. I would do anything for you," I

whisper.

Her face crumbles. "And you have."

I pull her into my arms and she washes me in tears as her broken words mew into my cheek. "I'm so sorry. I'm so sorry for the pain, for your knee, for my selfishness then and now." I feel her hands tighten on my back. "For Beth."

And the tidal wave of remorse rips the air from my lungs as I fall apart...but not alone.

"Nothing will ever tear us apart." She states it with the same determination as when she declared her success, when she was young. And her eyes fix on me, watery and bright, with conviction. "You are my everything Blake, and there is nothing on this earth that is going to stop us."

"I know."

A smile touches her lips. "You really are my soul mate."

"Yes."

She pushes up on her elbows, tugging on me until I move closer. Her arm comes around me as her nose caresses mine. "I knew it all along, because even in the beginning you made me feel glittery in my heart."

I smile. "That's just you. You have the best soul in the world. You are heaven to me. Warm and wonderful."

Her kisses are soft. "That warmth you feel, my love?"

"Yeah?"

"That's because of you, because of your love." She pulls back from my lips, tracing them slowly with hers. "You are the final composition in the music of my life."

I remember those words, the parallel of them

from that summer day when I let her go so long ago. They rattle the meager grasp I have on my composure.

"You're mine."

Rachel's eyes fill again, and she clings to me, tightening her grip. "It's a song that I promise will play forever. And when all the music is bled out of this God *forsaken* world, Blake, I will always find my song in you."

And just like before, her words absolutely destroy me.

But this time, when the torrential shared love between us pricks my heart, I don't cry alone.

I cry with her, without a secret between me and my love.

Chapter Twenty-six

What Victory Feels Like
May 20th, 2029
(1 year left)

The sparrows sing in the tree above us. I can see them, hopping around and lingering, despite the warble of Celeste's whine.

"Blake."

I glance over at Rachel. She gives me a smile that knows me so fully and so well, I feel exposed under the intensity.

"Can you pass me the musical toy?" I do and when her fingers brush mine I feel the charge into my bones. That is how it has been since I told her. Even here, in the mundane moment of lounging in the front yard, it's no less powerful. Everything between us is as sharp as a razor's edge, so blessedly deep and electric.

She winds the little plastic toy for Celeste, and I direct my eyes to the amber eyed toddler between us as she quiets and listens to the music play. She brushes her bangs out of her face as the rest of her hair splays on the blanket beneath us like she is floating in water.

Celeste is so very much a mix between Rachel and myself, our baby through and through. I marvel at her, and the bright smile she got from her mother when she looks at me and speaks. "Hi, Mommy."

"Hi, baby girl." When I look up at Rachel, she

is leaning back regarding me with that mirrored expression. "What?" I ask softly, putting my hand through Celeste's hair. She coos contentedly and I keep the motion going idly as I stare at Rachel.

"Just looking at you." Her dark eyes move over me and when she cocks her head, her curls catch the light. "You're so beautiful against the grass. It makes your eyes so green."

I feel the same way. "You, too."

She wets her lips, forming a smile. "Nothing on this earth will ever be as beautiful as you."

It makes my heart skip a beat, and I feel my blush move up my neck because of the sincerity she says it with. "I don't know if that is tr–"

"It is. Don't fight it. Just let me say it over and over, because it's the truth."

So, I do. I halt the words coming out of my mouth and form a smile instead. "Thank you."

"You're welcome, my love." She leans over, looking past me. "Emily! Get off your phone and enjoy the day!"

"Mom, come *on!*"

I roll my eyes.

"She just did that same motion. Wonder where she gets it from?" Rachel glances at me with a smile and pushes to her feet. She pauses beside me, her fingers gathering in my hair and scratching lightly against my scalp. "Emily, let's swing. I'll push you."

"I'm too old for that. God, why can't you just let me do my own thing?"

"Tell whoever it is you'll talk later, or I'm going to take that phone and read through every text on it."

I watch as Rachel approaches her and holds out her hand. Emily shifts from one foot to the other, somehow juggling her soccer ball deftly as she literally makes the phone disappear. I've never seen electronics vanish that quickly. She doesn't do it happily, not at all, wearing a very angry glare stunningly reminiscent of one of my own. She stomps the ball into a bounce and then kicks it into the bushes. And boy, does she have the temper her mother once had.

"Don't do that again," Rachel reprimands. "Now, come on."

And once Rachel gets her in the swing, Emily's not twelve anymore. She's a little girl laughing, effervescent and beautiful like her mother, like the woman staring at me again, and mouthing *I love you* between pushes.

I whisper it back, watching them.

"Celeste?" I wrangle our youngest into my arms and tickle her until she is breathless, under a canopy of shade and sunlight. With a heave and a grunt I lift her in my arms and carry her through the grass. It tickles between my toes, and smells like late spring, warm like my memories of kissing Rachel beneath the bleachers.

Her eyes are on me as we trade children and I push Emily with enough force to send her spinning with a whoop of excitement on her lips.

"You're next," I note to my wife with a grin.

She dazzles me with the look she gives me. "Oh, honey. You always have me spinning with that smile of yours."

"Ew, cut it out!" Emily yells as she twirls close and I push her away again.

It makes me laugh, but I must confess that I've never felt like this before, a returning hero.

I've been defined in so many *other* ways. A bitch

that wreaked havoc on everyone and everything in my youth. I've been a pregnant teen, wearing my scarlet letter as plainly as the baby bump that offset the backpack on my shoulders. The wife of a celebrity, and all the pomp and circumstance that came with it.

My titles range far and wide, troublemaker and heartbreaker, demon and angel alike. Doctor and patient. Mother and daughter. All the dichotomy that makes me human and real and *special*, despite my own heavy handed self-appraisal. But now, now I'm something else entirely.

I can see it reflected in the eyes of my wife when she looks at me like she is now. I'm her hero. It's similar to the look she had in the kitchen when I broke up with her, that defiant zealotry in her love for me. It makes me feel like if I even think one bad thing about myself, if I feel one shred of displeasure in my actions, she will kill it with a fury like I've never seen. It makes me feel safe and loved on a level I've never felt before, where I'm protected from even my own self-deprecating hand.

It is a victory that I never thought I would have. A release from purgatory, I didn't expect to find. It redefines everything, rearranges my schema, and makes me believe anything is possible for me. The look in her eyes breathes magic back into my life. It reminds me of all the victories I thought I had in my lives. It pales the times when I thought I found victory in the accolades to my beauty or a trophy on the shelf, cold cash I traded for my family time or my utopian countenance.

It colors the vibrant reality of what victory really is. Victory is in the moments we share. It's in the slow stretch of time between us, accommodating to feel like forever. It's in the emotions I hold close to my heart and the incredible love we share.

February 8th, 2028
(2 years left)
I never made it to this place. Not before. I keep pace with Rachel's breaths. "It's going to be okay." I touch her forehead, and her eyes blink up at me, looking to me for comfort.

"I didn't have a full appreciation for how rough this is." Her face twists and I hold her eyes, miming the breathing techniques she suddenly forgets when the pain hits. As a matter of fact, she forgets to breathe at all.

"Breathe with me." I hold her hand, squeezing it until her grip crushes back. Until she can put her lips together and actually take a breath.

She does until the muscles in her cheeks aren't as tight and I know the contraction is ending.

I've dimmed the lights for her, because they hurt her eyes. It's odd, but when all the chemicals in your body start firing, anything can happen. If she said that alligators made the pain better I'd be on the phone ordering one up from the Florida Everglades. Rachel was no different for me. When I had Emily, she rubbed my lower back until her fingers were sore, and sang to me until her throat was raw.

"Blake."

"Yeah baby?"

"I'm scared now."

I move closer to the hospital bed, caressing her hand. "What are you afraid of?"

"What if I can't do this?"

I smile, understanding. "But you're already

doing it. You're in labor, the pushing part is only a few minutes."

"What if I can't do it?"

I shake my head. "You will. Your body will do it, and it is beautiful and amazing and scary as hell because it happens without your consent and your control."

"Does the pain get worse?"

"It depends. It's different for everyone."

"Did it get worse for you?"

"It was more intense with Beth, I think because she was my fir..." Maybe I shouldn't say that to her. *Crap.*

Her eyes widen. "What? Because she was your first?"

I nod slowly. "Emily was easier for me because all my...well, everything had already been displaced, and stretched, and morphed. Once you've stretched everything through one delivery, it's faster and easier for the following."

Rachel huffs a sigh. "Should have made you do it." she teases.

I smirk when she gives me a very tired, pained look and then laughs softly.

"I would have gladly done it for you."

She shakes her head as her fingers brush through my hair. "No. You've been through enough. It's my turn to bear a little pain for the reward of our future."

I kiss her forehead and when I pull back she catches the back of my head, holding me close.

"I don't want to say this very loudly in case someone hears, but," she glances toward the curtain, "I feel like I'm being torn apart and I think I'm going to start crying soon."

I frown. "It's okay to cry, Rachel."

"You didn't cry."

I swallow slowly. "I wanted to be brave for you."

Her forehead presses to mine and I hold myself steady as I circle her shoulders.

"Honey?"

"Yes, my angel."

"I'm going to cry now." She sniffs. "Like, right now."

"I won't tell anyone. No one will ever know, just you and me," I soothe. "Go ahead."

It's only a tear or two, until the next contraction and then it's a few more as the incredible mystery of nature works its way through the body of my wife. I don't think I'll ever be able to express how life altering it is to watch someone you love so much and know so well, go through something so profound. When all their higher conceptual devices and self-actualized idealizations are stripped away, and they are reduced to their primal essences, that is when you really get to know someone. When psychology and nurturing give way to chemistry and biology and it's just them in that moment with you. And they become a part of raw nature.

"I love you. I love you. I love you." Her voice is so tired, but she just keeps saying it, over and over. I hold her hand, peppering the words back to her. It's four in the morning. I'm exhausted so I don't know how she keeps going after enduring an hour of this.

"Rachel, the contraction is starting again, I'm going to need you to push to the count of ten."

I glance at the obstetrician and slide my arm behind Rachel's back as she sits up. She's absolutely soaked through her hospital gown, and where her skin shows it sticks to mine as I hold her upright. "Breathe baby." I push the words into her ear and she nods quickly, pressing her forehead into my jaw and tightening her hand in mine.

I stare down at her, at the white of her knuckles where are hands are twisted, and further to where her legs are trembling. The obstetrician leans in, expectant hands touching her. "Ready. Push."

I feel it through her whole body as every muscle flexes to the point it feels like her bones will break. I don't hear his count, all I hear is the soft whine at the back of my wife's throat.

"Breathe."

We both do. "And again to the count of ten."

It feels like forever.

"Okay, stop and rest."

Rachel uncoils and I press kisses to her forehead.

"I can see her head ladies," the doctor announces. "But I'm going to need to make more space, because Rachel, you're just so narrow. I'm sorry but this is going to be uncomfortable for a moment. I only need to the count of ten."

Seriously, fuck this count to ten.

And his fingers probe, pushing in on her, stretching taut skin wider in accommodation. Rachel grabs for me on instinct, on impulse, tears in her eyes. I see the doctor hold out his hand, and the nurse press a silver instrument into it.

I swallow, holding her eyes. "It's going to hurt less in a second. I promise." And I hold her face to mine when the scalpel flashes, and she gives me more than a daughter.

She gives me a scar that is ours and ours alone.

I understand all of it, every silly little thing she

ever said about mine, when in the next contraction our daughter is born. It's the most beautiful secret I've ever shared.

I press a trembling kiss to Rachel's head as Celeste's cry rings out and dredges tears from her eyes.

"She's okay."

"Yeah, she's okay. Are you?"

"Yes, can I hold her?"

"Of course."

Rachel steals a shaken breath. "Will you hold us both?"

It puts a lump in my throat. "Always."

July 6th, 2028
(2 years left)

"Be careful!" Rachel calls to Emily as she walks away with her friends. Our daughter has mastered the backward wave, where she doesn't turn, she just salutes with a quick flick of her hand. Clearly, she is just too cool for us.

"She's probably not going to stop walking until she is on the other side of the carnival," I note.

"As far away as she can get from us, I'm sure."

I twist my hand in Rachel's. "Her loss."

Rachel laughs. "I doubt it. We are so boring to her."

I scoff. "How much living does someone have to do to be considered cool these days?"

"About two lifetimes, so you know you're cool to me." Rachel hip bumps me and then pulls me toward the games. "Now, go win me a stuffed bear."

I arch my brow at her as I pay the man a ticket, anyway. "Shouldn't you be giving me one?"

"I'll give you something, all right."

Even the young man behind the counter laughs at that. "Now the pressures on, it's gonna have to be a big bear to compete with that."

I smile. "You have no idea."

He hands me a bucket of baseballs, and rings a bell so loud it leaves my head ringing too.

"Now, step right up! We've got a lucky lassie here tonight!" He winks at me. "For her payment of ten tickets, she's assured herself a shot at any prize on the wall! All she has to do, is hit the three targets twice, lighting each and every one!"

The people passing by have stopped and I cover my face, chagrined. "This is terrible," I tell the young man.

"I'm sure you'll get over it when you win." His cool smile spreads to my face too, and I glance back at Rachel.

She's grinning so wide all I can see is the light in her smile.

I hit all the targets, twice, tipping the guy ten bucks for being so conspiratorially helpful with winning Rachel her pick of the bears on the wall. I even let a few children throw balls from what's left in my bucket. And when all is said and done, I'm breathlessly laughing and wandering around with my wife's hand in mine.

She clutches her teddy bear to her chest. "Did we ever do this before?"

I shake my head. "Not really."

"We failed each other so miserably before."

"But not this time."

"No, not this time." Her eyes light up when she notices the Ferris wheel. "Wanna ride with me? I have two tickets left."

I pull her into a kiss. "I would love to."

We ride the wheel wrapped in one another. I brush my fingers through her hair as the breeze pushes it around. I watch the light pattern over her eyes. "I'm glad we get to share this together."

"Me, too."

"I couldn't picture a better life."

"I could," I whisper, cuffing her jacket in my hand and pulling her to my mouth. "I could picture a life where we were in love from when we were little girls."

Rachel presses into my lips, turning her head so she can kiss me deeply. And she does, exploring my mouth with her tongue as the wheel turns. When she pulls back, we are cresting over the top again. "We have loved each other since we were little girls."

I smile, nudging her nose. "Even younger."

"Since kindergarten?"

I smirk. "Yeah and played in the grass together."

"Seesaw."

"Sandbox," I counter.

"Jungle gym."

"I don't think it would have worked out." We laugh into the night air.

We are at the top when the wheel grinds to a halt. I feel a nervous expectation hit my stomach as I look down over the side. "Did it break down? Shit."

"Yeah, it broke down."

I look at Rachel and her coy smile.

"Did you tell the guy to do this?"

She shrugs. "Maybe."

"You don't have to trap me to get fresh with me," I tease.

"It's kinda hot though with the added thrill of

this rocking little car." She shifts and the metal moves around us.

My heart is in my throat. "Don't do that."

"Nervous?" She does it a little softer and then tugs me against her mouth.

I'm able to wedge my words out between her warm kisses. "Not anymore."

Rachel's practically in my pants when she stops kissing me and pulls back. I stare at her quizzically. "What?"

She lifts a finger to her lips, a hesitant smile forming there. "Look at the car in front of us."

I turn my head slowly, making it look like I'm admiring the view. My eyes graze over two figures snuggled close to one another. They look like they are talking. And then I realize one is our daughter.

Emily leans on her arm after a moment, miming her words the same way Rachel does. And the girl across from her leans away looking down, it looks like her friend Savannah Jordan, the excellent pianist and terrifyingly bad soccer player.

Now I know why she endures playing, because of Em. Seeing that, and making the connection, pulls at my emotions, until Rachel puts her hand in mine. I come back to reality and feel myself slinking down, pulling the collar of my coat up. "Oh, my God. What do we do?"

"Spy like good parents, hello-o," Rachel says instantly ducking down a little too.

But then Emily laughs and it's that laugh that I've heard from Rachel a million times. The one that's just for me. It's the laugh that ends with two people staring at one another, and the inevitable conclusion that follows.

And I can't pull my eyes away even though I feel like I'm violating something by watching Savannah press forward swiftly and peck a chaste kiss to Emily's lips. It's a shock of a moment, and Emily pulls back, her eyes wide. She says something, and when Savannah answers, it's my daughter that connects their lips again, holding firm to the young girl.

I glance at Rachel. "Do we be mad?"

"I don't think so."

"God, she's only twelve."

"And sometimes we only have one chance to get it right," Rachel notes as she presses her face to my neck. "I hope she's happy."

I hear that laugh again, joined by Savannah's. "I'm sure she is."

"Me, too." She squeezes me tightly. "But no sleepovers anymore."

I smile wickedly. "The sleepovers aren't the problem. It's the pillows."

And then the laugh in the air is unmistakably my wife's.

October 26th, 2028
(2 years left)

Rachel gets up from the fireplace when I stride into the room dropping the strap-on on the sofa. I wink at her, at the way her eyes widen and take me in. "So, already naked."

I nod, looking down briefly. "As if I need the pretense of having you take off my clothes."

She grins. "I like that pretense, there is a certain pre-tease about it."

I raise my eyebrow and snicker at her play on words. "I could always go get dressed again." I feint leaving the room.

"Ha, no. That's okay." She pulls off her shirt and unsnaps her bra before my rapt gaze. She tosses them down and rolls her eyes at the focus on my face. "Oh, I see how it is, you get to watch."

"I know you like performing just for me."

She shrugs helplessly as she pops the buttons on the fly of her jeans and works them over her hips. She shifts her way out of them with a little shimmy. "Yeah, I'm an attention whore."

"But only for me, so it's okay."

"Very much so." Rachel steps out of her clothing pile, ruffling her hair out. "So, tell me how it went?"

She's talking about the moment in my other life I shared with her. The one we've set the stage for tonight. It used to be the pinnacle of hotness in my mind, but my God, what we've shared now dwarfs everything. "You were in my lap and I was using the strap-on."

Rachel regards me with a sparkle in her eye. "I like where this is going." She casts her eyes to the fireplace. "Did we have the lights on or…?"

"No, just the firelight."

"Sexy."

"It was."

"And it hides the baby weight. Even better."

I roll my eyes, to make her see how silly it sounds, and feint offence. "I know I still have some, you don't have to point it out, meanie."

She mock gasps. "I wasn't talking about you, I was talking about me."

I think she looks better now than she ever did before. Curvier and sexier. Luscious.

"You are without a doubt the most beautiful

you've ever been."

She blushes and it goes all the way to her toes from my compliment. "Thank you."

I'm trying to break her habit of self-deprecation, too.

Her hands rake through her hair again and she pulls her glasses off. It's all very sweet and charming as she folds them gently and sets them on the mantel. It's a stunning transformation. When she releases them it's like she's shedding the wife and mother I see in the daylight, in trade for the wild cat that comes out at night. The part that will forever be only for me.

When she turns back her eyes are smoldering. "Tell me more." She holds out her hand to me and I circle the sofa, smiling when she pushes me down on the cushions.

"Well," I draw the word out playfully as she slides into my lap. I can already feel her arousal, and I slide my fingers through it, watching her eyes widen at the contact. "You talked super sexy to me while you thrust on me and then..."

Rachel's lip quirks a lopsided smile and she presses her body to mine, arching sexily. I get distracted from what I was saying, and instead I wrap my hands in her pouring curls and kiss her neck. She sighs under the motions, dragging her nails up my arms, my neck, and into my hair.

My fingers trace again, gathering wetness to draw a line down the front of her body. I follow it with my tongue, listening to the satisfied groan she gives me.

"What else?" Her voice rumbles from beside my head.

I trail my tongue up to her ear. "After that, you

gave me permission to do anything I wanted to you."

Rachel moans softly and fists my hair, pulling my mouth into a searing kiss. When she moves back, her free hand trails down my chest, her fingers circling my nipple slowly.

"And what did you do to me after I said that?"

I cup her breasts, squeezing and kneading slowly. "Everything."

Her lips connect with mine over and over, and then she presses her face to mine. "Everything, huh?"

"Yeah."

Rachel presses closer, until I have to move my hands. Her fingers catch mine and hold them to the back cushion. Eyes hanging on mine, she smiles, slowing everything down between us. "Blake, if you want me to give it, you don't even have to ask. Anything, everything. I'm all yours." She flicks her eyes toward the strap-on. "On one condition."

I take a deep breath. "What is that?"

Now, she's got that hint of a blush on her cheeks and it makes me ache. "That you get me really, and I mean *really*, turned on before you put that thing anywhere else than the standard place." I blink at her, as her eyebrow arches suggestively.

"I don't think you let me do that last time."

Surrendering her grip on my hand, she traces over my cheek. "I'm a different woman, you've said it yourself. And you've most certainly earned the things I'm willing to give you in every respect. The experiences you've had, I want you to have them all with me. I'll give all that to you, because I love you."

"I love you, too."

"And because no matter what you're doing, you make me feel really, really good." She boggles at me.

"Like, really good."

I laugh. "And then, there's that, too."

But, even with what she is offering, I feel like there is something else I'm wanting. I stare at her thinking about what I really want to share with this incredible woman. My fingers tighten in hers. "I have an idea."

"Hmm?"

"Let me up."

She slides to the side and I scoot out. I flip the lights out, plunging the room into a warm flicker. When I return to the sofa, I clear my throat of the thickness I feel from seeing her bathed in firelight. My angelic little Rachel, who isn't really so very angelic right this moment. Not when she surprises me by sliding her fingers between my legs, then licks them with a whisper that sets me on fire. "I can't wait to put my mouth on you."

Her hands pull me into her and I crash my lips against hers. Drown in her. Filled to the brim with the heat of her passion and love. When she twists me, like she wants to resume our position, I break our kiss. "No, you sit down," I whisper.

When she does, I slide to the floor before her. "I have a different fantasy."

Her fingers brush through my hair and cup my cheek. "What fantasy is that?"

I smile up then. "Where you get to feel what I felt so you can understand what it meant to me."

Rachel smiles back. "What do you mean?"

"I think it's so much more intimate for you to have the same memories as me, than recreating them solely for myself."

She sobers, her eyes holding mine. "I do still

want to give you this moment again though, in this life with me."

"Tomorrow. Tonight, I want to be all yours."
I drag the strap-on over and work the harness up Rachel's calves, her thighs. And when she lifts her hips, I hand it to her as I set to licking up her leg slowly. Her hands move above my head, tightening the straps with a zip that puts a tingle up my spine.

I keep kissing and dragging my lips, tasting her skin and salivating over the taste of her in my mouth.

"Blake?"

I look up, summoned to her.

"Come to me, baby."

I climb into her lap, and straddle her. "Always."
Her hands caress softly, warm on my back, even with the fire behind me. Her kisses are so slow and painstakingly placed. They drag me into a delirium I never want to escape.

"You feel incredible."

"You too. I really have grown to like being vulnerable in your arms."

"I can see you being in control a lot, before."

I think about it. "I always was. I always have been even when it seemed like I wasn't."

She pulls me repeatedly into her slowly, miming the motion I know I'll be feeling soon. I loll my head back as her lips move slowly, inching down the front of me at the same pace as the drag of her fingertips.

"And right now?"

I stare at the ceiling, and then my eyes flutter closed. "I don't want to be in control anymore and it feels really good."

Rachel sits up a little, clearing space between us as her hand tightens on me. "Show me." I feel the brush of the strap-on against me, and she guides it right where I ache for her. I direct my eyes to hers and let the slow smile I feel in my heart, slide to my face.

Her lips catch mine, until she breaks the kiss, trailing over my neck and jaw. Her hand tightens further on my lower back, coaxing me on. "Show me how good I can make you feel."

Her hair tumbles through my hands, as I pull her close and with a roll of my hips, she's pressing into me. My words come out heated as the yearning ache is replaced by a different kind. "Whatever you want, however you want it," I arch in her arms, "I want you to take it."

"Anything?"

"Everything."

"You sure about that?"

I contemplate it as I remember what she was willing to offer me. "Yes, anything, but with the same condition you stipulated."

Rachel giggles. "I'll make sure of it, before I do the things I've dreamed of doing."

"What have you dreamed of doing to me that you haven't already done?"

"You'll see."

I moan at the sheer idea of it. "Don't ask me, just do it. Just take whatever you wa–" she grabs my butt and pushes me down into the rise of her hips. It steals every millimeter I have to give and while I'm surprised by it, it feels so good. I make sure she knows it, as I cry out her name.

"Like that?" Her hands jerk me back so she has more clearance and the look she pins me with, fucking uncages me.

"Just like that." I growl.

She moves fast and unyielding, mercilessly owning me. Her hands are everywhere, ushering breathy nonsensical words from my lips as I cling to her. It feels good to be controlled by someone I love and trust, especially like this. Her eyes work me over with the same intensity as her hands. I love her face, when it looks like she wants to consume me, when she is so in the moment.

It takes almost the whole night, but she absolutely takes everything I have to give, until I'm sore and exhausted and practically dehydrated. And just when I feel like I might not have anything more to give, she takes something else. She calls me *her* angel. When I'm at my most vulnerable, most intimate, most trusting, is when she presses the word into my ear and it takes me over the edge.

It liberates me of all the bad I've ever felt about myself.

Just like it did for her, once so long ago.

January 29th, 2029
(1 year left)
I kiss Hiram's forehead, and he opens his eyes to me. He can't speak, but his fragile smile hangs on his lips. The doctor said he wouldn't respond, so I forget the millions of things I was thinking. I say the only thing I can remember. The only thing that truly matters.

"I love you, Hiram. We all love you."

My voice breaks and because I want to be brave, I firm my lips in a line. I must be brave, for him, for my wife, for our family, as we say goodbye.

When I pull back, Deborah wipes her eyes. "It's all so sudden. Two days ago he was fine." I know her pain so well, the agony, the loss. The empty vacant hollow thud that echoes forever when you have to let go of the one you love unexpectedly.

But we made it. We made it here to this tiny hospital room, with walls too bland for the spirit of a man that is so incredibly wonderful. For someone who helped make me the woman I am. Whose voice buzzed in my ear so many times over the phone, who hugged me openly when I was happy, and held me in secret when I cried. He is the man that loved me like a father, since before he shook my hand in a smoky backyard.

He's the only father I've ever known.

I look up at Rachel, and her tears fall, dragging mine down with them.

When I look over, Hiram closes his eyes and I know it's the last time I'll see them. I know it, and despite myself it kills me all over again. I don't know how many hours Rachel and I sit alone, listening to his erratic breath. Deborah left with our girls, they all needed sleep. So my wife and I sit, shoulder to shoulder, hand in hand. There's no more tears, they've all been cried.

"I'm glad you told me about this," Rachel says softly from where her head is resting on my shoulder. "I got to live a life with my father that will have no regrets."

I nod. "You are a wonderful daughter."

"So are you." She turns to me, her eyes raw and tired. "He always loved you so much."

I can't cry. I can't. I say it over and over until I believe it's possible to keep myself steady. "I know. I love him, too."

Her hand squeezes mine. "We have to take care

of my mom." Her lip trembles. "I can't imagine what this is doing to her."

"We will, I promise." I hold her in my arms. "Because, I do know."

Her tears start then and fracture against the brittle walls holding me together.

"Even though I knew this was coming, and I've been slowly mourning since you told me, I still can't believe I'm here...that it's happening." She pulls back from my shoulder. "It's happening right now. Right now, all our lives are changing and we will never be the same again."

"No, we won't."

"Tell me we will be better."

I sniff lightly, directing my gaze to my father. "We have already been made better."

I mean it with everything I am and I hold Rachel against my chest as we fall asleep sitting on a narrow padded bench with the predawn Illinois sky in the window behind us. The last thing I see is Hiram tucked in the hospital bed and the clock winding down the hours until sunrise and my wife's hand in mine.

Then someone touches my knee and I lift my head to the darkness. The nurse is there, kneeling before us. Her eyes are sad and I know the look. I've worn it so many times in my life. "Your father's time has passed."

My mouth is dry, my heart breaking. "What?"

Rachel lifts her head in a jolt from the tone in my voice.

"His time has passed. I'm so sorry."

"Oh, Daddy." I don't hear anything more after Rachel's hushed agony. She moves out of my arms silently and I look up at the clock, at the time, at the twenty minutes that have passed since I closed my eyes.

He waited for us to fall asleep.

Forever a father to us.

I thank him, and I miss him, and I promise him I'll always guard his little girl.

And it starts with holding her while she cries.

March 4th, 2029
(1 year left)

There is one black hole in our home. The garage. It isn't like we have any reason to keep it immaculate, it isn't like either of us spend time there. As long as I can get to a rake and a shovel, the snow blower, and my gardening gloves, I'm happy.

But Rachel isn't happy about it. Not at all.

It is a radiant spring day, but instead of enjoying it outside somewhere with the kids, she's hell-bent on cleaning out this abyss.

"Where did all this stuff come from?"

I look over my shoulder at her. "I don't know... living maybe."

She pulls free a wrench and hands it to me. "Put it over there." She waves toward the piles she's making in the driveway.

I meander around, looking through the stacks. There is a grouping of paint cans, and a few of my books from college. I nudge them with my shoe. "Jesus I can't believe I read that much."

Rachel laughs. "Had I known you already were a doctor, I would have been a little bit bitter about all the money we spent on your books." When I look over my shoulder at her, she's smirking. "Shouldn't you be able to remember it all?"

"Theory and practice are two totally different things."

She shakes her head, rustling her wild ponytail. "I'm kidding." When I find the tool pile I drop the wrench into the bunch. It clangs loudly. "You know, Blake, maybe we should get a toolbox."

I dust my gloves on one another. "Yeah, no kidding. We have bought the same wrench four times. What is that one called with the spinny thing?"

"Adjustable wrench?"

"Isn't it a crescent wrench?"

"I don't know."

"Well, whatever, we've got four."

She snickers. "Well, then go punch your man card and get a toolbox."

I give her an appraising look, ready to say something smart to her, but instead I just smile.

"I love you." We say it at the same time.

"Jinx," I call and Rachel groans behind me.

I tease her by going back to the paint cans and crouching down to look at them. I hear her sigh. "Fine." I say her name three times so she can speak again.

"You know I can only shut up for two seconds, Blake Fortier."

"Yes, Rachel Fortier, I know this."

I sit down on the largest paint can. It's a huge container of flat white that we use every now and again to change the colors in the house. I love it, nesting over and over with her. We go through phases, blues, greens, raspberries and brown. I imagine someday the walls will be stripped and someone somewhere will think we were insane.

I direct my attention to Rachel when she grunts.

"Need help?"

"Nope, I've got it."

Rachel is moving a box and I watch the fluidity of her muscles as they move. I stare at her legs, at the cute shorts she's wearing. The very short shorts she's wearing, I notice when she bends over to look through another container.

She stands, staring down.

"What's wrong?" I ask, rising from my seat.

She looks up at me after a moment, a slow sad smile hovering on her lips. "You won't believe what I just found."

"What?"

"Our stuff."

"What stuff?"

She picks up a small box and it catches me completely off guard when I stop breathing at the image of glittering dust circling her as she comes out into the sunlight. She sets the box down and edges herself down onto the cement of the drive. She pats next to her, and I sit too.

She opens the flaps and I peer at the items inside. "Oh wow, I haven't seen one of these in a long time." I pull out a CD Rachel made for me. It's not of her singing, everything Rachel's ever put her voice to is safe inside; it's a music mix she made for me. "Wonder if we can still play it?"

She pops the case open, flashing sunlight across her handwriting that says, *With love, your Rachel.* "Looks like the disc is done. Damn."

I frown. "What did it have on it again? Paramore?"

"Yeah." She smiles at it. "And Katy Perry."

"Teenage dream." I remember instantly wearing out that song while we kissed after school. "Jesus, it's been a long time."

Rachel nods, setting it aside. Her hands go back into the box and tug free a plastic baggie with a pressed rose inside it. I know what it is as the emotion fills her face. "Oh wow."

I blink at the memories. "That's the flower I gave you on our date, isn't it?"

"Yeah, it is baby."

I take the plastic, holding the nineteen-year-old flower up against the blue sky. "It's held up so well. It makes me happy."

Rachel has tears in her eyes.

"What's wrong?" I lean forward and see the note in her hand. I know what note it is, the one I read a million times after we declared our love for one another. When she called me her soul mate for the first time. I can still recall every word.

"You didn't get rid of it?"

I shake my head. "Are you insane? How could I ever get rid of that?"

"I don't know, I just assumed after all these years…"

"No." I take the yellowing paper in my hand and slowly unfold it. "Never." I skim over Rachel's writing, and when I look up and see the grown woman who became my wife, the duality isn't lost on me. I pass her the note, and watch her eyes move over it as her lips form the words silently.

It makes me smile.

"I loved you so much then." She finally looks up at me. "I couldn't have done what you did."

I feel my brows furrow as I stare at the cement beside me. "I sometimes don't know how I did it either. I just didn't want you to ruin your life."

Her fingers find mine. "You're my best friend."

It takes my breath away every time. "You're mine, too."

Rachel pulls out a few other things, symbols of our friendship and love alike: a flier from a party we went to, movie ticket stubs, what was probably a receipt from a dinner we had but it's so faded I can't tell. It makes me sad when I see it.

But when I find my yearbook, it puts a whole new level of bitter sweetness into my heart. I flip to the most worn page of all, the place where the binding is cracked from all the times I held this page open and stared at it.

It's the picture of her and me. The image I coerced into being, that I prayed I would someday look at with her by my side. And now that I can, it hurts just as much as when I couldn't. "Do you remember this?"

Rachel leans over, her fingers feathering the page. "Oh, look at how young we were."

We were. It's hard to believe where the years have gone, how quickly they have blurred past me like the flip of a page. I can see it now, contrasting us to the two young girls smiling at the camera. In this image we are only a few years older than our *own* child.

"Look how happy we were."

"I've never been happier than I am now," Rachel notes, kissing my temple. "That little girl didn't have any idea what she was in for."

"I know, and neither did that one." I point at my picture and the secrets between us make Rachel smile.

I drag my finger down to her words written below the picture. It's where our loving epithet came from. It was once words scribbled on a page in the middle of homeroom, and has come to mean so much more.

    Always you, always.

    I wipe smudges of dust off Rachel's cheek and forehead. "Always you."

    "Always," we say together.

    Rachel's eyes widen. "Jinx."

    But I keep us both silent with my lips on hers.

Chapter Twenty-seven

Forced Hands
February 18th, 2030

The house is quiet; deep darkness, pulled like a cape over us. The girls are sleeping, dreaming beautiful dreams.

I hope.

I hope for so many things to come in the next few hours.

My fingers move slowly over the pages of writing before me. I've written this story as long as I can remember. Our life. I've lived it and then committed it to the innocent lines of paper that bear the weight of a world so heavy, I'm surprised the table doesn't collapse under it.

I'm surprised I haven't either.

I've bled my heart, bore the wreck of my choices from clumsy hands; yet, somehow I've found a gift greater than I ever thought I would. It's in the woman standing in the kitchen right now stirring sugar into our coffee mugs. Well, my coffee mug, hers is tea. My eyes hang on her in the dark, her hand moving, her outline superimposed against the rest of our home. She is the mother of my children and my salvation.

My hope.

Rachel quietly carries the cups to the table and sets them down. Her hands are trembling, and the coffee spills a little, peppering the page before me in brown. I smooth it away with my fingertips.

"I'm so sorry, Blake." Her voice sounds broken, like spilling the coffee and wetting my page will somehow end everything. Her fingers drag a piece of paper towel over where I am writing. She looks down at me, and in her eyes I see such fear.

"Don't be afraid."

Her gaze goes to the digital clock in the kitchen, to where it announces the time in blinding green.

11:48 p.m

"How can I not be?"

She takes her seat beside me, the seat she has always sat in. Every dinner, every day. It's her place, to my right. Rachel has always been my right-hand girl and always will be. I think it as her shoulders crumble and she cups her hands over her face, pressing shaken elbows to the wood of our kitchen table.

"I think I'm gonna be sick. I have such a shitty feeling right now." She sniffs behind the shield of her hands until they find their way into her hair and ruffle through it. "I can't get over the twisting ache in my stomach." When she looks at me, I fix my gaze on the papers.

"We have our plan."

She nods. "Yes, but just in case, tell me everything about what happened tomorrow again."

Only in our world could we use past tense about a day that hasn't come yet.

I push the page I've been writing on toward her. "I outlined everything that happened, here. I got up at five, left the house for work at six."

"You were working downtown, in the high-rise medical suites on Madison Avenue, right?"

"Yes." I point to the page. "I made it there at about quarter to seven. I had patients from seven to nine, then went to Saint James for an hour to fix some records for a resident."

"And then you went back and had more patients from what? Eleven to noon?" She pulls the list closer so she can see it in the non-existent light. "Twelve thirty."

"And then you came."

Rachel glances up at me sliding her glasses off the bridge of her nose. She folds them slowly. "And I brought you flowers."

She said those same words before, with the same smile.

"Yes."

"What was I doing before?"

"I don't know." I shake my head and then pause. "Well, that isn't true, I just haven't thought about it in a long time."

"What do you remember?"

"I checked the bank account, you bought the flowers from the corner shop on 35th and Broadway at 12:16 p.m. You were at home before that."

"And then I came to your office and we talked. When did I leave?"

"A little before one."

"And then..." She draws her expression into a line so sharp, it's hard to look at. "It all happened at 1:15 p.m."

"No. I looked at the clock when I felt something, it was one seventeen on the dot. I know it."

Rachel blinks at the glasses in her hands. "What time did I die, Blake?"

She's never asked me, not once in all these

talks we've had. I physically jolt back from the table, because the image of the blue bordered, pink and white page that made up her death certificate flashes clearly before me.

I close my eyes against it, even though I can still see it.

I'll never forget.

Ever.

"They pronounced you dead at 1:22 p.m."

The words carve my mouth on the way out and leave my heart bleeding.

"So, five minutes." She shakes her head with a bitter smile. It looks like she wants to ask me more, but the answer to her question is something I'll never part with. "I didn't have much of a fight in me. I'm sorry."

"Oh, God, don't say that." Hearing those words when I know different, when I know how hard she fought to stay with me, puts a lump in my throat. "It's not true. You were as valiant as you've always been."

Rachel pulls my hand in hers, twisting her fingers until they lock with mine. "If it happened now, you would see what kind of fight I have. I have too much to live for."

I stare at the surety in her eyes until my tears come and blur her. "But that isn't going to happen," I press, wiping my cheeks. "It's never going to happen."

She tightens her fingers in mine. "No, we are all staying home. No patients for you, no practice for me. No practice for Emily, either. Nothing. No one is leaving this house."

I nod. "And Celeste isn't going anywhere."

Rachel licks her lips where they are dry. "I don't understand that part, those dreams." She frowns.

"There's no way Celeste got in a car with someone we didn't know, and alone even. I wouldn't let that happen and neither would you."

I absolutely agree. Not to mention, she can't even be in the front yard alone. Not without me, or Rachel, or Emily to watch her.

It bothers me.

I take a sip of coffee to steady my nerves. It probably isn't the best thing, because when it hits my stomach it churns from the splash of acidity. I rub a hand there, like I can smooth away the ache.

"Feel sick?"

I nod numbly. "Yeah."

"Me, too."

"But we have a plan," I reaffirm more for my own benefit than hers.

Rachel smiles slightly. "We have a plan."

I can't hold her eyes any longer and I look away, past the dining room and into the family area. On the wall I can see the painting we painted, the tree stretching out forever.

Forever.

Rachel's hand tightens and when I look back at her, she is staring into the kitchen. I can see where her eyes are pinned on the clock and it makes my heart ache.

❧❧❧❧

February 19th, 2030
12:00 a.m

It's midnight. Midnight on the day I've been so afraid of.

It's here.

The thought shoots across my synapses and Rachel turns back, her eyes wild and desperate. "Blake?"

"I know."

Rachel's breath winds, her chest moving faster, until the panic is so deep in her eyes I feel it too. Her chair scrapes back, she throws herself in my arms as I grab for her. I grab for her like I'll never be able to hold her again, as if she's sliding through my fingers like water, like the sunlight I've lived my life in. If I'm not diligent in my grip, I fear I'll lose everything. Her hands are in my hair, on my shoulder, fingers clutching tightly. "Don't let me go. Please."

"I won't."

She pulls me with her roughly, pressing up on her toes to crash our mouths together as we stumble into the living room. "Please," she begs between the movements of her lips.

I hold her tighter, stumbling down the hallway. "I won't."

"I love you." She hops into my arms and I heave her up higher, fitting together to hold her close as her legs wrap and her mouth makes love to mine. I wouldn't have been able to do this before, not without fixing my knee. In this beautiful world we've made though, I'm strong enough to hold her here, strong enough to hold everything together. But it wouldn't have been possible without her.

"I love you."

I get us to the bedroom door, and Rachel's back pushes it open. We fall into one another on the bed. "I love you," she whispers hotly as we cling to each other by the lips in the hopes that love is stronger than fate. In the hopes that our best laid plans don't go astray.

❧❧❧❧

But life is the thing that happens between the lines of a plan. It tears everything asunder, like hands tearing paper. It all begins with the ring of the phone and the silence that follows it. As soon as the shrill sound crashes over our breakfast table, I know it for what it is. It's fate, calling us home. I go still, and Rachel lifts her head duly beside me.

"Don't answer it," she whispers without looking at me.

"I won't."

"Mommy the phone! You have to get it!" Celeste says excitedly, pointing at where the phone sits in its cradle by my desk. It makes me sick that fate's devices are in the voice of my child.

When the next ring screams, Rachel flinches. The only motion left as we sit frozen, is Rachel's tendrils tumbling back into place.

The third ring cuts off and my eyes go wide, as wide as Rachel's when she looks at me.

"Mother, it's Saint James!" It's Emily, she answered it in the other room. "They're saying it's important!"

I hold my wife's gaze. "I'll tell them no. No matter what it is."

"Okay."

She watches me. I can feel her eyes as I get up. I swallow before reaching out and picking up the phone. "Hello."

"Doctor Blake Fortier?" I don't recognize the woman's voice.

I stare at Rachel, turned in her chair to see me.

"Yes, this is she?"

"This is Doctor Sandra Milligan."

I blink, I have no idea who this is even though the name is oddly familiar. "Sandra Milligan?" Rachel's eyes widen in question and I shrug. "How can I help you?"

She clears her throat. "It is with great pleasure I get to tell you your name has made the short list as a candidate for Physician of the Year. You have been nominated by a committee of your peers for this distinguished award."

I open my mouth to speak, but my words die before they fully form. Rachel's staring at me so intensely I feel like I might combust. "I appreciate the nomination for the award. Thank you."

My wife beams and I raise my hand to still her because the woman begins speaking again. "Would it be too short a notice to meet at say," she pauses, "one?"

"Meet today at one?"

Rachel's face slips, I don't miss it. The time the woman just uttered might as well be a curse.

"Yes."

It's very divisive that this would happen today. It almost feels like my fate is a living, breathing, *baiting,* thing. If it is, then it is ridiculously deluded to think that I would be coerced by awards. Nothing but my family matters to me anymore. And, rightfully so. "Doctor Milligan, I apologize, but I can't accommodate a meeting today. Perhaps, tomorrow?"

My eyes waiver from Rachel's to fix on Celeste. She's stacking her fruit on her plate, while I listen to the silence on the other end of the line. "I don't see how that would be a problem."

"Good, I'm glad to hear it. What would be a good time?"

"Noon? We could make it a business lunch as we discuss the steps necessary to be eligible."

"I look forward to it. Would you like one of my assistants to set up a reservation for lunch at The Capital Grille?"

"That sounds good. Thank you, Doctor Fortier."

"Thank you again for the opportunity."

I open my mouth to say more, but close it. The line disconnects. When I fix my eyes on Rachel, she's standing beside the kitchen table, wrapped in a long silk robe. She smiles and slides her hand to Celeste's back.

I turn the phone over and press the end button for good measure even though the call has disappeared from the display. I stare at the time in the window, 10:54 am. I sigh, a little shaken, and set it down.

When I get back to the table, Rachel regards me thoughtfully. "So."

"So."

She peppers my head with kisses, "You're up for an award?"

I nod, sliding a piece of fruit from my plate over to Celeste's, so she can build her tower one peach wedge higher.

"Good, you deserve it."

I'm distracted. "It just feels weird. This didn't happen before."

"No, it happened before," Rachel confirms eerily and then smiles. "You had three by now, didn't you?" She dusts toast off her fingertips with a grin and turns in her chair again, angling her voice toward the back of the house. "Emily? Did you want something more than some fruit?"

"It's almost lunch time." I blink. "The day is speeding past."

Rachel chews her lip. "Yes, faster than I can stand in this second." She sighs, turning away again. "Emily! Earth to Emily!"

She doesn't answer.

I peek around the corner of the kitchen wall, to where the family room's intersecting hallway shoots down to the bedrooms. "I think her door is closed because I can't see light on the wall."

"She's probably on that damn phone again with Savannah."

Celeste laughs happily. "Damn."

Rachel sighs with a roll of her eyes. "I was better with our first."

I shrug. "Remember the f-u-c-k-you phase Emily went through? I think this is pretty mild in comparison."

Rachel snorts. "But she didn't learn *that* from us. Our daughter just said d-a-m-n because of me. Emily learned the 'f' word from that terrible–"

"Preschool," we finish simultaneously.

Rachel presses a kiss to my lips. She grows thoughtful. "I'm so proud of you and your fancy award."

With a nudge of her nose on mine she gets up, clearing the plates. "Can I ask you a question?"

"Yeah."

"Were we like Emily? Always together or on the phone?"

I laugh, staring at her until she turns back to me. "We're still like that, aren't we?" I arch my brow at her, nodding. She laughs dryly and turns to the sink.

I listen to the water pour over her hands while

I wipe Celeste's face. She gets fussy and I pick her up, carrying her over to the sink. Every child is different, and where Emily wanted to be in the dirt, Celeste just wants to be in the water. Rachel turns the faucet, cooling the tap before I lean Celeste over so she can play in it.

"Bubbles?" Rachel asks softly, plugging the sink. She swirls enough dish soap that it foams.

Celeste is in the suds flinging them around happily. I get some in my hair and I roll my eyes. "Now I'm trapped here cause if I take her away she's gonna cry," I whisper.

"Do you have somewhere else to be?"

I glance at the grin on her lips as she smoothes away the soap on my hair. "No, I really don't."

"Good." We watch her play for a while until Rachel takes Celeste from my arms. "Can you go ask Emily if she wants anything else before I'm officially done as chef until lunch?"

"Yeah." I press a kiss to the two girls before I meander my way to the bedrooms.

Emily's door is, in fact, closed. I lean beside it. "Em? Are you still hungry? Your mom is under the impression that cereal and fruit isn't enough to hold you over for an hour until lunch."

"Em?"

For a moment, I wonder if I did something to annoy her because she doesn't answer me. Then I roll my eyes because she has these ridiculously good headphones that block out everything.

Especially, me and Rachel.

"Em?" I raise my voice and knock. Finally, I get tired of being ignored in the house I pay for. "I'm coming in." I press the door open.

And her room is empty.

My eyes fix on the headphones I was just thinking about. They are strewn across her bed, neon pink against the stark white and purple comforter.

Okay, I tell myself, don't panic.

I swallow. "Emily?" I push the door open wider, my eyes tracing her soccer posters, and the magenta accent wall fringed in zebra print. Her clothes are everywhere, like she was in a whirlwind to find something to wear.

I stare at her open closet, at the empty hook that normally has her favorite faux fur fringed jacket.

I reach out for it and hold the hanger in my hand. I don't understand why it's shaking, until I raise my voice and hear the panic in my own tone. "Emily?"

Maybe she's in our room. Sometimes she likes to watch TV in there. I bolt out the door and head across the hall. Rachel has made the bed, and even the clothing from our turbulent lovemaking has been removed.

But the room is empty.

I head to Celeste's room, to the bathroom down the hall. I unceremoniously barge into the empty room and walk right out.

"Emily!"

This time I sound as scared as I feel, and my voice is as empty as the back of the house.

"Blake?" It's Rachel, her voice raised in empathetic concern. I rush into the family room. When Rachel looks at me with Celeste in her arms, I show her the hanger like it should mean something. I can't get words out of my mouth.

"What is that?"

"Emily's coat." It's all I can say as I grab the

front door and tug it open. It whips a cold chill into the warmth of our home.

"What?" Rachel looks like she's going to be sick. "Where's Emily?"

At her tone, Celeste starts crying.

I swallow, willing back my tears. "I don't know." I close the door behind me, running down the steps. My breath plumes from my lips as I scramble for air. I look up and down the street, then run as fast as I can to the back gate and flip the latch. I claw my way around the trash cans, and trip into the small yard.

The sheer wall of panic that hits me then, when I see the empty stillness of the yard, makes my knees give out. "Emily!"

When I can get my feet back under me, I run to the front yard. I don't know what I'm doing here. I spin in a circle and my eyes fall on the tire swing.

My memories of the dreams that have chased me, burn against the image before me. I've had the dream for nine years now. I know it well. And the little girl was Celeste's age. I lick my lips. A three year old, nine years ago.

"Oh my fucking God."

"Mrs. Fortier?"

I turn quickly, startled. It's Savannah. She's unmistakable with her ebony hair and eyes bluer than ice.

"Savannah, where's Emily?" I sound really angry, so much so, the girl before me blanches.

"I don't know."

Like hell she doesn't know, but then I realize, I'm the bad guy. I'm the parent getting angry. I'm not the Hiram or the Deborah, right now I'm *my* parents. "Please Savannah, tell me. If you know anything, I need to know it now. I am very worried."

She wars with the knowledge she has. "She had a tryout for a musical and we were going to meet up afterward. It was supposed to be a surprise for you guys."

"Text her." I calm my voice and resist the temptation to grab her arm and haul her phone out of her hand. "I need you to get on the phone and text her right now."

Savannah stares at my hand as it forms into a fist. "Okay. Do you want me to tell her to come home?"

"Tell her to get out of the car she is in, go to the closest restaurant and call home."

"Is she okay? What's happening?"

"Nothing. I just need you to do it right now."

And she does, while I shiver and wait breathlessly for a response. I flex my fingers against the February frost, aching all the way into my bones.

"She normally answers pretty fast. She hasn't just yet, but..." Savannah regards me. "I'm sorry. Can I come inside while we wait?"

"Okay."

꙳.꙳.꙳.꙳

Inside I stare at the clock. It's 12:15. Emily still hasn't messaged back. I clutch the keys to my car in my hands, twisting and untwisting them from between my fingers. I have to leave. If Emily doesn't message in the next few minutes, I have to leave.

It takes an hour to get to midtown in lunchtime traffic.

I stare at Rachel. I might only have five more minutes with her, because if I can't find Emily then...

What?

12:16 p.m.

"Anything?" Rachel asks.

"No, I'm sorry Mrs. Fortier. She might be in the tryout already."

Fuck. I pull up the call that rang through earlier. "She was here at 10:54." I should have left right away. I might have been able to catch up to her. "I need to leave."

When I say the words Rachel literally drops to the sofa cushions, like I punched her in the stomach. "No. You can't leave."

"It's...12:17 now. If I don't leave–" I don't have to finish the thought.

"You are *not* leaving without me." Rachel says it with all the venom of a woman fighting for her family.

"Well, I'm not driving like a maniac with Celeste in the car. And I need to drive fast. You have to stay."

"Like hell, I'm staying."

"I'll watch her." I turn to the right, looking toward the diminutive girl on the sofa. When Savannah draws both our gazes, she looks like she wants to melt away from speaking. Then, she firms her jaw. "I have two little brothers, don't worry."

"Okay."

Rachel grabs her keys. "My car. I have more acceleration." Rachel points her keys at Savannah. "Keep trying Emily and the second you get her, text us. Our numbers are on the fridge."

"Okay."

❧❧❧❧

When she says she has more acceleration, she really means she just has *no* qualms about driving at a speed that rattles the speedometer. It took us longer to get into the car than it did to get the car on the highway. Rachel's foot is on the floorboard, and she's lane changing like her life depends on it.

I just hope it doesn't.

I check my phone. Nothing.

Those hands of hers hold the wheel, all-encompassing and in control. She finds holes in lanes that don't exist, that are made by sheer will alone, as the snow covered landscape gives away to the even more desolate crag of buildings. The closer we get, the bigger they become, until the granite sky is blocked by towering blocks of black.

"Where is she going to be?" Rachel asks. "Fuck!" She checks her mirror, slams her foot to the ground and catches rubber at seventy. It's a testament to her reflexes and the Audi's pick up. She swerves in front of a truck and the blast of his horn nearly deafens me.

I look back at the middle finger the driver is giving us. "In Midtown."

She boggles at me. "Where exactly in Midtown, Blake?"

"I'm not sure, but everything happens on Vanderbilt Avenue."

She shudders a breath. "Check your phone."

I do. "I don't have any messages."

"Fuck."

I don't say anything. I can't. I hold the arm rest as Rachel exits the expressway with enough velocity that the tires squeal holding the lane. "Slow down! Jesus."

She doesn't answer me, she just points to the clock.

1:06 p.m.

Eleven minutes.

Just eleven minutes.

"Rachel." My throat is choked tight.

"Don't you say it," she whispers in a rush. "Don't you say it to me."

I close my eyes fighting my panic to remember anything from the dream. The buildings, the storefronts. Anything. It's a blank, all I see is the little girl in the car. All I see is *our* little girl. The lights reflected on the window as her burning hazel eyes take in the massive buildings.

"Wait." I hit the dash. "She passes the Neiman Marcus, on 35th!"

Rachel checks her mirrors again and yanks the wheel hard enough that she's almost in my seat. "When?"

"I don't know."

"What do you *mean* you don't know!"

"I don't know, Rachel!"

When we hit 35th Street it's a maze of cars straggling around, looking for purpose on the crowded lanes. For the first time in what feels like forever, we pull to a stop.

1:08 p.m.

The clock's digits might as well be burned into my retinas. The humidity from my rapid breathing has put a fog over the window and I roll it down. I lean out, looking up and down the street for any sign of the dark car that carries Emily.

"Anything?"

"No. You?"

"No."

I glance at Rachel as the neon countdown burns the space between us. "We need to split up, cover more ground."

"No."

My words put her to action and she makes space for the car using the bicycle lane and by wedging her driver's side tires on the median. She's so close to the cars we pass, I can see the drivers eyes widen as we slide by. Pedestrians yelp and move aside, stunned to see a car halfway up the curb.

"Rachel."

"No."

"Listen to me."

"No."

1:12 p.m.

"Rachel, you have to listen to me!"

And something in the way I say it breaks the dam on her composure. When her words come, they are ragged. "No, I don't want you to leave my sight."

"But, Emily..."

"I know." Her tears fall. "I don't know what to do."

I grab her hand tightly, and her foot depresses the brake at the red light in front of us. "You have to let me out. Go down to Broadway and double back." Even as I say it, I know she'll never get back in 5 minutes.

4 minutes.

If she doesn't find Emily, I'll never see her again.

I think it, and it puts tears in my eyes as we sit in the cold car, at a red light, on this day.

Oh my God, I'll never see her again.

"You have to let me go." And when I say those words, her eyes waiver because I think she can hear in my voice what I'm saying.

"I can't." Her hand tightens in mine. "I can't."

"You have to." I ease a breath and grab the car door handle. It feels frozen in my fingers. "We can find her."

"Blake?"

I don't know where I find the strength to pop the car door open, and lie to her. "Baby we'll find her. I know we will."

"Okay."

A second is about as long as it takes for me to get out and close the car door. I stare at Rachel's face, her lips drawn, eyes frightened. She's staring at me, her eyes following my hand as I take a step back from the car.

And let her go.

In the milliseconds before the light goes green, I memorize her. Remember her face. It's the smile and eyes and everything I have loved the only way I could. The *best* I could. When the light turns I see everything I've earned spill to her face in her tears, and the whispered *I love you* on her lips.

In that moment, I watch her fear morph into something much stronger. It's the strength I never had, the strength that will carry her the rest of her life without me. Determination hardens her eyes and she guns it at the light. She literally hits the accelerator so hard that the car rattles on it's chassis as it screams away from me.

I'm left in the drizzle watching her whip into a lane and vanish in the rush of cars.

My hands find my hair and I tangle it in my fingers.

I can't believe she let me go.

I can't believe I *let* her.

I can't believe it's over.

I don't even realize I have my phone in my hand until it rings. It sounds like it's a million miles away. On the other side of the world. I race through the intersection, darting between cars as I gather my tatters and the pieces of my heart I once left here. Pieces that are finally coming home.

I lift the phone to my ear as the time screams in my face.

1:14 p.m.

"Angel?"

"Baby?"

Her voice saying the epithet steals all the breath from my lungs. I wheeze, "Yeah?"

I squint through the rain as I run. I run like I did when I was young, through the willows and over the rivers, unfaltering and strong. I don't miss the parallel. How I've come full circle in my life. How in this beautiful world, I'm brave enough to do this, for her. For *me*.

"I'm almost down to Broadway! I don't see her! Where are you?"

I heave a breath and turn the corner at a full tilt run. "Vanderbilt."

"No, you were looking for her!" Her voice whistles with pain. "Don't do this to me!"

"I'm sorry. It's a risk I can't take."

She doesn't say anything. All I hear is the rev of her car's engine like it's spawning from the ground beneath me. She's coming.

But she isn't going to make it.

1:15 p.m.

I burst onto Vanderbilt Avenue, heaving as I struggle for air. In my ear, her car's horn blares in accent of her words. "You lied to me! How could you lie to me?"

"Because I will do anything to protect you both.

I love you that much." A calming wave of euphoria passes through me at the admittance. "Rachel?"

"What!"

I press a smile to my lips so she hears I'm not upset. Mournful, but fully aware that *this* was how it was supposed to be. That somehow in our other life, it was supposed to be me here. Not her. The realization fixes the broken disjointed parts of my existence. "Baby."

"What?"

"It's okay."

"No!" I hear her car's horn, hot and angry. "No, no, don't you do this to me!"

"It's okay, sweetheart."

"Fuck if it's okay, if you do this you will end everything!" She sobs. "You will end me!"

I clear my throat, holding back tears. "No. I won't, be brave baby. Not everything will end. Not the things that matter the most."

Rachel's sobbing cuts like a knife. "You matter the most to *me*!" The car door pops open and I can hear her breath rushing, her feet on the pavement.

Racing to me.

And it's funny how in a world like this, in a place where life spins it's dizzying circles, I find such comfort in knowing it will go on this time, even if it's without me.

A world where babies are born and where people die.

1:16 p.m.

But it's not *for* me. It never was. No, this was a world where Rachel and our girls were supposed to be. The woman that made it possible, made everything possible, was meant to survive this. No matter how afraid I am, in my heart I know the best of me will continue on despite it all. And that is all that matters.

That she's safe. That they *both* are this time. *Any* sacrifice is worth that.

"I love you, Rachel. I have *always* loved you."

"No, please! No! I love you!" Her cries are harder, because of the defeat she must feel. Her feet aren't moving anymore.

"Don't ever forget it, okay?" In her silence I see the car coming. It puts a rush to my words. "Tell me you'll never forget how much I love you."

"How could I *ever* forget it? I love you like that, too."

That puts tears in my eyes, and it blurs the vehicle racing toward me. It softens the hard edges of fate and the darkness of truth. The truth that everything I've done in my life has driven me here. My transgressions and sacrifices the sharp line I cut my path on. A path I *had* to find to become the best version of me. The *me* that could love her enough. That could love all of them *enough* to right the universe's wrong and not fall to my knees in defeat.

1:17 p.m.

I rush to the curb, renewed in my conviction. "I promise you will see me again."

Her final words are her final gift to me. She says them with the same conviction she's had throughout her life. "You're my *One*, Blake. I'll find you and I'll fix everything."

"I'll be waiting, angel."

And I step off the curb, because I believe her. Believe *in* her.

In the *us* I've finally learned how to give it *all* for. Always.

About the Author

Stephanie Kusiak grew up in an idyllic neighborhood in Orange County, California. She spent her formative years watching after her brothers, rescuing stray animals and learning all she could about the supernatural from her grandmother over Sunday brunches. As a writer, she realistically captures the humanizing elements in life and focuses on the characters that live in her worlds. She is known on the internet for her steamy erotica and her poignant emotional twists. Her interests include, playing the piano, karaoke singing, online gaming and perusing local farmers' markets. She currently works in the financial sector and resides in Aliso Viejo, California with her wife and their tortoiseshell cat, Sydney.

Printed by BoD™in Norderstedt, Germany

9 781939 062581